Praise for Jennifer L. Armentrou  D1581318

'The beginning of Armentrout's new Lux series is a thrilling ride from start to finish…This series is guaranteed to hold your attention and have you begging for more' *RT Book Reviews*

'*Obsidian* is fast-paced and entertaining. I couldn't put this one down. Who knew aliens could be sexy?' *YA Fantasy Guide*

'Witty, refreshing and electrifying' Shortie Says

'One of those books you get lost in reading and finish in one sitting. Each book is a fast-paced read with a great plot and strong characters. A must-read for young adult book lovers' Hypable.com

'An engrossing, sexy nail-biter! I'm delighted to join the Daemon invasion' Nancy Holder, *NYT* bestselling author of *Wicked*

'This is the stuff swoons are made of. Fans of *Obsidian* will devour the high-stakes plot and beautifully crafted chemistry' Wendy Higgins, *NYT* bestselling author of *Sweet Evil*

'I LOVED *OBSIDIAN*! Get ready to devour this book in one sitting, fall hard for Daemon, and be desperate for book two!' Deborah Cooke, bestselling author of *Dragonfire*

'Take some really hot, sizzling character chemistry, two stubborn love interests who know how to push each other's buttons, and add in some awesome out-of-this-world characters and you've got the makings for one fabulously written story' Mundie Moms

'An incredibly thrilling action packed story from start to finish' @TheBookCafe

Jennifer L. Armentrout lives in West Virginia. All the rumors you've heard about her state aren't true. Well, mostly. When she's not hard at work writing, she spends her time reading, working out, watching zombie movies, and pretending to write. She shares her home with her husband, his K-9 partner named Diesel, and her hyper Jack Russell Loki. Her dreams of becoming an author started in algebra class, where she spent her time writing short stories...therefore explaining her dismal grades in math. Jennifer writes Adult and Young Adult Urban Fantasy and Romance.

Find out more at www.jenniferarmentrout.com

Also by Jennifer L. Armentrout and available from Hodder:

Obsidian

The First Lux Novel

Jennifer L. Armentrout

HODDER

First published in the United States of America in 2011
by Entangled Publishing, LLC

This paperback edition first published in Great Britain in 2015
by Hodder & Stoughton
An Hachette UK company

1

A CIP catalogue record for this title is available from the British Library

Paperback ISBN 978 1 473 61586 1
eBook ISBN 978 1 444 79927 9

Printed and bound by Clays Ltd, St Ives plc

Hodder & Stoughton policy is to use papers that are natural, renewable
and recyclable products and made from wood grown in sustainable forests.
The logging and manufacturing processes are expected to conform
to the environmental regulations of the country of origin.

Hodder & Stoughton Ltd
338 Euston Road
London NW1 3BH

www.hodder.co.uk

For my family and friends. Love ya like I love cake.

Chapter 1

I stared at the pile of boxes in my new bedroom, wishing the Internet had been hooked up. Not being able to do anything with my review blog since moving here was like missing an arm or a leg. According to my mom, "Katy's Krazy Obsession" was my whole life. Not entirely, but it was important to me. She didn't get books the way I did.

I sighed. We'd been here two days, and there was still so much left to unpack. I hated the idea of boxes sitting around. Even more than I hated being here.

At least I'd finally stopped jumping at every little creaking sound since moving to West "By God" Virginia and this house that looked like something straight out of a horror movie. It even had a turret—a freaking turret. What was I supposed to do with that?

Ketterman was unincorporated, meaning it wasn't a *real* town. The closest place was Petersburg—a two or three stoplight town near a few other towns that probably didn't have a Starbucks. We wouldn't get mail at our house. We would have to drive *into* Petersburg to get our mail.

Barbaric.

Like a kick in the face, it hit me. Florida was gone—eaten by the miles we'd traveled in Mom's mad dash to start over. It wasn't that I missed Gainesville, the weather, my old school, or even our apartment. Leaning against the wall, I rubbed the palm of my hand over my forehead.

I missed Dad.

And Florida *was* Dad. It was where he'd been born, where he met my mom, and where everything had been perfect…until it all fell apart. My eyes burned, but I refused to cry. Crying didn't change the past, and Dad would've hated to know I was still crying three years later.

But I missed Mom, too. The Mom before Dad had died, the one who used to curl up on the couch beside me and read one of her trashy romance novels. It seemed like a lifetime ago. It certainly was half a country ago.

Ever since Dad died, Mom had started working more and more. She used to want to be home. Then it seemed like she wanted to be as far away as possible. She'd finally given up on that option and decided we needed to drive far away. At least since we'd gotten here, even though she was still working like a demon, she was determined to be more in my life.

I had decided to ignore my inner compulsive streak and let the boxes be damned today, when the smell of something familiar tickled my nose. Mom was cooking. This was so not good.

I raced downstairs.

She stood at the stove, dressed in her polka-dotted scrubs. Only she could wear head-to-toe polka dots and still manage to look good. Mom had this glorious blonde hair that was stick straight and sparkling hazel eyes. Even in scrubs she made me look dull with my gray eyes and plain brown hair.

And somehow I ended up more...round than her. Curvy hips, puffy lips, and huge eyes that Mom loved but made me look like a demented kewpie doll.

She turned and waved a wooden spatula at me, half-cooked eggs splattering onto the stove. "Good morning, honey."

I stared at the mess and wondered how best to take over this fiasco in the making without hurting her feelings. She was trying to do mom-stuff. This was huge. Progress. "You're home early."

"I worked almost a double shift between last night and today. I'm set to work Wednesday through Saturday, eleven till nine a.m. That leaves me with three days off. I'm thinking of either working part time at one of the clinics around here or possibly in Winchester." She scraped out the eggs onto two plates and set the half-burned offering in front of me.

Yum. Guess it was too late for an intervention, so I rifled through a box resting on the far counter marked 'Silverware & Stuff.'

"You know how I don't like having nothing to do, so I'm going to check into them soon."

Yeah, I knew.

And most parents would probably saw off their left arm before thinking of leaving a teenaged girl at home alone all the time, but not mine. She trusted me because I never gave her reason not to. It wasn't for lack of trying. Well, okay, maybe it was.

I *was* kind of boring.

In my old group of friends in Florida, I wasn't the quiet one, but I never skipped class, maintained a 4.0, and was pretty much a good girl. Not because I was afraid to do anything reckless or wild; I didn't want to add to Mom's troubles. Not then...

Grabbing two glasses, I filled them with orange juice Mom must have picked up on her way home. "Do you want me to get groceries today? We have nothing."

She nodded and spoke around a mouthful of eggs. "You think of everything. A grocery trip would be perfect." She grabbed her purse off the table, pulling out cash. "This should be enough."

I pocketed the money into my jeans without looking at the amount; she always gave me too much in the first place. "Thanks," I mumbled.

She leaned forward, a twinkle in her eyes. "So...this morning I saw something interesting."

God only knows with her. I smiled. "What?"

"Have you noticed that there are two kids about your age next door?"

My inner golden retriever kicked in and my ears perked up. "Really?"

"You haven't been outside, have you?" She smiled. "I'd thought for sure you'd be all over that disgusting flower bed by now."

"I plan on it, but the boxes aren't unpacking themselves." I gave her a pointed look. I loved the woman, but leave it to her to somehow forget that part. "Anyway, back to the kids."

"Well, one is a girl who looks about your age, and there's a boy." She grinned as she stood. "He's a hottie."

A tiny piece of egg caught in my throat. It was seriously gross to hear Mom talking about boys my age. "Hottie? Mom, that's just weird."

Mom pushed off from the counter, picked up her plate from the table, and headed to the sink. "Honey, I might be old, but my eyes are still working fine. And they were really working earlier."

I cringed. Double gross. "Are you turning into a cougar? Is this some sort of midlife crisis I need to be concerned about?"

Rinsing off her plate, she glanced over her shoulder. "Katy, I hope you'll make an effort to meet them. I think it would be nice for you to make friends before school starts." Pausing, she yawned. "They could show you around, yes?"

I refused to think about the first day of school, new kid and all. I dumped my uneaten eggs in the garbage. "Yeah, it would be nice. But I don't want to go banging on their door, begging them to be my friends."

"It wouldn't be begging. If you put on one of those pretty sundresses you wore in Florida instead of this." She tugged on the hem of my shirt. "It would be flirting."

I glanced down. It said My Blog Is Better Than Your Vlog. There wasn't a thing wrong with it. "How about I show up in my undies?"

She tapped her chin thoughtfully. "That would definitely make an impression."

"Mom!" I laughed. "You're supposed to yell at me and

tell me that's not a good idea!"

"Baby, I don't worry about you doing anything stupid. But seriously, make an effort."

I wasn't sure how to 'make an effort.'

She yawned again. "Well, honey, I'm going to catch up on sleep."

"All right, I'll get some good stuff at the store." And maybe mulch and plants. The flower bed outside was hideous.

"Katy?" Mom had stopped in the doorway, frowning.

"Yeah?"

A shadow flickered over her face, darkening her eyes. "I know this move is hard for you, especially before your senior year, but it was the best thing for us to do. Staying there, in that apartment, without him…It's time we started living again. Your dad would have wanted that."

The lump in my throat I thought I'd left in Florida was back. "I know, Mom. I'm fine."

"Are you?" Her fingers curled into a fist. The sunlight coming through the window reflected off the gold band around her ring finger.

I nodded quickly, needing to reassure her. "I'm okay. And I'll go next door. Maybe they can tell me where the store is. You know, make an effort."

"Excellent! If you need anything, call me. Okay?" Mom's eyes watered on another long yawn. "I love you, honey."

I started to tell her that I loved her, too, but she disappeared upstairs before the words were out of my mouth.

At least she was trying to change, and I was determined to at least try and fit in here. Not hide in my room on my laptop all day like Mom was afraid I'd do. But mingling with kids I'd never met wasn't my thing. I'd rather read a book and stalk my blog comments.

I bit my lip. I could hear my dad's voice, his favorite phrase encouraging me, "Come on, Kittycat, don't be a bystander." I squared my shoulders. Dad had never let life pass *him* by…

And asking about the nearest store was an innocent-enough reason to introduce myself. If Mom was right and they *were* my age, maybe this wouldn't turn out to be such an epic fail of a move. This was stupid, but I was doing it. I hurried across the lawn and across the driveway before I chickened out.

Hopping onto the wide porch, I opened the screen door and knocked, then stepped back and smoothed the wrinkles out of my shirt. *I'm cool. I got this.* There is nothing weird about asking for directions.

Heavy footsteps came from the other side, and then the door was swinging open and I was staring at a very broad, tan, well-muscled chest. A naked chest. My gaze dropped and my breath sort of…stalled. Jeans hung low on his hips, revealing a thin line of dark hair that formed below his navel and disappeared under the band of the jeans.

His stomach was ripped. Perfect. Totally touchable. Not the kind of stomach I expected on a seventeen-year-old boy, which is how old I suspected he was, but yeah, I wasn't complaining. I also wasn't talking. And I was staring.

My gaze finally traveling north again, I noted thick, sooty lashes fanning the tips of his high cheeks and hiding the color of his eyes as he looked down at me. I needed to know what color his eyes were.

"Can I help you?" Full, kissable lips turned down in annoyance.

His voice was deep and firm. The kind of voice accustomed to people listening and obeying without question. His lashes lifted, revealing eyes so green and brilliant they couldn't be real. They were an intense emerald color that stood out in vibrant contrast against his tan skin.

"Hello?" he said again, placing one hand on the doorframe as he leaned forward. "Are you capable of speaking?"

I sucked in a sharp breath and took a step back. A wave of embarrassment heated my face.

The boy lifted an arm, brushing back a wavy lock of hair on his forehead. He glanced over my shoulder, then back to me. "Going once..."

By the time I found my voice, I wanted to die. "I...I was wondering if you knew where the closest grocery store is. My name is Katy. I moved next door." I gestured at my house, rambling like an idiot. "Like two days ago—"

"I know."

Ooooo-kay. "Well, I was hoping someone would know the quickest way to the grocery store and maybe a place that sold plants."

"Plants?"

For some reason, it didn't sound as though he was asking me a question, but I rushed to answer anyway. "Yeah, see, there's this flower bed in front—"

He said nothing, just cocked a brow with disdain. "Okay."

The embarrassment was fading, replaced by a growing surge of anger. "Well, see, I need to go buy plants—"

"For the flower bed. I got that." He leaned his hip against

the doorframe and crossed his arms. Something glittered in his green eyes. Not anger, but something else.

I took a deep breath. If this dude cut me off one more time… My voice took on the tone my mother used when I was younger and was playing with sharp objects. "I'd like to find a store where I can buy groceries and plants."

"You *are* aware this town has only one stoplight, right?" Both eyebrows were raised to his hairline now as if he were questioning how I could be so dumb, and that's when I realized what I saw sparkling in his eyes. He was laughing at me with a healthy dose of condescension.

For a moment, all I could do was stare at him. He was probably the hottest guy I'd ever seen in real life, and he was a total douche. Go figure. "You know, all I wanted was directions. This is obviously a bad time."

One side of his lips curled up. "Anytime is a bad time for you to come knocking on my door, kid."

"Kid?" I repeated, eyes widening.

A dark, mocking eyebrow arched again. I was starting to hate that brow.

"I'm not a kid. I'm seventeen."

"Is that so?" He blinked. "You look like you're twelve. No. Maybe thirteen, but my sister has this doll that kinda reminds me of you. All big-eyed and vacant."

I reminded him of *a doll*? A *vacant* doll? Warmth burned in my chest, spreading up my throat. "Yeah, wow. Sorry to bother you. I won't be knocking on your door again. Trust me." I started to turn, leaving before I caved to the rampant desire to slam my fists into his face. Or cry.

"Hey," he called out.

I stopped on the bottom step but refused to turn around and let him see how upset I was. "What?"

"You get on Route 2 and turn onto U.S. 220 North, not South. Takes you into Petersburg." He let out an irritated breath, as if he were doing me a huge favor. "The Foodland is right in town. You can't miss it. Well, maybe *you* could. There's a hardware store next door, I think. They should have things that go in the ground."

"Thanks," I muttered and added under my breath, "Douchebag."

He laughed, deep and throaty. "Now that's not very ladylike, Kittycat."

I whipped around. "Don't ever call me that," I snapped.

"It's better than calling someone a douchebag, isn't it?" He pushed out the door. "This has been a stimulating visit. I'll cherish it for a long time to come."

Okay. That was it. "You know, you're right. How wrong of me to call you a douchebag. Because a douchebag is too nice of a word for you," I said, smiling sweetly. "You're a dickhead."

"A dickhead?" he repeated. "How charming."

I flipped him off.

He laughed again and bent his head. A mess of waves fell forward, nearly obscuring his intense green eyes. "Very civilized, Kitten. I'm sure you have a wild array of interesting names and gestures for me, but I'm not interested."

I did have a lot more I could say and do, but I gathered my dignity, pivoted, and stomped back over to my house, not giving him the pleasure of seeing how truly pissed I was. I'd always avoided confrontation in the past, but this guy was flipping my bitch switch like nothing else. When I reached my car, I yanked open the door.

"See you later, Kitten!" he called out, laughing as he slammed the front door.

Tears of anger and embarrassment burnt my eyes. I shoved the keys into the ignition and threw the car into reverse. 'Make an effort,' Mom had said. That's what happens when you make an effort.

Chapter 2

Chapter 2

It took the entire drive into Petersburg for me to calm down.
Even then there was still a hot mix of anger and humiliation
swirling inside me. What the heck was wrong with him? I
thought people in small towns were supposed to be nice, not
act like the son of Satan.

I found Main Street with no problem, which literally
seemed to be the *main* street. There was the Grant County
Library on Mount View, and I reminded myself I needed
to get a library card. Grocery store options were limited.
Foodland, which actually read FOO LAND, brought to you
by the missing letter D, was where Douchebag had said it
would be.

The front windows were plastered with a missing person's
picture of a girl about my age with long dark hair and
laughing eyes. The data below said she'd last been seen over
a year ago. There was a reward, but after she'd been missing

for that long, I doubted the reward would ever be claimed. Saddened by that thought, I headed inside.

I was a speed shopper, wasting no time strolling aisles. Throwing items into the cart, I realized I'd need more than I thought since we only had the bare necessities at home. Soon, my cart was filled to the rim.

"Katy?"

Lost in thought, I jumped at the soft female voice and dropped a carton of eggs on the floor. "Crap."

"Oh! I am so sorry! I startled you. I do that a lot." Tan arms shot out and she picked up the carton and placed it back on the shelf. She grabbed another one and held it in her slender hands. "These won't be cracked."

I lifted my gaze from the egg carnage slowly oozing bright yolks all over the linoleum floor and was momentarily stunned. My first impression of the girl was that she was too beautiful to be standing in a grocery store with a carton of eggs in her hand.

She stood out like a sunflower in a field of wheat.

Everyone else was a pale comparison. Her dark hair was curly and longer than mine, reaching her waist. She was tall, thin, and her almost perfect features held a certain innocence. She reminded me of someone, especially those startling green eyes. I gritted my teeth. What were the odds?

She grinned. "I'm Daemon's sister. My name is Dee." She placed the undamaged carton of eggs in my cart. "New eggs!" She smiled.

"Daemon?"

Dee gestured at a hot-pink purse in the front of her cart. A cell phone was lying on top of it. "You talked to him about thirty minutes ago. You stopped by...asking for directions?"

So the dickhead had a name. Daemon—seemed fitting. And of course his sister would be as attractive as him. Why not? Welcome to West Virginia, the land of lost models. I was starting to doubt I was going to fit in here. "Sorry. I wasn't expecting anyone to call out my name." I paused. "He called you?"

"Yeah." She deftly pulled her cart out of the way of a toddler running amok through the narrow aisle. "Anyway, I saw you guys move in, and I've been meaning to stop by, and when he said you were here, well, I was so excited to meet you I ran over. He told me what you looked liked."

I could only imagine *that* description.

Curiosity filled her face as she watched me with her intense green eyes. "Although, you don't look anything like he said, but anyway, I'd know who you were. It's hard not to know pretty much everyone's face around here."

I watched a grubby little kid climb up the bread rack. "I don't think your brother likes me."

Her brows furrowed. "What?"

"Your brother—I don't think he likes me." I turned back to the cart, fiddling with a package of meat. "He wasn't very... helpful."

"Oh no," she said and then laughed. I looked at her sharply. "I'm sorry. My brother is moody."

No shit. "I'm pretty sure that was more than being moody."

She shook her head. "He was having a bad day. He's worse than a girl, trust me. He doesn't hate you. We're twins. Even I want to kill him on days that end with a Y. Anyway,

Daemon's kind of rough around the edges. He doesn't get along with...people."

I laughed. "You think?"

"Well, I'm glad I ran into you here!" she exclaimed, changing the subject yet again. "I wasn't sure if I would've been bothering you if I popped over, with you getting settled in and all."

"No, it wouldn't have been a bother." I tried to keep up with the conversation. She went from one topic to the next like someone in bad need of Ritalin.

"You should've seen me when Daemon said you were our age. I almost ran home to hug him." She moved excitedly. "If I'd known he was going to be so rude to you, I would have been likely to punch him instead."

"I can imagine." I grinned. "I wanted to punch him, too."

"Imagine being the only girl in the neighborhood and stuck with your annoying brother most of the time." She glanced over her shoulder, delicate brows creasing.

I followed her gaze. The little boy now had a carton of milk in each hand, which reminded me that I needed milk. "Be right back." I headed over to the refrigerated section.

Finally, the mother of the child had rounded the corner, yelling, "Timothy Roberts, you put that back right now! What are you—?"

The kid stuck out his tongue. Sometimes being around children was the perfect abstinence program. Then again, not like I needed a program. I carried my milk back to where Dee waited, staring at the floor. Her fingers twisted over the handle of her cart, squeezing until her knuckles bleached.

"Timothy, get right back here this instant!" The mother

grabbed his chubby arm. Strands of hair had escaped her severe bun. "What did I tell you?" she hissed. "You don't go near *them*."

Them? I expected to see someone else. Except it was Dee and...me. Confused, I glanced at the woman. I was shocked to see her dark eyes filled with disgust. Pure revulsion, and behind that, in the way her lips pressed into a hard line and trembled, there was also fear.

And she was staring at Dee.

Then she gathered the squirmy boy into her arms and hurried off, leaving her cart in the middle of the aisle.

I turned to Dee. "What the heck was that about?"

Dee smiled, but it was brittle. "Small town. The locals are weird around here. Don't pay any attention to them. Anyway, you must be so bored after unpacking and then grocery shopping. That's like two of the worst things ever. I mean, hell could be devised of those two things. Think of an eternity of unpacking boxes and grocery shopping?"

I couldn't help grinning as I struggled to keep up with Dee's nonstop chatter while we finished loading our carts. Normally, someone like that would wear me out in five seconds, but the excitement in her eyes and the way she kept rocking back on her heels was sort of contagious.

"Do you have more stuff to get?" she asked. "I'm pretty much done. I really came to catch you and was sucked down the ice cream aisle. It calls to me."

I laughed and looked at my full cart. "Yeah, I hope I'm done."

"Come on then. We can check out together."

As we waited in the checkout aisle, Dee rattled on, and I

forgot about the weird incident in the milk aisle. Dee believed Petersburg needed another grocery store—because this one didn't carry organic food—and she wanted organic chicken for what she was making Daemon fix her for dinner. After a few minutes I got past the difficulty of keeping up with her and actually started to relax. She wasn't bubbly, just really...*alive*. I hoped she rubbed off on me.

The checkout line moved quicker than it did in larger cities. Once outside, she stopped next to a new Volkswagen and unlocked the trunk.

"Nice car," I commented. They had money, obviously, or Dee had a job.

"I love it." She patted the rear bumper. "It's my baby."

I shoved groceries in the back of my sedan.

"Katy?"

"Yeah?" I twirled the keys around my finger, hoping asshat brother aside, she wanted to hang out later. There was no telling how late Mom was going to sleep.

"I should apologize for my brother. Knowing him, I'm sure he wasn't very nice."

I sort of felt sorry for her, being that she was related to such a tool. "It's not your fault."

Her fingers twisted around her key ring, and her eyes drifted to mine. "He's really overprotective, so he doesn't take well to strangers."

Like a dog? I almost smiled, but her eyes were wide and she looked genuinely scared I wouldn't forgive her. Having a brother like him must suck. "It's no big deal. Maybe he was just having a bad day."

"Maybe." She smiled, but it seemed forced.

"Seriously, no worries. We're good," I said.

"Thanks! I'm totally not a stalker. I swear." She winked. "But I'd love to hang out this afternoon. Got any plans?"

"Actually, I was thinking of tackling the overgrown flower bed in the front. You wanna help?" Having company might be fun.

"Oh, that sounds great. Let me get these groceries home, and I'll head straight over," she said. "I'm really excited to garden! I've never done that."

Before I could ask what sort of childhood didn't include at least the obligatory tomato plant, she'd dashed off to her car and zoomed out of the parking lot. I pushed off my bumper and headed toward the driver's side. I opened the car door and was about to climb in when the feeling of being watched crept over me.

My eyes darted around the parking lot, but there was only a man in a black suit and dark sunglasses staring at a missing person's picture on a community corkboard. All I could think of was *Men in Black*.

The only thing he needed was that little memory-wiper device and a talking dog. I would've laughed, except nothing about the man was funny…Especially since he was now staring right back at me.

• • •

A little past one that afternoon, Dee knocked on the front door. When I stepped outside, I found her standing near the steps, rolling back on the heels of her wedge sandals. Not what I'd consider "gardening" attire. The sun cast a halo around her dark head and she had an impish grin on her face. In that moment, she reminded me of a fairy princess. Or maybe a cracked-out Tinker Bell, considering how hyper she was.

"Hey." I stepped out onto the porch, closing the door quietly behind me. "My mom's sleeping."

"I hope I didn't wake your mom," she mock whispered.

I shook my head. "Nah, she'd sleep through a hurricane. It's happened, actually."

Dee grinned as she sat on the swing. She looked timid, hugging her elbows. "As soon as I came home with groceries, Daemon ate half a bag of *my* potato chips, two of *my* fudge pops, and then half of the peanut butter jar."

I started laughing. "Wow. How does he stay so..." *Hot*. "Fit?"

"It's amazing." She pulled her legs up and wrapped her arms around them. "He eats so much we usually have to run two to three trips a week to the store." She looked at me with a sly glint in her eyes. "Of course, I can eat you out of house and home too. I guess I shouldn't be talking."

My envy was almost painful. I wasn't blessed with a fast metabolism. My hips and butt could attest to that. I wasn't overweight, but I really hated it when Mom referred to me as 'curvy.' "That's so not fair. I eat a bag of chips and gain five pounds."

"We're lucky." Her easy grin seemed tighter. "Anyway, you must tell me all about Florida. Never been there."

I propped myself up on the porch railing. "Think nonstop shopping malls and parking lots. Oh, but the beaches. Yeah, it's worth it for the beaches." I loved the heat of the sun on my skin, my toes squishing in the wet sand.

"Wow," Dee said, her gaze darting next door as if she were waiting for someone. "It's going to take a lot for you to get used to living here. Adapting can be...hard when you're out of your element."

I shrugged. "I don't know. It doesn't seem that bad. Of course when I first found out, I was like, you have *got* to be kidding me. I didn't even know this place existed."

Dee laughed. "Yeah, a lot of people don't. We were shocked when we came here."

"Oh, so you guys aren't from here either?"

Her laugh died off as her gaze flicked away from mine. "No, we're not from here."

"Did your parents move here for work?" Although I had no idea what sort of jobs were around this place.

"Yeah, they work in the city. We don't see them a lot."

I had the distinct impression there was more to it. "That must be hard. But...a lot of freedom, I guess. My mom is rarely here either."

"I guess you understand then." A strange, sad look filled her eyes. "We kind of run our own lives."

"And you'd think our lives would be more exciting than this, right?"

She looked wistful. "Have you ever heard of, be careful what you wish for? I used to think that." She toed the swing back and forth, neither of us rushing to fill the ensuing silence. I knew exactly what she meant. I can't remember how many times I'd lain awake at night and hoped Mom would snap out of it and move on—and welcome West Virginia.

Dark clouds seemed to roll in out of nowhere, casting a shadow across the yard. Dee frowned. "Oh no! It looks like we're going to get one of our famous afternoon rainstorms. They usually last a couple of hours."

"That's too bad. I guess we better plan to garden tomorrow instead. Are you available?"

"Sure thing." Dee shivered in the suddenly chilly air.

"Wonder where this storm came from. It seemed to come out of nowhere, didn't it?" I asked.

Dee jumped up from the swing, wiping her hands on her pants. "Looks that way. Well, I think your mom is up, and I need to wake Daemon."

"Sleeping? That's a little late."

"He's weird," Dee said. "I'll be back tomorrow, and we can head to the garden shop."

Laughing, I slid off the rail. "Sounds good."

"Great!" She skipped down the steps and twirled around. "I'll tell Daemon you said hi!"

I felt my cheeks turn a fiery red. "Uh, that won't be necessary."

"Trust me, it is!" She laughed and then sprinted to the house next door. *Joy.*

Mom was in the kitchen, coffee in hand. As she faced me, steaming brown liquid sloshed over the counter. The innocent look on her face gave it away.

Grabbing a towel, I walked over to the counter. "She lives next door, her name is Dee, and I ran into her while I was at the grocery store." I swiped the towel over the splotches of coffee. "She has a brother. His name is Daemon. They're twins."

"Twins? Interesting." She smiled. "Is Dee nice, dear?"

I sighed. "Yes, Mom, she's very nice."

"I'm so happy. It's about time you came out of your

shell."

I didn't realize I was in a shell.

Mom blew softly and then took a sip, eyeing me over the rim. "Did you make plans to hang out with her tomorrow?"

"You would know. You were listening."

"Of course." She winked. "I'm your mother. That is what we do."

"Eavesdropping on conversations?"

"Yes. How else am I supposed to know what is going on?" she asked innocently.

I rolled my eyes and turned to go back into the living room. "Privacy, Mom."

"Honey," she called from the kitchen, "there is no such thing as privacy."

Chapter 3

The day my Internet was hooked up was better than having a hot guy check out my butt and ask for my phone number. Since it was Wednesday, I'd typed up a quick "Waiting on Wednesday" post for my blog featuring this YA book about a hot boy with a killer touch—can't go wrong there—apologized for my extended absence, responded to comments, and stalked a few other blogs I loved. It was like coming home.

"Katy?" Mom yelled up the stairs. "Your friend Dee is here."

"Coming," I shouted back and closed the lid of my laptop.

I skipped down the stairs, and Dee and I headed off to the hardware store, which wasn't anywhere near FOO LAND like Daemon had said. They had everything needed for me to fix that gross flower bed out front.

Back home, we each grabbed a side of a bag and hauled it

out of my trunk. The bags were ridiculously heavy and by the time we'd gotten them out of the car, sweat poured off of us.

"Want to get something to drink before we drag those bags over to the flower beds?" I offered, arms aching.

She wiped her hands against each other and nodded. "I need to lift weights. Moving stuff sucks."

We headed inside and grabbed iced tea. "Remind me to join the local gym," I joked, rubbing my puny arms.

Dee laughed and twisted her sweat-soaked hair from her neck. She still looked gorgeous, even red-faced and tired. I'm sure I looked like a serial killer. At least now we knew I was too weak to do any real damage. "Umm. Ketterman. Our idea of a gym is dragging your garbage can to the end of a dirt road or hauling hay."

I dug up a hair tie for her, joking about the uncoolness of my new small-town life. We'd only been inside ten minutes tops, but when we went back out, all the bags of soil and mulch were stacked next to the porch.

I glanced at her, surprised. "How did they get over here?"

Dropping down on her knees, she started pulling up the weeds. "Probably my brother."

"Daemon?"

She nodded. "He's always the thankless hero."

"Thankless hero," I muttered. Not likely. I'd sooner believe the bags levitated over here on their own.

Dee and I attacked the weeds with more energy than I thought we had. I've always felt pulling weeds was a great way to let off steam, and if Dee's jerky movements were any indication, she had a lot to be frustrated about. With a brother like hers, I wasn't surprised.

Later, Dee stared at her chipped nails. "Well, there went my manicure."

I grinned. "I told you, you should've gotten gloves."

"But you're not wearing any," she pointed out.

Lifting my dirt-stained hands, I winced. My nails were usually chipped. "Yeah, but I'm used to it."

Dee shrugged and went over and grabbed a rake. She looked funny in her skirt and wedge sandals, which she insisted were the height of gardening couture, and dragged the rake over to me. "This is fun, though."

"Better than shopping?" I joked.

She seemed to consider it seriously, scrunching her nose. "Yeah, it's more…relaxing."

"It is. I don't think when I'm doing stuff like this."

"That's what's nice about it." She started raking the faded mulch out of the bed. "Do you do it to avoid thinking?"

Sitting back, I ripped open another bag of mulch. I wasn't sure how to answer that question. "My dad…he loved doing things like this. He had a green thumb. In our old apartment, we didn't have a yard or anything, but we had a balcony. We made a garden up there, together."

"What happened to your dad? Did your parents get divorced?"

I pressed my lips together. Talking about him wasn't something I did. Like ever. He'd been a good man—a great father. He didn't deserve what happened to him.

Dee paused. "I'm sorry. It's none of my business."

"No. It's okay." I stood, brushing the dirt off my shirt. When I looked up, she was leaning the rake against the porch. Her entire left arm blurred. I could see the white railing through it. I blinked. Her arm was solid again.

"Katy? You okay?"

Heart pounding, I dragged my eyes to her face and then back to her arm. It was whole. Perfect. I shook my head. "Yeah, I'm okay. Um...my dad, he got sick. Cancer. It was terminal—in the brain. He'd been getting headaches, seeing things." I swallowed, looking away. Seeing things like I did? "But other than that, he'd been fine right up to the diagnosis. They started him on chemo and radiation, but everything... went to shit so quickly. He died about two months later."

"Oh, my God, Katy, I'm so sorry." Her face was pale, voice soft. "That's terrible."

"It's okay." I forced a smile I didn't feel. "It was about three years ago. It's why my mom wanted to move. A new start and all that jazz."

In the sunlight, her eyes glistened. "I can understand that. Losing someone doesn't get easier with time, does it?"

"No." By the sound of it, she knew what it felt like, but before I could ask, the door to her house swung open. Knots formed in my stomach. "Oh no," I whispered.

Dee twisted around, letting out a sigh. "Look who's back."

It was past one in the afternoon, and Daemon looked as if he'd just rolled out of bed. His jeans were rumpled, hair tousled and all over the place. He was on the phone, talking to someone as he rubbed a hand along his jaw.

And he was shirtless.

"Doesn't he own a shirt?" I asked, grabbing a spade.

"Unfortunately, I don't think so. Not even in the winter. He's always running around half-dressed." She groaned. "It's disturbing that I have to see so much of his...skin. Yuck."

Yuck for her. And hot damn for me. I started digging several holes in strategic places. My throat felt dry. Beautiful face. Beautiful body. Horrible attitude. It was the holy trinity of hot boys.

Daemon stayed on the phone for about thirty minutes, and his presence had a swamping effect. There was no ignoring him, not even when I had my back to him—I could feel him watching. My shoulder blades tingled under his heavy stare. Once I glanced over, and he was gone, only to return a few seconds later with a shirt on. Damn. I kind of missed the view.

I was patting down new soil when Daemon swaggered over, dropping a heavy arm over his sister's shoulder. She tried to wiggle free, but he held her close. "Hey, Sis."

She rolled her eyes, but she was grinning. A look of hero-worship filled her eyes as she gazed at him. "Thanks for moving the bags for us."

"Wasn't me."

Dee rolled her eyes. "Whatever, butthead."

"That's not nice." He pulled her closer, smiling—really smiling, and it was a nice look on him. He should try it more often. Then he glanced over at me and his eyes narrowed, as if he just realized I was there, in *my* yard. The smile was completely gone. "What are you doing?"

I glanced down at myself. It seemed pretty obvious considering I was covered with dirt and there were several plants scattered around me. "I'm fixing—"

"I wasn't asking you." He turned to his red-faced sister. "What are *you* doing?"

I was not going to let him get to me again. I shrugged

and picked up a potted plant. Yanking the plant out of its container, I ripped roots right along with it.

"I'm helping her with the flower bed. Be nice." Dee punched him in the stomach before squirming free. "Look at what we've done. I think I have a hidden talent."

Daemon turned his eyes on my landscaping masterpiece. If I had to pick a dream job right now, it would be working with landscaping and the outdoors. Yeah, I sucked butt in the wilderness, but I was at my best with my hands sunk deep into the dirt. I loved everything about it. The numbing it brought, the way everything smelled earthy and rich, and how a little water and fresh soil could bring life back into something that was faded and dying.

And I was good at it. I watched every show on TLC. I knew where to place plants that needed more sun and ones that thrived in the shadows. There was a layered effect, taller and leafy, sturdier plants in the back and flowers in the front. All I had to do was put down soil and *voila*!

Daemon arched a brow.

My insides tightened. "What?"

He shrugged. "It's nice. I guess."

"Nice?" Dee sounded as offended as I felt. "It's better than nice. We rocked this project. Well, Katy rocked it. I kind of just handed her stuff."

"Is this what you do with your spare time?" he asked me, ignoring his sister.

"What—are you deciding to talk to *me* now?" Smiling tightly, I grabbed a handful of mulch and dumped it. Rinse and repeat. "Yeah, it's kind of a hobby. What's yours? Kicking puppies?"

"I'm not sure I should say in front of my sister," he replied, his expression turning wolfish.

"Ew." Dee made a face.

The images I got then were totally R-rated, and I could tell by his smug expression he knew it. I grabbed more mulch.

"But it's not nearly as lame as this," he added.

I froze. Pieces of red cedar floated from my fingers. "Why is this lame?"

His look said *do I really need to explain*? And yeah, gardening wasn't the height of coolness. I knew that. But it wasn't lame. Because I liked Dee, I clamped my mouth shut and started spreading the mulch out.

Dee pushed her brother, but he didn't move. "Don't be a jerk. Please?"

"I'm not being a jerk," he denied.

I raised my eyebrows.

"What's that?" Daemon said. "You have something to say, *Kitten*?"

"Other than I'd like for you to never call me *Kitten*? No." I smoothed the mulch out, then stood, admiring our work. Casting Dee a look, I grinned. "I think we did good."

"Yes." She pushed her brother again, in the direction of their house. He still didn't move. "We did good, lameness and all. And you know what? I kind of like being lame."

Daemon stared at the freshly planted flowers, almost like he were dissecting them for a science experiment.

"And I think we need to spread our lameness to the flower bed in front of our house," she continued, her eyes filling with excitement. "We can go to the store, get stuff and you can—"

"She's not welcome in our house," Daemon snapped, turning to his sister. "Seriously."

Surprised by the venom in his words, I took a step back.

Dee, however, did not. Her delicate hands balled into fists. "I was thinking we could work on the flower bed, which is *outside*—not inside—the last time I checked."

"I don't care. I don't want her over there."

"Daemon, don't do this," Dee whispered, her eyes filling with tears. "Please. I like her."

The remarkable happened. His face softened. "Dee..."

"Please?" she asked again, bouncing like a little girl asking for her favorite toy, which was odd to watch given how tall she was. I wanted to kick Daemon for turning his sister into someone clearly starving for friendships.

He cursed under his breath, folding his arms. "Dee, you have friends."

"It's not the same, and you know it." Her movements mimicked his. "It's different."

Daemon glanced over at me, his lip curling. If I still held the spade, I might've chucked it at his head. "They're your friends, Dee. They're like you. You don't need to be friends with someone...someone like *her*."

I'd kept quiet up to that point, because I had no idea what was going on and I didn't want to say anything that might upset Dee. Dickhead was her brother, after all, but that—*that* was way too much. "What do you mean, someone like me?"

He tilted his head to the side and let out a long breath.

His sister's eyes darted from me to him nervously. "He didn't mean anything by it."

"Bullshit," he muttered.

Now my hands were clenching into fists. "What the *hell* is your problem?"

Daemon faced me. There was a strange look on his face. "You."

"I'm your problem?" I took a step forward. "I don't even know you. And you don't know me."

"You are all the same." A muscle popped in his jaw. "I don't need to get to know you. Or want to."

I threw my hands up, frustrated. "That works perfectly for me, buddy, because I don't want to get to know you either."

"Daemon," Dee said, grabbing his arm. "Knock it off."

He smirked as he watched me. "I don't like that you're friends with my sister."

I said the first thing that came to mind. Probably not the smartest, and normally I wasn't the type of person to fire right back, but this guy got under my skin and made me see red. "And I don't give two shits what you like."

One second he was standing next to Dee and the next he was right in front of me. And I mean, *right in front of me*. He couldn't have moved that fast. It was impossible. But there he was, towering over me and staring down.

"How...how did you move...?" I took a step back, words failing me. The intensity in his eyes sent shivers down my arms. *Holy crap...*

"Listen closely," he said, taking a step forward. I took one back, and he matched my steps until my back bit into one of the tall trees. Daemon bent his head down, his unnatural green eyes taking up my whole world. Heat rolled off his body. "I'm only going to tell you this once. If anything happens to my sister, so help me—" He stopped, taking a deep breath as his gaze dropped to my parted lips. My breath caught. Something flickered in his eyes, but they narrowed again, hiding whatever had been there.

The images were back. The two of us. Hot and sweaty. I bit my lip and tried to make my expression blank, but yet again I knew he could tell what I was thinking when his expression turned annoyingly smug. Beyond annoying.

"You're kind of dirty, Kitten."

I blinked. Deny. Deny. Deny. "What did you say?"

"Dirty," he repeated, voice so low I knew Dee couldn't hear him. "You're covered in dirt. What did you think I meant?"

"Nothing," I said, wishing he'd back the hell up. Daemon being this close wasn't exactly comforting. "I'm gardening. You get dirty when you do that."

His lips twitched. "There are a lot more fun ways to get... dirty. Not that I'd ever show *you.*"

I had a feeling he knew each way intimately. A flush spread over my cheeks, down my throat. "I'd rather roll around in manure than anything *you* might sleep in."

Daemon arched a brow and then spun around. "You need to call Matthew," he said to his sister. "Like now and not five minutes from now."

I stayed against the tree, eyes wide and unmoving until he disappeared back into his house, the door slamming shut behind him. I swallowed, looking at a distraught Dee. "Okay," I said. "That was intense."

Dee dropped down on the steps, her hands in her face. "I really love him, I do. He's my brother, the only—" She cut herself off, lifting her head. "But he's a dick. I know he is. He wasn't always like that."

Speechless, I stared at her. My heart was still racing, pumping blood way too fast. I wasn't sure if it was fear or adrenaline that was making me dizzy when I finally pushed away from the tree and approached her. And if I wasn't afraid, I kind of wondered if I should be.

"It's hard having friends with him around," she murmured, staring at her hands. "He runs them all off."

"Gee, I wonder why." Actually, I did wonder why. His possessiveness seemed a bit off the charts. My hands were still shaking, and even though he was gone, I could still *feel* him—the heat he'd thrown off. It had been…exciting. Sadly.

"I'm so, so sorry." She jumped up from the steps, opening and closing her hands. "It's just that he's overprotective."

"I get that, but it's not like I'm some dude trying to molest you or something."

A grin peeked through. "I know, but he worries a lot. I know he'll…calm down, once he gets to know you."

I doubted that.

"Please tell me he hasn't run you off, too." She stepped in front of me, brows furrowed. "I know you probably think hanging out with me isn't worth—"

"No. It's okay." I ran a hand over my forehead. "He didn't run me off—he won't."

She looked so relieved I thought she'd collapse. "Good. I have to go, but I'll fix this. I promise."

I shrugged. "There's nothing to fix. He isn't your problem."

A strange look crossed her face. "But he kind of is. I'll talk to you later, okay?"

Nodding, I watched her head back to her house. I grabbed the empty bags. What the hell had that been about? Never in my life had someone disliked me so strongly. Shaking my head, I dumped the bags in the trash.

Daemon was hot, but he was a jerk. A bully. And I'd meant what I said to Dee. He wasn't going to scare me off from being friends with his sister. He'd just have to deal with it. I was here to stay.

Chapter 4

I skipped posting on my blog on Monday, mainly because it was usually a "What are you reading" type thing and I wasn't reading anything new at the moment. I decided my poor car needed a bath instead. Mom would be proud if she had been up, seeing that I was outside during the summer and not chained to my laptop. Other than the occasional gardening stint, I was typically a shut-in.

The sky was clear and the air carried a light musky scent mingled with pine. Soon after I'd gotten started with cleaning the inside of my car, I was amazed at how many pens and hair ties I found. Seeing my book bag on the backseat caused me to cringe. In a couple of weeks I'd be starting a new school, and I knew Dee would be surrounded by friends — friends that Daemon probably approved of, which wasn't me, because he obviously thought I was a crack dealer.

Next, I got out a bucket and hose and soaped up most

of the car, but when I reached over the top of the roof, all I ended up doing was soaking myself and dropping the sponge a dozen times. No matter which side I tried to attack the roof from, it wasn't working

Cursing, I started picking out pieces of gravel and grass from the sponge. I wanted to launch it into the nearby woods. Frustrated, I ended up tossing the sponge into the bucket.

"You look as if you could use some help."

I jumped. Daemon stood a few feet away from me, hands in the front pockets of his faded jeans. His bright eyes sparkled in the sunlight.

His sudden appearance had startled me. I hadn't even heard him. How could someone move so damn quietly, especially as tall as he was? And hey, he had a shirt on. I wasn't sure if I should be grateful or disappointed. Mouth aside, he was drool-worthy. I snapped out of it, preparing myself for the inevitable verbal smackdown.

He wasn't smiling, but at least he didn't look like he wanted to kill me this time. If anything, his expression took on a mask of grudging acceptance, probably how I looked when I had to give a book I'd been excited about a less than stellar review.

"You looked as though you wanted to throw that again." He gestured to the bucket with his elbow and the sponge floating on top of the suds. "I figured I'd do my good deed for the day and intervene before any innocent sponges lose their lives."

I brushed a few strands of damp hair out of my eyes, not sure what to say.

Daemon bent quickly and snatched up the sponge, squeezing

out the excess water. "You look like you got more of a bath than the car. I never thought washing a car would be so hard, but after watching you for the last fifteen minutes, I'm convinced it should be an Olympic sport."

"You were watching me?" Kind of creepy. Kind of hot. *No! Not hot.*

He shrugged. "You could always take the car to the car wash. It would be a lot easier."

"Car washes are a waste of money."

"True," he said slowly. He knelt down and began cleaning a spot I'd missed on the fender around the tire before tackling the roof of the car. "You need new tires. These are about bald and winter's crazy around here."

I didn't care about my tires. I couldn't figure out why he was here, talking to me, when the last time we'd spoken, he'd acted like I was the antichrist and practically had me pinned to a tree, talking about ways to get dirty. And why hadn't I brushed my hair this morning?

"Anyway, I'm glad you were out here." He finished with the roof in record time and picked up the hose. He flashed a half grin at me and started spraying the car with water, the suds running down the sides like an overflowing cup. "I think I'm supposed to apologize."

"You *think* you're supposed to?"

Daemon faced me, eyes narrowed against the bright sun, and I barely dodged the spray of water as he tackled the opposite side of the car. "Yeah, according to Dee I needed to get my ass over here and make nice. Something about me killing her chances of having a 'normal' friend."

"A normal friend? What kind of friends does she have?"

"Not normal," he replied.

He preferred "not normal" friends for his sister? "Well, apologizing and not meaning it kind of defeats the purpose of apologizing."

He made an affirmative noise. "True."

I stared at him. "Are you serious?"

"Yeah," he dragged the word out, working his way around the car as he continued to rinse off the soap suds. "Actually, I don't have a choice. I have to make nice."

"You don't seem like a person who does anything he doesn't want to do."

"Normally I'm not." He moved around to the back of the car. "But my sister took my car keys and until I play nice, I don't get them back. It's too damn annoying to get replacements."

I tried to stop it, but I laughed. "She took your keys?"

He scowled, returning to my side. "It's not funny."

"You're right." I laughed. "It's freaking hilarious."

Daemon shot me a dirty look.

I folded my arms. "I'm sorry, though. I'm not accepting your not-so-sincere apology."

"Not even when I'm cleaning your car?"

"Nope." I smiled at the way his eyes narrowed. "You may never see those keys again."

"Well, damn, there went my plan." A begrudging smile toyed with the corners of his mouth. "I figured that if I really don't feel bad, then at least I could make up for it."

Part of me was annoyed, but there was another part of me that was amused—reluctantly amused. "Are you normally this warm and sparkly?"

He headed past me and turned the water off. "Always. Do you usually stare at guys when you stop over, asking for directions?"

"Do you always answer the door half-naked?"

"Always. And you didn't answer my question. Do you always stare?"

Heat infused my cheeks. "I was *not* staring."

"Really?" he asked. That half grin was there again, hinting at dimples. "Anyway, you woke me up. I'm not a morning person."

"It wasn't that early," I pointed out.

"I sleep in. It is summer, you know. Don't you sleep in?"

I pushed back a strand of hair that had escaped my ponytail. "No. I always get up early."

He groaned. "You sound just like my sister. No wonder she loves you so much already."

"Dee has taste...unlike some," I said. His lips twitched. "And she's great. I really like her, so if you're over here to play big, bad brother, just forget it."

"That's not why I'm here." He gathered up the bucket and various sprays and cleansers. I probably should have helped him sort things out, but it was fascinating watching him take charge of my little cleaning project. Although he kept tossing me the odd half smile, I could tell this little exchange was awkward for him. Good.

"Then why are you here, other than delivering a crappy apology?" I couldn't stop staring at his mouth when he spoke. I bet he knew how to kiss. Perfect kisses too, ones that weren't wet and gross, but the kind that curled toes.

I needed to stop looking at him in general.

Daemon placed all the supplies on the porch steps and straightened. Stretching his arms over his head, his shirt rode up, revealing a tantalizing glimpse of muscles. His gaze lingered on my face, and warmth blossomed in my belly. "Maybe I'm just curious why she is so enamored. Dee doesn't take well to strangers. None of us do."

"I had a dog once that didn't take well to strangers."

Daemon stared at me a moment, then laughed. It was a deep, rumbling sound. Nice. Sexy. Oh God, I looked away. He was the kind of boy that broke hearts and left a long line of them shattered behind him. He was trouble. Maybe the fun kind of trouble, but he was also a jerk. And I didn't do jerks. Not that I *did* anyone.

I cleared my throat. "Well, thanks for the car thing."

Suddenly, he was right in front of me again. So close that his toes almost touched mine. I sucked in a sharp breath, wanting to back up. He needed to stop doing that. "How do you move so fast?"

He ignored the question. "My little sis does seem to like you," he said, as if he couldn't figure out why.

I bristled and tilted my head back but focused my gaze over his shoulder. "Little? You're twins."

"I was born a whole four minutes and thirty seconds before she was," he boasted, his eyes meeting mine. "Technically she is my little sister."

My throat felt dry. "She's the baby in the family?"

"Yep, therefore I'm the one starved for attention."

"I guess that explains your poor attitude then," I retorted.

"Maybe, but most people find me charming."

I started to respond, but made the mistake of looking into

his eyes. I was immediately snared by the unnatural color, reminded of the purest, deepest parts of the Everglades. "I have…a hard time believing that."

His lips curved slightly. "You shouldn't, Kat." He picked up a loose section of hair that had escaped my clip, twirling the hair around his finger. "What kind of color is this? It's not brown or blonde."

My cheeks itched with heat. I snatched my hair back. "It's called light brown."

"Hmm," he said, nodding. "You and I have plans to make."

"What?" I sidestepped his large body, dragging in a deep breath as I gained some distance. My heart was pounding. "We don't have any plans to make."

Daemon sat down on the steps, stretching out his long legs and leaning back on his elbows.

"Comfortable?" I snapped.

"Very." He squinted up at me. "About these plans…"

I stood a few feet from him. "What are you talking about?"

"You remember the whole 'getting my ass over here and playing nice' thing, right? That also involves my car keys?" He crossed his ankles as his gaze slid over to the trees. "Those plans involve me getting my car keys back."

"You need to give me a little more of an explanation than that."

"Of course," he sighed. "Dee hid my keys. She's good at hiding stuff, too. I've already torn the house apart, and I can't find them."

"So, make her tell you where they are." Thank God I

didn't have any siblings.

"Oh, I would, if she was here. But she's left town and won't be back until Sunday."

"What?" She'd never mentioned going out of town. Or family nearby. "I didn't know that."

"It was a last-minute thing." He uncrossed his ankles and one foot started to tap an unheard rhythm. "And the only way she'll tell me where the keys are hidden is by me earning bonus points. See, my sister has this thing about bonus points, ever since elementary school."

I started to smile. "Okay...?"

"I have to earn bonus points to get my keys back," he explained. "The only way I can earn those points is by doing something nice for you."

I busted out laughing again. The look on his face was awesome. "I'm sorry, but this is kind of funny."

Daemon drew in a deep, disgusted breath. "Yeah, it's real funny."

My laughter faded. "What do you have to do?"

"I'm supposed to take you swimming tomorrow. If I do that, then she'll tell me where my keys are hidden—and I *have* to be nice."

He had to be kidding, but the longer I stared at him, I realized he was being serious. My mouth dropped open. "So the only way you get your keys back is by taking me swimming and by being nice to me?"

"Wow. You're a quick one."

I did laugh again. "Yeah, well, you can kiss your keys good-bye."

Surprise shone on his face. "Why?"

"Because I'm not going anywhere with you," I told him.

"We don't have a choice."

"No. *You* don't have a choice, but I do." I glanced at the closed door behind him, wondering if Mom was somewhere trying to listen in. "I'm not the one with missing keys."

Daemon watched me for a moment, and then he grinned. "You don't want to hang out with me?"

"Uh, no."

"Why not?"

I rolled my eyes. "For starters, you're a jerk."

He nodded. "I can be."

"And I'm not spending time with a guy who's being forced to do it by his sister. I'm not desperate."

"You're not?"

Anger whipped through me, and I took a step forward. "Get off my porch."

He seemed to consider it. "No."

"What?" I sputtered. "What do you mean no?"

"I'm not leaving until you agree to go swimming with me."

Steam should be coming out of my ears. "Fine. You can sit there, because I'd rather eat glass than spend time with you."

He laughed. "That sounds drastic."

"Not nearly," I shot back, heading up the stairs.

Daemon twisted around, catching my ankle. His grip was loose, his hand incredibly warm. I looked down at him, and he smiled at me, as innocent as an angel. "I'll sit here all day and night. I'll camp out on your porch. And I won't leave. We have all week, Kitten. Either get it over with tomorrow and be done with me, or I'll be right here until you do agree. You won't be able to leave the house."

I gaped at him. "You can't be serious."

"Oh, I am."

"Just tell her we went and that I had a great time." I tried to pull my foot free, but he held on. "Lie."

"She'll know if I'm lying. We're twins. We know these things." He paused. "Or are you too shy to go swimming with me? Does the idea of getting almost naked around me make you uncomfortable?"

I grabbed the railing and yanked on my foot. The *butthead* was only lightly holding me, but my foot wouldn't budge. "I'm from Florida, idiot. I've spent half my life in a bathing suit."

"What's the big deal?"

"I don't like you." I stopped pulling and stood there. His hand seemed to hum around my skin. It was the weirdest feeling ever. "Let go of my ankle."

Very slowly, he lifted each finger while holding my stare. "I'm not leaving, Kitten. You're going to do this."

My mouth opened as did the door behind us. Stomach dropping, I turned to see Mom standing there in all her fuzzy-bunny pajama glory. Oh, for the love of God.

Her eyes went from me to Daemon, completely misinterpreting everything. The glee in her eyes made me want to vomit on Daemon's head. "You live next door?"

Daemon twisted around and smiled. He had perfect white, straight teeth. "My name is Daemon Black."

Mom smiled. "Kellie Swartz. Nice to meet you." She glanced at me. "You two can come inside if you want. You don't have to sit outside in the heat."

"That's really nice of you." He stood and elbowed me, and not very gently. "Maybe we should go inside and finish talking about our plans."

"No," I said, glaring at him. "That won't be necessary."

"What plans?" Mom asked, smiling. "I support plans."

"I'm trying to get your lovely daughter to go swimming with me tomorrow, but I think she's worried you wouldn't like the idea." He chucked me on the arm and I almost fell into the railing. "And I think she's shy."

"What?" Mom shook her head. "I have no problem with her going swimming with you. I think it's a great idea. I've been telling her she needs to get out. Hanging out with your sister is great, but—"

"*Mom*." I narrowed my eyes at her. "That's not really—"

"I was just telling Katy here the same thing." Daemon dropped his arm over my shoulders. "My sister is out of town for the next week. I thought I'd hang with Katy."

My mom smiled, pleased. "That is so sweet of you."

I wrapped my arm around his narrow waist, digging my fingers into his side. "Yeah, that's sweet of you, Daemon."

He sucked in a sharp breath and let it out slowly. "You know what they say about boys next door...."

"Well, I know Katy doesn't have plans tomorrow." She glanced at me, and I could practically see her envisioning Daemon and my future children. My mom was not normal. "She's free to go swimming."

I dropped my arm and wiggled out from underneath Daemon's. "Mom..."

"It's okay, honey." She started back inside, giving Daemon a wink. "It was nice to finally meet you."

Daemon smiled. "You, too."

The moment my mom shut the door behind her, I whirled around and pushed Daemon, but he was like a brick wall. "You jerk."

Grinning, he backed down the steps. "I'll see you at noon, Kitten."

"I hate you," I hissed.

"The feeling's mutual." He glanced over his shoulder. "Twenty bucks says you wear a one-piece swimsuit."

He was insufferable.

Chapter 5

When the first cracks of light came through the windows, I rolled onto my side, still half asleep.

I groaned.

I had to hang out with Daemon today. And I'd tossed and turned all night, dreaming about a boy with shocking green eyes and a bikini that kept coming undone. Grabbing the latest novel I was reviewing from my nightstand, I spent the morning lounging in bed and reading, desperately trying to think of anything but our upcoming adventure.

When the sun was nearly high in the sky, I set the book aside, threw off the covers, and headed to the shower.

A few minutes later, I was standing in a towel and staring at my swimsuit options. Horror filled me. Daemon had been right. The idea of being half naked around him did make me want to spew my Tater Tots. Even though I couldn't stand him, and I actually think he might be the first person I ever hated, he was…he was a *god*. Who knew the kind of girls he was used to seeing in bathing suits.

Even though I wouldn't touch him for all the money in the world, I was big enough to admit there was a part of me that wanted him to want *me*.

I only had three bathing suits that could be considered acceptable: a razorback one-piece. Plain and boring. A two-piece that was a bikini top and boy shorts, and a third that was a red two-piece bikini.

I could have chosen a tent and I'd still feel uncomfortable.

Throwing the one-piece back into the closet, I held up the other two. My reflection stared back at me, a suit on each side, and I took a hard look at myself. Light brown hair fell to the middle of my back, and I was nervous of ever cutting it. My eyes were a plain gray — not magnetic or compelling like Dee's. My lips were full but not as expressive as my mom's.

I spared a glance at the red suit. I was always reserved, more cautious than my mom would ever be. The red bathing suit was anything but cautious. It was flirty, sexy even. Something I clearly was not and, well, that bothered me. Reserved, practical Katy was safe and boring. That was who I was. Why my mom felt okay to leave me alone all the time, because I would never do anything that would make her blink twice.

The kind of girl Daemon expected he could easily boss around and intimidate. He probably expected me to wear a one-piece and keep my shorts and top on since he'd taunted me. What had he said when he first met me? That I looked like a thirteen-year-old?

A red hot feeling sparked inside me.

Screw him.

I wanted to be exciting and bold. Maybe I even wanted to shock Daemon, prove him wrong. Without a second thought, I threw the plain suit into the corner and laid the red one on my small desk.

My decision was made.

I put on the tiny scraps in record time, and a pair of denim shorts and a tank top that had pretty flowers on it over the top to hide my audacity. Once I found my sneakers, I gathered up a towel and headed downstairs.

My mom was lingering in the kitchen, the standard coffee cup in hand. "You slept late. Did you sleep well last night?" she asked expectantly.

Sometimes I wondered if my mom was psychic. Shrugging, I shuffled by her and grabbed the orange juice. I concentrated way too hard on making toast while she continued to stare at my back. "I've been reading."

"Katy?" she said after what seemed like forever.

My hand shook a bit as I buttered my toast. "Yeah?"

"Is…is everything working out for you here? Do you like it?"

I nodded. "Yeah, it's nice."

"Good." She took a deep breath. "Are you excited about today?"

My stomach dropped as I faced her. Part of me wanted to throttle her for helping trap me in Daemon's plans, but she didn't know any better. I knew she worried I was going to hate her for yanking me out of everything I loved and insisting we move here. "Yeah, I guess so," I lied.

"I think you will have a good time," she said. "Just be

careful."

I shot her a knowing glance. "I doubt I'll get into any trouble swimming."

"Where are you guys going?"

"I don't know. He didn't say. Somewhere nearby I'm sure."

My mom made her way to the door. "You know what I mean. He's a good-looking boy." Then she gave me the *I've been there so don't try anything* look before she left.

Breathing a sigh of relief, I washed out her coffee cup. I didn't think that I could sit through another birds and bees conversation, especially not now. The first one had been traumatic enough.

I shuddered at the memory.

I was so caught up reliving that horrible mother-daughter bonding moment, I jumped when someone banged against the front door. My heart flipped as I looked at the time.

11:46 a.m.

After taking a calming breath, I stumbled over my own feet to get to the door. Daemon stood with a towel thrown casually over his shoulder.

"I'm a little early."

"I can see," I said, voice flat. "Change your mind? You could always try lying."

He arched a brow. "I'm not a liar."

I stared at him. "Just give me a second to grab my stuff." I didn't wait for his reply. I swung the door shut in his face. It was childish, but I felt like I'd scored a small victory. I went to the kitchen and grabbed my sneakers and stuff before returning and opening the door again. Daemon was right where I'd left him.

Nervous excitement fluttered in my belly as I locked the front door and followed Daemon down the driveway. "Okay, so where are you taking me?"

"What fun would it be if you knew?" he asked. "You won't be surprised then."

"I'm new to town, remember? Everywhere is going to be a surprise for me."

"Then why ask?" He cocked a smug eyebrow.

I rolled my eyes. "We aren't driving?

Daemon laughed. "No. Where we're going you can't drive. It's not a well-known spot. Most locals don't even know about it."

"Oh, I'm special then."

"You know what I think, Kat?"

I peeked at him and caught him watching me with such serious intensity I flushed. "I'm pretty sure I don't want to know."

"I think my sister finds you very special. I'm starting to wonder if she's onto something."

I smirked. "But then there's all kinds of *special* now, isn't there, Daemon."

He seemed startled to hear his name. After a beat the intensity was gone, and he led me down the road and across the main highway. He had me curious when we entered the dense tree line on the other side of the road.

"Are you taking me out to the woods as a trick?" I asked, half serious.

He glanced over his shoulder, lashes hiding his eyes. "And what would I do out here to you, Kitten?"

I shivered. "The possibilities are endless."

"Aren't they?" He made his way easily around the thick brush and vines tangled together on the floor of the woods.

I was having a hell of a time not breaking my neck on the many exposed roots and moss-covered rocks. "Can we pretend we did this?"

"Trust me, I don't want to be doing this either." He jumped over a fallen tree. "But bitching about it isn't going to make it any easier." Turning around, he offered me his hand.

"You're such a joy to talk to." I briefly considered ignoring it, but I placed my hand in his. Static passed from his skin to mine. I bit down on my lip as he helped me over the downed tree before dropping my hand. "Thank you."

Daemon looked away and continued walking. "Are you excited about school?"

What? Like he cared? "It's not exciting being the newbie. You know, the whole sticking out like a sore thumb. Not fun."

"I can see that."

"You can?"

"Yeah, I can. We only have a little bit more to go."

I wanted to question him further, but why put the effort into it? He'd give me another vague answer or innuendo. "A little bit? How long have we been walking?"

"About twenty minutes, maybe a little longer. I told you it was fairly hidden."

Following him over another uprooted tree, I saw a clearing ahead beyond the trees.

"Welcome to our little piece of paradise." There was a sardonic twist to his lips.

Ignoring him, I walked into the clearing. I was amazed.

"Wow. This place is beautiful."

"It is." He stood next to me, one hand cupping his eyes against the glare from the sun bouncing off the smooth surface of the water.

I could tell from the stiff set of his shoulders, this place was special to him. Just knowing that kind of made my stomach flutter. I reached up and put my hand on his arm, and he turned to face me. "Thank you for bringing me."

Before Daemon could open his mouth and ruin the moment, I dropped my hand and deliberately looked away.

A creek divided the clearing, expanding into a small, natural lake. It rippled in the soft breeze. Rocks erupted from the middle, flat and smooth-looking. Somehow, the land had been cleared in a perfect circle around the water. Large patches of flat, grassy land and wildflowers blossomed in the full sun. It was peaceful.

I went to the water's edge. "How deep is it?"

"About ten feet in most parts, twenty feet on the other side of the rocks." He was right behind me, doing that creepy, quiet walking thing. "Dee loves it here. Before you came, she spent most of her days here."

To Daemon, my arrival was the beginning of the end. The apocalypse. Kat-mageddon. "You know, I'm not going to get your sister in trouble."

"We'll see."

"I'm not a bad influence," I tried again. Things would be much easier if we could just get along. "I haven't ever gotten into trouble before."

He slipped around me, eyes on the still waters. "She doesn't need a friend like you."

"There isn't anything wrong with me," I snapped. "You know what? Forget this."

He sighed. "Why do you garden?"

I stopped, hands clenching. "What?"

"Why do you garden?" he asked again, still staring at the lake. "Dee said you do it so you don't think. What do you want to avoid thinking about?"

Was this caring and sharing time now? "It's none of your business."

Daemon shrugged. "Then let's go swimming."

Swimming was the last thing I wanted to do. Drowning him? Maybe. But then he kicked off his sneakers and took off his jeans. Underneath, he had on swim trunks. Then he whipped his shirt off in one quick motion. *Dayam*. I'd seen guys without their shirts on before. I lived in Florida, where every guy felt the need to walk around half-dressed. Hell, I'd seen *this* half-naked guy before. This shouldn't be a big deal.

But man, I was so wrong.

He had a great build, not too big but more muscles than any boy his age should have. Daemon moved with a fluid grace to the water, his muscles flexing and stretching with every step.

I wasn't sure how long I stood staring after him before he finally dived into the water. My cheeks were warm. I exhaled, realizing I'd been holding my breath. I needed to get a grip. Or a camera to memorialize this moment, because I bet I could make money from a video of him. I could make a fortune... As long as he never opened his mouth.

Daemon broke the surface several feet away from where he went under, water glistening in his hair and on the tips of his lashes. His dark hair was slicked back, bringing more focus on his eerie green eyes. "Are you coming in?"

Recalling the red bathing suit I'd decided to wear, I wished I could run away. My earlier confidence had evaporated. I toed off my shoes with slow, deliberate movements, pretending to enjoy the surroundings while my heart threw itself against my ribs.

He watched for a few moments, curious. "You sure are shy, aren't you, Kitten?"

I stilled. "Why do you call me that?"

"Because it makes your hair stand up, like a kitten." Daemon was laughing at me. He pushed back farther, the water lapping at his chest. "So? Are you coming in?"

Good God, he wasn't going to turn around or anything. And there was a challenge in his stare, as if he expected me to chicken out. Maybe that's what he wanted—expected. There was no doubt in my mind that he knew he had an effect on girls.

Practical, boring Katy would've gone into the lake fully clothed.

I didn't want to be her. That was the whole purpose of the red bathing suit. I wanted to prove to him I wasn't easily intimidated. I was determined to win this round.

Daemon looked bored. "I'm giving you one minute to get in here."

I resisted the urge to flip him off again and took a deep breath. It wasn't as if I was getting naked, not really. "Or what?"

He moved closer to the bank of the lake. "Or I come and get you."

I scowled at him. "I'd like to see you try that."

"Forty seconds." He watched me with an intense, piercing gaze as he drifted closer.

Rubbing my hand down my face, I sighed.

"Thirty seconds." He taunted from an even shorter distance.

"Jesus," I muttered, yanking my shirt off. I thought twice about throwing it at his head. I raced to shed my shorts when he called out the last taunting reminder.

I stepped toward the edge with my hands on my hips. "Happy?"

Daemon lost his smile and stared. "I'm never happy around you."

"What did you say?" My eyes narrowed on his blank expression. He did *not* say what I thought he did.

"Nothing. You better get in before that blush reaches your toes."

Flushing even more under his scrutiny, I turned and walked toward the edge of the lake where the drop-off wasn't steep. The water felt great, easing the uncomfortable heat prickling my skin.

I stumbled for anything to say. "It's beautiful out here."

He watched me for a moment and then thankfully disappeared under the water. Water dripped down his face when he popped back up. Needing to cool my face off, I went under. The cold rush was invigorating, clearing my thoughts. Resurfacing, I pushed the long clumps of hair out of my face.

Daemon eyed me from a few feet away, his cheeks above the waterline and his breath blowing the occasional bubble to break the surface tension. Something in his gaze beckoned me closer.

"What?" I asked after a stretch of silence.

"Why don't you come here?"

There was no way I was going near him. Not even if he dangled a cookie in his hand. Trust and his name didn't go together. I twisted around, dipping under the water, heading for the rocks I'd seen in the middle of the lake.

I reached them in a few strong strokes and pulled myself out of the water, onto the warm, hard surface. I started squeezing the water out of my hair. He treaded water in the middle of the lake. "You look disappointed."

Daemon didn't respond. A curious, almost confused look crossed his face. "Well…what do we have here?"

I dangled my feet into the water and made a face at him. "What are you talking about now?"

"Nothing." He waded closer to me.

"You said something."

"I did, didn't I?"

"You're strange."

"You're not what I expected," he said in a hushed voice.

"What does that mean?" I asked as he made a grab for my foot, and I moved my leg out of his reach. "I'm not good enough to be your sister's friend?"

"You don't have anything in common with her."

"How would you know?" I shifted again as he reached for the other leg.

"I know."

"We have a lot in common. And I like her. She's nice and she's fun." I scooted back, completely out of his grasp. "And you should stop being such a dick and chasing off her friends."

Daemon was quiet, and then he laughed. "You're not really like them."

"Like who?"

Another long moment passed. The water lapped around his shoulders, tiny ripples echoing from his chest as he pushed away.

Shaking my head, I watched him disappear under the water again. I leaned back and closed my eyes. The way the warmth of the sun fell against my upturned face, and the way the heat from the rock seeped through my skin, reminded me of dozing off at the beach. Cool water tickled my toes. I could stay here all day, basking in the sun. Minus Daemon, it would've been perfect.

I had no idea what he meant by the whole not like them or needing a friend like me. It had to be more than him being a psycho overprotective brother. Pushing up, I expected to see him floating on his back, but he had disappeared. I didn't see him anywhere. I stood up, careful of the sloping rock, and scanned the lake, studying the twinkling surface for a mass of black, wavy hair.

I made another turn on the rock as unease bubbled in my stomach. Did he leave me here as a joke? But wouldn't I have heard him?

I waited, thinking that any second he would break out of the water, lungs gasping for breath, but seconds turned into a minute, and then another. I kept searching the calm surface for any sign of Daemon, growing more frantic with each sweep of my eyes.

I dragged my hair behind my ears, cupping my hand

against the harsh sun. There was no way he could've held his breath this long. No way.

My breath hitched, then turned to ice in my tight chest. This was wrong. I scrambled across the rock and peered down into the still water.

Had he hurt himself somehow?

"Daemon!" I screamed.

There was no response.

Chapter 6

"Daemon!"

A hundred thoughts raced through my head. How long had he been under? Where had I seen him last? How long would it take for me to get help? I didn't like Daemon, and yeah, I might have briefly considered the idea of drowning him, but I didn't really wish the guy dead.

"Oh my God," I whispered. "This can't be happening."

I couldn't afford to think anymore. I had to do something. Just as I took a small step to dive into the water, the surface heaved and Daemon burst from the water. Surprise and relief rushed through me, followed by the intense urge to vomit. And then hit him.

He levered himself onto the rock, the muscles of his arms popping from the strain. "Are you okay? You look a little freaked out."

Snapping out of it, I grabbed his slippery shoulders in

an effort to assure my queasy stomach he was alive and not brain damaged from lack of oxygen. "Are you okay? What happened?" Then I smacked his arm. *Hard.* "Don't you ever do that again!"

Daemon threw his hands up. "Whoa there, what is your problem?"

"You were under the water for so long. I thought you drowned! Why would you do that? Why would you scare me like that?" I hopped to my feet, dragging in a deep breath. "You were under the water *forever.*"

He frowned. "I wasn't down there that long. I was swimming."

"No, Daemon, you were down there a long time. It was at least ten minutes! I looked for you, called for you. I...I thought you were dead."

He climbed to his feet. "It couldn't have been ten minutes. That's not possible. No one can hold their breath that long."

I swallowed. "You apparently can."

Daemon's eyes searched mine. "You were really worried, weren't you?"

"No shit! What part of '*I thought you drowned*' don't you understand?" I was shaking.

"Kat, I came up. You must not have seen me. I went right back down."

He was lying. I knew it in every bone in my body. Was he just able to hold his breath for an extremely long time? But if that was the case, why wouldn't he say so?

"Does this happen often?" he asked.

My gaze snapped back to his. "Does what?"

"Imagining things." He waved his hand. "Or do you have a horrible issue with telling time."

"I wasn't imagining anything! And I know how to tell time, you jerk."

"Then I don't know what to tell you." He stepped forward, which wasn't very far on the rock. "I'm not the one imagining that I was underwater for ten minutes when it was like two minutes tops. You know, maybe I'll buy you a watch the next time I'm in town, when I have *my* keys back."

For some stupid reason, one I would probably never know, I'd forgotten the reason why we were here. Somewhere between seeing him half naked and then thinking he was dead, I'd lost my mind.

"Well, make sure you tell Dee we had a *wonderful* time so that you can get your stupid keys back," I said, meeting his eyes. "Then we won't need a replay of today."

The smug smile was plastered across his face. "That's on you, Kitten. I'm sure she'll call you later and ask."

"You'll have your keys. I'm ready—" My foot slipped over the wet rock. Thrown off balance, my arms flailed in the air.

Moving lightning fast, his hand shot out and grabbed mine, pulling me forward. The next thing I knew I was against his warm, wet chest and his arm was around my waist.

"Careful there, Kitten. Dee would be pissed at me if you end up cracking your head open and drowning."

Understandable. She'd probably think he did it on purpose. I started to respond but couldn't. There wasn't much separating our skin in terms of clothing. My blood was pumping way too fast. It had to be the whole almost-drowning incident.

A strange edginess swamped me as we stared at each other, the slight wind brushed along wet skin that wasn't pressed against one another, making the parts plastered together seem even hotter.

Neither of us spoke.

His chest rose and fell, the deep bottle-green of his eyes shifting by degrees. It was a powerful, almost electric feeling that coursed through me—answering something in him?

Well, that was strange, foolish, and illogical. He hated me.

Then Daemon released my waist and stepped back. He cleared his throat, his voice thick. "I think it's time we head back."

I nodded, disappointed and not even sure why I was disappointed. His mood swings made me feel as if I were on one of those crappy tilt-a-whirls that wouldn't end, but there…there was just something about him.

We didn't speak as we dried off and dressed. We started back home silently. It seemed neither of us had anything to say, which was actually nice. I liked him better when he'd lost the ability to speak.

But when we reached the driveway, he cursed under his breath. It felt like a blast of arctic air had swept between us. I followed his troubled gaze. There was a strange car in his driveway, one of those expensive Audis that cost my mom's salary. I wondered if it was his parents, and if this was going to turn into Kat-mageddon round two.

Daemon's jaw flexed. "Kat, I—"

A door opened and closed, banging off the side of the house. A man in his late twenties, early thirties stepped out onto the porch. His light brown hair didn't match Daemon's and Dee's dark waves. Whoever he was, he was handsome and dressed nicely.

And he also looked pissed.

The man came down the steps two at a time. He didn't even look at me. Not once. "What's going on here?"

"Absolutely nothing." Daemon folded his arms. "Since my sister is not home, I'm curious as to why you're in my house?"

Okay. Definitely not family.

"I let myself in," he replied. "I didn't realize that would be a problem."

"It is now, Matthew."

Matthew. I recognized the name from the phone call Dee had to take. Finally, the man's steely gaze zeroed in on me. His eyes widened slightly. They were a bright, startling blue. His lip curled as he looked me up and down. Not in a checking me out kind of way, either, but like he was sizing me up. "Of all people, I'd think you'd know better, Daemon."

Oh hell, here we go again. I was beginning to wonder if I was flying a freak flag. The air was rife with tension, and all because of me. It didn't make any sense. I didn't even know this guy.

Daemon's eyes narrowed. "Matthew, if you value the ability to walk, I wouldn't go there."

Weirded out to the max, I stepped to the side. "I think I should go."

"I'm thinking Matthew should go," Daemon said, stepping in front of me, "unless he has another purpose other than sticking his nose where it doesn't belong."

Even Daemon couldn't block the revulsion in the man's stare. "I'm sorry," I said, voice wavering, "but I don't know what's going on here. We were just swimming."

Matthew's gaze swung on Daemon, who squared his shoulders. "It's not what you're thinking. Give me some credit. Dee hid my keys, forced me take her out to get them back."

A hot flush swept through me. Did he really need to tell some dude I was a pity date?

And then the man laughed. "So this is Dee's little friend."

"That would be me," I said, crossing my arms.

"I thought you had this under control." He gestured toward me, sounding as if I were a homicidal clown standing next to Daemon. "That you'd make your sister understand."

"Yeah, well, why don't you try to make her understand," Daemon retorted. "So far, I'm not having much luck."

Matthew's lips thinned. "Both of you should know better."

A crack of thunder startled me as they stared at one another. Lightning streaked overhead, momentarily blinding. Once the light receded, dark, tumultuous clouds rolled in. Energy crackled around me, flashing across my skin.

Then Matthew turned away, casting another dark look in my direction before heading inside Daemon's house. The moment the door slammed shut behind him, the clouds parted. I stared at Daemon, mouth hanging open.

"What...what just happened?" I asked.

He was already walking into the house, the door smacking off the frame once again like a shot in a canyon. I stood there, not sure what happened. I looked up at the clear sky. No trace of the violent storm. I'd seen that happen a hundred times in Florida, but what occurred seemed way too freakish. And thinking back to the lake, I wasn't sure what had happened, but I knew Daemon had been underwater far too long. I also knew there was something not normal about him.

About all of them.

Chapter 7

Dee called that night, and even though I wanted to tell her that my time with Daemon hadn't been all puppy dog tails and rainbows, I lied. I told her he was *great*. He *earned* his keys and then some. Otherwise, she might make him take me on another outing.

I almost felt bad for lying when she sounded happy.

The next week crawled by. I had endless time to dread the fact there was only a week and a half left before school started. Dee still hadn't come back from visiting family or whatever she was doing. Left alone and bored out of my mind, I'd gotten reacquainted with the Internet intimately.

It was early Saturday evening when Daemon unexpectedly showed up at my door, hands shoved into the pockets of his jeans. His back was to me, head tipped back as he stared up at the cloudless blue sky. A few stars were starting to appear but the sun wouldn't truly set for another couple of hours.

Surprised to see him, I walked outside. His head whipped down so fast I thought he would pull a muscle. "What are you doing?" I asked.

His brows slanted low. Several seconds passed and then his lip tipped up at one corner. He cleared his throat. "I like staring at the sky. There's something about it." His gaze returned to the sky. "It's endless, you know."

Daemon almost sounded deep. "Is some crazy dude going to run out of your house and yell at you for talking to me?"

"Not right now, but there is always later."

I wasn't sure if he was being serious or not. "I'm okay missing 'later.'"

"Yeah. Busy?"

"Other than messing with my blog, no."

"You have a blog?" He faced me, leaning back against the post. Derision pinched his features.

He'd said blog like it was a crack habit. "Yeah, I have a blog."

"What's your blog's name?"

"None of your business," I said, smiling sweetly.

"Interesting name." He returned my smile with a half grin. "So what do you blog about? Knitting? Puzzles? Being lonely?"

"Ha. Ha, smartass." I sighed. "I review books."

"Do you get paid for them?"

I laughed out loud at that. "No. Not at all."

Daemon seemed confused by that. "So you review books and you don't get paid if someone buys a book based on your review?"

"I don't review books to get paid or anything." Although

that would be sweet, which reminded me I needed to get a library card. "I do it because I like it. I love reading, and I enjoy talking about books."

"What kind of books do you read?"

"All different kinds." I leaned against the post opposite of him, craning my neck back to meet his steady gaze. "Mainly I prefer the paranormal stuff."

"Vampires and werewolves?"

Man, how many questions could he ask? "Yeah."

"Ghosts and aliens?"

"Ghost stories are cool, but I don't know about aliens. ET really doesn't do it for me and a lot of readers."

One single eyebrow arched. "What does it for you?"

"Not slimy green space creatures," I replied. "Anyway, I also appreciate graphic novels, history stuff—"

"You read graphic novels?" Disbelief colored his tone. "Seriously?"

I nodded. "Yeah, so what? Are girls not supposed to like graphic novels and comics?"

He stared at me a long moment, then jerked his chin toward the woods. "Want to go on a hike?"

"Uh, you know I'm not good with the whole hiking thing," I reminded him.

A grin appeared. There was an edge to it. Rough. Sexy. "I'm not taking you up on the Rocks. Just a harmless little trail. I'm sure you can handle it."

"Did Dee not tell you where your keys were?" I asked, suspicious.

"Yeah, she did."

"Then why are you here?"

Daemon sighed. "I don't have a reason. I thought I would just stop over, but if you're going to question everything, then you can forget it."

I watched him go down the steps as I chewed on my lip. This was crazy. I'd been dying of boredom for days. Rolling my eyes, I called out, "All right, let's do this."

"Are you sure?"

I agreed, with a hefty amount of trepidation. "Why are we going behind my house?" I asked when it was evident where he was leading me. "The Seneca Rocks are that way. I thought most trails started over there." I pointed to the front of my house, to where the tips of the monstrous sandstone-looking structures loomed over everything.

"Yeah, but there are trails back here that will take you around and it's quicker," he explained. "Most people here know all the main trails that are crowded. There used to be a lot of boring days out here, and I found a couple of them off the beaten trail."

I made a face. "How far off the beaten track are we talking?"

He chuckled. "Not *that* far."

"So it's a baby trail? I bet this is going to be boring for you."

"Anytime I get to go out and walk around is good. Besides it's not as if we'll hike all the way to Smoke Hole Canyon. That's a pretty big hike from here, so no worries, okay?"

"All right, lead the way."

We stopped off at Daemon's to grab a couple of water bottles and then took off. We walked on in silence for a few minutes and then he said, "You're very trusting, Kitten."

"Stop calling me that." It was a little difficult to keep up with his long-legged pace, so I trailed a few steps behind him.

He glanced over his shoulder without a misstep. "No one has ever called you that before?"

I picked my way around a large, prickly bush. "Yeah, people call me Kitten all the time. But you make it sound so..."

His brows shot up. "Sound so what?"

"I don't know, like it's an insult." He'd slowed, and now I was walking beside him. "Or something sexually deviant."

He turned his head away, laughing. The sound had my muscles tensing.

"Why are you always laughing at me?"

Shaking his head, he grinned down at me. "I don't know, you just kind of make me laugh."

I kicked a small rock. "Whatever. So what was up with that Matthew dude? He acted as if he hated me or something."

"He doesn't hate you. He doesn't trust you," he muttered the last words.

I shook my head, bewildered. "Trust me with what? Your virtue?"

He barked out a laugh, and it took him a few moments to respond. "Yeah. He's not a fan of beautiful girls who have the hots for me."

"What?" I tripped over an exposed root. Daemon caught me easily, setting me back on my feet the minute I was steady. The brief contact had my skin tingling through my clothes. His hands lingered on my waist only a few seconds before he dropped them. "You're joking, right?"

"Which part?" he asked.

"Any of that!"

"Come on. Please don't tell me you don't think you're pretty." He considered my silence. "No guy has ever said you're pretty?"

He wasn't the first person to say anything nice about me, but I guess I never cared before. Previous boyfriends told me I was pretty, but I never considered that a reason for someone disliking me. Looking away, I shrugged. "Of course."

"Or...maybe you're not aware of it?"

I shrugged again as I focused on the trunks of old trees, about to change the subject and deny the other part of his statement. I most definitely did not have the hots for this arrogant guy.

"You know what I've always believed?" he said softly.

We were still standing in the path, only the sounds of a few birds echoing around us. My voice drifted away on a light breeze. "No."

"I've always found that the most beautiful people, truly beautiful inside and out, are the ones who are quietly unaware of their effect." His eyes searched mine intently, and for a moment we stood there toe to toe. "The ones who throw their beauty around, waste what they have? Their beauty is only passing. It's just a shell hiding nothing but shadows and emptiness."

I did the most inappropriate thing possible. I laughed. "I'm sorry, but that was the most thoughtful thing I've ever heard you say. What alien ship took the Daemon I know away, and can I ask them to keep him?"

He scowled. "I was being honest."

"I know, but it's just that was really…wow." And here I was, ruining probably the nicest thing he would ever say to me.

He shrugged and began leading me down the trail again. "We won't go too far," he said after a few minutes. "So you're interested in history?"

"Yeah, I know that makes me a nerd." I was also grateful for the change in subject.

His lips twitched at that. "Did you know this land was once traveled by the Seneca Indians?"

I winced. "Please tell me we aren't walking on any burial grounds?"

"Well…I'm sure there *are* burial grounds around here somewhere. Even though they just traveled through this area, it's not a stretch that some died on this very spot and—"

"Daemon, I don't need to know that part." I gave him a light push on the arm.

He had that weird look again and shook his head. "Okay, I'll tell you the story and I'll leave some of the more creepy but natural facts out."

A long branch stretched across the path, and Daemon held it up for me to duck under, my shoulder brushing against his chest as I passed before he dropped the branch and took the lead again. "What story?"

"You'll see. Now pay attention…A long time ago, this land was forest and hills, which isn't too different than today with the exception of a few small towns." His finger drifted over the lower hanging branches as we walked, pushing the lower ones aside for me. "But imagine this place so sparsely populated that it could take days, even weeks, before you reached your nearest neighbor."

I shivered. "That seems so lonely."

"But you have to understand that was the way of life hundreds of years ago. Farmers and mountain men lived a few miles away from one another, but the distance was all traveled by foot or horse. It wasn't usually the safest way to travel."

"I can imagine," I responded faintly.

"The Seneca Indian tribe traveled through the eastern part of the United States, and at some point, they walked this very path toward the Seneca Rocks." His gaze met mine. "Did you know that this very small path behind your house leads right to the base of them?"

"No. They always seem so far off in the distance I never thought of them as being that close."

"If you stayed on this path for a couple of miles you'd find yourself at the base of them. It's a pretty rocky patch even the most experienced rock climbers stay away from. See, the Seneca Rocks spread from Grant to Pendleton County, with the highest point being Spruce Knob and an outcropping near Seneca called Champe Rocks. Now they are kind of hard to get to, since it usually involves invading someone's property, but it can be worth it if you can scale way beyond nine hundred feet in the sky," he finished wistfully.

"That sounds like fun." Not. I couldn't keep the sarcasm from my voice, so I offered a pained smile. I didn't want to spoil the mood. This was probably the longest Daemon and I had ever spoken without some statement earning him the finger.

"It is if you're not afraid of slipping." He laughed at my expression. "Anyway, the Seneca Rocks are made out of quartzite, which is part sandstone. That's why it sometimes has a pinkish tint to it. Quartzite is considered a beta quartz. People who believe in...abnormal powers or powers in... nature, as a lot of Indian tribes did at one time, believe that any form of beta quartz allows energy to be stored and transformed, even manipulated by it. It can throw electronics and other stuff off, too — hide things."

"Ooo-kay." He shot me a stern look, so I decided not to interrupt anymore.

"Possibly the beta quartz drew the Seneca Tribe to this area. No one knows since they weren't native to West Virginia. No one knows how long any of them camped here, traded, or made war." He paused for a few moments, scanning the terrain as if he could see them there, shadows of the past. "But they do have a very romantic legend."

"Romantic?" I asked as he led me around a small stream. I couldn't imagine anything romantic about something thrusting nine hundred feet in the sky.

"See, there was this beautiful Indian princess called Snowbird, who had asked seven of the tribe's strongest warriors to prove their love by doing something only she had been able to do. Many men wanted to be with her for her beauty and her rank. But she wanted an equal.

"When the day arrived for her to choose her husband, she set forth a challenge so only the bravest and most dedicated warrior would win her hand. She asked her suitors to climb the highest rock with her," he continued softly, slowing down so we were walking side by side on the narrow path now. "They all started, but as it became more difficult, three turned back. A fourth became weary and a fifth crumpled in exhaustion. Only two remained, and the beautiful Snowbird stayed in the lead. Finally, she reached the highest point and turned to see who was the bravest and strongest of all warriors. Only one remained a few feet behind her and as she watched, he began to slip."

I was quickly caught up in the legend. The idea of making seven men fight and face possible death to win your hand was unimaginable to me.

"Snowbird paused only for a second, thinking that this brave warrior obviously was the strongest, but he was not her equal. She could save him or she could let him slip. He was brave, but he had yet to reach the highest point like she had."

"But he was right behind her? How could she just let him fall?" I decided that this story sucked if Snowbird let the guy fall.

"What would you do?" he asked curiously.

"Not that I would ever ask a group of men to prove their love by doing something incredibly dangerous and stupid like that, but if I ever found myself in that situation, as unlikely—"

"Kat?" he chided.

"I would reach out and save him, of course. I couldn't let him fall to his death."

"But he didn't prove himself."

"That doesn't matter," I argued. "He was right behind her and how beautiful could you truly be if you let a man fall to his death just because he slipped? How could you even be capable of love or worthy of it, for that matter, if you let that happen?"

He nodded. "Well, Snowbird thought like you."

Relieved, I smiled. If she hadn't, this would've been a pretty crappy romance story. "Good."

"Snowbird decided that the warrior was her equal and with that, her decision had been made. She grabbed the man before he could fall. The chief met them and was very pleased with his daughter's choice in mate. He granted their marriage and made the warrior his successor."

"So is that why the rocks are called Seneca Rocks? After the Indians and Snowbird?"

He nodded. "That's what the legend says."

"It's a beautiful story, but I think the whole climbing several hundred feet in the air to prove your love is a little excessive."

He chuckled. "I'd have to agree with you on that."

"I'd hope so or you'd find yourself playing with cars on an interstate to prove your love nowadays." I wanted to bite my tongue the minute the words were out of my mouth. I hope he didn't think I meant for *me*.

He gave me a hard look. "I don't foresee that happening."

"Can you get to where the Indians climbed from here?" I asked curiously.

He shook his head. "You could get to the canyon, but that's serious hiking. Not something I would suggest you doing by yourself."

I laughed at the thought. "Yeah, I don't think you have to worry about that. I wonder why the Indians came here. Were they looking for something?" I stepped around a large boulder. "It's hard to believe that a bunch of rocks brought them here."

"You never know." His lips pursed and he was quiet for a moment before speaking again. "People tend to look on the beliefs of the past as being primitive and unintelligent, yet we are seeing more truth in the past every day."

I peered up at him, trying to gauge if he was being serious. He sounded much more mature than any boy our age. "What was it that made the rocks important again?"

He glanced down at me. "It's the type of rock...." His eyes widened suddenly. "Kitten?"

"Would you stop calling me—?"

"Be quiet," he hissed, gaze fixed over my shoulder. He placed his hand on my arm. "Promise me you won't freak out."

"Why would I freak out?" I whispered.

Tugging me toward him, he caught me off guard. I placed my hands on his chest to stop from tumbling over. His chest seemed to...hum under my hands. "Have you ever seen a bear?"

Dread pushed through my calm and blossomed. "What? There's a bear—?" I pulled out of his grasp and spun around.

Oh, yeah, there was a bear.

No more than fifteen feet from us, a big bear, black and furry, sniffed the air with its long whiskered muzzle. Its ears twitched at the sound of our breathing. For a moment I was kind of stunned. I'd never seen a bear, not in real life. There was something majestic about the creature. The way its muscles moved under the heavy coat of fur, how its dark eyes watched us as intently as we watched it.

The animal moved closer, stepping under the rays of light that broke through the branches overhead. The fur had turned a glossy black in the sunlight.

"Don't run," he whispered.

Like I could move even if I wanted to.

The bear made a half bark, half growl as he rose onto his hind legs, standing at least five feet tall. The next sound was an honest-to-God roar that sent shivers through me.

This wasn't good at all.

Daemon started yelling and waving his arms, but it didn't faze the bear. The animal dropped onto all fours, his massive shoulders shaking.

The bear rushed us.

Unable to breathe past the ball of fear choking me, I squeezed my eyes shut. Eaten alive by a bear was so wrong. I heard Daemon curse and even though my eyes were closed, a blinding flash of light pierced my thin eyelids. There was an accompanying blast of heat that blew my hair back. And then the flash came again, but darkness followed this time, swallowing me whole.

Chapter 8

When I opened my eyes again, there was a strange metallic taste in my mouth. Rain smacked off the roof and thunder rolled in the distance. Lightning struck somewhere nearby, filling the air with a fine current of electricity. When did it start raining? The skies had been clear, blue, and perfect the last I remembered.

I drew in a shallow breath, confused.

My shoulder was pressed against something warm and hard. Turning my head, I felt the object rise up sharply and then slowly ease back down. It took me a second to realize it was a chest my cheek was pressed into. We were on the swing, his arm around my waist keeping me securely pinned to his side.

I didn't dare move.

Every inch of my body became aware of his. How his thigh was molded to mine. The deep, even breaths moving his stomach under my hand. How his hand curved around my waist, his thumb moving in idle, soothing circles at the hem of my shirt. Each circle inched the material up a little, exposing my skin until his thumb was against the curve of my waist. Flesh against flesh. I was hot and shivery. A feeling I had little experience with.

His hand stilled.

Pushing up, I looked into a pair of startling green eyes. "What…what happened?"

"You passed out," he said, pulling his arm away from my waist.

"I did?" I scooted back, putting distance between us as I brushed my tangled hair out of my face. The metallic taste was still on the roof of my mouth.

He nodded. "I guess the bear scared you. I had to carry you back."

"All the way?" Dammit. I missed that? "What…what happened to the bear?"

"The storm scared it. Lightning, I think." He frowned as he watched me. "Are you feeling okay?"

Suddenly, a bright streak of light blinded us for a moment. Moments later, booming thunder overshadowed the rain. Daemon's expression was cast in shadows.

I shook my head. "The bear was scared of a storm?"

"I guess so."

"We got lucky then," I whispered, glancing down. I was drenched, as was Daemon. The rain was coming down even harder, making it difficult to see more than a couple of feet off the porch, giving the sense we were in our own private world. "It rains here like it does in Florida." I didn't know what else to say. My brain felt fried.

Daemon nudged my knee with his. "I think you may be stuck with me for a few more minutes."

"I'm sure I look like a drowned cat."

"You look fine. The wet look works for you."

I scowled. "Now I know you're lying."

He shifted beside me, and without a word, I felt his fingers lift my chin toward him. A crooked smile lifted his full lips. "I wouldn't lie about what I thought."

I wished I had something clever to say, maybe even a little flirty, but his intense stare sent any coherent thought scattering.

Confusion flashed in his eyes as he leaned forward, his lips parting slightly. "I think I understand now."

"Understand what?" I whispered.

"I like to watch you blush." His voice barely above a murmur as his thumb traced circles on my cheek.

He lowered his head, resting his forehead against mine. We sat like that, the two of us, caught in something that hadn't been there before. I think I stopped breathing. My heart seemed to take several stuttered steps and then freeze, anticipation welling up through me, threatening to spill over in any given second.

I didn't even *like* him. He didn't like me. This was insane, but it was happening.

Lightning struck again, this time much closer. The following snap of thunder didn't even startle us. We were in our own world. And then his crooked smile slipped from his face. His own eyes were confused and desperate, but still searching mine.

Time seemed to slow, every second stretching out before me, tantalizing and torturing every breath I took. Waiting, wanting to show him whatever he was looking for as his eyes darkened to a deep green. His face strained, as if he were waging an internal battle. Something in his eyes made me feel very unsure.

I knew the second he made up his mind. He took a deep breath and his beautiful eyes closed. I felt his breath against my cheek, slowly moving to my lips. I knew I should pull back. He was bad, bad news. But my own breath caught in my throat. His lips were so close to mine, I desperately wanted to meet him halfway, to rush forward to test if his lips were as pillow soft as they looked.

"Hey guys!" Dee called out.

Daemon jerked back, sliding in one fluid movement and putting a healthy distance between us on the swing.

I sucked in a sharp breath, surprise and disappointment churning in my stomach. My body was still tingling as if it had been deprived of oxygen. We'd been so absorbed in each other, neither of us had noticed the rain had stopped.

Dee came up the steps, her smile fading as her gaze went from her brother to me. She squinted her eyes. I was sure my face was blood red, making it obvious that she'd interrupted something. But she only stared at her brother, her lips forming a perfect, pouty O.

He grinned at her. The same lopsided grin that gave the impression that he was secretly laughing. "Hey, there, sis. What's up?"

"Nothing," she said, eyes narrowing. "What are *you* doing?"

"Nothing," he replied, jumping from the swing. He

glanced at me over one broad shoulder. "Just earning bonus points."

His words whipped through the pleasant haze as he hopped off the porch and ambled toward his own house. I glanced at Dee, wanting to chase after Daemon and dropkick him. "Was almost kissing me a part of the deal to get his keys back or to keep you happy?" My voice was tight. My skin *hurt*.

Dee sat beside me on the swing. "No. That was never a part of the deal." She blinked slowly. "Was he about to kiss you?"

I felt my cheeks burn even hotter. "I don't know."

"Wow," she murmured, her eyes wide. "That was unexpected."

And this was awkward. I didn't want to even think about what would've happened if she hadn't showed, and definitely not while she was sitting here. "Uh, you went to visit family?"

"Yeah, I had to before school started. Sorry I didn't get a chance to tell you. It kind of happened all of a sudden." Dee paused. "What were you and Daemon doing earlier...before the almost-kissing part?"

"We went on a walk. That's all."

"That's odd," she continued, watching me closely. "I had to steal his keys, but he got them back."

My face scrunched. "Yeah, thanks for that, by the way. There's nothing like a boy being blackmailed into hanging out with you to boost the self-esteem."

"Oh, no! It wasn't like that at all! I thought he needed... motivation to be nicer."

"He must really value his car," I muttered.

"Yeah...he does. Has he been spending a lot of time with

you while I was gone?"

"We haven't spent that much time together. We went to the lake one day and then just today. That's all."

A curious look crossed her features, and then she smiled. "Did you guys have a good time?"

Unsure of how to answer, I shrugged. "Yeah, he was actually pretty decent. I mean, he has his moments, but it wasn't all bad." If I didn't count the fact he was being forced into spending time with me, had almost kissed me for *bonus points*.

"Daemon can be nice when he wants." Dee pushed back on the swing, using one foot on the floor to keep it moving. "Where did you guys go for a walk?"

"We followed one of the trails and talked, but then we saw a bear."

"A bear?" Her eyes widened. "Holy crap, what happened?"

"Uh, I sort of passed out or something."

Dee stared at me. "You passed out?"

I flushed. "Yeah, Daemon carried me back to the porch and yeah, well, the rest is whatever."

She was watching me closely again, curious. Then she shook her head. Changing the subject, she asked if she'd missed anything else while she was gone. I filled her in while my mind was completely elsewhere. Dee mentioned something about watching a movie later before she left. I think I agreed.

Long after I'd gone inside and pulled on a pair of old sweats, I was still confused over Daemon. He'd seemed almost likeable during our hike before flashing back to Super Douche. Flushing and frustrated, I flopped on the bed and stared at the ceiling.

There was a network of tiny cracks in the plaster. My gaze traveled over them as my mind replayed the events leading up to the "almost kiss." My stomach flipped thinking about how close his lips had been to mine. Worse yet was the knowledge that I had wanted him to kiss me. Like and lust must not have anything in common.

• • •

"Let me get this straight." Dee frowned from where she'd perched herself on the old recliner in desperate need of being reupholstered. "You have no idea where you want to go to college?"

I groaned. "You sound like my mom."

"Yeah, well, you're entering your senior year." Dee paused for a second. "Don't you guys start applying as soon as school starts?"

Dee and I were sitting in my living room flipping through magazines when my mom had oh-so-casually walked in and dropped a stack of college brochures on the coffee table. Thanks, Mom. "Shouldn't you be applying? You're one of 'us,' too."

The interest that had been sparkling in her eyes dulled. "Yeah, but we're talking about you."

I rolled my eyes and laughed. "I haven't decided what I want to do. So I don't see the need to pick a school."

"But every school offers the same thing. You could pick a place—any place you wanted to go. California, New York, Colorado—oh, you could even go overseas! That would be awesome. That's what I'd do. I'd go somewhere in England."

"You can," I reminded her.

Dee lowered her eyes. She shrugged. "No, I can't."

"Why not?" I pulled my legs up and crossed them. It didn't seem as though money was a problem for them, not when you looked at the cars they drove or the clothes they wore. I'd asked her if she had a job, and she'd said she had a monthly allowance that kept her cushy. Parental remorse at always staying in the city for work and all. Nice gig if you can get it.

Mom was great at giving me cash if I needed it, but I sincerely doubted she'd ever pony up three hundred bucks a month for a fun, new car for me. Nope. I'd have to keep on loving my little sedan, rust and all. Point A to Point B, I always reminded myself. "You can go wherever you want, Dee."

Dee's smile was tinged with sadness. "I'll probably stay here when I graduate. Maybe enroll in one of those online universities."

At first I thought she was joking. "You're being serious?"

"Yeah, I'm kind of stuck here."

I was intrigued by the idea of someone being stuck anywhere. "What's sticking you?"

"My family is here," she said quietly, looking up. "Anyway, that movie we watched last night gave me nightmares. I hate the whole idea of a haunted house with ghosts in it, watching you sleep."

Her swift change of subject didn't pass me by. "Yeah, that movie was pretty creepy."

Dee made a face. "It reminds me of Daemon. He used to stand over me when I was sleeping, because he thought it was funny." Her delicate shoulders shuddered. "I'd get so mad at him! I don't care how deep of a sleep I was in, I could still feel him staring at me and I'd wake up. He would laugh and laugh."

I smiled at the image of Daemon as a little boy teasing his twin. That picture was completely replaced by the full-grown Daemon. I sighed, beyond frustrated, and closed the magazine.

I hadn't seen him since the evening on my porch, but it was only Monday. Two days without seeing him seemed commonplace. And it wasn't as if I wanted to see him.

Looking up, I watched Dee flip to the back of her magazine. She always did that, going to the horoscopes in the back. She held her right hand against her chin, tapping her lips with one painted purple nail.

The finger blurred, nearly fading out. Air around her seemed to hum.

I blinked several times. The finger was still there. Great. I was hallucinating again. I threw the magazine aside. "I need to go to the library. I need new books to read."

"We can plan a trip and go book shopping." She hopped in her chair, excited all over again. "I want to check out that book you reviewed on your blog the week before you moved here. The one with the kids with superpowers."

My little heart did a happy dance. She'd read my blog. I didn't even remember telling her the name. "That would be fun, but I was thinking about going to the library tonight. I can't beat it when it's free. Do you want to come with me?"

"Tonight?" she questioned, eyes widening. "I can't tonight, but I can go tomorrow night."

"It's no big deal if you can't go. I've been thinking about going for a couple of days, but I keep putting it off, and I need brain candy before I have to read school stuff."

Dark hair swung around her impish face as she shook her head. "Oh, it's no big deal. I don't mind going with you. I can't go tonight. I have plans already. If I didn't, I'd go."

"It's okay, Dee. I can go to the library alone, and then we can go shopping later. I pretty much know my way around town now. Not as if I can get lost or anything. It's only like... five blocks." I paused, and then quickly asked about her plans for the evening, trying to change the subject.

Dee's lips were firm. "Nothing, just friends are back in town."

My innocent question obviously put her on the spot, and she seemed reluctant to say what she was actually doing. She shifted on the recliner, focused on her nails. I felt like I'd pried, but I didn't understand how that question could have made her uncomfortable. There was also a part of me hurt and disappointed I wasn't included.

"I hope you guys have fun tonight," I lied. Well, not a real lie. But at least half of a lie. I'm not proud of it, but there you have it. Right or wrong, I felt left out.

Dee squirmed in her seat as she watched me. Her eyes squinted, much like they'd done the day on the porch. "I think you should wait until I can go with you. There have been a couple of girls who've gone missing recently."

Going to the library wasn't going to a house that cooked meth, but I remembered the missing poster I'd seen the other day and shrugged. "Okay, I'll think about it."

Dee stayed until it was nearly time for my mom to go to

work. On the way out, she stopped at the edge of the porch. "Really, if you can wait until tomorrow night, I'll go to the library with you."

I agreed once more and gave her a quick hug. I missed her the moment she left. The house was too quiet without her.

Chapter 9

After dinner with Mom, I headed out. It didn't take very long to get into town and find the library again. The streets, which during the few times I had been in town had always been populated, were now pretty much deserted. On the ride down, the skies had started to cloud over, too, giving the entire downtown an eerie ghost town feeling.

In spite of the weirdness that was my life at the moment and the lingering icky feeling I felt over Dee not inviting me out with her friends, I smiled as I walked into the library. Thoughts of the twins and everything else vanished as I rounded the corner of the quiet library and saw stacks of books lining the walls. As with gardening, in the stillness of the library, I felt at peace.

Stopping by one of the empty tables, I let out a little breath of happiness. I was always able to lose myself in reading. Books were a necessary escape I always gladly jumped into headfirst.

Time passed faster than I realized, and the library took on a gloomy aura. Libraries were always shadowy as daylight ended, but the unnatural darkening of the sky outside added to the creepy feeling. I didn't know how late it was until the librarian turned off most of the lights, and I was having trouble making my way back to the front desk. By then, I couldn't wait to be out of the drafty and creaky place.

A flash of lightning lit up the bookshelves and thunder rolled outside the windows. I hoped I could make it to my car before it started pouring. Clutching the books I wanted to check out to my chest, I hurried to the front desk. I was done in record time, barely having the time to say thank you before the librarian turned her back and dashed off to lock up.

"Well then," I muttered under my breath.

The impending storm had turned dusk to night, making it seem much later than it was. Outside, the streets were still barren. I looked behind me, thinking about staying until the rain passed, but the final light in the library snicked off.

I gritted my teeth and shoved my books into my backpack before heading out. I stepped out onto the pavement, and the sky opened in a torrential downpour, soaking me within seconds. I tried my best to keep my backpack from getting wet as I fumbled with my keys and hopped back and forth. The rain was freaking freezing!

"Excuse me, miss?" A gravelly voice interrupted my struggles. "I was hoping you could help me?"

Intent on getting the door open and the books out of the rain, I didn't hear anyone approach. I shoved my backpack into the car and tightened the hold on my purse as I turned toward the sound. A man came out of the shadows and stood under the streetlight. Rain coursed down his light-colored hair, plastering the longish strands to his head. His wire-framed glasses slipped down the bridge of his crooked nose as he stood with his arms wrapped around his chest, his thin body shivering slightly.

"My car back there," he gestured behind him, shouting a bit to be heard over the rain pounding against the hood, "has a flat tire. I was hoping you had a tire iron."

I did, but every fiber in my body was telling me to say no. Even though the man looked as if he couldn't throw a stone very far. "I'm not sure." My voice was smaller than I intended. I pushed at my wet hair and cleared my throat. I shouted back, "I don't know if I have one or not."

The man's smile was weary. "I couldn't have picked a better time, could I?"

"No, you couldn't." I shifted from one foot to the next.

Part of me wanted to leave him there with an apology, but then there was this other part of me—a huge part of me—that was never good at telling people no. I chewed my lower lip as I hovered by the door. I couldn't leave him in the rain. The poor man looked about to crumple over any second. Pity for him pushed away the sense of dread that always came when you were confronted with the unknown.

I couldn't leave him stuck in the rain when I knew I could help. At least the rain was starting to let up.

My decision made, I forced a weak smile. "I can check. I may have one."

The man beamed. "You would be a savior if you did." He stayed where he was, not moving any closer, probably sensing my initial distrust. "The rain seems to be letting off, but by those dark clouds coming in I think we may be in for a heck of a storm."

I shut the driver's side door and headed to the rear of the car. Opening the trunk, I ran my hand along the carpeted bottom, searching for the release to the spare tire. "I think I may have one, to be honest."

My back was to the stranger for only a few seconds when I felt a rush of chilly air stir the hair at the back of my neck. Adrenaline coursed through my veins, sending my heart slamming against my ribs and painful tendrils of fear burrowing through my stomach.

"Humans are so stupid, so gullible." His voice was as cold as the wind on my neck.

Before my brain could register his words, an icy, wet hand closed over mine in a painful grip. His breath was sticky against my neck, striking a chord of finality. I didn't even have a chance to respond.

Using my hand, he swung me around. A cry escaped my throat as pain shot up my arm. I was face to face with him now, and he didn't seem as helpless as he had before. Actually, he seemed to have grown taller—broader.

"If—if you want money you can take whatever I have." I wanted to throw the purse at him and take off.

The stranger smiled and then pushed me. *Hard*. The impact of the rough asphalt knocked the air out of me and jarred my wrist in scorching pain. With my good hand, I grabbed my purse and shoved it at him. "Please," I begged. "Just take it. I won't say anything. Just take it. I promise."

My attacker crouched in front of me, lips curved in a sneer

as he took my purse. Behind the glasses, his eyes seemed to shift colors. "Your money? I don't need your money." He tossed the purse aside.

I stared as little gasps of breath wheezed in and out of my lungs. I couldn't keep up with the idea that this was happening. If he wasn't robbing me, then what did he want? My mind shrunk from that line of thinking, instead echoing in terror: *No. No. No.*

I couldn't keep my head afloat in the rush of thoughts and images that flooded me. But my body was moving, and I was scooting away from him, banging into the curb. Fear swamped me. I knew I needed to scream. I felt it welling up in my throat. I opened my mouth.

"Don't scream," he warned, his voice a biting command.

I felt the muscles in my legs tense. I twisted, pulling my knees up, getting ready to run. I could make it. He wouldn't expect it. I could make it. *Now!*

His arms shot out in a blur, grabbing both legs and yanking. My left arm and that side of my face hit the pavement, skin grating against rough cement in blinding pain. My eye started to swell in a matter of seconds and warm blood trickled down my arm. My stomach heaved. I tried to pull my legs out of his grip, kicking when that failed. He grunted, but held on.

"Please! Let me go." I tried again to kick my legs loose. The road scraped my arms, sending more pain and something stronger.

Anger coursed through me, pushing at the fear, trying to overcome it. The combination sent me into heady action. I kicked and bucked, pushed and shoved, but nothing seemed to budge him. Not even an inch.

"Let go of me!" This time I yelled, the sound torn from my throat until it was raw.

He moved quickly, his face fading in and out like I'd seen Dee's hand do. And then he was on top of me, his hand covering my mouth. His weight was unbearable even though he'd appeared so small before, so helpless. I couldn't breathe, couldn't move. He was crushing me, but the thought of what was to come next nearly destroyed me.

Someone had to have heard me. It was my only hope.

He lowered his head, sniffing my hair. A shudder of revulsion rolled through me. He hissed. "I was right. You have their trace." He moved his hand from my mouth and gripped my shoulders. "Where are they?"

"I…I don't understand," I choked out.

"Of course you don't." His face contorted with disgust. "You're nothing but a stupid, walking mammal. Worthless."

I squeezed my eyes shut. I didn't want to look at him. I didn't want to see his face. I wanted to go home. *Please…*

"Look at me!" When I didn't he shook me again. My head cracked against the ground. The fresh new pain startled me and my one good eye opened against my will. He grabbed my chin with his icy hand. My gaze flickered across his face and finally settled on his eyes. They were vast and empty. I'd never seen anything like it.

And in those eyes I saw something worse. Worse than being robbed, worse than being degraded and abused. I saw death in them—my death—without an ounce of remorse.

"Tell me where they are." Each word was bitten out.

His voice sounded muffled, as though underwater, or

maybe that was me. Maybe I was drowning.

"Fine," he spat. "Maybe you need a little encouragement."

Within a second, his hands wrapped around my throat and he squeezed. Before I had a chance, the last breath that I'd taken for granted was cut off. Panic clawed through my chest as I tried prying his fingers off my neck, my legs kicking out in a vain attempt at freedom. His grip dug into my fragile windpipe.

"Are you ready to tell me?" he challenged. "No?"

I didn't know what he was talking about. My wrist was no longer throbbing; the torn flesh of my arms and face no longer seemed to sting with such fierceness as before, because new pains were replacing the old. There was no air, no more air. My heart pounded in my chest, demanding oxygen. The pressure in my head threatened to explode. My legs were going numb. Tiny lights danced through my vision.

I was going to die.

I would never see my mom again. Oh God, she would be devastated. I couldn't die this way, for no reason. I begged silently, prayed someone would find me before it was too late, but everything was fading. I slipped into an inky abyss. The pressure wasn't bad now. The rawness in my throat seemed to ease. The pain was leaving. I was leaving, fading into the darkness.

Suddenly, his hands were gone, and there was a fleshy sound of a body hitting the road in the distance. It felt like I was at the bottom of a deep well and the source of the noise was too far above.

But I could breathe again. I gluttonously ate each breath, drawing the beautiful air down my bruised throat, already feeding my starved organs. I started to cough as I gulped air.

Someone cried out in a soft, musical language I'd never heard before, and then there was another curse and punch being thrown. A body landed next to me, and I rolled slightly. Pain caused me to wince, but I welcomed it. It meant I was alive.

They were fighting in the shadows. One of them—a man—grabbed another, holding him several feet into the air. The strength was shocking, brutal. Inhuman. Impossible.

Rolling up, I was wracked by another round of coughing. I leaned over, putting weight on my wrist, and yelped.

"Dammit!" a deep voice exploded.

There was a flash of intense red-yellow light. Streetlamps down the street exploded, casting the entire block in darkness. I doubled over as I heaved. Gravel crunched and tips of hiking boots came into view. I threw my arm out to keep whoever it was back.

"It's okay. He's gone. Are you okay?" A gentle hand was on my shoulder, steadying me. In a distant part of my brain, I thought his voice sounded familiar. "Just sit still." I tried to lift my head, but dizziness nearly stole my breath. My vision blurred and then cleared. My left eye was now swollen shut and throbbed with each beat of my pulse. "Everything is okay."

A warmth started in my shoulder, flowing down my arm and circling my wrist, easing sore muscles and delving deeper. I was reminded of days lying out on white beaches, basking in the sun.

"Thank you for..." My words trailed off as my rescuer's face swam into focus. High cheekbones, straight nose, and full lips formed before my eyes. A face that was striking and so cold that it could not possibly belong to the same heat that was slowly swallowing my entire body. Vibrant, rare green eyes met mine.

"Kat," Daemon said. Concern was etched in his forehead. "Are you still with me?"

"You," I whispered as my head lulled to the side. I vaguely noticed it was no longer raining.

He arched a coal-black brow. "Yes, it's me."

Dazed, I glanced down where he was holding my wrist. It wasn't throbbing any longer but his touch was doing something else. I jerked my arm back, confused.

"I can help you," he insisted, reaching for me again.

"No!" I shrieked and it *hurt*.

He hovered a moment longer and then straightened, his eyes glancing down at my wrist. "Whatever. I'll call the police."

I tried not to listen to him as he spoke to the police on the phone. Eventually, I was able to catch my breath. "Thank…you." My voice was hoarse, and it hurt to speak.

"Don't thank me." He dragged his fingers through his hair. "Dammit, this is my fault."

How was this his fault? My brain wasn't working correctly yet, because that didn't make much sense. I leaned back carefully and peered up—way up—and I immediately wished I hadn't. He looked fierce. And protective.

"See something you like, Kitten?"

I dropped my gaze…to his clenched hands. His knuckles weren't even scratched. "Light—I saw light."

"Well, they do say there is light at the end of the tunnel."

I shrank away from the reminder I'd almost died tonight.

Daemon crouched down. "Dammit, I'm sorry. That was thoughtless. How bad are you hurt?"

"My throat...It hurts." I touched it gently and winced. "So does my wrist. I'm not...sure if it's broken." I lifted my arm gingerly. It was swollen and already turning an attractive shade of blue and violet. "But there was a flash...of light."

He studied my arm. "It might be broken or sprained. Is that all?"

"All? The man...he was trying to kill me."

His eyes narrowed. "I understand that. I was hoping he didn't break anything important." He stopped for a second, thinking. "Like your skull?"

"No...I don't think so."

He let out a breath. "Okay, okay." He stood and looked around. "Why were you out here anyway?"

"I...wanted to go to the library." I had to stop till the rawness in my throat subsided. "It wasn't that...late. It's not... like we are in a crime-ridden...city. He said he needed help... flat tire."

His eyes were wide with disbelief. "A stranger approaches you for help in a dark parking lot and you go and help him? That has to be one of the most careless things I've heard in a long time." He crossed his arms and stared down at me. "I bet you think things through, right? Accept candy from strangers and get into vans with a sign that reads free kittens?"

I gasped.

He began to pace. "Sorry wouldn't have been helpful if I didn't come, now would it?"

I ignored the last statement. "So why were...you out here?"

My throat was finally feeling slightly better. It still hurt like a bitch, but at least every word wasn't like being pulled across concrete.

Daemon stopped pacing and ran a hand over his chest, above his heart. "I just was."

"Geez, I thought you guys were supposed to be nice and charming."

He frowned. "What guys?"

"You know, the knight in shining armor and saving the damsel in distress kind." I stopped at that point. I must've hit my head.

"I'm not your knight."

"Okay..." I whispered. I slowly pulled my legs up and rested my head on my knees. Everything hurt, but not as bad as it did when that man had his hands around my throat. I shivered at the thought. "Where is he now?"

"He took off. Long gone by now," Daemon assured. "Kat...?"

I lifted my head. His hulking frame loomed over me as he stared at me. His gaze was unnerving, piercing. I didn't know what to say. I didn't like how Daemon's body cast a shadow from the moonlight, and I made a move to try and stand.

"I don't think you should stand." He kneeled again. "The ambulance and police should be here any minute. I don't want you passing out."

"I'm not going...to pass out," I denied, finally hearing the sirens.

"I don't want to have to catch you if you do." He examined his knuckles for a few moments. "Did ...did he say anything to you?"

I wanted to swallow so badly, but it hurt too much. "He said...I had a trace on me. And he kept asking...where they were. I don't know why."

He hurriedly looked away, drawing a sharp breath. "He sounds like a lunatic."

"Yeah, but...who did he want?"

Daemon turned back to me, a deep scowl on his face. "A girl stupid enough to help a homicidal maniac with his *tire* maybe?"

My lips pressed into a hard line. "You're such an ass. Has... anyone ever told you that?"

He flashed a genuinely amused smile. "Oh, Kitten, every single day of my blessed life."

I stared at him in disbelief again. "I don't even know what to say..."

"Since you already said thank you, I think nothing is the best way to go at this point." He stood with fluid grace. "Just please don't move. That's all I ask. Stay still and try not to cause any more trouble."

I frowned and it hurt.

My not-so-charming knight stood over me, legs braced apart and arms at his sides as if ready to protect me again. What if the guy came back? That must be what Daemon was worried about.

My shoulders started to shake, my teeth quickly joining in the fun. Daemon whipped his shirt off and pulled the warm cotton over my head, careful not to let even a whisper of cloth touch my damaged face. His scent wrapped around me and for the first time since the attack, I felt safe. With Daemon. Go figure.

As if my body recognized I didn't need to fight anymore, I started slipping sideways, and I knew I was going to black my other eye when my head hit the pavement because I was most definitely about to pass out for the second time in as few days. I briefly wondered why I was cursed to always faint in front of Daemon, and then folded to the ground like a paper sack.

Chapter 10

I didn't make it a habit to frequent hospitals. I hated them as much as I hated country music. To me, they smelled of death and disinfectant. They reminded me of Dad, and the time that had clocked away while the cancer hollowed his eyes and chemo bloated his body.

This hospital was no different, but the visit was a little more complex.

It involved the police, a frantic mother, and my surly, dark-haired savior, who still hovered near the little room they'd shoved me in. As rude and ungrateful as it was, I was doing my best to ignore him.

My mom, who'd been on shift at the hospital when the ambulance brought me in *with* a police escort, kept randomly reaching over and stroking my arm or face—the good side at least. As if that motion reminded her that I was alive and breathing and only bruised. I hated myself for it, but it was starting to annoy me.

I was feeling the height of bitchiness.

My head and back were aching something fierce, but the pain in my wrist and arm were the worst. After tons of poking, prodding, and half a dozen X-rays, nothing was broken. I had a sprained wrist and a torn tendon in my arm, in addition to numerous deep bruises and scratches. A brace already encased my left hand and forearm.

There was this elusive promise of pain medication that had yet to arrive.

The police officers were kind, if a little too brusque. They asked every question imaginable. I knew it was important I tell them everything I could remember, but the shock was beginning to wear off and the adrenaline had long since faded. All I wanted was to go home.

They thought it was an attempted robbery gone wrong until I told them he hadn't asked for any money. After I'd told them what the attacker had said, they believed he may have been ill or possibly a drug addict coming down from a high.

When the police were done asking me questions, they moved on to Daemon. They seemed to be on familiar terms with him. One even clapped him on the shoulder and smiled. They were buddies. How sweet. I didn't get a chance to listen to what he was telling them because my mom had taken over the interrogation.

I wanted them all to stop and go away.

"Miss Swartz?"

Surprised to hear my last name, I was pulled out of my own thoughts. One of the younger deputies was at my bed again. I couldn't remember his name, and I was too tired to even look for a name tag. "Yes?"

"I think we are pretty much done for tonight. If you remember anything else, please call us immediately."

I nodded and wished I hadn't. I grimaced as pain shot through my head.

"Honey, are you okay?" Mom asked, her tone pitched in worry.

"My head, it hurts."

She stood. "I'll go find the doctor so we can get those meds in you." She smiled gently. "Then you won't feel a thing."

That is what I needed, wanted—would love.

The deputy turned to leave but stopped. "I don't think you have anything to worry about. I—"

The crackle of his radio interrupted anything else he was about say. The dispatcher's voice broke through the static. "All available units, we have code 18 on Well Springs Road. Victim is a female, approximately sixteen to seventeen years of age. Possible DOA. EMT on the scene."

Whoa. What were the odds that I'd be attacked on the same night another teenage girl died in such a small town? It had to be a coincidence. I glanced at Daemon. His eyes were narrowed. He'd heard it, too.

"Jesus," the deputy said, then clicked on his radio. "Unit 414 leaving hospital and en route." He turned from the bed, still talking into the radio, and left.

With the exception of Daemon lounging against the wall by the curtain, the room was empty. He raised a curious brow at me. I chewed on my lower lip and turned my head away, causing another ripple of pain to go from one temple to the other. I stayed like that until my mother came rushing back to my bed with the doctor in tow.

"Honey, Dr. Michaels has good news."

"As you already know, you have no broken bones and it also looks like you don't have a concussion. Once we can release you, you can go home and rest," he said, rubbing the area where speckles of gray peppered the hair near his temples. He glanced at Daemon before focusing on me again. "Now, if you start experiencing dizziness or nausea, vision issues or loss of memory, we need you back here immediately."

"Okay," I said, eyeing the pills. I'd agree to anything at this point.

After the doctor left, Mom hovered as I took the small plastic cup and pills from her, swallowing them quickly. I didn't even care what they were.

On the verge of tears again, I reached for my mom's hand, but was interrupted by an excited voice in the hallway.

Dee rushed into the room, her face pale and worried. "Oh no, Katy, are you okay?"

"Yes. Just a little banged up." I lifted my arm and gave a weak smile.

"I can't believe this has happened." She turned to her brother. "*How* could this have happened? I thought you—"

"Dee," Daemon warned.

She darted away from her brother, lingering on the other side of my bed. "I'm so sorry about this."

"It's not your fault."

She nodded, but I could tell she was harboring guilt.

My mom's name was called over the loudspeaker. Her face strained, she excused herself and promised to be back in a few seconds.

"Can you leave soon?" Dee asked.

I dragged my attention back to her. "I guess so." I paused. "As long as my mom comes back."

She nodded. "Did…you see the guy who attacked you?"

"Yeah, he said some crazy stuff." I closed my eyes, and it seemed to take longer than normal to reopen them. "Something about finding 'them'. I don't know." I shifted on the hard bed. The bruises didn't hurt as much. "Weird."

Dee paled. "I hope you can leave soon. I hate hospitals."

"I do, too."

Her nose wrinkled. "They have…such a strange smell to them."

"That's what I've always told Mom, but she thinks I make it up."

Dee shook her head. "No, it's not you. They have this… musty smell."

My eyelids flickered open again and focused on Daemon. He had his eyes closed as he leaned his head against the wall but I knew he was listening to everything. Dee talked about taking me home if my mom couldn't leave. I was struck again by the twins. Daemon and Dee didn't belong here, but I did. I could blend easily with the whitewashed walls and pale green curtains. I was as plain as the linoleum, but these two seemed to light the room with their flawless beauty and demanding presence.

Ah, the medication was kicking in. I was poetic. And high. *Bliss.*

Dee shifted, and my view of Daemon was blocked. I immediately felt panic rising and struggled to move until I could see him again. My pulse quieted the moment my gaze settled on his still form. He didn't fool me. He was trying to pretend he was relaxed, leaning against the wall like that with his eyes closed and all, but his jaw was clenched and I knew he was like a coiled spring, filled with vigilant energy.

"You're handling this well. I'd be totally freaked out, rocking in the corner somewhere." Dee smiled.

"I'll freak out," I murmured. "Give me time."

I wasn't sure how much time passed before my mother returned with a bothered expression on her pretty face. "Honey, I'm sorry to disappear on you," she said in a rush. "There was a bad accident, and they're bringing in multiple victims. You may have to stay here awhile. I have to stay, at least until we determine if we need to move them to a larger hospital. A bunch of nurses are off, and the hospital isn't staffed to handle this type of crisis."

I stared at her dumbfounded. I felt my bitchiness gaining ground. Screw everyone else. I'd nearly died tonight, and I wanted my mom.

"Ms. Swartz, we can take her home," Dee said. "I'm sure she wants to go home. I know I would and it would be no problem for us to do it."

I begged Mom with my eyes to take me home herself. "I would feel better if she was here or with me, in case she does have a concussion and, well, I don't want anything else to happen."

"We would never let anything happen." Dee's gaze was steady. "We'll take her right home and stay with her. I promise."

I could tell Mom was wrestling with the need to keep me close and her responsibility to those injured in the accident. I felt contrite for making her choose. Plus I knew seeing me in the hospital had to be a painful reminder of Dad. My eyes darted to Daemon, and the bitchiness eased from my shoulders. I gave my mom a weak smile. "It's okay, Mom. I'm feeling a lot better, and I'm sure nothing else is wrong. I don't want to stay here."

Mom sighed, wringing her hands. "I can't believe this would happen on tonight of all nights."

Her name was called over the loudspeaker once more. She did something very uncharacteristic and cussed. "Dammit!"

Dee immediately jumped up. "We can do it, Mrs. Swartz."

Mom glanced at me and then the door. "Okay, but if she seems in any way out of character," she turned to me, "or if your head starts hurting more, call me immediately. No! Call 9-1-1."

"I will," I reassured her.

She leaned down and kissed me swiftly on the cheek. "Get some rest, honey. I love you." Then she was off, rushing down the hallway.

Dee grinned impishly as I looked at her. "Thank you," I said. "But you don't have to stay with me."

She frowned. "Yes, I will. No arguments." She dashed from my side. "I'll go see what I can do to spring you from this place."

I blinked and she was gone, but Daemon had inched closer. His expression was stoic as he stood at the foot of my bed. I closed my eyes. "Are you going to insult me again? Because I'm not up to...pear for that."

"I think you meant par."

"Pear. Par. Whatever." I opened my eyes and found him staring.

"Are you really okay?"

"I'm great." I yawned loudly. "Your sister acts as if this is her fault."

"She doesn't like it when people get hurt," he said softly. "And people tend to get hurt around us."

A chill snaked around my insides. Even though his expression was blank, his words were heavy with pain. "What does that mean?"

He didn't answer.

Dee came back then, a grin on her face. "We're good to go, with doctor's orders and all."

"Come on, let's get you home." Daemon moved to the side of my bed and, surprisingly, he helped me sit up and then stand.

I stumbled a few steps, having to stop. "Whoa, I feel buzzed."

Dee's face was sympathetic. "I think the pills are starting to work."

"Am I...slurring yet?" I asked.

"Not at all," Dee laughed.

I sighed, exhausted to the point of almost falling over. My body was whisked up into the air and against Daemon's hard chest before being deposited gently into a wheelchair. "Hospital rules," Daemon explained, and wheeled me out, stopping only long enough for me to sign a couple of forms before steering me toward the parking lot.

He helped me into Dee's backseat, mindful of the arm brace, by carrying me again and placing me into the rear. "I can walk, you know."

"I know." He walked around and slid in next to me.

I tried to keep on my side of the car and my head up, because I doubted he'd appreciate me lying on him, but once Daemon settled next to me, my head sort of fell to his chest. He stiffened for a moment and then placed an arm around my shoulder. The warmth of him quickly seeped into my bones. It felt right, at that moment, to be nestled against him. I felt safe, and it reminded me of the heat that had come off his hand earlier.

I snuggled the good side of my face against the soft fabric of his T-shirt and thought his arm tightened around me, but that could've been the pills. By the time the car started, I was already drifting away, one thought colliding into the next without any coherence.

I wasn't sure if I was dreaming or not when I heard Dee speak, her voice sounding muted and far away. "I told her not to go. I could still see it."

"I know." There was a pause. "Don't worry. I'm not going to let anything happen this time. I swear."

Silence followed by more hushed whispers. "You did something, didn't you?" she asked. "It's stronger now."

"I didn't...mean to." Daemon shifted slightly, smoothing the hair off my face. "It just happened. Shit."

Several long moments passed, and I struggled to stay awake. But the events of the night were weighing too heavily on me, and finally I succumbed to the warmth of Daemon and the blissful silence.

· · ·

When I opened my eyes again, daylight peeked through the heavily curtained living room, catching small particles of dust that hung in a lazy pattern over the peaceful head of Dee. She was a few feet away, curled up on the recliner in a deep sleep. Her small hands were folded neatly under her cheek and lips slightly parted. She looked more like a china doll than a real person.

I smiled and immediately winced.

The spark of pain cleared the haze from my head and the fear from last night doused my veins in ice water. I lay there for several moments, taking deep, calming breaths as I tried to gain control of my spiraling emotions. I was alive—thanks to Daemon, who apparently was also my pillow.

My head was in his lap. One of his hands was resting on the curve of my hip. My heart sped up. He couldn't have been comfortable, sitting up all night.

Daemon stirred. "You okay, Kitten?"

"Daemon?" I whispered, trying to gain control of my spiraling emotions. "I...sorry. I didn't mean to sleep on you."

"It's okay." He helped me sit up. The room spun a little. "Are you okay?" he asked again.

"Yeah. You stayed here all night?"

"Yeah," was all he said.

I remembered Dee volunteering but not him. Waking up with my head in *his* lap was the last thing I'd expected.

"Do you remember anything?" he asked quietly.

My chest squeezed tight. I nodded, expecting it to hurt

more than it did. "I was attacked last night."

"Someone tried to mug you," he said.

No, that wasn't right. I remembered a man grabbing my purse, then falling down, but he hadn't wanted my money. "He wasn't trying to mug me."

"Kat—"

"No." I tried standing up, but his arm returned, forming a band of steel around me that I couldn't break. "He didn't want my money, Daemon. He wanted *them*."

Daemon stiffened. "That doesn't make any sense."

"No shit." I frowned as I moved my arm and found that the splint was heavy. "But he kept asking about where *they* were and about a trace."

"The guy was insane," he said, voice low. "You realize that, right? That he wasn't right in the head. That nothing he said means anything."

"I don't know. He didn't seem crazy."

"Trying to beat the crap out of a girl isn't crazy enough for you?" His brows rose. "I'm curious what you think is crazy."

"That's not what I meant."

"Then what did you mean?" He shifted, careful not to jar me, which kind of surprised me. "He was a random lunatic, but you're going to make it bigger than it is, aren't you?"

"I'm not making this anything." I took a steadying breath. "Daemon, that wasn't a normal lunatic."

"Oh, you're an expert in crazy people now?"

"A month with you and I feel I have a master's degree in the subject," I snapped. Glaring at him, I scooted away. My head swam.

"You okay?" He reached out, placing a hand on my good arm. "Kat?"

I shook his hand off. "Yeah, I'm okay."

Shoulders stiff, he stared straight ahead. "I know you're probably messed up after what happened last night, but don't make this into something it's not."

"Daemon—"

"I don't want Dee worried that there is an idiot out there attacking girls." His eyes were hard. Cold. "Do you understand me?"

My lip trembled. Part of me wanted to cry. Another part wanted to whale on him. So all his caring was about his sister? How silly of me. Our eyes locked. There was such intensity in his, as if he were willing me to understand.

Dee yawned loudly.

I jerked away, breaking contact first. Of course, score one for Daemon.

"Good morning!" Dee chirped as one or both of her legs dropped to the ground, sounding surprisingly heavy for someone as slender as she was. "Have you guys been awake long?"

Another sigh, much louder and more annoyed than the first pushed through Daemon's hard lips. "No, Dee, we just woke up and were talking. You were snoring so loudly we couldn't stay asleep any longer."

Dee snorted. "I doubt that. Katy, are you feeling...okay this morning?"

"Yeah, I'm a little sore and stiff, but overall okay."

She smiled but her eyes were still hooded with guilt. Which made no sense. She tried to smooth down her curls, but they sprung back into disarray as soon as she removed her hands. "I think I'm going to make you breakfast."

Before I could respond, she dashed off to the kitchen and I heard numerous doors open and close, pots and pans clanging against each other. "Okay."

Daemon stood and stretched. The muscles of his back were taut under his shirt. I looked away.

"I care more about my sister than I do anything in this universe," he said quietly. Each word punctuated by truth. "I'd do anything for her, to make sure she's happy and she's safe. Please don't worry her with crazy stories."

I felt infinitely small. "You're a dick, but I won't say anything to her." When I looked up, I found it hard to concentrate when his eyes were as bright as they were. "Okay? Happy?"

Something flickered over his face. Anger? Regret? "Not really. Not at all."

Neither of us looked away again. There was a heavy quality to the air, tangible.

"Daemon!" Dee called from the kitchen. "I need your help!"

"We should go see what she's doing before she destroys your kitchen." He rubbed his hands down his face. "It's possible."

Keeping quiet, I followed him out into the hallway, where the light spilled in from the open door. I winced at the abrupt brightness and suddenly remembered I hadn't brushed my hair or my teeth yet. I cringed away from Daemon. "I think I need to...go."

He raised an eyebrow at me. "Go...where?"

I felt my cheeks turn hot. "Upstairs. I need a shower."

Surprisingly, he didn't fire back with the door I'd left open. He nodded and disappeared into the kitchen. At the top of the stairs, my fingers mindlessly went to my lips and then another shiver rolled through me. How close to dying did I come last night?

"Is she really going to be okay?" I heard Dee ask.

"Yeah, she'll be fine," Daemon responded patiently. "You have nothing to worry about. Nothing is happening. Everything was taken care of when I came back here."

I crept closer to the landing.

"Don't look like that. Nothing will happen to you." Daemon sighed with real frustration this time. "Or her, okay?" Another gap of silence followed. "We should've expected something like this."

"Did you?" Dee asked, her voice rising sharply. "Because I was trying not to. I was trying to hope that we could have a friend—a real one—without them getting…"

Their voices lowered, becoming unintelligible. Were they talking about me? They had to be, but that didn't make sense. I stood in absolute confusion, trying to figure out what they could be talking about.

Daemon's voice rose, "Who knows, Dee? We will see how it plays out." He paused and then laughed. "I think you are beating those eggs to death. Here, let me have them."

I listened a few more moments as they bantered back and forth like normal before I peeled myself away from my spot. Without warning, another stolen conversation quickly resurfaced. The night before, as I coasted in and out of consciousness in the car, I'd overheard both of them whispering worries that I couldn't comprehend.

I wanted to shrug off the nagging feeling that they were hiding something. I hadn't forgotten Dee's weird aversion to me going to the library. Or the strange light I'd seen outside the library that reminded me so much of the light in the woods, when I'd seen the bear and passed out, something that I'd never done before in my life. And then there was the day at the lake, when Daemon had turned into Aquaman.

I walked numbly to my bathroom and flipped on the light, expecting to see my face busted up. I tilted my head to the side, a startled gasp escaping my throat. I knew my cheek had been scraped raw last night. The pain I remembered. And my eye swollen shut. But my eye was only slightly bruised, my cheek pink, as if new skin had already grown. My gaze drifted along my neck. The bruises there were faint, as if the attack had happened days ago and not last night.

"What the heck?" I whispered.

My wounds were almost healed, with the exception of my encased arm...but that too barely ached. Another loose memory poked through, of Daemon leaning over me in the road, his hands warm. Had his hands...? No way. I shook my head.

But as I stared at myself, I couldn't shake the nagging feeling that something was going on here. The twins knew it. Things didn't add up.

Chapter 11

The Sunday before school was scheduled to start, Dee took me into town to pick up notebooks while she replaced almost everything she used for school with a new item. We only had three more days of vacation and then we had Labor Day. I was already yearning for it. Before we headed home, Dee was hungry as usual, and we stopped at one of her favorite places.

"It's quite a...quaint restaurant," I said.

Dee smirked, her sandaled foot continuously tapping. "Quaint? It would be quaint to a big city gal like you, but it's the place to be here."

I stole another quick glance around. The Smoke Hole Diner wasn't bad; it was actually kind of cute in an earthy, down-home way, and I did like the clusters of rocks and stones that jutted out around the table's edge.

"It's a lot busier in the evening and after school," she added between sips. "It's hard to get a seat then."

"You come here often?" I found it kind of hard to imagine beautiful Dee hanging out here, eating hot turkey sandwiches and drinking milkshakes.

But there she was, on her second hot turkey sandwich and her third milkshake. Ever since I met Dee, I had been constantly amazed by the amount of food she could consume in one sitting. It was actually a little disturbing.

"Daemon and I come here at least once a week for their lasagna. It is to die for!" Her eyes lit up with a mixture of excitement and longing.

I laughed. "You must love their food, but thanks for inviting me out today. I'm glad to get out of the house since Mom is home. She has been hovering over me every second she's there."

"She's worried."

I nodded, toying with my straw. "Especially after news broke about the girl who died the same night. Did you know her?"

Dee looked down at her plate, shaking her head. "Not very well. She was in a grade lower than us, but a lot of people knew her. Small town and all. I thought I read they weren't sure if she was murdered? That it looked like a heart attack." She paused, her lips pursed as she looked over my shoulder. "Strange."

"What?" I asked, turning to see what she was looking at and turned back around to face her as fast as I could. It was Daemon.

Dee's head was cocked to the side, her dark hair falling carelessly around her. "I didn't know he would be here."

"Oh, man, it's he who shall not be named."

Laughter erupted from Dee, drawing attention from everyone in the diner. "Ah, that was funny."

I sunk in my seat. After the morning he and his sister made me breakfast, he'd avoided me and that was fine. I had wanted to thank him for sort of saving my life. A proper thank you that didn't end in insults, but the few times I'd been able to catch him, he stopped only long enough to give me a look that warned me not to even think about approaching him.

Daemon might be the most physically flawless male I'd ever seen—his face was something that any artist would die to get a chance to sit and sketch—no light reflected badly off him. But he could also be the biggest jerk on the planet.

"He's not going to come over here, right?" I whispered to Dee, who suddenly looked very amused.

"Hello, sis."

I sucked in a deep breath at the sound of his husky voice. I slid my bandaged arm under the table. I was positive if he saw it, it would remind him of how inconveniencing I'd been.

"Hey there," Dee said as she rested her chin on her hand. "What are you doing here today?"

"I'm hungry," he responded dryly. "This is where people come to eat, isn't it?"

I stared very intently at my half-eaten burger and fries, moving them around on my plate, praying to whoever was listening that I could fade into the rustic-colored booths until he left. I forced myself to think about anything—books, television shows, movies, Daemon, the grass outside—

"That is, except you, who must come here to play with her food?"

Aw, dammit. I plastered the brightest smile I could muster and steeled myself. My smile faltered the instant I met his eyes. He looked at me expectantly, as if he knew what I was really thinking, wanted me to fight back. "Yeah, see my mom normally takes me out to Chuck E. Cheese's for dinner so I'm a little out of my element. Missing the ball pen and all."

Dee snorted and looked up at her brother. "Isn't she great?"

"Just lovely." He crossed his arms, his tone as dry as ever. "How's your arm?"

His question took me off guard. My arm actually felt fine. I wanted the splint off, but my mom refused to let me even shower without it. "It's better. It's okay. Thank you — "

"Don't," he cut me off, running a hand through a mess of black waves. "Your face looks a lot better, by the way."

I subconsciously placed a hand on my cheek. "Well... thanks, I think." I looked at Dee with disbelief and mouthed the words *my face* to her.

She exchanged an amused look with me before turning back to her brother. "Are you going to join us? We were just about finished."

It was Daemon's turn to snort. "No, thank you."

I returned to poking my food around on my plate. As if the idea of eating with us was the most absurd thing.

"Well, that's too bad." Dee didn't miss a beat.

"Daemon, you're here already!"

I glanced up at the sound of a very excited female. A small, pretty blonde waved from the main entrance. Daemon waved back, not as joyously, and I watched as she practically bounced over to our table. When she reached Daemon she stretched up and gave him a quick kiss on his cheek before wrapping a possessive arm around his.

An ugly, hot feeling unfurled in my belly. He had a girlfriend? I glanced at Dee. His sister didn't look happy.

The girl finally looked down at our table. "Hey, Dee, how are you doing?"

Dee returned her smile with a very tight one. "Great Ash, how have you been?"

"I've been *really* good." She nudged Daemon as if that was a private joke between the two of them.

I couldn't breathe.

"I thought you were leaving again?" Dee asked, her usually warm eyes turning sharp. "With your brothers and coming back when school starts?"

"Changed my mind." She glanced up at Daemon again, who was beginning to shift uncomfortably.

"Hmm, interesting," Dee responded, her expression taking on a very catlike quality. "Oh, how rude of me. Ash, this is Katy." She gestured over at me. "She's new to our exciting little town."

I forced myself to smile at the girl. I had no reason to be jealous or to care, but damn, this girl was pretty.

Ash's smile faded. She took a step back. "This is *her*?"

My eyes darted to Dee.

"I can't do this, Daemon. Maybe you guys can be okay with this, but I'm not." Ash tossed her blonde hair back with a tan hand. "This is wrong."

Daemon sighed. "Ash…"

Her full lips thinned. "No."

"Ash, you don't even know her." Dee came to her feet.

"You're being ridiculous."

The traffic in the diner literally stopped. Everyone stared.

I felt heat, a mixture of embarrassment and anger, creep across my face as I stared at Ash. "I'm sorry, but did I do something?"

Ash's extraordinarily bright blue eyes fixed on me. "Yeah, how about breathing, for starters?"

"Excuse me?" I said.

"You heard me," Ash snapped. Then she turned to Daemon. "Is this why everything is going to shit in a handbasket? Why my brothers are running around the country—"

"That's enough." Daemon grabbed Ash's arm. "There's a McDonald's down the street. We'll get you a Happy Meal. Maybe that'll make you happier."

"What's going to shit?" I demanded. The urge to get up and rip out her hair was hard to ignore.

Ash's glare burned into me like twin lasers. "*Everything* is going to shit."

"Well, this was fun." Daemon cocked a brow at his sister. "I'll see you at home."

I watched them leave, boiling with anger. But under that anger was also hurt.

Dee plopped back in the seat. "Oh, my God, I'm sorry. She's a complete bitch."

I looked at her as my hands shook. "Why did she say those things to me?"

"I don't know. She might be jealous." Dee toyed with her straw, not meeting my eyes. "Ash has a thing for Daemon, always had. They used to date."

My brain got hung up on the words 'used to' for a second.

"Anyway, she heard about him coming to your rescue that night. Of course she's going to hate you."

"Are you serious?" I didn't believe her. "All of that because Daemon saved me from being *killed*?" Frustrated, I slammed my splint down on the table and winced. "And Daemon treats me like I'm a total terrorist. Ridiculous."

"He doesn't hate you," she replied quietly. "I think he wants to, to be honest. But he doesn't. That's why he acts like that."

That made no sense to me. "Why would he want to hate me? I don't want to hate him, but he makes it hard not to."

Dee glanced up, her eyes full of tears. "Kat, I'm sorry. My family is a little weird. So is this town. So is Ash. See, her family is…is a friend of our family. And all of us have a lot in common."

I stared at her, waiting for her to explain how in the hell that had anything to do with Ash's bitchiness.

"They're triplets, you know?" Dee sat back against the booth, staring listlessly at her plate. "She has two brothers, Adam and Andrew."

"Wait." I gaped at her. "You're telling me there is a set of triplets here and you guys are twins?"

Her face scrunched up as she nodded.

"In a town with a population of, like, five hundred?"

"I know, it's weird," she said, glancing up. "But we do have it in common and all of us are kind of tight-knit. Small towns don't do well with weird. And I'm sort of dating her brother Adam."

I gaped. "You have a boyfriend?" When she nodded, I shook my head. "You've never mentioned him before."

She shrugged, looking away. "It's not something I thought about bringing up. We don't see each other a lot."

I clamped my mouth shut. What girl doesn't talk about her boyfriend? If I had one, I'd talk about him, at least mention him once. Maybe twice. I stared at Dee with new eyes, wondering how much more she wasn't telling me. Sitting back, my gaze drifted beyond Dee, and it was like a switch being thrown.

I started noticing things—little things.

Like how the redheaded waitress with a pencil stuck in her bun kept glancing over at me and touching the shiny, black gemstone on her necklace. Then there was the old man sitting at the bar, food untouched, staring at us while muttering under his breath. He looked a bit crazy. My eyes flitted around the diner. A lady in a business suit caught my eye. She sneered and turned back to her companion. He glanced over his shoulder, and his face paled.

Quickly, I turned back to Dee. She looked oblivious to it all, or maybe she was trying real hard to ignore it. Tension clotted the air. It was like an invisible line had been drawn somewhere and I'd skipped right over it. I could feel all of them, dozens of eyes, settling on me. All of their gazes filled with distrust and an emotion far, far worse.

Fear.

· · ·

The last thing I wanted to be wearing was a splint on my first day at a new school, but since my mom was insistent that I'd wait until my checkup tomorrow after school, I was stuck with more than the 'Look, a new girl!' reactions I got the moment I stepped into the halls of PHS. I had those looks plus 'Look, a new girl who's been beaten up!' too.

Everyone stared as if I were a two-headed alien rolling up into school. I wasn't sure if I should feel like a celebrity or an escaped mental patient. No one spoke to me.

Luckily, PHS was easy to navigate and find classes. I was used to high schools that were at least four stories tall, had multiple wings, and open campuses. PHS had a couple of floors, but that was it.

I found my homeroom class easily and sat through curious stares and a few tentative smiles. I didn't see my neighbors until second period, and it was Daemon who strolled in seconds before the bell rang, with an easy smile on his full lips. Conversations practically ceased. Several of the girls around me even stopped scribbling in or on their notebooks.

Daemon had a sort of rock star entrance with that deadly swagger. He had everyone's attention, especially when he shifted his trig textbook from one hand to the other and then ran his fingers through the tousled waves of his thick hair, letting it fall back over his forehead. His jeans hung low on his hips, so when he lifted his arm, he flashed a row of golden skin that somehow made math all the more interesting.

A girl with reddish hair sighed next to me and said under her breath, "God, what I wouldn't do for a piece of that. A Daemon sandwich should be on the menu."

Another girl giggled. "That is terrible."

"Along with the Thompson twins as a side dish," the redhead replied, flushing as he drew close.

"Lesa, you're such a ho-bag," laughed the brunette.

I hastily averted my eyes to my notebook, but I still knew

he'd taken the seat directly behind me. The entire length of my back tingled. A second later, I felt something poke me in my back. Biting down on my lip, I glanced over my shoulder.

His smile was lopsided. "How's the arm, Kittycat?"

Excitement and dread warred inside me. Did he write on my back? I wouldn't be surprised if he had. I felt my cheeks redden at the sparkle in his green eyes. "Good," I said, tucking my hair back. "I get the splint off tomorrow, I think."

Daemon tapped his pen off the edge of the desk. "That should help."

"Help with what?"

He circled the pen in the air, apparently encompassing my fashion sense. "With what you've got going on there."

My eyes narrowed. I didn't even want to know what he was referencing. There was nothing wrong with my jeans or my shirt. I looked like everyone else in the classroom, with the exception of kids who had their shirts tucked into their pants. I hadn't seen a cowboy hat or teased bangs yet. These kids looked like the kids in Florida, just with less potential for skin cancer.

Lesa and her friend had stopped talking, watching Daemon and me with openmouthed stares. I swore to God if Daemon said anything ignorant, I was going to lay him out in class. My splint was heavy enough to do damage.

Leaning forward, his warm breath danced along my cheek when he spoke. "Less people will stare without the splint is all I'm saying."

I didn't believe for one second that was all he was talking about. On top of that, with him this close to my face, *everyone* was staring. And we weren't looking away from each other.

We were stuck in the middle of an epic stare-down I refused to lose. Something passed between us, reminiscent of the strange current I'd felt with him before.

A boy on the other side of Daemon gave a low whistle. "Ash is going to kick your ass, Daemon."

Daemon's grin went up a notch. "Nah, she likes my ass too much for that."

The boy chuckled.

Eyes still on me, he tipped his desk forward even further. "Guess what?"

"What?"

"I checked out your blog."

Oh. Dear. Baby. Jesus. How did he find it? Wait. More importantly was the fact that he *had* found it. Was my blog now Googleable? That was awesomesauce with an extra heaping of sauce. "Stalking me again, I see. Do I need to get a restraining order?"

"In your dreams, Kitten." He smirked. "Oh wait, I'm already starring in those, aren't I?"

I rolled my eyes. "Nightmares, Daemon. Nightmares."

He smiled, his eyes twinkling, and I almost smiled back, but luckily the teacher started calling roll, forcing an end to, well, whatever was going on between us. I turned around in my seat, letting out a slow breath.

Daemon laughed softly.

When the bell rang, signaling the end of class, I couldn't get out of there quick enough. I did so without looking back to see what Daemon was doing. Math was going to suck butt more than it normally did if he sat behind me in class every day.

Out in the hallway, Lesa and her friend fell in step with

me. "You're new here," said the brunette. Observant.

Lesa rolled her dark eyes. "That's not obvious, Carissa."

Carissa ignored her friend, pushing her square-framed glasses up her nose as she deftly stepped out of the way of another stupid kid barreling through the crowded hall. "How do you know Daemon Black so well?"

Considering the first kids to talk to me were doing so because I'd been talking to Daemon, I wasn't thrilled. "I moved in next to them in the middle of July."

"Ah, I'm jealous." Lesa pursed her lips. "Half the population at this school would love to trade places with you."

I'd gladly change positions with them.

"By the way, my name is Carissa and that's Lesa if you hadn't figured it out yet. We've lived here our whole lives." Carissa waited.

"My name is Katy Swartz, from Florida." Oddly, they didn't have thick accents like I'd been expecting.

"You came here, to West Virginia, from Florida?" Lesa's eyes went wide. "Are you insane?"

I smiled. "My mom is."

"What happened to your arm?" Carissa asked as they followed me up the crowded stairs.

There were so many people in the stairwell I didn't want to announce what happened, but Lesa apparently knew. "She was mugged in town, remember?" She nudged Carissa with a curvy hip. "The same night Sarah Butler died."

"Oh yeah," Carissa said, frowning. "They're holding a memorial for her tomorrow during the pep rally. So sad."

Unsure of how to respond, I nodded.

Lesa smiled as we reached the second floor. I had English

at the end of the hall that I was pretty sure I shared with Dee. "Well, it's nice meeting you. We don't get a lot of new people here."

"Nope," Carissa agreed. "No new kids since the triplets arrived here when we were freshmen."

"You mean Ash and her brothers?" I asked, confused.

"And the Blacks," Lesa answered. "All six of them showed up within days of each other. Had the entire school going crazy."

"Wait." I stopped in the middle of the hall, earning a few nasty looks from people I knocked off course. "What do you mean all six of them? And all of them came here at the same time?"

"Pretty much," Carissa said, fixing her glasses. "And Lesa isn't kidding. It was crazy for months afterward. Can you blame us, though?"

Lesa stopped by a classroom door, brow wrinkling. "Oh, you didn't know there'd been three of the Blacks?"

Feeling even more confused, I shook my head. "No. There's Daemon and Dee, right?"

The warning bell rang, and both Lesa and Carissa glanced into the classroom filling up. It was Lesa who explained. "They were triplets, too. Dee and there were two brothers, Daemon and Dawson. They were completely identical, like the two Thompson boys. Couldn't tell them apart if your life depended on it."

I stared at them, rooted to the floor.

Carissa smiled sadly. "It's really sad. The one brother— Dawson—he disappeared a year ago. Everyone pretty much believes he's dead."

Chapter 12

I didn't have much time to ask Dee about this other brother in English AP because I was late getting to class. And I was still too hurt to broach the topic with her. I couldn't believe they had another brother and never once mentioned him. Or mention their parents, their significant others, or what they do when they take off for a day or two.

And he'd disappeared? Died? My heart ached for them even though they obviously hadn't told me everything. I knew what it was like to lose someone. On top of all of that, there was something just flat-out odd about the fact that two different families with triplets moved to the same small town in a matter of days, but Dee had said the Thompsons were friends of the family. Maybe it was planned.

After class, Dee was waylaid by Ash and a golden-haired boy who looked as though he could be a model. It took no stretch of the imagination to figure out that was one of her brothers. And when they'd left her, all Dee said was to meet together at lunch before we had to rush off to our next classes.

Bio was my next class, and Lesa was in that one. She sat at the table in front of me, smiling. "How's your first day going?"

"Good. Normal." Normal with the exception of everything I'd learned. "Yours?"

"Boring and long already," she replied. "I can't wait for this school year to be over. I'm ready to get the hell out of Dodge, move to a normal town."

"A normal town?" I laughed.

Lesa leaned back, placing her arms on my table. "This town is the epicenter of weirdness. Some of the people here, well, they don't act right."

A three-fingered hillbilly danced in my head, but somehow I doubted that was what she meant. "Dee said some of the people around here weren't friendly."

She snickered. "She'd say that."

I frowned. "What's that supposed to mean?"

Her eyes widened, and she shook her head. "I don't mean that as a bad thing, but some of the kids here and the folks in town aren't friendly toward her and the others like her."

"Others like her," I said slowly. "I'm not sure what that means."

"Me either." Lesa shrugged. "Like I said, people are weird around here. The town is weird. People are always claiming to see men in black running around—like black suits, not the actors. I think they're government. I've actually seen them myself. Then there's the other things people claim to see."

I remembered the guy at the grocery store. "Like what?"

Grinning, Lesa glanced toward the front of the room. The teacher hadn't arrived yet. She scooted even closer and lowered her voice to a whisper. "Okay, this is going to sound insane and let's get one thing straight. I don't believe any of this crap, okay?"

This sounded juicy. "Okay."

Her dark eyes twinkled. "People around here have claimed that they've seen these forms of light up near Seneca Rocks. Like these... people-shaped things of light. Some believe they're ghosts or aliens."

"Aliens?" I busted out laughing, drawing a few stares. "I'm sorry, but seriously?"

"Seriously," she repeated, grinning. "I don't believe it, but we actually get traffic around here from people looking for evidence. I kid you not. We're like Point Pleasant around here."

"Uh, you're going to have to fill me in on that."

"You ever heard of the Mothman?" When she saw my look, she laughed. "It's another crazy thing about this flying giant dragonfly that warns people before something bad happens. Up in Point Pleasant, some have reported seeing it before the bridge collapsed and killed a bunch of people. And days before that, they said they saw men in suits hanging around."

I opened my mouth to respond, but our teacher walked in. At first, I didn't recognize him. His light brown hair was styled back from his forehead. His polo was pressed, nothing like the worn shirt and jeans I'd last seen him in.

Matthew was Mr. Garrison, my bio teacher—the same guy who'd been at Daemon's house when we returned from the lake.

He picked papers off his desk and looked up, his gaze scanning the class. His eyes landed on me, and I felt the blood drain from my face.

"Are you okay?" whispered Lesa.

Mr. Garrison held my gaze a second longer and then looked away. I let out the breath I was holding. "Yeah," I whispered, swallowing thickly. "I'm okay."

I sat back in my chair, staring ahead blankly while Mr. Garrison launched right into class, going over our course material and labs we'd be participating in. The obligatory animal autopsy was scheduled, much to my dismay. The idea of cutting into animals, dead or not, gave me the creeps.

But not as badly as the creeps Mr. Garrison gave me. Throughout class, I'd feel his concentrated gaze on me, and it was as if he was seeing right through me. What the hell was going on around here?

• • •

The school cafeteria was near the gymnasium, a long and rectangular space that smelled of overcooked food and disinfectant. Yum. White tables filled the room and most of them were already occupied by the time I got there. Standing in line, I recognized Carissa.

She turned, spotted me, and smiled. "Spaghetti on the menu, or at least what they consider spaghetti."

Grimacing, I plopped some on my tray. "It doesn't look too bad."

"Not after you've seen the meatloaf." She added noodles to her plate, along with a side of salad. Then she picked up her drink. "I know. Chocolate milk and spaghetti do not go together."

"No, they don't." I giggled, grabbing a bottle of water. "Do they allow anyone off campus to eat?"

"No, but they don't stop us when we do." Carissa handed a few dollars to the lunch lady, then turned to me. "You have anyone to sit with?"

Forking over cash, I nodded. "Yeah, I'm sitting with Dee. You?"

"What?" she said.

I looked up. Carissa stared at me, openmouthed. "I'm sitting with Dee. I'm sure you can sit—"

"No, I can't." Carissa grabbed my arm and pulled me out of the line.

I arched a brow. "Really? Why? Are they social lepers or something?"

She pushed her glasses up her nose as she rolled her eyes. "No. They're pretty cool and all, but the last girl to do so, like, disappeared."

Knots formed in my stomach as I let out a nervous laugh. "You're kidding, right?"

"No," she said solemnly. "She disappeared around the same time their brother did."

I couldn't believe it. What else was I going to find out? Aliens? Men in black? The Mothman? That the tooth fairy was real?

Carissa glanced over at a table full of friends. A few seats were open. "Her name was Bethany Williams. She transferred to this school in the middle of her sophomore year, a little after they got here." She tipped her head to the back of the cafeteria. "And she struck up a relationship with Dawson, and they both disappeared around the start of junior year."

Why did that name sound familiar? Did it matter? There was so much I didn't know about Dee.

"Anyway, do you want to sit with us?" Carissa asked.

I shook my head, feeling bad for turning down her offer. "I promised Dee I would sit with her today."

Carissa relented with a weak smile. "Well, then maybe tomorrow?"

"Yes." I smiled. "Tomorrow, definitely."

Readjusting my book bag, I took my plate of food toward the back of the cafeteria. I saw Dee immediately. She was chatting with one of the Thompson brothers while she twisted her midnight hair around her finger. Across from the one golden-haired god was another with his back to me, half sitting on the table. I wondered which one was her 'kind of' boyfriend. The table was full, except for two open spaces. All guys except Dee.

Then I saw Ash's ultra shiny cap of blonde hair from behind the boy on the table. Oddly enough, she was sitting higher than everyone else. A moment later I realized why.

She was sitting on Daemon's lap. Her arms were draped around his neck, and I watched her press her chest right up against him, smiling at what he said.

Hadn't he tried to kiss me on the porch? I was pretty sure I hadn't imagined that. Daemon was a douchebag to the highest order.

"Katy!" Dee exclaimed.

Everyone at the table looked up. Even the one twin turned in his seat. His sky blue eyes widened upon seeing me.

The other twin sat back, folding his arms. The scowl on his face was a work of art.

"Sit," Dee said, smacking the top of the table across from her. "We were talking about—"

"Wait," Ash said. Her red painted lips twisted into a pout. "You did not invite *her* to sit with us? Really?"

The knots returned in full force, rendering me speechless.

"Shut up, Ash," grumbled the twin that had turned around. "You're going to make a scene."

"I'm not going to make anything happen." Her arm around Daemon's neck tightened. "She doesn't need to sit with us."

Dee sighed. "Ash, stop being a bitch. She's not trying to steal Daemon from you."

My cheeks flamed as I stood there awkwardly. Anger rolled off Ash in waves, spreading across the table, smacking into me.

"That's not what I'm worried about." Ash snickered, her gaze drifting over me as her lip curled. "For real."

The longer I stood there, the stupider I felt. My eyes bounced from Dee to Daemon, but he was looking over Ash's shoulder, his jaw working.

"Just sit," Dee said, motioning me forward. "She'll get over it."

I started to put my plate down.

Daemon whispered, and Ash smacked his arm. Not lightly either. He pressed his cheek into her neck, and that dark and unwanted feeling sprung up deep inside me.

I dragged my eyes away from them, focusing on Dee. "I don't know if I should."

"You shouldn't," Ash snapped.

"Shut up," Dee said, and then to me she said sweetly, "I'm sorry I know such hideous bitches."

I almost smiled, but there was a burning in my chest that was spreading up my throat, down my back. "Are you sure?" I heard myself say.

Daemon lifted his head from Ash's neck long enough to rake a long, confusing look over me. "I think it's obvious if you're wanted here or not."

"Daemon," hissed Dee, her cheeks red. She turned to me, tears in her eyes. "He's not being serious."

"Are you being serious, Daemon?" Ash turned in his lap, head cocked to the side.

My heart was already pounding in my chest when his eyes met mine. His were sheltered. "Actually I was being serious." He leaned over the table, staring up at me through thick lashes. "You're not wanted here."

Dee spoke again, but I was beyond hearing. My face felt like it was on fire. People around us were starting to stare. One of the Thompson boys was smirking while the other looked as though he wanted to crawl underneath the table *for me*. The rest of the kids at the table were staring at their plates. One of them snickered.

I'd never been more humiliated in my life.

Daemon turned away, staring over Ash's shoulder again.

"Run along," Ash said, flicking her long, slender fingers at me.

All the faces staring up at me, a mixture of pity and secondhand embarrassment, threw me back three years. To the first day I'd returned to school after my dad had died. I broke down in English class, crying when I learned we'd be reading *A Tale of Two Cities*, my dad's favorite story. Everyone had stared at me. Some felt bad. Others looked embarrassed for me.

It reminded me of the same looks the police and the nurses had given me at the hospital the night I'd been attacked, reminding me of how helpless I'd been.

I'd hated those looks then.

And I hated them now. There was no excuse for what I did next except that I wanted to — needed to...

Hands clenching the edges of the plastic tray, I leaned over the table and turned my plate upside down over Daemon's and Ash's heads. Chunks of noodles and spaghetti sauce fell. Most of the red gunk hit Ash and the noodles covered Daemon's broad shoulder. One long, stringy noodle slid over Daemon's ear and hung there, flopping around.

There was an audible gasp that rang out through the surrounding tables.

Dee smacked a hand over her mouth, her eyes wide and full of barely restrained laughter.

Shrieking, Ash leaped from Daemon's lap, her hands out to her sides, palms up. One would think I dumped blood on her considering the horrified look on her face. "You...you..." she sputtered, wiping the back of her hand down her sauce-stained cheek.

Daemon plucked a noodle off his ear and seemed to inspect it before he dropped it on the table. Then he did the oddest thing of all.

He laughed.

He really laughed — a deep, stomach rumbling kind of

laughter that reached his minty eyes and warmed them, causing them to sparkle like his sister's.

Ash lowered her hands, balling them into fists. "I will end you."

Daemon jumped up, throwing his arm around the girl's tiny waist. Whatever amusement he felt was long gone. "Calm down," he ordered softly. "I mean it. *Calm down*."

She pulled against Daemon but didn't make it far. "I swear to all the stars and suns, I will destroy you."

"What does that mean? Are you watching too many cartoons again?" I was so over this bitch. I tested the weight of my arm in the splint and seriously thought about hitting someone for the first time in my life.

For a second, I swore her eyes started to glow a bright amber from behind her irises. And then Mr. Garrison was suddenly there, standing at the edge of our table. "I believe that's enough."

Like a switch being thrown, Ash sat down in her own seat. The edge on her rage dissipated as she eyed me and grabbed a fistful of napkins off the table.

Daemon slowly picked a clump of long noodles off his shoulder and dropped it on the plate without speaking. I kept expecting him to explode on me, but like his sister, it looked as if he were trying not to laugh again.

"I think you should find another place to eat," Mr. Garrison said, voice low enough that only the people at our table could hear. "Do so now."

Stunned, I grabbed my book bag and waited for him to tell me to see the principal or for other teachers in the room to intervene but that never came. Mr. Garrison stared at me. He waited. Then it struck me. He was waiting for me to leave.

Like the rest of them were.

Nodding numbly, I turned around and walked out of the cafeteria. Eyes followed me, but I kept it together. I didn't break when I heard Dee call out my name. And I didn't break when I passed a dumbfounded-looking Lesa and Carissa.

I wasn't going to break. Not anymore. I was tired of this shit with Daemon's, well, whatever she was. I hadn't done a single thing for her to treat me this way.

I was done with being pushover Katy.

Chapter 13

I'd made a name for myself by the end of the day. I became the 'Girl Who Dumped Her Food on *Them.*' I expected backlash in every hallway and class, especially when I spotted one of the Thompson boys in my history class or a freshly clothed Ash sulking by her locker.

It never came.

Dee apologized profusely before gym class started, and then hugged for what I did. She tried to talk to me while we lined up for volleyball, but I was...numb. There was no mistaking the fact that Ash hated me. Why? It couldn't be because of Daemon. It was more than that. I didn't know what.

After school I drove home, trying to figure out everything that had happened since I moved here. The first day I'd felt something on the porch and in the house. The day at the lake, Daemon had sprouted gills. The flash of light with the bear and at the library had to be the same. And all that junk Lesa had been saying.

Once I got home, though, and saw several packages on my front porch, all the crap from the day disappeared. A few had smiley faces on them. Squealing, I grabbed the boxes. Books were inside—*new release* books I'd preordered *weeks* ago.

I hurried upstairs and powered up my laptop. I checked on the review I'd posted last night. No comments. People sucked. But I did gain five new followers. People rocked. I closed out the page before I started redesigning everything. Then I googled "people of light" and after initial results gave me a bunch of Bible-study groups, I typed in "Mothman."

Oh. Dear. Lord.

West Virginians were crazy. Down in Florida, every once in a while someone claimed to see Big Foot out in the Glades or the chupacabra, but not a giant flying whatever he was. He looked like a huge satanic butterfly.

Why in the hell was I looking at this?

It was insane. I stopped myself before I started searching for aliens in West Virginia. As soon as I went downstairs, there was a knock on my door. It was Dee.

"Hey," she said, "can we talk?"

"Sure?" I shut the door behind me and walked outside. "My mom's still asleep."

She nodded as I sat on the swing. "Katy, I am so, so sorry about today. Ash is a complete bitch sometimes."

"It's not your fault she acted like that," I said, meaning it. "But what I don't get is why she and Daemon acted like that." I stopped, feeling that stupid burn in my throat. "I shouldn't have dumped my food on them, but I've never been more embarrassed in my life."

Dee sat beside me, crossing her ankles. "I think it was actually kind of funny, what you did and not what they did. If I'd known they were going to be so terrible about everything I would've made sure they didn't."

Water under the bridge, I guessed.

She drew in a deep breath. "Ash isn't Daemon's girlfriend. She wants to be, but she's not."

"It didn't look that way to me."

"Well, they do…hang out."

"He's using her?" Disgusted, I shook my head. "What a douche."

"I think it's mutual on both sides. Honestly, they did date last year for a little bit, but then it cooled off. Today was the most I'd seen him pay attention to her in months."

"She hates me," I said after a few minutes, sighing. "I don't care about that right now. I wanted to ask you something."

"Okay."

I bit my lip. "We're friends, right?"

"Of course!" She looked at me with wide eyes. "Honestly, Daemon scares everyone off and you've lasted the longest, and, well, I think you're like my best friend."

I was relieved to hear that. Not the part about me lasting the longest, because that sounded weird. Like they broke their friends or something. "Same here."

She smiled broadly. "Good, because I would've felt stupid for saying that if you decided you didn't want to be friends anymore with me."

The sincerity in her voice struck a chord in me. Suddenly, I wasn't sure that I wanted to question her. Maybe it was something she didn't want to talk about because it was too painful. In the short time I'd known we'd grown close, and I didn't want to upset her.

"Why did you ask?" she prodded.

I tucked my hair back, staring down at the floor. "Why didn't you ever tell me about Dawson?"

Dee froze. I don't even think she breathed, to be honest. Then she ran a hand up and down her arm, swallowing. "I guess someone told you about him at school?"

"Yeah, they told me he disappeared with a girl."

Pressing her lips together, she nodded. "I know you probably think it's weird that I'd never mentioned him, but I don't like talking about him. I try not to even think about him." She looked at me, eyes glistening with tears. "Does that make me a bad person?"

"No," I said fiercely. "I try not to think about my dad, because it hurts too much sometimes."

"We were close, me and Dawson." She wiped a hand across her face. "Daemon was always the quiet one, off doing things on his own, but Dawson and I were super close. We did *everything* together. He was more than a brother. He was my best friend."

I didn't know what to say. But it certainly explained the almost desperate quality to Dee's friendship, and that common feeling we each recognized in the other. Loneliness. "I'm sorry. I shouldn't have brought it up. I didn't understand and…" And I was a nosy bitch.

"No, it's okay." She twisted toward me. "I would be curious, too. I totally understand. And I should've told you. I'm such a crappy friend that you find out about my other brother from kids at school."

"I was confused. There's been so much..." I trailed off, shaking my head. "Nothing. When you're ready to talk about him, I'm here. Okay?"

Dee nodded. "There's been so much what?"

Talking to her about all the weird crap wouldn't be good. And I had promised Daemon not to talk about the attack. I forced a smile. "It's nothing. So do you think I have to watch my back now? Go into the Witness Protection Program?"

She let out a shaky laugh. "Well, I wouldn't try to talk to Ash anytime soon."

Figured that much. "What about Daemon?"

"Good question," she said, glancing away. "I have no idea what he'll do."

. . .

The next day, I was dreading second period. My stomach was twisted, and I'd been unable to eat breakfast without wanting to hurl. There was no doubt in my mind that Daemon believed revenge was a dish best served in my face.

As soon as Lesa and Carissa arrived at class, they demanded to know what possessed me to dump my plate of spaghetti on Daemon's and Ash's heads.

I shrugged. "Ash was being a bitch." I'm sure I seemed a lot more confident than I felt. I actually wanted to take the whole thing back. Sure, Ash was being rude and embarrassed me, but hadn't I done the same thing to her? If I was the girl who dumped spaghetti on *them*, then she was the dumpee and that's got to be more embarrassing.

I was ashamed. I'd never done anything to make anyone feel bad before. It was as though Daemon's obnoxious personality was rubbing off on me, and I didn't like it. I decided it would be best for everyone if I stayed the hell away from him from now on.

Eyes wide, Lesa leaned across the aisle. "And what about Daemon?"

"He's always an ass," I told them.

Carissa took off her glasses and giggled. "I honestly wish I'd known you were going to do that. I would've filmed it."

Thinking about that being up on YouTube, I cringed as I watched the door.

"Rumor around school is you and Daemon hooked up over the summer." Lesa seemed to wait for me to confirm the rumor. Not in this lifetime.

"People are ridiculous."

I held their gazes until Carissa coughed and asked, "You're going to sit with us today?" She put her glasses back on with a push on the bridge.

Surprised, I blinked at her. "You still want me to sit with you after yesterday?" I was figuring I'd be eating my lunches in the restroom for the rest of the year.

Lesa nodded. "Are you kidding? We think you rock. We don't have any problems with them, but I'm sure there have been a few students who've wanted to do that."

"And it was pretty badass," Carissa added, grinning. "You were like a food ninja."

I laughed, relieved. "I'd love to, but I'm only here until fourth period. I'm getting my splint off today."

"Oh, you're going to miss the pep rally," Lesa said. "Poor you. Are you going to the game tonight?"

"No. Football isn't my thing."

"Neither is it ours, but you still should go." Lesa popped in her seat, her tight curls bouncing around her heart-shaped face. "Carissa and I usually go just to get out and do something. There's isn't much to do around here."

"Well, there are the field parties after the games." Carissa pushed her bangs out of her glasses. "Lesa always drags me to them."

Lesa rolled her eyes. "Carissa doesn't drink."

"So?" Carissa said.

"And she doesn't smoke, have sex, or do anything interesting." Lesa dodged out of the way of Carissa's swinging hand. "Yawn."

"Excuse me if I have standards." Her eyes narrowed on Lesa. "Unlike some."

"I have standards." Lesa faced me, a slight grin on her face. "But around here, you kind of have to lower them."

I started to laugh.

And then Daemon walked into class. I sunk in my seat, biting my lip. "Oh God."

Wisely, both girls stopped talking. I picked up my pen, pretending to be engrossed in the notes I'd taken yesterday. Turned out, I hadn't taken many notes, so I wrote the date on my notebook very slowly.

Daemon took the seat behind me, and my stomach jumped clear into my throat. I was going to vomit. Right here, in class, in front—

He poked me in the back with his pen.

I froze. Him and that goddamn pen. The poke came again, this time with a little force behind it. I swung around, eyes narrowed. "What?"

Daemon smiled.

Everyone around us was staring. It was like a repeat of lunch. I bet they were wondering if I was going to dump my backpack on his head. Depending on what he said, there was a good chance it could happen. I doubted I'd get away with it this time, though.

Tipping his chin down, he stared at me through his wickedly long lashes. "You owe me a new shirt."

My jaw hit the back of my chair.

"Come to find out," he continued softly, "spaghetti sauce doesn't always come out of clothes."

Somehow I found my ability to speak. "I'm sure you have enough shirts."

"I do, but that was my favorite."

"You have a favorite shirt?" I arched a brow.

"And I also think you ruined Ash's favorite shirt, too." He started to grin again, flashing a deep dimple in one cheek.

"Well, I'm sure you were there to comfort her during such a traumatic situation."

"I'm not sure she'll recover," he replied.

I rolled my eyes, knowing I should apologize for what I'd done, but I couldn't find it in me. Yeah, I was becoming a terrible person. I started to turn around.

"You owe me. Again."

I stared at him for a long moment. The warning bell rang, but it seemed far away. My chest lurched. "I don't owe you anything," I said, low enough for only us to hear.

"I have to disagree." Leaning closer, he tipped the edge of his desk down. There were only a few inches between our mouths. Totally inappropriate amount of space, really, since we were in class, and he had a girl on *his* lap yesterday. "You're nothing like I expected."

"What did you expect?" I was sort of turned on by the fact I had surprised him. Weird. My eyes dropped to his poetic lips. Such a waste of a mouth.

"You and I have to talk."

"We have nothing to talk about."

His gaze dropped, and the air suddenly felt steamy. Unbearable. "Yes," he said, voice low, "we do. Tonight."

Part of me wanted to tell him to forget the whole talking thing, but I gritted my teeth and nodded. We did need to talk if at least for me to tell him we shouldn't ever talk again. I wanted to find the nice Katy he'd had gagged and put in the corner.

The teacher cleared his throat. Blinking tightly, I saw that we had the entire class transfixed. Flushing to the roots of my hair, I turned around and gripped the edges of my desk.

Class began, but the heat in the air was still there, coating my skin in anticipation. I could feel Daemon behind me, his eyes on me. I didn't dare move. Not until Lesa stretched beside me and dropped a folded note on my desk.

Before the teacher could catch on, I opened the note and slid it under my book. When he turned back to the chalkboard, I lifted the edge of my textbook.

Holy Hawt Chemistry, Batman!

I looked over at her, shaking my head. But there was a fluttering deep in my chest, a breathlessness that shouldn't be there. I didn't like him. He was a jerk. Moody. But there had been brief moments that I'd spent with him—like a nanosecond—when I thought I might have seen the *real* Daemon. At least a *better* Daemon. And that part made me curious. And the other side, the jerky one, yeah, that part didn't make me curious.

It sort of excited me.

Chapter 14

I tried paying attention in my classes, but my mind was on Daemon and what he wanted to talk to me about tonight. Thankfully, I only had to muscle through half a day before it was time to go get my splint removed.

As expected, my arm was completely fine.

On the way home, I stopped at the post office. There was a ton of junk mail in our box, but also a few yellow envelopes, which brought a big ole smile to my face. *Media Mail* was stamped across them. Gathering my goodies, I headed home and piddled around the house. Anxious energy jolted through my system like I'd chugged one of those cheap energy drinks.

I changed several times, settling on a little sundress after going through my closet and finding nothing I wanted to wear. Changing didn't get rid of the anxious feeling.

What did Daemon want to talk about?

I ended up rearranging my *entire* blog design trying

to pass time. And that only made me more anxious about everything, because I was sure I'd screwed up my header and the banner at the bottom. Only when a book release countdown widget had completely disappeared, lost to the realm of the Internet, did I force myself away from the computer.

Turned out I had a while to wait and see. It was after eight when Daemon showed up at my door, a few minutes after my mom left for Winchester. He was leaning against the railing, staring up at the sky like usual. With the moonlight slicing over half of his face and the rest cast deep in shadows, he didn't seem real.

Then Daemon zeroed in on me, his gaze sliding over my dress and then back up. He looked as if he were about to speak but thought twice.

Gathering up my courage, I walked over and stopped beside him. "Is Dee home?"

"No." He returned to staring at the night sky. There were a thousand twinkling stars. "She went to the game with Ash, but I doubt she will stay long." Daemon paused, glancing down at me. "I told her I was going to hang out with you tonight. I think she'll come home soon to make sure we haven't killed each other."

Looking away, I hid my grin. "Well, if you don't kill me, I'm sure Ash will be more than glad to do so."

"Because of the spaghetti-gate or something else?" he asked.

I shot him a sidelong look. "You looked mighty comfy with her in your lap yesterday."

"Ah, I see." He pushed off the railing, coming to stand

beside me. "It makes sense now."

"It does?" I held my ground.

His eyes gleamed in the dark. "You're jealous."

"Whatever." I forced a laugh. "Why would I be jealous?"

Daemon followed me down the steps until we were standing in my driveway. "Because we spent time together."

"Spending time together isn't a reason to be jealous, especially when you were forced to spend time with me." I realized how lame it was that I *was* sort of jealous. Ugh. "Is this what we need to talk about?"

He shrugged. "Come on. Let's take a walk."

Watching him, I smoothed my hands over my dress. "It's kind of late, don't you think?"

"I think and talk better when I walk." He held a hand out to me. "If not, I turn into the dickhead Daemon you're not very fond of."

"Ha. Ha." I stared at his hand. There was a fluttering in my stomach. "Yeah, I'm not holding your hand."

"Why not?"

"Because I'm not going to hold hands with you when I don't even like you."

"Ouch." Daemon placed his hand over his chest, wincing. "That was harsh."

Yeah, he needed better acting classes. "You're not going to take me out in the woods and leave me there, are you?"

"Sounds like a fitting case of revenge, but I wouldn't do that. I doubt you'd last very long without someone to rescue you."

"Thanks for the vote of confidence."

He tossed me a brief grin, and we walked in silence for a

few minutes, crossing the main access road. The night air was definitely chilly compared to when I'd first put the dress on, and I was beginning to wish I put tights on, too. Fall was well on its way.

Soon we had moved deep into the woods, where the moonlight struggled to make it through the thick trees. Daemon reached in his back pocket and pulled out a thin flashlight that gave off a surprisingly large amount of light. Every cell in my body seemed to be aware of how close he was while we walked in a cocoon of darkness, the light bouncing in front of us with each step. And I hated each of my traitorous cells with a vengeance.

"Ash isn't my girlfriend," he said finally. "We used to date, but we're friends now. And before you ask, we're not *that kind* of friend even though she was sitting on my lap. I can't explain why she was doing that."

"Why did you let her?" I asked, wanting to smack myself afterward. It wasn't my business and I didn't care.

"I don't know, honestly. Is being a guy a good enough reason?"

"Not really," I said, staring at the ground. I could barely see my feet.

"Didn't think so," he replied. I couldn't see his expression and I needed to, because I could never tell what he was thinking and sometimes, well, his eyes were at war with his words. "Anyway, I'm…I am sorry about the whole lunch thing."

Surprised he apologized, I stumbled over a rock. He caught me easily, his breath warm on my cheek before he backed off. My skin tingled, but I pulled back. Daemon apologizing for the lunch debacle was like being doused with cold water. I wasn't sure what was worse: him not knowing he'd been a jerk or fully aware of what he'd been doing to me.

"Kat?" he said softly.

I glanced at him. "You embarrassed me."

"I know—"

"No, I don't think you do know." I started walking, hugging my elbows. "And you pissed me off. I can't figure you out. One minute you aren't bad and then you are the biggest ass on the planet."

"But I have bonus points." He caught up with me, always shining the light far enough ahead of me so I could easily make out exposed roots and rocks. "I do, right? Bonus points from the lake and our walk? Did I get any from saving you that night?"

"You got a lot of bonus point for your *sister*." I shook my head. "Not for me. And if they were my bonus points, you've lost most of them by now."

He was quiet for a few moments. "That blows. It really does."

I stopped. "Why are we talking?"

"Look, I am sorry about that. I am." He let out a long breath. "You didn't deserve the way we acted."

I didn't know what to say to that. He sounded genuine and almost sad, but it wasn't as if he didn't have a choice in how he acted. Searching for something to say, I settled on what probably wasn't going to take well. "I'm sorry about your brother, Daemon."

He came to a complete stop, nearly hidden in the shadows. There was such a long gap in silence I wasn't sure he'd ever respond. "You don't have any idea what happened to my brother."

My insides were tight. "All I know is that he disappeared—"

Daemon's hand opened and closed at his side, the other dangling the flashlight straight down. "That was a while ago."

"It was last year," I pointed out gently. "Right?"

"Oh, yeah, you're right. Just seems longer than that." He looked away, half of his face coming out of the shadows. "So how did you hear about him?"

I shivered in the chilled air. "Kids were talking about it at school. I was curious why no one ever mentioned him or that girl."

"Should we have?" he asked.

Glancing at him, I tried to gauge his expression but it was too dark. "I don't know. Seems like a pretty big deal that people would talk about."

Daemon started walking again. "It's not something we like to talk about, Kat."

That was understandable, I supposed. I struggled to keep up with him. "I don't mean to pry—"

"You don't?" His voice was tight, movements stiff. "My brother is gone. Some poor girl's family will probably never see their daughter again, and you want to know why no one told *you?*"

I bit my lip, feeling like a jerk. "I'm sorry. It's just that everyone is so…secretive. Like, I don't know anything about your family. I've never seen your parents, Daemon. And Ash hates my guts for no reason. It's weird that there are two sets of triplets that moved *here* at the same time. I dumped food on your head yesterday, and I didn't get in trouble. That's plain weird. Dee has a boyfriend she's never mentioned. The town—it's odd. People stare at Dee like she's either a princess or they're afraid of her. People stare at *me*. And—"

"You sound like those things have something in common."

I could barely keep up with him. We were moving deeper into the woods, almost near the lake by now. "Do they?"

"Why would they?" His voice was low and taut with frustration. "Maybe you're feeling a little paranoid. I would be if I'd been attacked after moving to a new town."

"See, you are doing it now!" I pointed out. "Getting all uptight because I'm asking a question, and Dee does the same thing."

"Do you think maybe it's because we know you've been through a lot and we don't want to add to it?"

"But how can you add to it?"

He slowed in his pace. "I don't know. We can't."

I shook my head as he stopped near the edge of the lake and flipped off the flashlight. In the night, the water gleamed like a shined onyx. A hundred stars reflected off the still surface like the night sky, but less infinite. It seemed as if I could reach out and touch them.

"The day at the lake," Daemon said after a few moments. "There were a few minutes when I was having a good time."

My breath caught hearing that. There were a few minutes that I'd enjoyed it, too. I tucked my hair back. "Before you turned into Aquaman?"

Daemon was quiet, his shoulders unnaturally tense. "Stress will do that, make you think things are happening that aren't."

Looking at him, his striking features lit by the pale moonlight, he didn't seem real. The exotic eyes, the curve of his jaw, all of it seemed more defined out here. Daemon stared at the dark sky, a brooding and pensive look to his face.

"No, it doesn't," I said finally. "There is something...odd here."

"Other than you?" he said.

Several responses lined up, but I pushed them away. Arguing with him in the middle of the woods at night wasn't on the top of my list of things to do. "Why did you want to talk, Daemon?"

He clasped a hand on the back of his neck. "What happened yesterday at lunch is only going to get worse. You can't be friends with Dee, not like the kind of friend you want to be."

A hot flush crawled down my cheeks, spreading over my neck. "Are you serious?"

Daemon lowered his hand. "I'm not saying you have to stop talking to her, but pull it back. You can still be nice to her, talk to her at school, but don't go out of your way. You're only going to make it harder on her and yourself."

Every hair on my body rose all at once. "Are you threatening me, Daemon?"

Our eyes locked. His were full of...*what*? Regret? "No. I'm telling you how it's going to be. We should head back."

"No." I dug in, staring at him. "Why? Why is it wrong if I'm friends with your sister?"

A second passed, and his jaw tensed. "You shouldn't be out here with me." He drew in a harsh breath, his eyes wide.

He took a step forward. A warm breeze kicked up, scattering fallen leaves and tossing my hair back. The gust seemed to come from behind Daemon, almost as if it were fueled by his mounting anger. "You aren't like us. You are *nothing* like us. Dee deserves better than you, people that are like her. So leave me alone. Leave my family alone."

It was a smack in the face, only worse. Out of everything I was expecting him to say, he went for a doozy. I drew in a deep breath, but it hitched in my throat. I took a step back, blinking away the rush of angry tears.

Daemon didn't take his eyes off me. "You wanted to know why. That's why."

I swallowed thickly. "Why...why do you hate me so much?"

For a brief second, the mask cracked and pain contorted his features. It was so quick, I couldn't be sure I'd actually seen it. He didn't answer.

The tears building in my eyes were about to spill down my cheeks. I refused to cry in front of him, to give *him* that kind of power. "You know what? Screw you, Daemon."

He looked away. "Kat, you can't—"

"Shut up!" I hissed. "Just shut up." I headed around Daemon and started walking. My skin felt hot and cold, my insides burned with fire and ice. I was going to cry. I knew it. That was what that choking feeling was in the back of my throat.

"Kat," Daemon called out. "Please wait up."

I picked up my pace until I was almost running.

"Come on, Kat, don't walk so far ahead. You're going to get lost. At least take the flashlight!"

As if he cared. I wanted to be free of him before I lost it. There was a good chance I'd hit him. Or I'd cry, because whether I liked him or not, what he had said *hurt*. Like there was something wrong with me.

I stumbled over a few branches and rocks on the ground I couldn't see, but I knew I could find my way back to the road. And I could hear him behind me, his feet snapping twigs as he kept up with me.

Raw hurt opened up in my chest. I stomped ahead, needing to get home, to call Mom and somehow convince her that we needed to move, like, tomorrow.

Run away.

My hands curled into fists. Why should I run away? I hadn't done anything wrong! Angry and disgusted with myself, I tripped over a root sticking out of the ground. I nearly fell flat on my face. I grumbled.

"Kat!" Daemon cursed from behind me.

I gained my footing and rushed forward, relieved to see the road up ahead. I nearly broke into a dead run. I could hear his footfalls now, echoing in the distance. I reached the dark road, wiping the back of my hands over my face. Shit. I *was* crying.

Daemon yelled, but his voice was drowned out by the twin headlights of a truck racing toward me, no more than fifty feet away. I was too shocked to move.

It was going to hit me.

Chapter 15

A loud crack of thunder—only more powerful—reverberated through the valley. It was like a sonic blast that shook me to the very core. There was no time for the driver to see me or stop. I threw up my arms, as if they could somehow protect me. The truck's loud roar filled my ears. I braced myself for the bone-shattering impact, my last thought of my mom and what my mangled body was going to do to her, but the impact never came.

I could've kissed the bumper; it was that close. My hands mere inches from the hot grille. Slowly, I lifted my head. The driver sat motionless behind the wheel, eyes wide and empty. He didn't move, didn't blink. I wasn't even sure if he was breathing.

A cup of coffee was in his right hand, frozen halfway to his mouth. Frozen—everything was frozen.

A metallic taste filled the corners of my mouth. My mind

balked.

The engine was still running, roaring in my face.

I turned from the frozen driver to see Daemon. He seemed to be concentrating, his breathing heavy and his hands were clenched at his sides.

And his beautiful eyes were different. Wrong. I took another step back, now out of the path of the truck, my hand held in front of me, as if to ward him from coming close to me.

"Oh my God..." I whispered, my already pounding heart faltering for a mere beat.

Daemon's eyes glowed iridescent in the dark, lit from the inside. The light seemed to be growing more intense, and his fists started to shake, the trembling moving up his arms until his entire body seemed to be reverberating in tiny, miniscule waves.

And then Daemon began to fade out, his body, along with his clothes, disappearing and being replaced by an intense reddish-yellow light that swallowed him whole.

People made of light.

Holy crap...

Time seemed to stop. No, *time had already stopped*.

Somehow, he'd kept that truck from hitting me. Stopped a seven-ton truck from surely breaking every bone in my body with what? A word? Thought?

So much power.

It caused the air to vibrate around us unnaturally. The ground shivered under his sheer strength. I knew if I tried hard enough I could reach down and feel it quake.

In the distance I heard Dee, confusion pouring from her

voice, calling to us. How had she found us?

Right. Daemon was lighting up the entire street—he was *that* bright.

I looked back to the truck and saw that not only was it shaking, but the driver was, too. It was trying to break past the invisible barrier that seemed to hold it frozen in time. The metal beast shuddered and the engine screamed, the driver's foot still on the gas pedal.

I ran, not out of the road, but beyond that. I vaguely heard the truck howl past me. I ran up the twisting road that led to our houses, nestled at the mouth of nowhere. I briefly saw Dee running up to me before I dodged her. I only knew *she* had to be like *him*.

What were they? They weren't human. What I saw was not possible. No human could do that.

No human could stop a truck on command, stay underwater for several minutes, or fade in and out. All the strange things I'd been noticing seemed to make sense now.

I continued to run, past my driveway, having no idea where I was running or why. My brain wasn't working. Instinct had taken over. Branches ripped at my hair, at the pretty dress I'd worn. I tripped over a large rock, but I pushed myself from my knees to keep moving.

Suddenly, there were footsteps racing behind me. Someone called out to me, but I didn't stop, pushing faster into the dark woods ahead of me. I was not thinking at this point. I only wanted to get away.

A curse sounded from close behind, and then a hard body crashed into me. I went down, surrounded in warmth. Somehow, he managed to cushion the brunt of the fall with his own body by twisting in midair. Then he rolled me under him, pinning me.

I pushed on his chest and tried to kick him. None of it worked. I closed my eyes, too afraid to see if his eyes still held that eerie glow. "Get off!"

Daemon grabbed my shoulders, shaking me gently. "Stop it!"

"Get away from me!" I screamed at him, trying to inch away, but he held me down.

"Kat, stop it!" he yelled again. "I'm not going to hurt you!"

How could I believe him? Some small part of my brain that was still thinking reminded me that he *had* saved my life. I stopped thrashing.

Daemon stilled above me. "I won't hurt you, Kat." His tone was softer, but still laced with fury as he tried to control me without doing any real damage. "I could never hurt you."

His words made my stomach quiver. Something inside me answered, believed him even as my mind rebelled at the idea. I didn't know what part of me was that foolish, but it seemed to be the part winning. My breathing still rough, I tried to calm down. He loosened his hold on me, but he still loomed above. His breath was ragged against my cheek.

Pulling back, Daemon put a finger under my chin to turn my head to face him. "Look at me, Kat. You need to look at me right now." I kept my eyes closed. I didn't want to know if his eyes were still freaky. Daemon shifted up, moving his hands from my shoulders to my cheeks. I should've made my escape then, but the moment his warm hands touched my cheeks, I couldn't move. Carefully, his fingers smoothed over my face.

"Please." His voice lost its furious edge.

Letting out a shaky breath, I opened my eyes. His gaze searched mine. His eyes were still that strange, intense green, but they were his. Not the ones I'd seen minutes before. The pale light of the moon broke through the trees above, slowly sliding over his high cheekbones, bouncing off his parted lips.

"I'm not going to hurt you," he said again softly. "I want to talk to you. I need to talk to you, do you understand?"

I nodded, unable to make my throat work.

He closed his eyes briefly, a soul-wrenching sigh escaping his lips. "Okay. I'm going to let you up, but please promise me you won't run. I don't feel like chasing you anymore right now. That last little trick nearly wiped me out." He paused, waiting for my answer. His face did look tight with fatigue. "Say it, Kat. Promise me you won't run. I can't let you run out here by yourself. Do you understand?"

"Yes," I barely croaked out.

"Good." He slowly let go and leaned back, his left hand moving down my cheek in a small gesture he seemed unaware of. I remained frozen on the ground until he crouched on his heels.

Under his weary gaze, I scooted away until my back was against a tree. Once he seemed satisfied that I wouldn't take off, he sat in front of me.

"Why did you have to walk out in front of the truck?" he asked, but didn't wait for an answer. "I was trying everything to keep you out of this, but you had to go and ruin all of my hard work."

"I didn't do it on purpose." I raised a trembling hand to

my forehead.

"But you did." He shook his head. "Why did you come here, Kat? Why? I—we were doing well and then you show up and everything is thrown to hell. You have no idea. Shit. I thought we'd get lucky and you'd leave."

"I'm sorry I'm still here." Pulling my legs away from him, I tucked them against my chest.

"I'm always making this worse." He shook his head, looking as if he wanted to curse again. "We're different. I think you realize that now."

I rested my forehead against my knees. I took a moment to gather what I had left of my thoughts and lifted my head. "Daemon, what are you?"

He smiled ruefully and rubbed at his head with the heel of his palm. "That is hard to explain."

"Please tell me. You need to tell me, because I'm about to lose it again," I warned him. I wasn't lying. The control that I had obtained started to slip the longer he was silent.

Daemon's gaze was intense as he spoke. "I don't think you want to know, Kat."

His expression, his voice were so sincere they filled me with a deep sense of dread. I knew whatever he was going to tell me was going to change my life forever. Once I learned what he and his family were, I could never take it back, never go back. I would be inexplicably changed. Even knowing all that, I had already passed the point of no return. The old Katy would be running again. I was sure of it. She'd rather pretend none of this happened. But I was different now, and I had to know. "Are you...human?"

Daemon's short laugh was without humor. "We're not

from around here."

"You think?"

His brows rose. "Yeah, I guess you've probably figured out we're not human,"

I took a shaky breath. "I was hoping I was wrong."

He laughed again but there was very little humor in his voice. "No. We're from far, far away."

My stomach dropped to my toes, and my arms around my legs tightened. "What do you mean by 'far, far away'? Because I'm suddenly seeing visions of the beginning of *Star Wars*."

Daemon stared at me hard. "We're not from this planet."

Okay. There. He said what I'd pretty much already figured was the truth, but that told me nothing. "What are you? A vampire?"

He rolled his eyes "Are you serious?"

"What?" Frustration whipped through me. "You say you're not human, and that limits the pool of what you can be! You stopped a truck without touching it."

"You read too much." Daemon exhaled slowly. "We're not werewolves or witches. Zombies or whatever."

"Well, I'm glad about the zombie thing. I like to think what's left of my brains are safe," I muttered. "And I don't read too much. There's no such thing as that. But there's no such thing as aliens either."

Daemon leaned forward quickly, placing his hands on my bent knees. I froze at his touch, my senses ran hot and cold at once. His stare penetrated me, locked me onto him. "In this vast, neverending universe, do you think Earth—this place—is the only planet with life?"

"N-no," I stammered. "So that kind of stuff...that's normal for your... Hell, what do you call yourselves?"

He leaned his head back as the seconds skipped by, and my heart doubled its beats in wait for his answer. He seemed to be wrestling with how much to tell me, and I was pretty sure whatever it might be, I wasn't going to like it....

Chapter 16

This was one of those moments in my life that I didn't know if I should laugh, cry, or run away as fast as possible.

Daemon smiled tightly. "I can tell what you're thinking. Not that I can read your mind, but it's written all over your face. You think I'm dangerous."

And a jerk...and hot, but I wasn't admitting that. And an alien life form? I shook my head. "This is crazy, but I'm not scared of you."

"You're not?"

"No." I laughed, but it sounded a bit crazed—totally unconvincing. "You don't look like an alien!" It seemed important to point that out.

He arched a brow. "And what do aliens look like?"

"Not...not like you," I sputtered. "They aren't gorgeous—"

"You think I'm gorgeous?" He smiled.

I shot him a dark look. "Shut up. Like you don't know that everyone on this planet thinks you're good-looking." I grimaced, shocked to even be having this conversation. "Aliens—if they exist—are little green men with big eyes and spindly arms or...or giant insects or something like a lumpy little creature."

Daemon let out a loud laugh. "ET?"

"Yes! Like ET, asshole. I'm so glad you find this funny. That you want to screw with my head more than you guys have already screwed with it. Maybe I hit my head or something." I started to climb to my feet.

"Sit down, Kat."

"Don't tell me what to do!"

He stood fluidly, arms out to his sides. That creepy glow filled his eyes, like two orbits of pure light. "Sit. Down."

I sat down. With a one-fingered wave, of course. He might be all about sharing his alien-ness with me now, Mr. Badass Alien, but I instinctively knew he wouldn't hurt me.

"Will you show me what you really look like? You don't sparkle, do you? And please tell me I didn't almost kiss a giant brain-eating insect, because seriously, I'm gonna—"

"Kat!"

"Sorry," I muttered.

Daemon closed his eyes and inhaled. Light appeared over the center of his chest, and like back at the road, he started to vibrate and then fade out until nothing but this brilliant reddish-yellow light surrounded him. Then the light took form. Two legs, a torso, arms, and a head made of nothing but light. A light so intense it lit up everything around us, turning night into day.

I shielded my eyes with a trembling hand. "Holy shit."

And when he spoke, it wasn't out loud. It was in my head. *This is what we look like. We are beings of light. Even in human form, we can bend light to our will.* There was a pause. *As you can see, I don't look like a giant insect. Or...sparkle.* Even in my head I could hear the disgust on that last one.

"No," I whispered. Out of all the paranormal books I'd read and reviewed, no one glowed like *this*. Some glittered in the light. Others had wings. No one was a freaking giant sun.

Or a lumpy little creature, which I find offensive, by the way. One arm made of light stretched out toward me. A hand and fingers formed, opening palm up. *You can touch me. It won't hurt. I imagine that it's pleasant for humans.*

For humans? Sweet. Baby. Jesus. Swallowing nervously, I raised one hand. Part of me didn't want to touch him, but to see this, to be next to something so...so, well, out of this world, I had to. My fingers brushed over his, and a jolt of electricity danced over my hand, up my arm. The light hummed along my skin.

I sucked in a sharp breath. Daemon had been right. It didn't hurt. His touch was warm, heady. It was like touching the surface of the sun without being burned. I curled my fingers around his, watching as the light grew until I could no longer see my hand. Little bands of light flicked out from his hand, licking over my wrist and forearm.

Figured you'd like it. He pulled his hand free and stepped back. His light slowly faded, and then Daemon was standing in front of me—human Daemon. I felt the loss of his warmth immediately. "Kat," he said, this time out loud.

All I could do was stare at him. I'd wanted the truth, but

actually hearing it—seeing it—was totally different.

Daemon seemed to read my expression, because he slowly sat back down. He looked relaxed, but I knew he was more like a wild animal, coiled and ready to spring in case I made the wrong move. "Kat?"

"You're an alien." My voice was weak.

"Yep, that's what I've been trying to tell you."

"Oh...oh, wow." I curled my hand back to my chest, staring at him blindly. "So where are you from? Mars?"

He laughed. "Not even close." He closed his eyes briefly. "I'm going to tell you a story. Okay?"

"You're going to tell me a story?"

Nodding, he dragged his fingers through his tousled hair. "All of this is going to sound insane to you, but try to remember what you saw. What you know. You saw me do things that are impossible. Now, to you, nothing is impossible." He paused, seemed to gather himself. "Where we're from is beyond the Abell."

"The Abell?"

"It's the farthest galaxy from yours, about thirteen billion light years from here. And we're about another ten billion or so. There is no telescope or space shuttle powerful enough to travel to our home. There never will be." He glanced down at his open hands, his brow lowered. "Not that it matters if they did. Our home no longer exists. It was destroyed when we were children. That's why we had to leave, find a place that is comparable to our planet in terms of food and atmosphere. Not that we need to breathe oxygen, but it doesn't hurt. We do it out of habit now more than anything else."

Another memory tugged loose. "So you don't need to

breathe?"

"No, not really." He looked sort of sheepish. "We do out of habit, but there are times we forget. Like when we're swimming."

Well, that explained how Daemon had stayed underwater for so long. "Go on."

He watched me for a few moments, then nodded. "We were too young to know what the name of our galaxy was. Or even if our kind felt the need to name such things, but I do remember the name of our planet. It was called Lux. And we are called Luxen."

"Lux," I whispered, recalling one of my freshman classes. "That's Latin for light."

He shrugged. "We came here in a meteorite shower fifteen years ago, with others like us. But many came before us, probably for the last thousand years. Not all of our kind came to this planet. Some went farther out in the galaxy. Others must've gone to planets they couldn't survive on, but when it was realized that Earth was sort of perfect for us, more came here. Are you following me?"

I stared blankly. "I think. You're saying there're more like you. The Thompsons—they're like you?"

Daemon nodded. "We've all been together since then."

That explained Ash's territorial nature, I guessed. "How many of you are here?"

"Right here? At least a couple hundred."

"A couple hundred," I repeated. Then I remembered the strange looks in town—the people at the diner and the way they'd looked at me...because I was with Dee—an alien. "Why here?"

"We…stay in large groups. It's not…well, that doesn't matter right now."

"You said you came during a meteorite shower? Where's your spaceship?" I felt stupid for even saying that.

He raised a brow at me, looking like the Daemon I knew. "We don't need things such as ships to travel. We are light — we can travel with light, like hitching a ride."

"But if you're from a planet millions of light years away and you travel at the speed of light… It took you millions of years to get here?" My old physics teacher would be proud.

"No. The same way I saved you from that Mack truck, we're able to bend space and time. I'm not a scientist, so I don't know how it works, just that we can. Some better than others."

What he said didn't sound sane at all, but I didn't stop him. Like he pointed out, what I saw earlier did not make any sense so maybe I was no longer the judge of what did make sense.

"We can age like a human, which allows us to blend in normally. When we got here, we picked our…skin." He noticed my wince with another shrug. "I don't know how else to explain that without creeping you out, but not all of us can change our appearances. What we picked when we got here is what we're stuck with."

"Well, you picked good then."

The corners of his lips twitched up as he ran his fingers over blades of grass in front of him. "We copied what we saw. That only seems to work once for most of us. And how we grew up to look alike, well, our DNA must've taken care of the rest. There are always three of us born at the same

time, in case you're wondering. It's always been that way."
He paused, lifting his gaze. "For the most part, we're like
humans."

"With the exception of being a ball of light I can touch?"
I let out a low breath, blown away.

His lips twitched again. "Yeah, that, and we're a lot more
advanced than humans."

"How advanced is a lot?" I asked quietly.

He smiled a little then, running his hands over the grass
again. "Let's say if we ever went to war with humans, you
wouldn't win. Not in a billion years."

My heart turned over heavily and I scooted back again,
not even realizing I'd been leaning forward, toward him.
"What is some of the stuff you can do?"

Daemon's eyes flicked up to mine briefly. "The less you
know is probably for the best."

I shook my head. "No. You can't tell me something like
this and not tell me everything. You…you owe that to me."

"The way I see it, you owe me. Like three times over," he
replied.

"How three times?"

"The night you were attacked, just now, and when you
decided Ash needed to wear spaghetti." He ticked them off
on his fingers. "There better not be a fourth."

"You saved my life with Ash?"

"Oh yeah, when she said she could end you, she meant
it." He sighed, tipping his head back and closing his eyes.
"Dammit. Why not? It's not like you don't already know. All
of us can control light. We can manipulate it so that we're not
seen if we don't want to be. We can dispel shadows, whatever.

Not only that, but we can harness light and use it. And trust me when I say you don't ever want to be hit with something like that. I doubt a human could survive."

"Okay..." I barely breathed. "Wait. When we saw the bear, I saw a flash of light."

"That was me, and before you ask, I didn't kill the bear. I scared it off. I'm not sure why you passed out. You were close to my light. I think it had an effect on you. Anyway, all of us have some sort of healing properties, but not all of us are good at it," he continued, lowering his chin. "I'm okay at it, but Adam—one of the Thompson boys—can practically heal anything as long as it's still somewhat alive. And we're pretty much indestructible. Our only weakness is if you catch us in our true form. Or maybe cut our heads off in human form. I guess that would do the trick."

"Yeah, cutting off heads usually does." My mind was going completely blank, only capable of processing what he was telling me and about one line of coherent thought every minute or so. My hands slid to my face and I sat there, cradling my head. "You're an alien."

He raised his brows at me. "There is a lot we can do, but not until we hit puberty, and even then we have a hard time controlling it. Sometimes, the things we can do can get a little whacked out."

"That has to be...difficult."

"Yes it is."

I lowered my hands, curling them above my chest. "What else can you do?"

He watched me closely as he spoke. "Promise not to take off running again."

"Yes," I agreed, thinking what the hell. Not like I could get more freaked out.

"We can manipulate objects. Any object can be moved, animated or not. But we can do more than that." He picked up a fallen leaf and held it between us. "Watch."

Smoke immediately started wafting from it. Bright, orange flames erupted from the tips of his fingers, curling over the leaf. Within seconds it was gone, but his flames still crackled over his fingers.

I scooted forward, placing my fingers near the fire. Heat blew off his fingers. I pulled my hand back, looking at him. "The fire doesn't hurt you?"

"How can something that's a part of me hurt?" He brought his flaming fingers over the ground. Embers flew from his hand, but the ground remained untouched by the fire. He shook his hand. "See. All gone."

Eyes wide, I inched closer. "What else can you do?"

Daemon smiled and then he was gone. Pushing back, I looked around. He was leaning against the tree several feet away.

"How...in the world—wait! You've done that before. The creepy, quiet, moving thing. But it's not that you're quiet." I sat back against the tree, dazed. "You move that fast."

"Fast as the speed of light, Kitten." He reappeared in front of me and slowly sat down. "Some of us can manipulate our bodies past the form we chose originally. Like shift into any living thing, person or creature."

I stared at him. "Is that why Dee fades out sometimes?"

He blinked. "You've seen that?"

"Yes, but I figured I was seeing things." I stretched out

my legs a little. "She used to do it when she was feeling comfortable, it seemed. Just her hand or the outline of her body would fade in and out."

Daemon nodded. "Not all of us have control over what we can do. Some struggle with their abilities."

"But you do?"

"I'm just that awesome."

I rolled my eyes, but then I sat up straighter. "What about your parents? You said they work in the city, but I've never seen them."

His gaze fell to the ground again. "Our parents never made it here."

An ache for him and Dee filled my chest. "I'm...I'm sorry."

"Don't be. It was a long time ago. We don't even remember them."

That seemed sad. Even though my memories of my dad seemed worn over the years, I still had them. And I had so many questions about how they survived without parents, someone taking care of them when they were little. "God, I feel so stupid. You know, I thought they worked out of town."

"You aren't stupid, Kat. You saw what we wanted you to see. We are very good at that," he sighed. "Well, apparently not good enough."

Aliens...Wow, those crazy people Lesa were talking about were right. They'd probably seen one of them. Maybe the Mothman was real. And the chupacabra really was out sucking goat blood.

Daemon's odd eyes flashed for a moment, and then they settled on my face. "You're handling this better than I expected."

"Well, I'm sure I'll have plenty of time to panic and have a mini breakdown later. I will probably think that I have lost my mind." After I spoke, something occurred to me. "Can... can you all control what others think? Read minds?"

He shook his head. "No. Our powers are rooted in what we are. Maybe if our power—the light—was manipulated by something, who knows. Anything would be possible."

As I stared at him, anger and disbelief warred inside me. "This whole time I thought I was going crazy. Instead, you've been telling me I'm seeing things or making shit up. It's like you've given me an alien lobotomy. Nice."

His eyes opened, a flash of anger sparked through them along with something else that I couldn't decipher. "I had to," he insisted. "We can't have anyone knowing about us. God knows what would happen to us then."

Forcing myself to let it drop for the time being, I asked, "How many...humans know about you?"

"There are some locals who think we're God only knows what," he said. "There's a branch of the government that knows of us, within the Department of Defense, but that's about it. They don't know about our powers. They can't," he nearly growled, meeting my eyes. "The DOD thinks we're harmless freaks. As long as we follow their rules, they give us money, our homes, and leave us alone. So when any one of us goes power crazy it's bad news for several reasons. We try not to use our powers, especially around humans."

"Because it would expose what you are."

"That and..." He rubbed his jaw. "Every time we use our power around a human, well, it leaves a trace on that person, enables us to see that they've been around another one like us. So we try not to ever use our abilities around humans, but you...well, things never went according to plan with you."

"When you stopped the truck, did that leave a...*trace* on me?"

He blinked and looked away.

"And when you scared the bear away? That's traceable by others like you?" I swallowed down the cold lump of fear. "So the Thompsons and any other alien around here know I've been exposed to your...alien mojo?"

"Pretty much," he said. "And they aren't exactly thrilled about it."

"Then why did you stop the truck? I'm obviously a huge liability to you."

Daemon slowly turned back to me. His eyes were sheltered, closed. Again, he didn't answer.

I drew in a deep breath, ready to run, fight. "What are you going to do with me?"

When he did speak, his voice wavered. "What am I going to do with you?"

"Since I know what you are, that makes me a risk to everyone. You...can light me on fire and God knows what else."

"Why would I have told you everything if I were going to do anything to you?"

Good point. "I don't know."

He moved forward, and when I flinched away from him, he stopped short of touching me. "I'm not going to do anything to you. Okay?"

I bit my lip. "How can you trust me?"

He paused again and then finally reached out to take my chin in his hand. "I don't know. I just do. And honestly, no one would believe you. And if you made a lot of commotion, you'd bring the DOD in, and you don't want that. They will do anything to make sure the human population isn't aware of us."

I remained still and quiet as Daemon still held me in his soft grip. Several emotions swept through me. Looking at him now, as his presence encircled me, it was all too easy to fall into something I knew I would probably never resurface from. I pulled back. "So that's why you said all those things earlier? You don't hate me?"

Daemon glanced down at his still-outstretched hand. He lowered it. "I don't hate you, Kat."

"And this is why you don't want me to be friends with Dee, because you were afraid that I'd find out the truth?"

"That, and you're a human. Humans are weak. They bring us nothing but trouble."

My eyes narrowed. "We aren't weak. And you're on our planet. How about a little respect, buddy."

Amusement flickered in his emerald eyes. "Point taken." He paused, his eyes roaming over my face. "How are you handling all of this?"

"I'm processing everything. I don't know. I don't think I'm going to freak out anymore."

Daemon stood. "Well then, let's get you back before Dee thinks I killed you."

"Would she really think that?"

A dark look crept over his face. "I'm capable of anything, Kitten. Killing to protect my family isn't something I'd hesitate over, but that's not what you have to worry about."

"Well, that's good to know."

He tilted his head to the side. "There are others out there who will do anything to have the powers that the Luxen have, especially mine. And they will do anything to get to me and my kind."

Anxiety clawed its way back into my chest. "And what does that have to do with me?"

Daemon crouched before me, his gaze roaming the dense forest surrounding us. "The trace I've left on you from stopping the truck can be tracked. And you're lit up like the Fourth of July right now."

My breath caught.

"They will use you to get to me." Daemon reached out, pulling a leaf from my hair. His hand lingered near my cheek for a second before dropping to his knee. "And if they get ahold of you...death would be a relief."

Chapter 17

Bright light pushed through the windows, piercing the darkness that I'd been so comfortable in. I groaned and pushed my head into the soft pillow. My mouth was dry and my head throbbed viciously. I didn't want to wake up yet. I couldn't remember exactly why I thought it was best I stay asleep as long as possible, but I knew there must be a good reason.

My muscles ached as I rolled over and pried my eyes open. Two vibrant green eyes stared intently into mine. I choked on a scream and jumped in surprise. In my shock, my legs tangled in the light blanket and I stumbled out of the bed.

"Holy mother…" I croaked.

Dee caught me, holding me upright while I untangled my legs. "Sorry, I didn't mean to scare you."

I pushed at the blanket until it settled in a messy puddle

at my feet. My legs were bare. And the oversized shirt was so not mine. My cheeks flushed when I remembered Daemon tossing the shirt into the room. It had his scent, a lush mix of spice and the outdoors.

"What are you doing here, Dee?"

The tips of her cheeks flushed as she sat down on the chaise lounge across from the large bed. "I was watching you sleep."

I made a face. "Okay, that's creepy."

She looked even more embarrassed. "It wasn't like I was *watching you*, watching you. It was more like waiting for you to wake up." She pushed at her tousled hair. "I wanted to talk to you. I *needed* to talk to you."

I sat on the bed. Dee did look tired, almost as if she hadn't slept all night. There were dark smudges under her eyes and her arms hung lifelessly at her sides. "Still, it was a little unexpected." I paused. "And still creepy."

Dee rubbed at her eyes. "I wanted to talk to you…" She trailed off.

"Okay, I…need a moment."

She nodded and leaned her head back against the pale cushions, closing her eyes. After a quick look around their guest room, I headed to the bathroom. I found my toothbrush, plus other personal things on their sink I'd picked up from my house when Daemon had brought me back.

I turned on the water until it was drowning out all the sound around me. I finished brushing my teeth and started to wash my face. One look in the mirror told me I didn't look any more rested than Dee did. I looked like hell. My hair was a tangled mess. There was a red line that etched across my cheek like a fine scratch. I cupped my hands under the hot water, splashing my face. The scratch stung.

Funny how a little spark of pain unleashed something more powerful than the fleeting ache it caused. Memories of last night crashed through me. I remembered *everything*.

And felt dizzy.

"Oh my God." I gripped the cool marble of the sink until my knuckles throbbed. "My best friend's an alien."

Spinning around, I threw open the door. Dee stood on the other side, her hands folded behind her back. "You're an alien."

She nodded slowly.

I stared at her. Maybe I should've felt fear or more confusion, but that wasn't what burned inside me. Curiosity. Intrigue. I stepped forward. "Do it."

"Do what?"

"The alien light bulb thing," I said.

Dee's lips spread into a wide smile. "You're not afraid of me?"

I shook my head. How could I be afraid of Dee? "No. I mean, I'm a little blown away by everything, but you're a freaking alien. That's kind of cool. Bizarre, but definitely on the cool side of things."

Her lip trembled. Tears turned her eyes into shimmering jewels. "You don't hate me? I like you, and I don't want you to hate me or be scared of me."

"I don't hate you."

Dee popped forward, moving faster than my human eyes could register. She gave me a surprisingly strong hug and pulled back, sniffling. "I was so worried all night, especially since Daemon refused to let me talk to you. All I could think was I'd lost my best friend."

She was still the same Dee, alien or not. "You haven't lost me. I'm not going anywhere."

A second later she about squeezed the life out of me. "Okay. I'm starving. Get changed and I'll make us breakfast."

She disappeared out of the room in a blink of an eye. That would take some getting used to. I grabbed the change of clothes I'd nabbed last night after telling my mom I was staying over at Dee's house. I quickly changed, then headed downstairs.

Dee was already making breakfast and chatting on her cell phone. The clang of pots and the soft lure of running water muted most of what she was saying. Snapping the phone closed, she spun around.

Then she was in front of me, pulling me to the kitchen table. "When everything happened last night, all I could think is that you must believe we're a bunch of freaks."

"Well..." I started. "You sure aren't normal."

She giggled. "Yes, but normal is so boring sometimes."

I cringed at her choice of words and went to pull out the chair. It moved before I could touch it, sliding back several inches. Startled, I glanced up. "You?"

Dee grinned.

"Well, that was handy." I sat slowly, hoping it didn't get moving again. "So you're as fast as light?"

"I think we might be a little faster." She popped over to the stove. She placed her hand over the skillet. It immediately started crackling under her palm. Over her shoulder, she grinned.

The stove wasn't turned on, but the scent of cooked bacon filled the air.

I leaned forward. "How are you doing that?"

"Heat," she said. "It's faster this way. Takes me seconds to fry up pig."

And it really was only minutes when she handed me a plate of eggs and bacon. Between the moving super-fast and the microwave hand, I was starting to get a bad case of alien envy.

"So what did Daemon tell you last night?" She sat down, a mountain of eggs on her plate.

"He showed me some of your cool alien tricks." The food smelled delicious and I was starving. "Thank you for the breakfast, by the way."

"You're welcome." She pulled her hair up into a messy knot. "You have no idea how hard it's been pretending to be something we're not. It's one of the reasons why we don't have a lot of close friends that are...human. That's why Daemon's all 'Human equals no friend' or whatever."

I toyed with my fork while she devoured half her plate in seconds. "Well, now you don't have to pretend anymore."

Her eyes lifted, sparkling. "Want to know something cool?"

Coming from her, I could only imagine what it was going to be. "Yeah."

"We can see things that humans can't. Like the energy you all put off around you. I think new age people call them auras or whatever. It represents their energy, or some could call it life force. It changes when their emotions change, if they are feeling sick."

My fork stopped halfway to my mouth. "Can you see mine now?"

She shook her head. "You have a trace around you right now. I can't see your energy, but it was a pale pink when I met you, which seems normal. It used to get really red when you'd talk to Daemon."

Red probably represented anger. Or lust.

"I'm not good at reading it though. Some powers come more easily to others, but Matthew rocks at reading energies."

"What?" I set my fork back down. "Our biology teacher is an alien? Holy crap…all I can think of is that movie *The Faculty*." But it made sense, the way he'd acted when he saw Daemon and me together, the strange looks in class.

Dee choked on her orange juice. "We don't snatch bodies."

I hoped not. "Wow. So you guys have like normal jobs."

"Yep." Jumping from her chair, she glanced at the door. "Want to see what I'm good at?"

When I nodded, she moved back from the table and closed her eyes. The air around her seemed to hum softly. A second later she went from teenage girl to a form made out of light, and then a wolf.

"Um," I cleared my throat. "I think I've discovered how the legend of werewolves got started."

She padded over to me and nudged my hand with her warm nose. Unsure of what I should do, I patted her on the top of her furry head. The wolf let out a bark that sounded more like a giggle and then backed off. A few seconds later, it was Dee again.

"And that's not all. Look." She shook her arms. "Don't

freak out."

"Okay." I clenched my glass of OJ.

Closing her eyes, her body faded into the light and then she became someone totally different. Light brown hair fell past her shoulders and her face was a bit paler. Eyebrows arched over large, doe eyes, and her rosy-colored lips formed a half smile. She was shorter, a little more normal looking.

"Me?" I squeaked. I was staring at *me*.

"Hey," Dee-as-me said. "Can you tell us apart?"

Heart pounding, I started to stand but didn't make it. My mouth moved but no words came out. "This is...weird." I squinted. "Does my nose really look like that? Turn around." She did. I shrugged. "My butt doesn't look bad."

The exact replica of me laughed and then faded out. For a moment I could see the outline of a body, but I could see the fridge through the center. A second later she was Dee. She sat down again. "I can look like anyone except for my brother. I mean, I can look like him, but that would be gross." She shuddered. "All of us can shift, but I can hold the form for like forever. Most of us can only mimic for a few minutes tops." Her chest swelled with pride.

"Have you guys ever done that? Been someone else around me?"

She shook her head. "Daemon would have a shit fit if he knew I'd done that. It doesn't leave a huge trace on you, but you're all kinds of lit up right now, so it doesn't matter."

"So Daemon can do that too? Morphing into a kangaroo if he wanted to?"

Dee laughed. "Daemon can do about anything. He's one of the most powerful of us. Most of us can do one or two things easily—the rest is a struggle. Everything is easy for him."

"He's just so awesome," I muttered.

"Once he actually moved the house a little bit," Dee said, nose wrinkled. "He totally broke the foundation."

Sweet Jesus…

I took a sip of my juice. "And the government doesn't know you can do any of that?"

"No. At least, we don't think they do," Dee said. "We've always hidden our abilities. We know that it would scare humans to know we can do things. And we also know that people would take advantage of that. So we try not to risk exposure."

I let that soak in as I took another drink. My brain felt like it was two seconds from blowing up. "So why did you guys come here? Daemon said something happened to your home."

"Yeah, something happened all right." Dee picked up the dishes and headed to the sink. Her back was rigid as she cleaned the dishes. "Our planet was destroyed by the Arum."

"The Arum?" Then I got it. "Dark? Right? Are those the people that are out to like steal your abilities?"

"Yes." She glanced over her shoulder, nodding. "They're our enemies. Pretty much the only enemies of the Luxen besides humans, if they decided to stop being kosher with us being here, I guess. The Arum are like us—only opposite, coming from our sister planet. They destroyed our home. My mom used to tell me a bedtime story that when the universe was formed it was filled with the purest light, shining so brightly it made the shadows envious. The Arum are the children of the shadows, jealous and determined to suffocate all light in the universe, not realizing for one to exist so must the other. Many Luxen feel that every time an Arum is killed, a light in the universe fades away. It's the only thing I remember about Mom."

"And your parents died in this war?" I asked, then immediately regretted doing so. "I'm sorry. I shouldn't have asked that."

Dee stopped washing the dishes. "No, it's okay. You should know, but it shouldn't scare you."

I didn't know how their parents' deaths could scare me, but I had begun to feel alarmed by what I might find out.

"There are Arum here. The government thinks they're Luxen. We have to keep it that way or there's a chance the DOD could learn of our powers through the Arum." Dee faced me, placing her hands on the edge of the sink. "And now, you're like a beacon to them."

Appetite gone, I pushed my plate away. "Is there any way to get the trace off?"

"It will fade over time." Dee forced a smile. "Until then it would be good to stick around us, especially Daemon."

Goodie goodie gumdrops. But it could be worse. "Okay, so it fades…eventually. I can deal with that if that's my only problem."

"It's not," she said. "We need to make sure the government doesn't know that you know the truth. Their job is to make sure we don't expose ourselves. Can you imagine if the human population knew we existed?"

Images of rioting and looting flickered in my head, which was how we reacted to everything we didn't understand.

"And they will do anything to make sure we stay secret." Dee's eyes locked onto mine. "You can never tell anyone, Katy."

"I wouldn't. I would never do that." The words rushed from me. "I would never betray any of you like that." And I meant it. Dee was like a sister to me. And Daemon was... well, he was whatever, but I would never betray them. Not after they trusted me with something so amazing. "I won't tell anyone."

Dee knelt beside me and she placed her hand on mine. "I trust you, but we can't let the DOD find out about you, because if they ever did, then you'd disappear."

Chapter 18

"Katy, you've been so quiet today. What's on your mind?"

I winced, wishing my mother wasn't so good at reading me. "I'm just tired." I forced a smile for her benefit.

"Are you sure that all?"

Guilt ate at me. I rarely spent time with my mother, and I wished I hadn't been distracted. "I'm sorry, Mom. I guess I am a little out of it today."

She started washing our dinner dishes. "How are things with Daemon and Dee?"

We'd made it all day without talking about them. "They're doing great. I think I may go watch a movie with them later."

She smiled. "Are you going with both of them?"

I narrowed my eyes. "Mom, please."

"Honey, I'm your mother. I do have a right to ask."

"I'm not sure, really. I don't even know if we are going.

It was just an idea." I grabbed an apple out of the fruit bowl and took a bite. "What are you doing with your evening, Mom?"

She tried to look nonchalant. "I'm going out and having coffee with Mr. Michaels tonight."

"Mr. Michaels? And who is he?" I asked between bites. "Wait. Is he that fine-looking doctor at the hospital?"

"Yes, the one and only."

"Is this a date?" I leaned against the counter, grinning around the apple. "Go Mom."

My mother blushed—actually blushed. "It's just coffee. Not a date."

That explained why she kept picking out dresses today, going as far as making me choose at least two of the pretty things from her closet. "Well, I hope you have fun on your not a date, but sounds like a date."

Smiling, she chattered on about her evening plans and then about a patient she had yesterday. Before she left to get ready, she brought me a couple of dresses she'd found in the back of her closet. "Well, if you go out tonight, why don't you wear one of these? You'll look pretty in them. They always looked too young for me to wear."

My nose scrunched. "Mom, I'm not the one who has a date tonight."

She scoffed. "I don't either."

"Whatever!" I yelled as she raced up the stairs.

It didn't take her long to get ready and leave. Since it wasn't technically a date, she was meeting him at a little diner in town. I hoped she had a good time; she deserved to have fun. Since Dad had passed away, I don't think she had even looked twice at a guy. Which meant Mr. Michaels must be special.

Other than Dee mentioning that we should get together, there hadn't been any plans for the night. I knew Daemon was keeping an eye on me from next door all day, but I'd refused to let him hover at my house. They'd told me the Arum were stronger at night and preferred to attack then. I felt pretty safe during the day. I'd wanted to spend a normal day of reading and blogging and hanging out with my mom.

But it was strange going about normal stuff after such a huge secret. I felt like they should be out stopping accidents, curing world hunger, and saving kittens caught in trees.

Tossing the apple core in the garbage, I fiddled with the ring on my finger as I looked over the dresses on the table. I wouldn't be wearing them on a date anytime soon.

A sharp knock on the back door jarred me out of my thoughts. I went to the door and Daemon stood there. Even dressed in casual jeans and a plain white shirt that strained against his upper body, he looked utterly magnificent. It was unsettling. And what was even more unnerving was the way he stood there and stared at me. His brilliant jade gaze was intense and consuming.

"Hey?" I said.

He nodded, giving me no clue what kind of mood he was in.

Oh boy. "Um, do you want to come in?"

He shook his head. "No, I thought maybe we could go do something."

"Do something?"

Amusement flashed in his eyes. "Yeah. Unless you have a

review to post or a garden that needs tending."

"Ha. Ha." I started to shut the door in his face.

He threw his hand out, easily stopping it without touching it. "Okay. Let me try that again. Would you like to do something with me?"

Not really, but I was curious. And a part of me was beginning to understand why Daemon was so standoffish. Maybe—just maybe—we could do this without wanting to kill one another. "Where did you have in mind?"

Daemon pushed away from the house and shrugged. "Let's go to the lake."

"I'll check the road before I cross this time." I followed him, avoiding his amused look. I shoved my hands in the pockets of my shorts and decided to not beat around the bush. "You're not taking me out in the woods because you changed your mind and decided your secret is not safe with me, are you?"

Daemon busted out laughing. "You're very paranoid."

I snorted. "Okay, that is coming from an alien who apparently can toss me into the sky without touching me."

"You haven't locked yourself in any rooms or rocked in any corners, right?"

I rolled my eyes and began walking again. "No Daemon, but thanks for making sure I'm mentally sound and all."

"Hey." He threw up his hands. "I need to make sure you aren't going to lose it and potentially tell the entire town what we are."

"I don't think you need to worry about that for several reasons," I replied dryly.

Daemon gave me a pointed look. "You know how many

people we've been close to? I mean, really close to?"

I made a face. It wasn't hard to imagine what he meant. Oddly, I found myself not liking those images.

His chuckle was deep and throaty. "Then one little girl goes and exposes us. Can you see how hard that is for me to...trust?"

"I'm not a little girl, but if I could go back in time and do it all over I wouldn't have stepped out in front of that truck."

"Well that is good to know," he responded.

"But I don't regret finding out the truth. It explains so much. Wait, can you go back in time?" I asked seriously. The possibility hadn't crossed my mind before but now I honestly wondered.

Daemon sighed and shook his head. "We can manipulate time, yes. But it's not something we'd do, and only going forward. At least I've never heard of anyone being able to bend time to the past."

My eyes felt like they were going to pop out. "Jesus, you guys make Superman look lame."

He smiled as he dipped his head down to avoid a low-hanging branch. "Well, I'm not telling you what our kryptonite is."

"Can I ask you a question?" I asked after a couple of moments of us walking along the leaf-covered trail. When he nodded, I took a deep breath. "The Bethany girl that disappeared—she was involved with Dawson, right?"

He cut me a sharp sidelong glance. "Yes."

"And she found out about you guys?"

Several seconds passed before he answered. "Yes."

I glanced at him again. His face was stoic as he stared

straight ahead. "And that's why she disappeared?"

Again, there was a gap of silence. "Yes."

Okay. He was only going to give me one-word answers. Nice. "Did she tell someone? I mean, why did she...have to disappear?"

Daemon sighed heavily. "It's complicated, Kat."

Complicated meant a lot of things. "Is she...dead?"

He didn't answer.

I stopped, digging an odd-shaped pebble out of my sandal. "You're just not going to tell me?"

He grinned at me with infuriating ease.

"So why did you want to come out here?" I shook the rock out and put my sandal back on. "Because it's fun for you to be all evasive?"

"Well, it is amusing to watch your cheeks get all pink when you're frustrated."

I glared at him.

Daemon smirked and started walking again. We didn't say anything until we reached the lake. He went to the edge and glanced back to where I stopped a few feet behind him. "Besides the twisted fact that I like watching you get all bent out of shape, I figured you'd have more questions."

Well, it was sick he liked pissing me off. Even sicker was the fact I liked watching him get all pissy, too. "I do."

"Some I won't answer. Some I will." Daemon paused, looking thoughtful. "Might as well get all your questions out of the way. Then we don't have a reason to bring any of this up again, but you're going to have to work for those questions."

Never bring up the fact that they were *aliens*? Ha. Okay.

"What do I have to do?"

"Meet me on the rock." He turned back to the lake and kicked off his shoes.

"What? I'm not wearing a bathing suit."

"So?" He turned around, grinning. "You could almost strip down —"

"Not going to happen." I folded my arms.

"Figured," he replied. "Haven't you ever gone swimming in your clothes before?"

Yes. Who hadn't? But it wasn't even *that* warm. "Why do we have to go swimming for me to ask questions?"

Daemon stared at me a moment, then his lashes lowered, fanning his cheeks. "It's not for you, but for me. It seems like a normal thing to do." The tips of his cheekbones turned pink in the sun. "The day we went swimming?"

"Yes," I said, taking a step forward.

He looked up, his eyes meeting mine. The green churned slowly, giving an appearance of vulnerability. "Did you have fun?"

"When you weren't being a jerk and if I ignore the fact that you were bribed into it, then yes."

A smile pulled at his lips as he looked away. "I had more fun that day than I can remember. I know it sounds stupid, but —"

"It's not stupid." My heart lurched. At once, I sort of understood him better. Underneath it all, I think he wanted to be normal. "Okay. Let's do this. Just don't go underwater for five minutes."

Daemon laughed. "Deal."

I kicked off my sandals while he tugged off his shirt. I

tried not to stare at him, especially since he was watching me like he expected me to change my mind. Tossing him a quick grin, I stepped up to the water's edge and dipped my toes in. "Oh my God, the water is cold!"

He winked at me. "Watch this." His eyes took on that eerie glow, his whole body vibrating and breaking apart into a fiery ball of light...that flew up into the sky and dove straight in, lighting the lake like a pool light. He zipped around and around the rocks in the center, at least a dozen times in as many seconds. Show-off.

"Alien powers?" I asked, teeth chattering.

Water ran off his hair as he leaned over the edge of the rock, extending a hand. "Come in, it's a little warmer now."

Gritting my teeth in preparation for the icy water, I was shocked to discover its temperature wasn't too bad. It wasn't warm, but it wasn't icy cold anymore. Stepping all the way in now, I waded out to the rocks. "Any other cool talents?"

"I can make it so that you can't even see me."

I took his hand, and he pulled me out into the water and onto the rock, wet clothes and all. He let go, scooting back. Shivering, I welcomed the warmth of the sun-baked rock. "How can you do things without me seeing?"

Leaning back on his elbows, he looked unaffected by the cold swim. "We're made of light. We can manipulate the different spectrums around us, using them. It's like we're fracturing the light, if that makes any sense."

"Not really." I needed to pay more attention in science class.

"You've seen me turn into my natural state, right?" When I nodded, he went on. "And I sort of vibrate until I break apart into tiny particles of light. Well, I can selectively eliminate the light, which allows us to be transparent."

I pulled my knees to my chest. "That's kind of amazing, Daemon."

He smiled up at me, flashing a dimple in one cheek before he laid back on the rock, folding his hands behind his head. "I know you have questions. Ask them."

I had so many questions I wasn't sure which one to start with. "Do you guys believe in God?"

"He seems like a cool guy."

I blinked, not sure whether to laugh at that or not. "Did you guys have a God?"

"I remember there was something like a church, but that's all. The elders don't talk about any religion," he said. "Then again, we don't see any elders."

"What do you mean by 'elders'?"

"The same thing you'd mean. An old person."

I made a face at him.

He grinned. "Next question?"

"Why are you such an ass?" The words came out before I could think twice.

"Everyone has to excel at something, right?"

"Well, you're doing a great job."

His eyes opened, meeting mine for a second before closing. "You do dislike me, don't you?"

I hesitated. "I don't dislike you, Daemon. You're hard to…like. It's hard to figure you out."

"So are you," he said, eyes closed, face relaxed. "You've accepted the impossible. You're kind to my sister and to me — even though I admit I've been a jerk to you. You could've run right out of the house yesterday and told the world about us, but you didn't. And you don't put up with any of my crap," he added with a soft laugh. "I like that about you."

Whoa. Wait. "You like me?"

"Next question?" he said.

"Are you guys allowed to date people—humans?"

He shrugged. "Allowed is a strange word. Does it happen? Yes. Is it advised? No. So we can, but what would be the point? Not like we can have a lasting relationship when we have to hide what we are."

"So, you guys are like us in other, uh, departments?"

Daemon sat up, arching a brow. "Come again?"

I felt my cheeks flush. "You know, like sex? I mean, you guys are all glowy and stuff. I don't see how certain stuff would work."

Daemon's lips curled into a half smile, and that was the only warning he gave. Moving unbelievably fast, I was on my back and he was above me in a flash. "Are you asking if I'm attracted to human girls?" he asked. Dark, wet waves of hair fell forward. Tiny droplets of water fell off the ends, splashing against my cheek. "Or are you asking if I'm attracted to *you*?"

Using his hands, he lowered himself slowly. There wasn't an inch of space between our bodies. Air fled my lungs at the contact of his body against mine. He was male and ripped in all the places I was soft. Being this close to him was startling, causing an array of sensations to zing through me. I shivered. Not from the cold, but from how warm and wonderful he felt. I could feel every breath he took, and when he shifted his hips, my eyes went wide and I gasped.

Oh yeah, *certain stuff* was definitely working.

Daemon rolled off me, onto his back beside me. "Next question?" he asked, voice deep and thick.

I didn't move. I stared wide-eyed at the blue skies. "You could've just told me, you know?" I looked at him. "You didn't have to *show* me."

"And what fun would there be in telling you?" He turned his head toward me. "Next question, Kitten?"

"Why do you call me that?"

"You remind me of a little fuzzy kitten, all claws and no bite."

"Okay, that makes no sense."

He shrugged.

I searched my scattered thoughts for another question. I had so many, but he'd totally blown my train of thought to smithereens. "Do you think there are more Arum around?"

Only the barest hint of emotion flitted across his face. He tipped his head back, studying me. "They are always around."

"And they're hunting you?"

"It's the only thing they care about." He returned to staring at the sky. "Without our powers, they are like...humans, but vicious and immoral. They're into ultimate destruction and whatever."

I swallowed hard. "Have you...fought a lot of them?"

"Yep." He eased onto his side, using his hand to support his head. A lock of hair fell over his eye. "I've lost count of how many I've faced and killed. And with you lit up like you are, more will come."

My fingers itched to brush that strand of hair back. "Then why did you stop the truck?"

"Would you have preferred I let it pancake you?"

I didn't even bother responding to that. "Why did you?"

A muscle popped in his jaw as his gaze drifted over my upturned face. "Honestly?"

"Yes."

"Will it get me bonus points?" he asked softly.

Holding my breath, I reached up and brushed back the strand of hair. My fingers barely grazed his skin, but he sucked in a sharp breath and closed his eyes. I pulled my hand away, not sure why I'd done that. "Depends on how you answer the question."

Daemon's eyes opened. The pupils were white, strangely beautiful. He eased down on his back again, his arm against mine. "Next question?"

I clasped my hands together, over my stomach. "Why does using your powers leave a trace?"

"Humans are like glow-in-the-dark T-shirts to us. When we use our abilities around you, you can't help but absorb our light. Eventually, the glow will fade, but the more we do, the more energy we use, the brighter the trace. Dee blurring out doesn't leave much of anything. The truck incident and when I scared the bear, that leaves a visible mark. Something more powerful, like healing someone, leaves a longer trace. A faint one, nothing big so I'm told, but it lingers longer for some reason.

"I should've been more careful around you," he continued. "When I scared the bear I used a blast of light, which is kind of like a laser. It left a large enough trace on you for the Arum to see you."

"You mean the night I was attacked?" I whispered, my

voice hoarse.

"Yes." He dragged a hand down his face. "Arum don't come here a lot, because they don't think any Luxen are here. The beta quartz in the Rocks throws off our energy signature, hides us. That's one of the reasons why there are a lot of us here. But there must have been one coming through. He saw your trace and knew there had to be one of us nearby. It was my fault."

"It wasn't your fault. You weren't the one who attacked me."

"But I basically led him to you," he said, voice tight.

At first I couldn't speak. There was this horrible punched-in-the-gut type of feeling that spread to the tips of my fingers and down to my toes. I felt the blood drain out my face so fast it left me dizzy.

Suddenly, what that man had said made sense. *Where are they?* He'd been looking for them. "Where is he now? Is he still around? Is he going to come back? What—"

Daemon's hand found mine and squeezed. "Kitten, calm down. You're going to have a heart attack."

My eyes dropped to our hands. He didn't pull his away. "I'm not going to have a heart attack."

"Are you sure?"

"Yes." I rolled my eyes.

"He isn't a problem anymore," he said after a few seconds.

"You...you killed him?"

"Yeah, I kind of did."

"You kind of did? I didn't know there was any 'kind of' in killing someone."

"Okay, yes, I did kill him." There wasn't a single ounce of doubt or remorse in his voice, like killing someone didn't even faze him. I should be afraid, very afraid of him. Daemon sighed. "We're enemies, Kitten. He would've killed me and my family after absorbing our abilities if I didn't stop him. Not only that, he would've brought more here. Others like us would've been in danger. *You* would've been in danger."

"What about the truck? I'm glowing brighter now." I ignored the clenching in my stomach. "Will there be another?"

"Hopefully there are none nearby. If not, the traces on you should fade. You'll be safe."

He was guiding his thumb across my hand in a silent alphabet. It was sort of soothing, comforting. "And if not?"

"Then I'll kill them, too." He didn't hesitate. "For awhile, you're going to need to stay around me, until the trace fades."

"Dee said something like that." I bit my lip. "So you don't want me to stay away from you guys anymore?"

"It doesn't matter what I want." He glanced down at his hand. "But if I had my way, you wouldn't be anywhere near us."

I sucked in a sharp breath, pulling my hand free. "Gee, don't be honest or anything."

"You don't understand," Daemon replied. "Right now, you can lead an Arum right to my sister. And I have to protect her. She's all I have left. And I have to protect the others here. I'm the strongest. That is what I do. And while you're carrying the trace on you, I don't want you going anywhere with Dee if I'm not with you."

Sitting up, I glanced toward the shore. "I think it's time I head back."

His fingers wrapped around my arm. The skin tingled. "Right now, you can't be out there by yourself. I need to be with you until the trace fades."

"I don't need you to play babysitter." My jaw ached from how hard I was clenching it. The whole staying away from Dee pissed me off, but I understood. Doesn't mean his words didn't hurt. "I'll stay away from Dee until it fades."

"You're still not getting it." His grip didn't tighten, but I had a feeling he wanted to shake the crap out of me even though I knew he never would. "If an Arum gets ahold of you, they aren't going to kill you. The one at the library—he was playing with you. He was going to get you to the point that you'd beg for your life and then force you to take him back to one of us."

I swallowed. "Daemon—"

"You don't have a choice. Right now, you're a huge risk with the trace. You are a danger to my sister. I will not let anything happen to her."

His love for his sister was admirable, but did nothing to stop the flow of anger rushing through my veins. "And then after the trace fades? Then what?"

"I prefer that you'd stay the hell away from all of us, but I doubt that's going to happen. And my sister does care for you." He let go of my arm and leaned back, resting on his elbows. "As long as you don't end up with another trace, then I don't have a problem with you being friends with her."

My hands balled into fists. "I'm so grateful to have your approval."

His little half smile didn't reach his eyes. His smiles rarely did. "I've already lost one sibling because of how he felt for a human. I'm not going to lose another."

Anger was still simmering in me, but his words caught my attention. "You're talking about your brother and Bethany."

There was a pause and then, "My brother fell in love with a human...and now they're both dead."

Chapter 19

Like he'd turned off my bitch switch, all I could do was stare at him. There was a feeling in my gut that told me I already knew this stuff but hadn't wanted to acknowledge it. God, he was such a jerk, but my anger eased off, lessening and leaving uncertainty in its wake.

"What happened?" I asked.

He was staring over my shoulder, focused on the trees behind me. "Dawson met Bethany, and I swear to you, it was like love at first sight. Everything for him became about her. Matthew—Mr. Garrison—warned him. I warned him that it wasn't going to work. There was no way we can have a relationship with a human."

Pressing his lips together, he took a moment. "You don't know how hard it is, Kat. We have to hide what we are all the time, and even among our own kind, we have to be careful. There are many rules. The DOD and Luxen don't like the idea of us messing with humans." He paused, shaking his head. "It's as if they think we're animals, beneath them."

"But you're not animals," I said. They were definitely not like us, but they weren't beneath us.

"Do you know anytime we apply for something, it's tracked by the DOD?" He glanced at me, eyes troubled. Angry. "Driver's license, they know. If we apply for college, they see it. Marriage license to a human? Forget it. We even have a registration we have to go through if we want to move."

I blinked. "Can they do that?"

He laughed humorlessly. "This is your planet, not ours. You even said it. And they keep us in place by funding our lives. We have random check-ins, so we can't hide or anything. Once they know we're here, that's it."

Not sure what to say, I remained quiet. Everything about their life seemed controlled, chronicled. It was frightening and sad.

"And that's not all. We're expected to find another Luxen, and to stay there."

Alarm trickled through my system. Was he obligated to Ash? It seemed the wrong time to ask. And it seemed even more wrong that I wanted to ask. "That doesn't seem fair."

"It's not." Daemon sat up in one fluid motion, dropping his arms over his bent knees. "It's easy to feel human. I know I'm not, but I want the same things that all humans want." He stopped, shaking his head. "Anyway, something happened between Dawson and Bethany. I don't know what. He never said. They went out hiking one Saturday and he came back late, his clothing torn and covered with blood. They were closer than ever. If Matt and the Thompsons didn't have their suspicions before, they did then. That following weekend, Dawson and Bethany went out to the movies. They never came back."

I squeezed my eyes shut.

"The DOD found him the next day in Moorefield, his body dumped in a field like garbage." His voice was low, rough. "I didn't get to say good-bye. They took his body before I could even see him, because of the risk of exposure. When we die or get hurt, we resort back to our true form."

I ached for that—for him and Dee. "Are you sure he's... dead then, if you've never seen his body?"

"I know an Arum got him. Drained him of his abilities and killed him. If he were still alive, he would've found a way to contact us. Both his and Bethany's bodies were taken away before anyone could see. Her parents will never know what happened to her. And all we know is that he had to have done something that left a trace on her, enabling the Arum to find him. That's the only way. They can't sense us here. He *had* to have done something major."

My chest squeezed. I couldn't imagine what he and Dee had to have felt. My father's death had been expected. It hurt—it had felt like his sickness and eventual death was killing me—but he hadn't been murdered.

"I'm sorry," I whispered. "I know there's nothing I can say. I'm just so sorry."

He shifted slightly, lifting his head to the sky. In a second, the mask he wore slipped down. And there was the real Daemon. Still a total badass, but there was pain in him, a vulnerability in the lines of his face that I doubted anyone ever got to see. And suddenly, I felt like I was intruding, witnessing this moment. For it to be me, of all people, to see beneath the layers of attitude didn't seem right. It should've been someone he cared about, someone important to him.

"I...I miss the idiot," he said raggedly.

My heart clenched. The pain in his voice pricked at me. Not thinking, I turned and reached over, wrapping my arms around his all too stiff body. I hugged him, squeezing him as tightly as I could. And then I let him go before he overreacted and threw me off the rock.

Daemon still didn't move. He stared at me, eyes wide, like he'd never been hugged before. Maybe the Luxen didn't believe in hugs.

I lowered my gaze. "I miss my dad, too. It doesn't get any easier."

His breath expelled harshly. "Dee said he was sick but not what was wrong with him. I'm sorry...for you loss. Sickness isn't something we're accustomed to. What was it?"

I told him about my dad's cancer, which was surprisingly easy. And then I told him about better things—things my dad and I shared before he got sick. How I used to garden with him and we'd spend Saturday mornings during the spring searching for new plants and flowers.

And he shared memories of Dawson. The first time they hiked the Seneca Rocks. And the time that Dawson had morphed into someone else and couldn't figure out how to change back. We stayed there, somehow finding a peace in talking about them until the sun started to fade and the rock lost its warmth. And it was just me and him, in the dusk, staring at the stars filling the sky.

I was reluctant to leave, not because the water would be cold, but because I knew—*I knew*—that this little piece of the world we created, where we weren't arguing or hating one another, wouldn't last. It seemed that Daemon...needed someone to talk to, and I happened to be here. I asked the right questions. And it was the same for me. He was here. At least, that's what I was telling myself, because I knew tomorrow would be no different than the week before.

We had to go back to the real world. And Daemon wishing he'd never met me.

Neither of us spoke until we were on my porch. The light was on in the living room, so when I did speak, I kept my voice low. "What happens now?"

Daemon's hands were fists at his side as he looked away, not answering.

I started to turn, but in the time that it took for me to blink my eyes, Daemon was already gone.

• • •

"You didn't do anything for Labor Day?" Lesa pointed at Carissa behind her. "You live a life as exciting as Carissa."

Carissa rolled her eyes as she straightened her glasses. "Not all of us have parents who whisk us away for a quick weekend in North Carolina. We aren't as cool as you."

It wasn't like I could tell them I did have an exciting weekend, one involving almost getting hit by a truck and proving the existence of extraterrestrial life forms, so I shrugged and scribbled in my notebook. "Just hung out at home."

"I can see why." Lesa tipped her chin toward the front of

the classroom. "I would too if I lived next to that."

"You should've been born as a man," Carissa remarked, and I hid a smile. Those two were a riot; one as oppressed as the other was ballsy. I always felt like I was watching an insane tennis match between the angel on my left shoulder and the devil on my right.

But I didn't need to look up to see they were talking about Daemon. Last night I'd barely slept. Only thing I was certain come Tuesday morning, I wouldn't act like anything was different. I ignored him, which was what I did before I found out he was from far, far away.

And it worked right up until he sat behind me and I felt his pen poking against my back. Slowly, I set my pen down and casually turned around. "Yes?"

Sooty lashes lowered, but not before I saw the sparkle in his eyes. "My house. After school."

Lesa's audible intake of breath was sort of embarrassing.

I knew I had to hang out with Daemon until the damn trace thing faded, but I didn't take well to being ordered around. "I have plans."

His head moved an inch to the side. "Excuse me?"

A small, evil part of me reveled in his surprise. "I said I have plans."

A second of silence passed, and then he smiled. It wasn't as devastating as I expected, but pretty damn close. "You don't have plans."

"How would you know?"

"I do."

"Well, you're wrong." He wasn't. I didn't have any plans.

His gaze slid to the girls. "Is she hanging out with either

of you after school?"

Carissa opened her mouth, but Lesa cut her off. "Nope."

Some friends. "Maybe I wasn't hanging out with them."

Daemon tipped his desk forward, closing the space between us. "Besides them and Dee, what other friends do you have?"

I cut him a death look. "I have other friends."

"Yeah, name one."

Dammit. He called my bluff. "Fine. Whatever."

He gave me a sexy smirk and settled back in his seat, tapping his pen on his desk. Sending him one more look of pure hatred, I turned back around. Yeah, nothing had changed.

. . .

Daemon followed me home after school. Literally. He tailed me in his new Infiniti SUV. My old Camry, with its leaky exhaust and loud muffler, was no match for the speeds he wanted to go.

I'd brake-checked him several times.

He'd blown his horn.

It made me feel all warm and fuzzy inside.

As soon as I stepped outside of my car, he was right in front of the driver's side. "Jesus!" I rubbed my chest. "Would you please stop doing that?"

"Why?" He leaned his head down. "You know about us now."

"Yeah, but that doesn't mean you can't walk like a normal human being. What if my mom saw you?"

He grinned. "I'd charm her into believing she was seeing

things."

I shoved past him. "I'm having dinner with my mom."

Daemon popped in front of me, causing me to shriek. I swung at him, but he moved to the side. "God! I think you like to do that to piss me off."

"Who? Me?" His eyes were wide with innocence. "What time is dinner?"

"Six." I stomped up the steps. "And you are not invited."

"Like I want to eat dinner with you," he retorted.

I flipped him off without looking back.

"You have until 6:30 to be next door, or I'm coming after you."

"Yeah. Yeah." I went inside without looking back.

Mom was standing by the window in the living room, holding a picture frame she was dusting. It was her favorite picture of us. She'd stopped a random teenager and asked him to take our picture while we'd been at the beach. One smile from her and the kid couldn't help but obey. I remembered being embarrassed she'd stopped the boy. I looked sullen next to her, put out and frustrated. I hated that picture.

"How long have you been standing there?"

"Just long enough to see you give Daemon the middle finger."

"He deserved it," I grumbled, dropping my backpack on the floor. "I'm going over there after dinner."

She wrinkled her nose. "Do I even want to know?"

I sighed. "Not in a million years."

. . .

When I did show up next door, at 6:34, it sounded like World War III had erupted in the house. I'd let myself in since no one answered the damn door.

"I can't believe you ate all the ice cream, Daemon!"

I cringed and stopped inside the dining room. There was no way I was going into that kitchen.

"I didn't eat all of it."

"Oh, so it ate itself?" Dee shrieked so loudly I thought I heard the rafters in the ceiling shake. "Did the spoon eat it? Oh wait, I know. The carton ate it."

"Actually, I think the freezer ate it," Daemon responded dryly.

I grinned when I heard what sounded like the empty container hitting what suspiciously sounded like flesh.

Turning, I went back into the living room and piddled around until I heard footfalls behind me.

Daemon lounged against the frame of the door that led from the dining room to the living room. I slowly took him in. His hair carelessly disheveled and the faint light from the lamp bouncing over high cheekbones. His lips curved into a half smile, and even in the simple shirt and jeans, he looked... well, beyond words.

He took up the whole room, and he wasn't even in it.

One brow rose as he waited. "Kat?"

Mentally kicking myself, I looked away. "Did you get hit by an ice cream carton?"

"Yes."

"Damn. And I missed that."

"I'm sure Dee would love to do a replay for you."

I smiled a little at that.

"Oh, you think this is funny." Dee burst into the living room, car keys in hand. "I should be making you go to the store and get me Rocky Road, but because I like Katy and value her well-being, I'm going to get it myself."

That would mean I'd be left alone…Oh hell to the no. "Can't Daemon go?"

Daemon smiled at me.

"No. If the Arum comes around, he's only going to see your trace." Dee grabbed her purse. "You need to be with Daemon. He's stronger than me."

My shoulders fell. "Can't I go next door?"

"You do realize your trace can be seen from the outside?" Daemon pushed out of the doorway. "It's your funeral, though."

"Daemon," Dee snapped. "This is all your fault. My ice cream is not your ice cream."

"Ice cream must be very important," I said.

"It is my life." Dee swung her purse at Daemon but missed. "And you took it from me."

Daemon rolled his eyes. "Just get going and come right back."

"Yes, sir!" She saluted him. "You guys want anything?"

I shook my head.

Daemon did the blinking out and reappearing thing. He was now beside Dee and pulled her in for a quick hug. "Be careful."

There was no doubt in my mind that Daemon loved and cherished his sister. He'd gladly give his life for her. The way he was always looking out for her was more than admirable. There wasn't a good enough word for it. And it made me wish I had a sibling.

"As always." She smiled, gave me a quick wave, and darted out the door.

"Wow. Remind me never to eat her ice cream."

"If you do, even I wouldn't be able to save you." He flashed a sardonic grin. "So, Kitten, if I'm going to be your babysitter for the evening, what's in it for me?"

My eyes immediately narrowed. "First off, I didn't ask you to babysit me. And you made me come over here. And don't call me Kitten."

Daemon tipped his head back and laughed. The sound sent shivers through me, reminding me of waking up with him, my head in his lap. "Aren't you feisty tonight?"

"You ain't seen nothing yet."

Still chuckling, he turned toward the kitchen. "I can believe that. Never a dull moment when you're around." He paused. "Are you coming or not?"

I took a deep breath and exhaled slowly. "Going where?"

He pushed open the kitchen door. "I'm hungry."

"Didn't you just eat all of the ice cream?"

"Yeah, still hungry."

"Good Lord, aliens can eat." I stayed put.

Daemon glanced over his broad shoulder. "I have this strong inclination that I need to keep an eye on you. Where I go you go." He waited for me to move, and when I didn't, his smile turned devilish. "Or I can forcibly move you."

I was pretty sure I didn't want to know how he planned to do that. "All right, let's go." I shuffled past him and plopped down in a seat at the table.

Daemon grabbed a plate of leftover chicken. "Want some?"

I shook my head. Unlike them, I didn't eat ten square meals a day.

He was quiet as he moved around the kitchen. Since the night on the rock, we hadn't been at each other's throats. It wasn't like we were getting along, but it seemed like an undeclared truce existed. I had no idea what to do with him since we weren't trying to tick each other off.

Resting my cheek on my palm, I had a hard time pulling my eyes off him. He was broad and tall, but he moved like a dancer. Each step was smooth and supple. Even the simplest movement looked like a form of art.

Then there was his face.

At that moment, he peered up from his plate. "So how are you holding up?"

I tore my eyes from him and focused on the plate of food that was already half eaten. How long had I been staring at him? This was getting ridiculous. Did the trace turn me into a walking hormone? "I'm doing okay."

He took a bite of chicken and chewed slowly. "You are. You've accepted all of this. I'm surprised."

"What did you think I'd do?"

Daemon shrugged. "With humans, the possibilities are endless."

I bit my lip. "Do you think that we are somehow weaker than you because we're human?"

"It's not that I think you're weaker, I know you are." He eyed me over his glass of milk. "I'm not trying to be obnoxious by saying that. You are weaker than us."

"Maybe physically but not mentally or…morally," I countered.

"Morally?" He sounded confused.

"Yeah, like, I'm not going to tell the world about you guys to get money. And if I was captured by an Arum, I wouldn't bring them back to you all."

"Wouldn't you?"

Offended, I leaned back and folded my arms. "No. I wouldn't."

"Even if your life was threatened?" Disbelief colored his tone.

Shaking my head, I laughed. "Just because I'm human doesn't mean I'm a coward or unethical. I'd never do anything that would put Dee in danger. Why would my life be more valuable than hers? Now yours…debatable. But not Dee."

He stared at me for several seconds, then went back to his food. If I was expecting an apology I wasn't going to get one. Big surprise there.

"So how long will it take for this trace to fade?" My eyes went right back to him. Very annoying.

Daemon's eyes were intent and bright, the green hue seeming to burn through me. He took a long, healthy drink.

I swallowed, my throat dry.

"Probably a week or two, maybe less," he said, squinting. "It's already starting to fade."

It was weird that he was talking about this light around me that I couldn't see. "What do I look like? A giant light bulb or something?"

He chuckled, shaking his head. "It's a soft white glow

that's around your body, kind of like a halo."

"Oh, well that's not too bad. Are you done?" When he nodded, I grabbed his plate out of habit. Not to throw it at him, but mainly out of something to do. "At least I don't look like a Christmas tree."

"You look like the star atop the tree." His breath stirred the hair around my cheek.

Gasping, I turned around.

Daemon stood directly behind me. Our bodies separated only by a foot or two. Placing my hands on the edge of the counter, I dragged in a deep breath. "I hate it when you do that alien super-speed thing."

Smiling, he cocked his head to the side. "Kitten, what are we going to get into?"

A thousand images flashed. Thank God reading thoughts wasn't one of his alien powers. Such a strange thickness invaded the air around me, and this overwhelming yearning from deep inside sprung to life.

"Why not hand me over to the DOD?" I blurted out.

Daemon took a step back, surprised. "What?"

I wished I hadn't gone there, but I did, and there was no coming back from it. "Wouldn't everything have been easier for you if you handed me over to the DOD? Then you wouldn't have to worry about Dee or anything."

Daemon stood in silence. The color of his eyes went up a notch, becoming brighter. I wanted to take a step back, but there was nowhere to go.

Voice low, he said, "I don't know, Kitten."

"You don't know? You risk everything and you don't know why?"

"That's what I said."

I stared at him, bewildered by the fact that he'd put everything on the line and seemed to have no idea why. That was crazy to me. Absurd. Admittedly, it was unnerving, because it could mean many things.

Things I didn't dare acknowledge.

His arms quickly shot out, landing heavily against the counter. Bands of muscle created a very successful trap, pinning me in place without even touching. He lowered his head and dark waves spilled over his eyes. "Okay. I do know why."

At first I had no idea what he was talking about. "You do?"

Daemon nodded. "You wouldn't survive a day without us."

"You don't know that."

"Oh, I know." He tilted his head to the side. "Do you know how many Arum I have faced? Hundreds. And there have been times I barely escaped. A human doesn't stand a chance against them or the DOD."

"Fine. Whatever. Can you move?"

Standing his ground, Daemon smiled. God, he was exasperating. I could either stand here, stare at him like an idiot, or I could move past him. I opted for the latter. My plan was to muscle my way around him as quickly as possible.

Not that I got very far.

He was like a brick wall only a freight train could knock out of the way. He grinned wider, entertained by my lack of progress. "Asshole," I muttered.

Daemon laughed. "You have such a mouth on you. Do

you kiss boys with that thing?"

My cheeks heated. "Do you kiss Ash with yours?"

"Ash?" His smile disappeared and his eyes were suddenly hooded, less clear. "You would like to know that, wouldn't you?"

An unreasonable spark of jealousy flared in me, but I pushed it aside. I smirked. "No, thank you."

Daemon leaned in even more. His spicy and earthy scent surrounded me. "You aren't a very good liar, Kitten. Your cheeks get red whenever you lie."

Do they? Aw, hell. I tried pushing past him again, but he reached out, taking ahold of my arm. It wasn't a tight grip, but I still felt it down to my bone. His hand hummed. Tingles were sharp and startling, yet pleasant. I didn't want to look at him but I didn't seem capable of stopping myself.

We were too close and there was too much tension between us. His gaze burned as it latched onto mine. He lowered his head, and I forgot how to breathe. Fascinated, I watched his lips slowly curved into a smile. It was hard to pay attention to his words when he spoke, but they somehow made it through the strange fog clouding my brain.

"I have a strange idea that I should test this out."

"Test what?" My eyes dropped to his lips. I felt myself sway.

"I think you would like to know." He moved closer, his hand sliding up my arm and resting carefully at the nape of my neck. "You have beautiful hair."

"What?"

"Nothing." His fingers spread along the back of my neck, slowly weaving themselves through strands of loose hair.

His deft fingers moved against the base of my skull. My lips parted, and I waited.

He dropped his hand and reached out again as I stood there, eager — maybe too eager — to discover if he felt the same unexpected ache. If he was any bit as affected as I was.

Instead, Daemon plucked up a bottled water off the counter.

I slumped against the counter. What the holy hell.

His eyes danced with laughter as he turned back to the table. "What was it that you were asking, Kitten?"

"Stop calling me that."

He took a drink. "Did Dee pick up a movie or something?"

I nodded. "Yeah, she mentioned it earlier in class."

"Well, come on. Let's go watch a movie."

I pushed away from the counter and followed behind him. I lingered by the door as he held the DVD up and frowned. "Whose idea was this?"

I shrugged and then watched his brows rise as he read the blurb on the back. "Whatever," he muttered.

Clearing my throat, I took one step into the room "Look, Daemon, you don't have to sit and watch a movie with me. If you have other things you want to do, I'm sure I will be fine."

He glanced up from the movie and then shrugged. "I have nothing to do."

"Okay." I was still unsure. Imagining him enjoying a movie night with me was more farfetched than the idea of aliens living among humans.

I dragged myself across the room and sat on the couch as he fiddled with the movie. After sliding the disc in, he approached the couch and sat down on the far end. Then the television came on, and I would swear he'd left the remote by the T.V. It was probably a good thing I didn't have his power. I'd be beyond lazy.

He glanced at me, and I immediately faced the television.

"If you fall asleep during this movie, you'll owe me."

I turned to him with a frown. "Why?"

Daemon spared me a wolfish smile. "Just watch the movie."

I made a face, but remained quiet. Daemon shifted. The couch dipped and the distance between us grew smaller. I held my breath until I had to come up for air. He didn't seem to notice as the open credits rolled over the screen.

I stared at his profile and wondered for the hundredth time what he could be thinking and, like always, I came up empty. Out of frustration, I turned back to the movie and decided the strange pull I felt for him had to be my imagination. It couldn't be anything more.

Tense and unused to what I was feeling, I counted the minutes until Dee returned.

Chapter 20

Daemon was surprisingly subdued in math on Wednesday. The inevitable pen poke only came once, and that was to remind me the only plans I had after school were with him.

Yeah, whatever, like I could forget.

In bio, like the day before, Mr. Garrison's keen stare kept going back to me. I knew he saw the trace, and I had no clue what he was thinking. Daemon hadn't mentioned if he and Dee had said anything to the other Luxen. Throughout the day before, several teachers had given me weird looks. Today, one of the coaches I passed on the way to the cafeteria stopped in the middle of the hall and looked me up and down. Either he was a perv or an alien. Or both, which would be a winning combination.

While standing in the lunch line, I did everything in my power to not look toward the back of the cafeteria. Staring at the food, I stepped forward and nearly bounced off the back of a walking mountain.

Simon Cutters turned around and then looked down. He smiled when he saw me. "Hey there, Katy."

I handed my money to the checkout lady, and turned to Simon. "Sorry about that."

"No problem." He waited for me at the end of the line, his plate full of food. He ate almost as much as Dee. "Did you have a clue what Monroe was talking about in trig? I swear it was a different language."

Considering I'd spent most of the class ignoring the boy behind me…"I have no clue. I'm hoping someone took notes." I shifted my plate. "We have a test next week, right?"

Simon nodded. "Right before the game, too. I think Monroe does that—"

Someone reached in to grab a drink, forcing us to take a step back from one another, which wasn't necessary since anyone could've easily walked around us. When I inhaled the crisp scent, I realized who it was.

Daemon grabbed a carton of milk off the cart and flipped it. Passing me an unreadable glance, he turned to Simon. Both of them were the same height, but Simon was much broader. Still, Daemon gave off a more badass vibe.

"How you doing, Simon?" he asked, flipping the carton again.

Blinking as he backed up, Simon cleared his throat. "Good—doing good. Heading over to my—uh, my table." He looked at me nervously. "See you in class, Katy."

Frowning, I watched Simon trip over his own feet to get to his table. I turned back to Daemon. "Okay?"

"Are you planning on sitting with Simon?" he asked,

crossing one arm over his chest.

"What? No." I laughed. "I was planning on sitting with Lesa and Carissa."

"So am I," Dee chimed in, coming out of nowhere. She balanced a plate in one hand and two drinks in the other. "That is if you think I'd be welcomed?"

"I'm sure you will be." I glanced back at Daemon, but he was already heading back to his table. I stood there for a moment, confused. What the hell had that been all about? There were the Thompson twins and Ash, huddled together. A few of the other kids were chatting. I had no idea if they were aliens or not. Daemon sat down beside them, pulled out a book, and started thumbing through it. Ash looked up and didn't appear too thrilled. "Do you think anyone else will mind?" I asked finally.

"No. I hated that I didn't sit with you yesterday. And I think it's time for a change-up." Dee looked so hopeful I couldn't disagree. "Right?"

Lesa and Carissa were shocked into stunned silence for roughly five minutes after Dee joined me at their table, but she won them over and everyone relaxed pretty quickly.

Everyone but me.

Half the cafeteria watched me, probably waiting for me to get into another epic food fight with Blondie. It had been a week, and still everyone considered me the food ninja. Every so often, Ash glanced over at our table, a deep scowl on her beautiful face. She had on an electric blue tube top that matched her eyes. The white shirt she wore over it was unbuttoned, revealing that she had a kickass body.

God, what was up with alien DNA? I got that they were

otherworldly, but Jesus, did that include perfect breasts, too?

Dee nudged me with her elbow while Carissa and Lesa chatted with a freckle-faced boy at the end of the table. "What?" I asked.

She leaned into my shoulder, speaking so only I could hear. "What's going on with you and my brother?"

I took a bite of my pizza, mulling over how to answer that. "Nothing, you know, the same-old."

Dee arched a perfectly groomed brow. "Yeah, he was gone all day Sunday. And so were you. And while he was gone, a certain someone came looking for him."

My slice flopped in my hand.

She picked up her drink, smiling slightly. "I didn't get to tell you yesterday since he was up our butts, but you can't tell me you haven't noticed Ash giving you the stink eye."

"I have," Lesa cut in, plopping her elbows on the table. "She looks like she's wishing you dead."

I made a face. "Gee. That's nice."

"And you have no idea why?" Dee asked, angling her body so her back was to their table. "Pretend you're looking at me. Right now."

"I am looking at you right now," I pointed out, taking another bite of my pizza.

Lesa laughed. "Look over her shoulder, genius. Toward their table."

Rolling my eyes, I did as they instructed. At first, I noticed that one of the blond boys was turned in his seat, talking it up with a boy at the table in front of them. Then I shifted my gaze, and my eyes locked with Daemon's. Even though several tables separated us, my breath caught. There was something...wicked in those emerald-colored eyes. Consuming. I couldn't look away, and he didn't either. The distance between us seemed to evaporate.

A second later, he smirked and turned away, focusing on what Ash was saying to him. Drawing in a shallow breath, I focused on my friends.

"Yeah," Lesa murmured dreamily, "that's why."

"I...there's no reason." My face felt on fire. "Did you see him? He's only making the lip thing at me."

"That lip thing is sexy." Lesa glanced at Dee. "Sorry. I know he's your brother and all."

"It's okay. I'm used to it." Dee rested her chin in her hand. "Remember the day on the porch?"

I narrowed my eyes at her.

"What happened on the porch?" Lesa asked, curious enough that her dark eyes gleamed.

"Nothing," I said.

"They were like this close." Dee held up her finger and her thumb so that there was barely a centimeter between the two. "And I'm sure they've gotten closer."

My mouth dropped open. "We have not, Dee. We don't even like each other, like on a basic level."

Carissa took her glasses off and blew on them. "What's going on?"

Lesa filled her in, much to my horror. "Oh, yeah." Carissa nodded. "They were googley-eyed in class on Friday. It was pretty steamy, the whole 'I'm screwing you with my eyes' thing they had going on."

I choked on my drink. "That was not what we were doing. We were talking!"

"Katy, you were so doing it." Lesa picked up a napkin and started rolling it. "Nothing to be ashamed of. I'd do it if he'd be game."

I stared at her a second, then busted out laughing. "You guys are insane. There's nothing going on." I looked at Dee. "And you should know that."

"I know a lot of things," she said innocently.

My brows furrowed. "What's that supposed to mean?"

She shrugged and pointed at my second slice. "You going to eat that?"

I picked it up and handed it over. She ignored my look while she happily devoured my extra slice of pizza.

"Oh, did you guys hear about Sarah?" Carissa flipped closed her cell phone, looking up. "I almost forgot."

"No." Lesa glanced over at me. "Carissa's older brother Ben is friends with Sarah's brother. They go to WVU together."

"Oh." I turned my drink around and started peeling off the label. When I thought of Sarah, I thought of the hospital and how I'd heard about her death. And I thought of the Arum, and how they were around.

"Robbie told Ben that the police don't think it was a heart attack or a natural cause." Carissa looked around the table, lowering her voice. "Or at least no natural causes that they're aware of."

Dee lowered the pizza from her mouth. That's how I knew this was serious. "What do you mean?"

"Apparently, there was so much damage to her heart that there was no way it could be like that regardless of if she had any heart conditions," Carissa explained.

Dee shrugged. "I know, but what else could it be?"

I glanced at Dee, having an idea of what or who it could've been. After lunch, I dragged her to the side. "Was it one of them?" I asked. "One of the Arum?"

Dee bit down on her lip and then she tugged me away from the cafeteria doors and her brother, who was coming out of the room. Down the hall, she stopped. "It was, but Daemon took care of him."

I hesitated. "It was the same one who attacked me?"

"It was." Dee glanced behind her, lips thin. "Daemon thinks it was purely coincidental, that the Arum stumbled across her. She didn't know us. I swear."

That didn't make any sense to me. "Then why?"

Dee met my stare. "They don't need a reason, Katy. The Arum are evil. They kill us for our powers." She paused, paling. "And they kill humans for the fun of it."

Chapter 21

Astonishingly, things were sort of...normal now. My trace did fade in a week and a half. Daemon had acted like he'd been released from a twenty-year jail sentence, and he was never around when I was with Dee anymore. September and most of October passed without anything happening. Mom continued to work both jobs, and she had a couple more dates with Mr. Michaels. She liked him, and I was happy for her. It had been so long since I'd seen her smile not tinged with sorrow.

Carissa and Lesa both had been to my house, and many times we'd gone to the movies or the mall in Cumberland with Dee. Even though I'd grown close to the two human girls and had a heck of a lot more in common with them, I was closer to Dee. We did everything together—everything except talk about Daemon. She tried, several times.

"I know he likes you," she'd said once while we were

supposed to be studying. "I see the way he looks at you. He gets uptight if I even bring you up."

I'd sighed and closed my notebook. "Dee, I think the reason why he stares at me is because he's planning on ways to kill me and hide my body."

"That is so not the look he gives you."

"Then what's the look, Dee?"

She knocked her book off the bed and climbed to her knees, placing her hands over her chest. "It's the 'I hate you but I want you' look."

I giggled. "That was terrible."

"It's true." She lowered her hands. "We can date humans if we want to, you know. It's kind of pointless, but we can. And he's never paid attention to any other human."

"He's been forced to pay attention to me, Dee." I flopped onto my back on my bed. My stomach tightened at the thought of Daemon secretly wanting to be with me. Granted, I knew he was attracted to me. I *felt* it, but lust didn't have anything on like. "What about you? What's up with Adam?"

"Absolutely nothing at all. I don't know how Ash is attracted to Daemon. We grew up with them, and Andrew is like a brother to me. I don't think he feels any differently, either." She paused, her lower lip trembling. "I don't like any of my kind."

"Is there a…human boy you like?"

She shook her head. "No. But if there was, I shouldn't have to be afraid to like him. I have a right to be happy. It shouldn't matter if it's one of your kind or ours that does it."

"I completely agree."

Dee had lain down next to me, snuggling up. "Daemon

would freak if I fell for a human."

I almost smiled at that, but then I remembered their brother. Damn right, Daemon would freak. Maybe rightfully so, because if his brother hadn't fallen for a human, he'd still be alive.

I hoped for Dee's sake she never fell for one. Daemon would most definitely go nutso.

As it approached mid-October, it seemed like we'd gone backward in time. I was going to find that pen of his and destroy it. I'd lost count of how many times I was poked in the back long after the trace had faded from me. It seemed he lived to get under my skin.

And there was a part of me that kind of looked forward to it, only because it was entertaining...until one of us seriously got mad, especially when he was being downright antisocial.

Like Friday in class, Simon had asked if I wanted to study for our trig exam. Before I could even respond, Simon's backpack had flown off his desk, scattering its contents across the floor as if someone had swept his arm across his desk. Red-faced and confused, Simon had been successfully distracted by the laughing class while he gathered up his notebooks and scattered pencils.

I'd glanced back over my shoulder at Daemon, suspecting he was behind the flying backpack, but all he did was smile lazily at me.

"What's your deal?" I asked in the hallway after class. "I know you did that."

He shrugged. "So?"

So? I stopped by my locker, surprised to find that Daemon had followed me there. "That was rude, Daemon. You embarrassed him." Then I lowered my voice to a whisper, "And I thought using your…stuff would draw *them* here."

"That was barely a blip on the map. That didn't leave a trace on anyone." He lowered his head until the edges of his dark curls brushed my cheek. I was caught between wanting to crawl into my locker and crawl into *him*. "Besides, I was doing you a favor."

I laughed. "And how was that doing me a favor?"

Daemon smiled at me and then lowered his gaze so his thick, dark lashes shielded his eyes. "Studying math wasn't what he had in mind."

That seemed debatable, but I decided to play along. I wasn't backing down from him, not even when he could toss me in the air with a single thought. "And what if that's the case?"

"You like Simon?" His chin jerked up, anger flashing in his emerald eyes. "You can't possibly like him."

I hesitated. "Are you jealous?"

Daemon looked away.

And I seized the opportunity to finally have one thing to rub in his face and stepped forward. He didn't move or breathe. "You're jealous of Simon?" I lowered my voice. "Of a human? For shame, Daemon."

He sucked in a sharp breath. "I'm not jealous. All I'm trying to do is help you out. Guys like Simon want to get between your legs."

My cheeks flushed as I stared at him. "Why? You think that's the only reason why a guy might like me?"

Daemon smiled knowingly as he slowly backed up. "Just saying."

He left after that, disappearing into the crowded hall. Which was good, because if he'd stayed a moment longer I would have socked him. When I turned around, I saw Ash standing outside her class. Her look pretty much fried me on the spot.

No one was talking about Sarah. It wasn't that the school had forgotten her. It was just that they'd moved on, like most did. Knowing how and why she died was something I tried not to think about. When I did, my stomach soured like curdled milk. She died because Daemon saved me and the Arum had needed someone to take his anger out on.

And at night, I dreamed about the parking lot behind the library. I saw *his* face, the coldness and rage in his eyes as he squeezed the life out of me. Those nights, I woke with a scream stuck in my throat, covered in a cold sweat.

Other than the nightmares and the occasion alien-bully move on Daemon's part, there was nothing else that was out of the norm. It was like living next to normal teenagers.

Teenagers that didn't need to get up to change the television channel and got a little uptight after meteorite showers.

Dee had explained that the Arum used those atmospheric displays as a way to come down to Earth without being detected by the government. I didn't understand how, and she didn't explain, but for a few days after a shower or even a falling star, the siblings were on edge. They would also disappear, sometimes taking a three-day weekend or missing a Wednesday without any warning. Dee eventually explained that they'd been checking in with the DOD. They continued to tell me that the Arum weren't a problem, but I didn't believe them. Not when they took such great lengths to avoid discussing them.

But Dee was on edge for a whole different reason in class on Thursday. Homecoming was next weekend and she hadn't found a dress. She had a date with Andrew. Or was it Adam? I couldn't tell the incredible blond duo apart.

Everyone was excited about homecoming, it seemed. Streamers hung from the hallways. Banners announced the game against the other school and the dance. Tickets were selling left and right. Lesa and Carissa also had dates. Neither of them had dresses, from the sound of yesterday's lunch conversation.

I, on the other hand, didn't have a date.

They tried to convince me yesterday that going stag wasn't the height of social disaster, and I knew that, but standing along the wall all night or playing third wheel wasn't my cup of tea.

Everybody knew each other in a school as small as PHS. Couples had been together their entire high school stint. Friends were shacking up with one another to go to the dance. And I, having no real connection to anyone, seemed dateless. Total killer for the self-esteem.

After spending math class ignoring Daemon's attempts to tick me off, Simon appeared by my locker while I switched out one heavy, useless book for another heavy, useless book.

"Hey," I said, smiling. I hoped Daemon was nowhere nearby, because God only knew what he'd do. "You looked like you fell asleep in class today."

He laughed. "I kind of did. And I was dreaming about formulations. It was all very frightening."

I laughed, shoving the textbook into my backpack as I

nudged my locker door shut with my hip. "I can imagine."

Simon wasn't bad looking. Not if you had a thing for big, burly jocks who looked like they tossed bales of hay during the summer. He had arms the size of tree trunks and a charming-enough smile. Pretty blue eyes, too, and when he smiled, the skin around those baby blues crinkled. But his eyes weren't green, his lips not poetic.

"I've never seen you at any of our games," he said, his skin doing that crinkly thing. "Not a fan of football?"

Simon was the starting fullback or lineback. Honestly, I had no clue. "I went to one," I told him. And I'd left at halftime with Dee. Both of us had been bored out of our minds. "Football isn't my thing."

I expected him to leave after that because football was like a religion around here, but he leaned against the locker next to me, folding his arms over his chest. "So, I was wondering if you had plans next Saturday."

My eyes went up to the red and black banner above his head. Next Saturday was homecoming. My throat dried like a cornered animal, and my eyes got all buggy. "No. No plans at all."

"You're not going to the dance?" he asked.

Do I say I don't have a date or does that sound way too lame? I settled on shaking my head.

Simon looked relieved. "Would you like to go? Together?"

My first thought was to say no. I barely knew the guy, and I thought he'd been dating one of the limber cheerleaders, and I wasn't interested in him. But going with Simon didn't mean I was going to marry him. Or even date him. I would be going to a dance with him. And a horrible thought popped in my head.

I couldn't wait to see Daemon's face when he learned I had a date.

I told him yes, and we exchanged numbers and that was that. I was going to the homecoming dance, and now I also needed a dress. Mom would be thrilled by this. At lunch, I broke the news to Dee, thinking she'd be excited.

"Simon asked you to the dance?" Dee's mouth had dropped open. She even stopped eating for five whole seconds. "Did you say yes?"

I nodded. "Yeah, so what?"

"Simon has a reputation," Carissa said, eyeing me over the rim of her classes. "Like he wants to be the PHS bicycle."

"He wants to give everyone a ride," Lesa clarified with a shrug. "But he is cute. I like his arms."

"Just because he has a reputation, that doesn't mean I'm going to add to it." I poked my salad around my plate. Meatloaf had been on the menu today. So was not braving that. "And he was kind of cute when he asked."

"Him and Kimmy broke up a week or so ago," Carissa said. "Supposedly, he was cheating on her with Tammy."

Ah, Kimmy. That was the limber cheerleader's name. "Does he have a thing for girls' names that end in Y?"

Lesa snorted. "Aw, just like you. It's a match made in heaven."

I rolled my eyes.

"Well, whatever. You got a date. Now all of us can shop for dresses this weekend." Carissa clapped her hands. "Oh! And maybe we can carpool together. Sounds fun, right? How about you Dee?"

"Huh?" Dee blinked. Carissa repeated her question, and

Dee nodded with a faraway look in her eyes. "I'm sure Adam would be okay with that."

We made plans to go to Cumberland on Saturday, and Lesa and Carissa were practically bouncing in their seats. Dee didn't look excited. She didn't even look happy. And strangest of all, she didn't finish her lunch or eat half of mine.

• • •

When I left school that day, I had to walk all the way to the back of the parking lot since I'd been late that morning. The lot lined up with the track and football field, which was empty. It was a total bitch to park there. Cold wind whipped down from the mountains, blasting that entire area of the gravel lot.

"Katy!"

I turned around, recognizing the deep voice. My heart leapt in my throat. I didn't feel the wind anymore. Squeezing the strap on my bag, I waited for him to catch up to me.

Daemon stopped in front of me and reached out, fixing the twisted strap on my bag. "You know how to pick a parking spot."

Caught off guard by the gesture, it took me a moment to respond. "I know."

We made it to my car, and while I threw my bag in the backseat, Daemon waited beside me, his hands shoved into his pockets. There was a dark look to his gaze, a tightness to his lips.

My stomach dropped a little. "Is everything okay? It's not...?"

"No." Daemon ran a hand through his hair. "Nothing...

uh, cosmic-related."

"Good." I breathed a sigh of relief, leaning against the car next to him. "You scared me there for a second."

He twisted toward me, and like that, there were only a few inches between us. "I hear you're going with Simon Cutters to the dance."

I pushed back a strand of hair that blew across my face. The wind knocked it right back. "News travels fast."

"Yeah, it does around here." He reached out again, but this time he caught the piece of hair and tucked it back behind my ear. His knuckles brushed against my cheek. The slight touch brought that weird tingle, along with a shiver that had nothing to do with the cold. "I thought you didn't like him."

"He's not bad," I said. Kids were rolling out on the track, stretching and getting ready to run. "He's kind of nice, and he asked me."

"You're going with him because he asked you?"

Isn't that how things worked? I nodded. He didn't immediately respond while I fiddled with my car keys. "Are you going to the dance?"

Daemon inched closer, his knee brushing my thigh. "Does it matter?"

I bit back a string of curses. "Not really."

His body angled toward me. "You shouldn't go with someone just because he asked you."

I glanced down at the keys, wondering if I could stab someone in the eyeball with them. "I don't see why this has anything to do with you."

"You're my sister's friend, and therefore it has something to do with me."

I gaped at him. "That is the worst logic I have ever heard." I started around the car, but stopped at the hood. "Shouldn't you be more concerned with what Ash is doing?"

"Ash and I aren't together."

A stupid part of me liked the idea of them not being together. Shaking my head, I went for the driver's door. "Save your breath, Daemon. I'm not backing out because you have a problem with it."

Cursing under his breath, he followed me. "I don't want to see you get into any kind of trouble."

"What kind of trouble?" I yanked open my car door.

He caught the door. One dark eyebrow arched. "Knowing you, I can't even begin to imagine how much trouble you'd get in."

"Oh yeah, because Simon's going to leave a trace on me that attracts killer cows instead of killer aliens. Let go of my car door."

"You are so frustrating," he snapped, eyes flaring with irritation. "He has a reputation, Kat. I want you to be careful."

I stared at him for a moment. Could it be that Daemon was genuinely concerned about my well-being? As soon as that thought popped into my head I pushed it out. "Nothing is going to happen, Daemon. I can take care of myself."

"Fine." He let go of the door so fast that I yanked it back. "Kat—"

Too late. The door caught my fingers. I yelped as pain shot over my hand and up my arm. "Ouch!" I shook my hand, trying to ease the pain in my fingers. The pointer finger was bleeding. The rest would definitely be bruised and look like sausages by morning. Tears were already streaming down my cheeks. "Christ! That hurt."

Without warning or saying a word, his hand shot in, wrapping around my palm. A flash of heat went through my hand, tingling, spreading to the tips of my throbbing fingers and down to my elbow. In an instant the pain was gone.

My mouth dropped open. "Daemon?"

Our eyes locked. He dropped my hand as if I'd burned him. "Shit…"

"Did you…is there another trace on me?" I wiped the blood away from my finger. The skin was pink, but already sealed up. "Holy crap."

He swallowed. "It's faint. I don't think it will be a problem. I can barely see it, but you might—"

"No! It's faint. No one will see it. I'm fine. No more babysitting." I drew a shallow breath. Knots formed in my belly. "I can take care of myself."

Daemon watched me for a moment. "You're right. Obviously you can as long as it doesn't involve car doors. You've lasted longer than any human that's known about us."

• • •

Daemon's parting words hung over me like a thick, foreboding cloud the rest of the night and well into Saturday. I'd lasted longer than anyone else that had known the truth about them. I couldn't help but wonder when my time would be up.

I left with Dee, and we picked up the girls after lunch. It didn't take long to get to Cumberland and find the dress shop they'd wanted to go to. I'd expected there to be nothing left to pick from when we walked into the Dress Barn, but their racks were full.

Carissa and Lesa already had an idea of what they wanted: something tight. Dee seemed to navigate toward the pink and frilly. I wanted a dress that didn't look like it'd been bedazzled by a grandmother or swallowed by a bow factory.

Dee ended up picking out a red Grecian-style dress for me that cinched under the waist and hung loose around my hips and legs. It had a scallop neckline, a little daring but nothing like what Lesa and Carissa strutted out in.

"What I wouldn't do for a chest like that," Lesa muttered, looking disgusted as she stared at Carissa's chest spilling out of her dress. "It's not fair. I have an ass and no boobs."

Carissa eyed herself in the wall mirror while Dee tried on a pink knee-length dress she'd found. Twisting her hair up off her shoulders, Carissa grinned at her reflection. "What do you guys think?"

"You look hot," I told her. And she did. She had the perfect hourglass figure.

Dee stepped out, looking absolutely stunning in pink. Her dress had tiny straps and hugged her willowy frame. She took one look at herself, nodded, and went back in to change.

I exchanged a grin with Lesa. "Our opinion was not needed."

"Yeah, cause there isn't anything in this world that Dee doesn't look good in." She rolled her eyes, grabbing her dress to try on.

When it came my turn to try my dress on, I had to give it to Dee. She had a remarkable eye for style. The dress fit my body like it'd been made for me. With its built-in bra, it also made me feel like I could stand beside Carissa and not feel like a little girl. I twisted in front of the mirror, checking out the back. Not too bad.

"You should pull your hair up," Dee said, appearing beside me. She reached up, artfully twisting my long hair atop my head. "You have such a long neck. Show it off. I can do it for you if you like and your makeup, too."

I nodded, thinking it would be fun. "Thank you. I would've never thought I'd look good in this dress."

"You'd look good in any of these dresses." Dee let go of my hair. "Now you need shoes." She nodded over to the shoe racks. "Anything red or clear would work. The more strappy the better."

I poked around the shoes, thinking of a pair of strappy heels I had at home. God knows this dress was going to cost every last cent my mom had happily handed over this morning. I picked up a pair of red heels, though. They were divine.

A skeevy feeling coursed over me as I stood there. I glanced around. The girls were in the back, looking at clutches, and the clerk was behind the counter. The door opened, making a wind chime sound. No one was there.

The clerk looked up, frowning. Shaking her head, she returned to reading her magazine.

I shivered as my gaze crawled past the door to the windows in the front of the store. Beyond the garbed mannequins, a man stood on the sidewalk, looking in. His dark hair was combed back from his pale face. Most of his features were covered with a pair of oversized sunglasses that seemed out of place on such an overcast day. He was wearing dark jeans and a leather jacket.

And he gave me the creeps.

I moved behind the racks and pretended to be checking

out another dress. Casually, I lifted my head and peeked over the rack.

He was still there.

"What the hell?" I muttered. Either he was waiting for someone in here or he was a total creeper. Or an Arum. I refused to consider the last one. Glancing around the near-empty store, I was going to go with creeper.

"What are you doing?" Lesa came out, tugging on the zipper to a pink trumpet dress that gave her boyish figure curves. "Hiding behind racks?"

I started to point out the stalker, but when I looked at the window, he was gone. "Nothing." I cleared my throat. "You guys ready?"

She nodded, and I darted back to the dressing room and quickly changed. The whole time we checked out, I kept glancing at the window. That eerie feeling was still there, following us back to where Dee had parked. I expected the dude to jump out and scare the living crap out of me at any moment.

We folded up our dresses carefully and placed them in the trunk while Carissa and Lesa climbed in the backseat. Shutting the trunk, Dee turned to me. A small smile was on her face. "I didn't tell you this because I'm sure you would've changed your mind about the dress."

"What?" I frowned. "Does it make my butt look big?"

She laughed. "No. You looked stunning in it."

"Then what's the deal?"

Her smile turned downright mischievous. "Oh, you know, just that the color red is Daemon's favorite."

Chapter 22

The night of the dance I was full of nerves. A huge part of me wanted to call Simon and beg off, especially since he nixed the whole carpool idea from the get-go, but my mom had bought the dress and Dee had done an outstanding job making me look pretty.

My hair had been curled and twisted up, exposing my neck. A few strategically placed curls hung over my temples and rested on my bare shoulders. She even sprayed this vanilla-scented glittery stuff in my hair, so when I turned, my hair shimmered. My eyes were a warm brown due to the smoky outline she'd given them. I was also pretty sure she'd applied fake eyelashes, because my lashes had never been this long or thick. Her final touch before she rushed off to meet up with Lesa was the gloss she painted on my lips, turning them a perfect shade of ruby.

I inspected myself in the mirror before I went downstairs.

It was like staring at a stranger, and I made a mental note to wear makeup more often.

Mom started crying the moment she saw me. "Oh my God, honey, you look so beautiful." She went to hug me but stopped. "I don't want to ruin anything. Let me grab my camera."

Even I wouldn't begrudge her this moment. I waited until she returned and took a dozen pictures. Dressed in her nursing scrubs, she looked kind of funny snapping pictures.

"Now this Simon guy," she started, her forehead wrinkling. "You never talked about him."

Oh Lord. "We're friends. Nothing more, so you don't have a thing to worry about."

She gave me a motherly look. "Whatever happened with the boy next door—Daemon? You were hanging out with him a couple of times, right?"

I shrugged. That was a conversation I couldn't even begin to broach with my mom. "Uh, we're frenemies."

"What?" Her brows puckered.

"Nothing," I sighed, glancing at my hand. There wasn't a single mark on my fingers. There was a trace though, still lingering faintly, he said. "We're friends."

"Well, that's a shame." She reached out, smoothing down an errant curl. "He seemed like such a nice boy."

Daemon? Nice boy? Um, no. A loud engine from outside ended our conversation. I moved over to the window, peeking out. Good Lord. Simon's truck was the size of a submarine.

"Why didn't you two go to dinner like Dee was talking about?" my mother asked, gearing up the camera for another round of shots.

Since Simon had nixed the carpool idea, I'd nixed the dinner. Simon was meeting me here, which I wasn't too thrilled about, but meeting at the dance seemed stupid. Not to mention he had the tickets.

I didn't answer as I went to the door and opened it. Simon stood there, dressed in a tux. I was sort of surprised they had ones that fit him. His eyes, which seemed a little bleary, drifted down me in a way that turned my skin the color of my dress.

"You look hot," he said, thrusting out a corsage that went around my wrist.

I winced, hearing my mom clear her throat. Taking the corsage, I stepped aside and let Simon in. "Mom, this is Simon."

Simon stepped forward, shaking Mom's outstretched hand. "Now I see where Katy gets her looks from."

My mom arched a brow, turning into the Ice Queen. Simon had not made a fan. "Aren't you kind."

I slunk over to his side as I slipped my corsage on, grateful it was not one that had to be pinned on. Simon took having the epic amounts of pictures taken good-naturedly, wrapping his arm around my waist and smiling for the camera.

"Oh. I almost forgot." Mom disappeared into the living room, returning with a lacy black shawl. She draped it over my shoulders. "This will keep you warm."

"Thank you," I said, hugging it closer, more grateful for the coverage than she could ever imagine. The dress had seemed fine earlier, but now with Simon practically drooling on my cleavage I felt uncomfortable baring so much skin.

Mom pulled me aside while Simon waited outside. "Make sure you call me when you get home. If anything happens, call me. Okay? I'm working in Winchester tonight." She glanced out the door, frowning. "But I can leave if need be."

"Mom, I'll be fine." I leaned over, kissing her cheek. "I love you."

"Love you, too." She ushered me to the door. "You do look gorgeous."

Before the tears could fill her eyes again, I fled the house. Getting in the truck required strategic climbing. I was surprised that I didn't need a stepladder.

"Man, you do look hot." Simon popped a breath mint in his mouth before he backed out of the long driveway.

I hoped he wasn't planning to use those breath mints later. "Thanks. You look nice, too."

That was the extent of our conversation. Turns out Simon wasn't a witty conversationalist. Shocking. The ride to school was long and awkward, and I was gripping the edges of my shawl like there was no tomorrow. Several times he glanced over, smiled, and popped another breath mint.

I couldn't wait to get to the dance.

When we arrived in the parking lot, I found out why he was popping so many breath mints. Simon pulled a silver flask from the inside of his tux and took a long swig. He offered it to me next.

He was drinking. This was already starting off great. I declined the offer, already making plans to find another ride home. Drinking didn't bother me. Ending up with a drunk driver did.

Seeming not to care, he shoved it back in his jacket.

"Hold on. I'll help you get down."

Well, that was nice of him, because I was wondering how in the world I was supposed to get down. He opened the door and I smiled. "Thank you."

"Did you want to keep your purse in here?" he asked.

Oh, hell no. I shook my head and let the tiny clutch dangle from my wrist. Simon took my hand and helped me down from the truck. He pulled a little too hard, and I stumbled against his thick chest.

"Are you okay?" he asked, smiling.

I nodded, trying to ignore the icky feeling building in my stomach.

Outside, I could hear the steady thump of music from the gymnasium. We stopped before the fogged-over doors, and Simon pulled me toward him in an awkward hug.

"I'm glad you wanted to go to the dance with me," he said, his breath minty and tinged with the harsh smell of liquor.

"Same here," I said, trying to mean it. I placed my hands on his burly chest and pushed back. "We should go in."

Smiling, he slid his arms away. One of his hands slipped down my back, over the curve of my hip. I stiffened and told myself it was an accident. It had to be. He surely didn't just cop a feel like that. We hadn't even danced yet.

The gymnasium had been converted over to an autumn-themed dance. Strings of fall foliage hung from the ceilings and covered the doors. There were pumpkins and cornucopia horns full of leaves stacked in the corners and lining the stage.

As soon as we stepped inside, we were surrounded by

Simon's friends. Some of them looked me over and gave Simon a not-so-discreet high five or clap on the back. It was like now they could tell I had boobs, I was suddenly cool. Boys could be so juvenile. While they passed around the flask Simon had brought in, I exchanged strained greetings with the other guys' dates. They were all cheerleaders. Yawn.

I scanned the crowd, spying Lesa with her date. "I'll be right back."

Before Simon could stop me, I darted off toward her. She turned when her date nodded in my direction. I smiled. "You look gorgeous." I had to yell to be heard over the music.

"So do you!" She gave me a quick hug and then pulled back. "Is he behaving himself?"

"So far. Do you mind?" I placed my shawl and clutch on their table when she shook her head. "They did a nice job on this."

Lesa nodded. "Still a gym, though." She laughed. "It has that smell."

That was true. Carissa quickly joined us, tugging both of us out onto the dance floor minus the guys. I didn't mind. We danced with each other, giggling and being plain-out stupid. Lesa danced like a double-jointed hooker, and I think Carissa did the running man at one point.

I caught a glimpse of Dee talking to Adam near the stage. Giving the girls a quick wave, I made my way over to them. "Dee!"

She turned toward me, her eyes glistening under the dazzling lights. "Hey."

I stopped short, my eyes bouncing between them. Adam gave me a tight smile before stalking off into the throng of dancers. "Is everything okay?" I took her hand, squeezing it. "Have you been crying?"

"No. No!" She wiped under her eye with her free hand, using her pinky. "It's just that...I don't think Adam wanted to go with me, and I'm not sure I want to even be here. And it's..." She shook her head and pulled her hand free. "Anyway, you look great! That dress is to die for!"

My heart went out to her. It didn't seem fair that she was limited to who she could go out with. Especially considering every male Luxen I'd met was a douche. Since they all grew up together, it must be like going to the dance with her brother. "Hey," I said, getting an idea. "We can bail on this if you want. Go get movies and eat ice cream in our pretty dresses. Sounds like fun, right? We can rent *Braveheart*. You love that movie."

Dee laughed, eyes tearing up again as she pulled me in for a tight hug. "No. We're going to enjoy ourselves here. How's your date?"

I glanced around, not seeing him. "Probably drunk somewhere."

"Oh no." She brushed a strand of hair back. She'd worn her hair down and straightened it so that it fell over her shoulders like a wave of dark water. "Bad?"

"Not yet, but I was wondering if I could catch a ride home with you guys?"

"Of course." She started pulling me toward the dance floor. "We're probably going to the bonfire afterward. You can come with us or we can drop you off."

Simon hadn't mentioned a party. Maybe I'd get lucky and he'd forget about me. Dee and I skirted the edge of the floor, hand in hand. I'd almost given up on spotting Lesa in the mess, but then I came to a complete standstill.

There was a small candle covered in glass on a white table. It sent a soft flickering glow over Daemon's high cheekbones and full lips. Ash was nowhere in sight, and honestly I didn't care where she was.

Daemon's stare was so concentrated I took an unintentional step back, but we didn't break eye contact. A craving unfurled deep in my stomach, shooting through me like heated lightning, and that—that was the kind of feeling you couldn't force, couldn't even replicate if you wanted.

And then Simon was in front of me, capturing my hand and pulling me away from Dee and out onto the dance floor. It wasn't a slow dance, but he wrapped his beefy arm around my waist and pulled me against his chest anyway. The hard edge of his flask cut into my ribs.

"You disappeared on me," he said, his lips brushing my ear, dousing my neck in alcohol fumes. "I thought you up and left me."

"No, I saw friends." I tried pulling back, but I was stuck to him. "Where are your friends?"

"Huh?" he yelled, unable to hear me as the music increased. "There's a party tonight down in the Field. Everyone is going." One of his hands was low on my back, his finger resting on the flare of my bum. "We should go."

Dammit. "I don't know. Curfew," I yelled back, trying to maneuver his hand off my rear.

"So? It's homecoming. It's time to party."

I didn't bother responding. I was too busy avoiding his hands, which were *everywhere*. We danced another song before I could successfully extract myself, and the only reason I could was because Carissa saved me.

Things were all over the place then. I spied Ash sitting at the table, looking pissed while Daemon stared at the floor. Several bathroom breaks and dances later, I ended up back with Simon.

For a human, he sure knew how to sneak up on someone.

He didn't reek of alcohol this time around, but dammit, his hands were super friendly as we moved in a tight circle. I could feel every last inch of him, and he didn't seem to mind. I was starting to sweat when one of his hands dropped off my shoulder, narrowly avoiding my breast.

I jerked back, glaring at him. "Simon."

"What?" He looked innocent. "Sorry. My hand slipped."

His hand slipped my rosy red butt. I looked away, debating what to do. I needed to disappear. Quick.

"Mind if I cut in?" a deep voice asked from behind me.

Simon's blue eyes widened as I twisted around. Daemon stood there, a hard look on his face. He wasn't looking at me. His eyes were focused on Simon in challenge. As if he dared the boy to say no.

After a terse second, Simon released me. "Perfect timing. I needed to get a drink anyway."

He cocked a brow at Simon and then looked at me. "Dance?"

Having no idea what he was up to, I gingerly placed my hands on his shoulders. "This is a surprise."

He didn't say anything as he wrapped one arm around my waist and reached up, taking hold of one of my hands. The music slowed down until it seemed to crawl by in a haunting melody about love lost and found again. I stared up into those extraordinary eyes, stunned that he could hold me so… tenderly. My heart thudded as blood rushed to every point in my body. It had to be the dance, the dress—the way he filled out his tux.

He pulled me closer.

Excitement and dread warred inside me. The dazzling lights overhead reflected in his midnight hair. "Are you having a good time with…Ash?"

"Are you having a good time with Happy Hands?"

I bit down on my lip. "Such a constant smartass."

He chuckled in my ear, sending shivers through me. "The three of us came together—Ash, Andrew, and me." His hand rested above my hip, having a totally different impact on me. My skin tingled underneath the chiffon. Daemon cleared his throat as he glanced away. "You…you look beautiful, by the way. Really too good to be with that idiot."

A blush stole over my skin, and I lowered my gaze. "Are you high?"

"Unfortunately, no I'm not. Though, I am curious why you would ask."

"You never say anything nice to me."

"Good point," he sighed. Daemon moved a little closer and turned his head slightly. His jaw grazed my cheek and I jumped. "I'm not going to bite you. Or grope you. You can relax."

My witty retort died on my lips when he moved his hand from my hip and guided my head to his shoulder. The moment my cheek touched his tux covered shoulder, there was a dizzying rush of sensations. His hand settled on my lower back again and we moved slowly to the music. After awhile, he started humming under his breath, and I closed my eyes. This…this wasn't nice. It was thrilling.

"Seriously, how's your date going?" he asked.

I smiled. "He's a little friendly."

"That's what I thought." He turned his head, and for a moment his chin rested against my hair, then he lifted his head. "I warned you about him."

"Daemon," I said softly, wanting him not to ruin the mood. There was something peaceful about this, lulling. "I have him under control."

He snorted. "Sure looks like it, Kitten. His hands were moving so fast I was beginning to question if he was human or not."

I stiffened, my eyes opening. I counted to ten. I made it to three before he spoke again.

"You should sneak out of here and go home while he's distracted." His hand tightened around mine. "I can even get Dee to morph into you if need be."

Shocked that he'd go to that extreme, I pulled back and looked up at him. "It's okay if he gropes your *sister?*"

"I know she can take care of herself. You're out of your league with that guy."

We'd stopped dancing, oblivious to the other couples. Disbelief coursed through me. "Excuse me? I'm out of my league?"

"Look, I drove here. I can let Dee catch a ride with Andrew and take you home." He sounded like he had everything planned out. Then his eyes narrowed. "Are you actually considering going to the party with that idiot?"

"Are you going?" I asked, pulling my hand free from his. My other hand was still on his chest and his arm still circled my waist.

"It doesn't matter what I'm doing." Frustration punctuated each of his words. "You're not going to that party."

"You can't tell me what to do, Daemon."

His eyes narrowed, but I could see the eerie glow beginning to form in his eyes, overshadowing his pupils. "Dee is taking you home. And I swear, if I have to throw you over my shoulder and carry you out of here, I will."

My hand curled into a useless fist against his chest. "I'd like to see you try."

He smiled, eyes starting to gleam in the darkness. "I bet you would."

"Whatever," I said, ignoring the looks we were starting to get from everyone. Over his shoulder, I saw Mr. Garrison watching us, which worked to my benefit. "You're the one who's going to cause a scene carrying me out of here."

Daemon made a noise that really sounded like a growl.

Anyone in their right mind would've been terrified, and I should've been, considering I knew what he was capable of. I wasn't. "Because your local alien teacher is watching us as we speak. What do you think he's going to believe when you toss me over your shoulder, buddy?"

Every inch of him stiffened.

I smiled like the cat that ate an entire aquarium full of fish. "Thought so."

Surprisingly, he returned the smile. "I keep underestimating you, Kitten."

Stealth-mode Simon appeared before I had a chance to

gloat over that major win. "You ready?" Simon asked, glancing between Daemon and me. "Everyone is leaving for the party."

Damon's look dared me to not listen to him, and that's pretty much why I agreed. He didn't control my life. I did.

Chapter 23

The Field was about two miles outside of Petersburg, heading in the opposite direction of my house. It was literally a gargantuan harvested cornfield. Enormous bales of hay covered the landscape as far as I could see, lit in orange and red. I couldn't help but think the combination of dried hay and fire wouldn't end well.

Someone tapped a keg.

Correction: the combination of hay, fire, and cheap beer couldn't end well.

Simon had kept his hands to himself the whole way here, so I was feeling pretty good about my decision with the exception of the above foreseeable problem. He led me through the trampled cornstalks toward the fire.

"The girls are over there." He pointed to the other side of the fire where several girls were clustered together, sharing red plastic cups. "You should go say hi. Mingle a little."

I nodded, having no intention of going there.

"I'll get us a drink." He leaned in, squeezing my shoulders before heading off. The moment he reached the keg, he gave some other burly dude a high five and let out a loud, "Hooray!"

Quite a crowd was gathering around the fire, pushing back to the surrounding woods. Someone had pulled a truck up, turned on the radio, and left the doors open, making it nearly impossible to hear anything. Clutching the shawl around my shoulders, I moved along the edges, looking for a familiar face. Relieved, I saw Dee standing with the Thompson triplets. Beside them, Carissa and Lesa shared a blanket. Daemon was nowhere to be seen.

"Dee!" I called, weaving out of the way of a girl teetering in high heels. "Dee!"

She turned, and then seconds later, she waved her hand wildly. I took a step in her direction, and Simon appeared out of nowhere, two cups in hand.

"Oh my God," I said, stepping back. "You scared me."

Simon laughed, handing me a cup. "I don't see how. I was calling your name."

"Sorry." I took the drink, wrinkling my nose at the distinct smell. Taking a sip, I learned it didn't taste much better than it smelled. "It's kind of hard to hear with all the noise."

"I know. And we haven't had a chance to talk at all." Simon draped his arm over my shoulder, stumbling a little. "And that sucks. I've wanted to talk to you all night. Did you like the corsage?"

"It's beautiful. Thank you again." It was pretty, a combination of pink and red roses. "Did you get it in town?"

He nodded and then downed the contents of his cup as we moved away from the truck. "My mom works at a local florist shop. She made it."

"Wow. That's pretty cool." I plucked at it, careful not to spill any beer on it. "Does your dad work in town?"

"Nope, he commutes into Virginia." He tossed the cup to the side and pulled out the flask. "He's a lawyer," he boasted, unscrewing the lid with one hand. "Handles personal injury claims. His brother is a doctor in town, though."

"My mom—she's a nurse and works in Virginia, too." All of his movements were pulling on the shawl. It was halfway off my shoulders. "Do you know where you're going to college yet?" I asked, struggling for something to say. Friendly hands aside, he was sort of nice.

"Going to WVU with the buds." He frowned at my own untouched drink. "You don't drink?"

"Oh, no, I do." I took a sip to prove it. He smiled and looked off, talking about which of his friends were planning on going to Marshall instead of WVU. When he wasn't looking, I dumped half the cup out.

Simon kept on asking questions, interrupted every few minutes when one of his friends would swing by. I dumped most of my drink out, which earned me several refills. Simon told me to stand wherever we were as he hustled back and forth between the keg. By my third pretend cup, Simon was probably thinking I was a lush but at least he was getting a great workout.

Before I knew it, we were a good distance away from the bonfire, among the first cropping of trees. Each step became more difficult. Partly due to the uneven ground and my heels, and even the slightest bit of Simon's weight was hard to support.

Simon straightened and pulled his arm off my shoulders, taking the shawl along with him. It fluttered somewhere behind me, quickly blending in with the shadowy ground and thick undergrowth.

"Crap," I said, turning around, squinting.

"What?" he slurred a little.

"My shawl—I dropped it." I took a couple steps back toward the fire.

"Mmm, you look better without," he said. "That dress— dayum."

I shot him an annoyed look over my shoulder before returning to staring at...everything that looked black. "Yeah, well, it belongs to my mom, and she'll kill me if I lose it."

"We'll find it. Don't worry about it now."

Suddenly, his arm was around my waist, pulling me back. Startled, I dropped the cup of beer and let out a nervous laugh as I twisted out of his grasp. "I think I need to find it now."

"Can't it wait?" Simon took a step closer to me, and I took one back. He was standing in front of me, and I realized I was trapped between him and a tree. "We were talking, and there's this thing I'd wanted to do."

I glanced over at the bonfire. It seemed too far away now. "What?"

He placed a massive hand on my shoulder, and his grip was tight. The feeling that crept over me was more than just the ick factor. It was something else. It was more powerful, leaving a strange taste on the roof of my mouth, like when the Arum had spoken to me outside the library. He leaned in, pulling me forward at the same time, dipping his head.

I froze for a second, and that was all it took. His mouth was on mine, tasting of beer and breath mints. He made a sound and pushed forward. My back was against a tree before I could shove him back, and he still kept pushing forward, kissing my tightly sealed lips. I couldn't breathe. Placing my hands on his chest, I pushed until I was able to wrench my mouth free.

"Whoa there, Simon, that's too much," I said, dragging in air. I tried to wiggle myself free, but he was unmovable.

"Aw come on, it's not too much." His hand worked its way between me and the tree, until it was against my back, holding me in place.

I pushed again against his chest, angry. "I didn't come here for this!"

Simon laughed. "Everyone comes here for this. Look, we're both drinking, both having fun. There's nothing wrong with that. I won't even tell anyone if you don't want me to. Everybody knows you did it with Daemon over the summer."

"*What*?" I screeched. "Simon, let me—"

His sloppy, wet lips cut off my words. His tongue slipped into my mouth, and I wanted to puke. My heart rate tripled, and in an instant, I wished I'd listened to Daemon, that I had taken him up on his offer to go home, because this *was* out of my league.

I managed to get my head free. "Simon, *stop*!"

And then Simon *did* stop. I sagged against the tree, dazed and breathless. There was the sound of someone hitting the ground and then a wounded cry.

Someone was bending over a sprawled Simon, reaching down and picking him up by the scruff of his neck. "Do you have a problem understanding simple English?"

I recognized that deep baritone. It was the same voice Daemon had used the day I'd been gardening. Deadly quiet, dangerously low. He was breathing heavily as he stared at the cowering boy.

"Man, I'm sorry," Simon slurred, grasping Daemon's wrist. "I thought she—"

"You thought what?" Daemon lifted him onto his feet. "That no meant yes?"

"No! Yes! I thought—"

Daemon raised his hand, and Simon just…just *stopped*. Arms raised, hands splayed out in midair in front of his face. Blood that had been trickling out of his nose, stopped on his open mouth. Eyes wide and unblinking. A look of fear and drunken confusion was frozen on his face.

Daemon had frozen Simon. Literally.

I stepped forward. "Daemon, what…what did you do?"

He didn't look at me, his eyes trained on Simon. "It was either this or I'd kill him."

There was no doubt in my mind that he was capable of killing him. I poked Simon's arm. It felt real, but stiff. Like a corpse. I swallowed. "Is he alive?"

"Should he be?" he asked.

A look passed between us, heavy with understanding and regret.

Daemon's jaw tensed. "He's fine. Right now, it's like he's sleeping."

Simon looked like a statue, a drunk and pervy statue. "God, what a mess." I backed up, wrapping my arms around myself. "How long will he stay like this?"

"As long as I want," he replied. "I could leave him out here. Let the deer piss on him and the crows crap on him."

"You can't...do that, you know that? Right?"

Daemon shrugged.

"You need to turn him back, but first, I'd like to do something."

Daemon cocked a brow in curiosity.

Dragging in a deep breath, which still tasted like cheap beer, mints, and Simon's tongue, I kicked him straight between the legs. Simon didn't react, but he'd feel it later.

"Whoa." Daemon let out a strangled half laugh. "Maybe I should've killed him." He frowned when he saw the expression on my face. He turned back to Simon and waved his hand.

The boy doubled over, cupping his hands between his legs. "Shit."

Daemon pushed Simon back. "Get the fuck out of my face, and I swear if you so much as look at her again, it will be the last thing you do."

Simon was three shades whiter as he wiped his hand over his bloodied nose. His eyes darted from me to Daemon. "Katy, I'm sorry—"

"Get. Out. Of. Here," Daemon bit out, taking a threatening step forward.

Simon spun around and took off, stumbling and limping over bushes. Dead silence fell between us. Even the music seemed to have become muted. Daemon turned around slowly and stalked off. I stood there, shivering.

Daemon was going to leave me here.

I didn't blame him. He warned me several times, and I hadn't listened. Tears of anger and frustration burned my eyes.

But then he returned, clutching my shawl in his hands. He handed it to me, cursing under his breath. Hands shaking, I took the shawl from him and saw that his eyes were glowing. How long had they been like that? I could feel his eyes on me, heavy and intense.

"I know," I whispered, clutching the shawl to the front of my torn dress. "Please don't say it."

"Say what? That I told you so?" He sounded disgusted. "Even I'm not that much of an ass. Are you okay?"

I nodded and drew in a deep breath. "Thank you."

Daemon cursed again and then he was moving closer, dropping something warm that smelled like him over my shoulders. "Here," he said gruffly. "Put this on. It will...cover up everything."

I looked down. The lacy shawl did nothing to hide the ripped bodice of my dress. Flushing, I slipped my arms into his tux jacket. Tears were clogging my throat now. I was angry at Simon—at myself—and embarrassed. Once I had the jacket on, I hugged it and the shawl close. Daemon was never going to let me live this one down. Right now he might not be throwing it in my face, but there was always tomorrow.

Daemon's fingers brushed over my cheek, tucking a strand of hair that had fallen loose behind my ear. "Come on," he whispered.

I lifted up my head. There was an unexpected softness in his eyes. I swallowed the lump in my throat. Now he'd be nice?

"I'm taking you home."

This time it wasn't an arrogant command or assumption. It was just simple words. I nodded. After the disaster that happened and the fact I figured I had another trace on me, I wasn't going to argue. Then it struck me. "Wait."

He looked like he was ready to come through on his earlier threat and throw me over his shoulders. "Kat."

"Won't Simon have a trace on him, like me?"

If the thought had crossed his mind, it didn't look like it bothered him. "He does."

"But—"

Daemon was in my face in the blink of an eye. "It's not my problem right now."

Then he took my arm. His grasp wasn't tight, but it was firm. We didn't talk as he led me through the brisk night air toward his SUV parked near the main road. Several of the cars we passed were fogged up. Some were even moving. Every time I glanced at him, his eyes were narrowed and jaw clenched.

Guilt chewed through my insides like acid. What if the Arum were still around, and they saw the trace on Simon? Yeah, he was borderline date rapist, but what would the Arum do to him? We couldn't leave him out there, roaming around with a trace on him.

He let go of my arm and opened the passenger door of his SUV. I got in, wiggling the clutch's strap off my wrist and placing it beside me. I watched him head around the car, texting on his phone.

Daemon climbed into the driver's seat, passing me a sheltered look. "I let Dee know I was taking you home. When I got here, she said she saw you but couldn't find you."

Nodding, I started yanking on the seatbelt, but it wouldn't move. All my frustration rose up, and I pulled on it hard. "Dammit!"

Daemon leaned over me and pried my fingers off. In such a small space, there wasn't much room to move around and before I could protest, he was already tugging on the seatbelt. His jaw grazed my cheek and then his lips followed. There were quick touches, all accidental, but I found it hard to breathe nonetheless.

Daemon got the seatbelt unstuck and as he brought it across my stomach, the back of his knuckles grazed over the front of my dress. I jerked in the seat.

He lifted his head, startled. And I was just as surprised. Our mouths were nearly touching. His breath was warm and sweet. Intoxicating. His gaze dropped to my lips, and my heart started doing all kinds of crazy stuff in my chest.

Neither of us moved for what seemed like an eternity.

And then he clicked it in and returned to his seat, breathing raggedly. He clutched the steering wheel for several strained minutes while I tried to remember how important it was to take normal breaths and not gulps of air.

Without saying a word, he pulled out onto the road. There was a thick, strained silence in the car. The ride home was near torturous. I wanted to thank him again and ask about what he planned to do with Simon, but I had a feeling it wouldn't go over well.

I ended up resting my head back against the seat, feigning sleep.

"Kat?" he said, about halfway home.

I pretended I didn't hear him. Childish, I know, but I didn't know what to say. He was a complete mystery to me. Every action was in contradiction of another action. I could feel his eyes on me, and it was hard to ignore that. Just as hard as it was to ignore whatever it was between us.

"Shit!" Daemon exploded, slamming on the brakes.

My eyes snapped open, shocked to find a man in the middle of the road. The SUV skidded to a halt, throwing me forward and then the seatbelt painfully biting into my shoulder and yanking me back. Then the car simply turned off, engine, lights—everything.

Daemon spoke in a language that was soft and musical. I'd heard it before, when the Arum had attacked at the library.

I recognized the man in front of our car. He wore the same dark jeans, sunglasses, and leather jacket I'd seen the day outside the dress shop. And then another man appeared, nearly identical to him. I couldn't even see where he came from. He was like a shadow, slipping out from the trees. Then a third appeared, joining the other to stand behind the first guy. They didn't move.

"Daemon," I whispered, my heart leaping into my throat. "Who are they?"

A fierce light, blinding white, lit up in his eyes. "Arum."

Chapter 24

Fear rose so quickly it left me dizzy, almost numb. And how could I be so numb when surely I should be feeling a dozen emotions?

Daemon reached down and yanked up his pants leg. There was a ripping sound, like Velcro. He held something long, dark, and shiny. Only when he shoved it into my shaky hands did I realized it was some kind of black glass shaped into a dagger, sharpened to a fine point on one end and a leather binding on the other.

"This is obsidian—volcanic glass. The edge is wicked sharp and will cut through *anything*," he explained quickly. "It's the only thing on this planet, besides us, that can kill the Arum. This is their kryptonite."

I stared at him as my fingers wrapped around the leather sheath.

"Come on, pretty boy!" yelled the Arum in the front, his

voice sharp as razors and guttural. He had a thick, foreign-sounding accent. "Come out and play!"

Daemon ignored them and grabbed my cheeks, his hands steady and strong. "Listen to me, Kat. When I tell you to run, you run and you don't look back no matter what. If any of them—*any*—chase you, all you have to do is stab them anywhere with the obsidian."

"Daemon—"

"No. You run when I tell you to run, Kat. Say you understand."

There were three of them and only one of Daemon. The odds weren't good. "Please don't do this! Run with me—"

"I can't. Dee is at that party." His eyes met mine for a second. "Run when I tell you."

And then he turned, letting out a resigned sigh, and opened the car door. Daemon's shoulders squared, and his swagger was full of confidence. That cocky smile, the one I'd wanted to smack off his face many times, appeared on his lips.

"Wow," Daemon said. "You guys are uglier as humans than in your true form. Didn't think that was possible. You look like you've been living under a rock. See the sun much?"

The one in the front, presumably their leader, snarled. "You have your arrogance now, like all Luxen. But where will your arrogance be when we absorb your powers?"

"In the same place as my foot," Daemon replied, hands balling into fists.

The leader looked confused.

"You know, as in up *your ass*." Daemon smiled and the two Arum hissed. "Wait. You guys look familiar. Yeah, I know. I've killed one of your brothers. Sorry about that. What was his name? You guys all look alike to me."

Their forms started flickering in and out, turning from human to shade and back again. I reached for the door handle, clenching the dagger in my hand. Blood pumped through my body so fast, everything slowed down.

"I'll rip your essence from your body," the Arum growled, "and you will beg for mercy."

"Like your brethren did?" responded Daemon, voice low and cold. "Because he begged — he cried like a little girl before I ended his existence."

And that was it. The Arum bellowed in unison; the sound of howling winds and death. My breath caught in my throat.

Daemon threw up his hands and a great roar started under the car, shaking the road, and the trees thrashed outside. A loud crack sounded, like a blast of thunder, quickly followed by several more in succession. The earth seemed to shake and rumble.

I turned to the window and gasped. Trees were being ripped from out of the ground, their thick and gnarled roots dripping clumps of moist dirt. An earthy scent filled the air.

Oh my God, Daemon was *uprooting* trees.

One smacked right into the back of an Arum, taking him several feet down the road. Trees toppled over. Some landed in the road, cutting off the potential for any innocent driver to happen upon the scene. Branches broke off, flying through the air like daggers. The other two Arum avoided them, blinking in and out as they advanced on Daemon, the branches shooting through their shade form without resistance.

The ground under the SUV trembled. All along the side

of the road, chunks of the shoulder broke free from the road. Huge sections of asphalt spun into the air, turning bright orange as though heated from within, and zinged straight at the Arum.

Good God, I was so going to reconsider pissing Daemon off next time.

The Arum dodged the asphalt and trees, throwing back what looked like globs of oil. Where the murky stuff landed, the road smoked. Burnt tar filled the air.

Then Daemon was nothing but blinding white light, a being that was not human, but otherworldly, beautiful and frightening in the same breath. The glow heightened around his outstretched limbs, forming a crackling ball of energy that snapped. Light dripped onto the road. Power lines overhead snapped and then exploded. The Arum blinked out, but their shadows couldn't hide from Daemon's light. I could see them moving toward him still. One darted out to the side, rushing him.

Daemon brought his hands together and the blast that followed shook the car. Light erupted from him, zinging straight into the one nearest, sending the Arum spinning up into the air, where for a moment he was in a human form. Dark sunglasses shattered. Pieces floated in the air, suspended. Another clap followed and the Arum exploded in an array of dazzling lights that fell like a thousand twinkling stars.

Daemon threw out his arm, and the other Arum flew back several feet, spinning and tumbling through the air, but he landed in a crouch.

Run. The voice came in my head. *Run now, Kat. Don't*

look back. Run!

I threw the car door open and stumbled out. Falling to my knees, I scrambled down the ditch, wincing at the sound of the Arums' howls. I made it to the first tree that was still standing and stopped. Instinct told me to keep running, to do as Daemon instructed, but I couldn't leave him there. I couldn't *run away.*

With my heart leaping into my throat, I turned around. The two remaining Arum were circling him, fading out to nothing more than shadows and then reforming back into the tall, imposing figures.

Thick globs of midnight oil shot past Daemon, narrowly missing the halo of light surrounding him. One of the dark streams smacked into a tree on the other side of the road, splitting it in two.

Daemon retaliated by throwing balls of light at them, wicked fast and deadly. They whizzed through the air, forming walls of flames that fizzled out when they didn't hit one of the Arum. The Arum were not as fast as Daemon, but they managed to avoid each of his missiles. After about thirty were lobbed, I could tell Daemon's light form was slowing down, the time between bombs stretching longer and longer. I remembered what he'd said after he'd stopped the truck. Using his powers wore him out. He couldn't keep this up.

Terror trickled through me as I saw them close in on Daemon, their darkness nearly enveloping his light. A ball of bright red flames formed and shot out toward the Arum, but Daemon missed. The ball of fire skidded across the road, fizzing out harmlessly.

One of the Arum flickered out completely, while the other

kept throwing oily bombs at Daemon over and over, never slowing down. Daemon flickered in and out, reappearing a few feet away from each projectile. He was moving so fast, the entire scene started to look like I was watching it unfold under strobe lights.

Daemon was focused on the one Arum lobbing oil bombs and he didn't see the other reappear behind him. The shadowy arms wrapped around what appeared to be Daemon's head, bringing him down to his knees on the side of the road. I cried out, but the sound was lost in the Arum's laugh.

"Ready to beg?" the Arum in front of him taunted, taking human form. "Please do. It would mean a lot to hear the word 'please' leaking from your lips as I take everything from you."

Daemon didn't respond, but his light was crackling and intense.

"Silence to the end, eh? So be it." The Arum stepped forward, lifting his head. "Baruck, it is time."

Baruck forced Daemon to stand. "Do it now, Sarefeth!"

A part of my brain clicked off. I was moving without thinking, running toward the very thing Daemon had ordered me to run away from. The obsidian grew warm in my hand as I rushed up the gully, burning like coals. A heel on my shoe snapped off when it became tangled in the downed branches, but I kept going.

I wasn't brave. I was desperate.

Sarefeth turned into a shadow, thrusting an arm forward, into the center of Daemon's chest. Daemon's scream tore through me, heightening the fear, flipping it into anger and desperation. Daemon's light flared, blinding and concentrated. The ground shook with a giant tremor.

Only a few feet behind Sarafeth now, I threw my arm back, obsidian in hand, and jumped forward and brought it down with every ounce of strength I had. I expected to meet resistance, flesh and bone, but the obsidian cut through the shadow, like Sarefeth was made of nothing more than smoke and air, and I stumbled to my knees.

Sarefeth jerked back, pulling his arm free of Daemon's light. He spun around, his shadowy arms reaching for me. I scrabbled backward, falling down. The obsidian glowed in my hand, humming with energy.

And then Sarefeth stopped. Pieces of him broke free from his form, clumps of darkness drifting into the sky, obscuring the stars until all of him was there one minute and floating away the next.

Baruck released Daemon, taking a step back. For a moment he was in human form, dark jeans and a jacket, his expression horrified, gaze locked on the glowing obsidian in my grip. His eyes met mine for only a second. Vengeance had been promised in that minute stare. And then he was a shadow, pulling the darkness into him, fleeing toward the other side of the road like a coiled snake and disappearing into the night.

I scuttled over branches and cracked pavement in a mad dash to reach Daemon's side. He was still nothing more than light, and I had no idea where to touch him or how badly he was hurt.

"Daemon," I whispered, dropping to my bleeding knees in front of him. My lips, hands—everything—trembled. "Daemon, please say something."

His light flared, throwing off a wave of heat, but he made no sound or movement, not even a whisper of words in my thoughts. What if someone came by? How in the world could I explain *any* of this? And what if he was injured, dying? A sob rose in my throat.

My cell phone! I could call Dee. She'd know what to do. She had to. I started to stand when I felt a hand on my arm.

I whipped around and there was Daemon, in human form, kneeling on the ground, his head bowed but grip strong. "Daemon, oh God, are you okay?" I knelt, placing my hand on his warm cheek. "Please tell me you're okay? Please!"

He slowly lifted his head, placing his other hand on mine. "Remind me," he paused, drawing in a stuttered gasp, "to never piss you off again. Christ, are you secretly a ninja?"

I laughed and sobbed in the same breath. Then I threw my arms around him, almost knocking him flat on his back. I buried my face in his neck, inhaling his earthy scent. He didn't have a choice but to hug me back. His arms swept around me, a hand delving deep into the curls that had fallen loose.

"You didn't listen to me," he murmured against my shoulder.

"I never listen to you." I squeezed him hard. Swallowing, I pulled back a little, searching his weary but beautiful face. "Are you hurt? Is there anything I can do?"

"You've already done enough, Kitten." He stood, bringing me along with him. Drawing in a breath, he looked around. "We need to get out before anyone comes."

I wasn't sure how that would help. It looked like a tornado had come through here, but then Daemon backed off and waved his hand. All down the road, trees were lifted off the road and rolled to the sides, clearing the path. The action barely fazed him.

"Come on," Daemon said.

On the way back to the car, I remembered I still had the obsidian in my fist. The car started as soon as Daemon turned the key, much to our mutual relief.

"Are you okay? Hurt in any way?" he asked.

"I'm okay." I was shaking. "It's just…a lot, you know?"

He gave a short laugh, but then he hit the steering wheel with his fist. "I should've known there would be more coming. They travel in fours. Dammit!"

I held his obsidian closer, staring straight ahead. The adrenaline was fading and I was trying to process everything that had happened tonight. "There were only three of them."

"Yeah, 'cuz I killed the first one." He pulled his cell phone out of his pocket. "And I'm sure they were pissed about that."

We'd killed two more, so I figured that meant the one remaining would be really pissed. Angry aliens. A small, hysterical laugh bubbled up, and I clamped my mouth shut.

He called his sister then, ordering Dee to get the Thompsons and to stay with Mr. Garrison until it was daylight. Whereas the Arum were stronger at night, using the darkness to move undetected and feeding on the shadows, the Luxen were opposite, stronger during the day. Daemon gave them bare details of what had happened, and I heard him tell Dee I was okay.

"Kat, are you okay? Seriously?" he asked after he hung up, concerned.

I nodded. I was alive. *He* was alive. We were okay. But I couldn't stop shaking, couldn't forget the sound of Daemon's scream.

. . .

Daemon wanted me to stay the night at his place. His reasoning was the bare truth. There was another one out there, and until they knew where the Arum was, it was safer being with him. For the second time that night, I didn't argue. I didn't kid myself his invitation was out of concern for me. It was more from necessity.

After I called my mom and told her I was staying the night with Dee, which she protested but eventually relented to, Daemon took me up to the guest room I'd woken up in the morning after finding out about them. It seemed like a lifetime ago.

Daemon had been quiet since we arrived at his house, his thoughts a million miles away. He left me in the guest room with a pair of worn flannel pajama bottoms and a shirt that looked like it belonged to Dee. In the guest bathroom, I quickly stripped off the ruined dress, rolling it up and tossing it into their wastebasket. I never wanted to see it again.

The hot water couldn't soothe the ache in me. I'd never felt the way I did now. Every muscle screamed, and my mind was weary with exhaustion. I stepped out of the shower, my legs shaking, and even in the heat of the steamy bathroom I felt cold.

I slowly wiped the steam off the mirror, shocked by the reflection that peered back at me. My eyes were wide. My cheeks were ghastly pale and drawn tight over my cheekbones. I looked more like an alien than my friends did.

I laughed and then immediately cringed. It sounded choked and ugly, shocking in the quiet room.

Baruck would come back. Wasn't that why Daemon had been quiet? Knowing that the Arum would seek revenge against his family, there was nothing he could do. Or I could even hope to do.

"Are you okay in there?" Daemon called through the closed door.

"Yeah." I quickly ran my fingers through my damp hair, pushing thick sections off my face. "Yeah," I whispered again. I changed into the clothes he'd brought me, and they felt warm, smelling faintly of laundry detergent and crisp leaves.

He was sitting on the edge of the bed when I came back, looking tired and young. He'd already changed into a pair of sweats and a shirt.

"Are you okay?" I asked.

He nodded. "Whenever we use our powers, it's like... losing a part of ourselves. It takes a bit to recharge. Once the sun comes up, I'll be fine." He paused, meeting my eyes. "I'm sorry you had to go through any of this."

I stopped in front of him. Sorry wasn't something that was in his vocab often. Neither were his next words, I suspected.

"I didn't say thank you," he said, staring up at me. "You should've run, Kat. They would've...killed you without thinking twice. But you saved my life. Thank you."

Words stalled on my breath. I stared at him. "Will you stay with me tonight?" I rubbed my arms. "I'm not coming on to you. You don't have to, but—"

"I know." He stood, his brow wrinkling. "Just let me check the house again, and I'll be right back."

I climbed into the bed, tugging the covers up to my chin while I stared at the ceiling. Closing my eyes, I counted silently until I heard Daemon's footsteps. When I opened my eyes, he was standing in the doorway, watching me.

I'd scooted to the far edge of the bed, leaving him plenty of room. A strange thought ran through my brain as I watched him watching me. Had he ever been in a bed with a human girl? Seemed like such a stupid thing to even think about. Relationships with humans weren't prohibited. They just make little sense. And after everything that had happened, why would I be thinking about that?

Daemon locked the door, checked the large bay windows, and then wordlessly settled into the bed, his arms crossed over his chest, much like mine. We lay there, staring up at the ceiling. And my heart was racing. It could've been everything that had happened or the fact that Daemon was here, so close and alive, but I was hyper-aware of everything. Of his slow, steady breaths. The heat radiating off of his body. And my own need to be enveloped in that warmth.

A strained silence descended as I ran my fingers over the edge of the blanket. Then, against my will, I looked at him. Daemon stared back, a lopsided grin on his face.

A laugh bubbled out of me. "This...this is so awkward."

The skin around his eyes crinkled as his grin spread. "It is, isn't it?"

"Yes." I gasped for breath, giggling. It seemed wrong to laugh after everything that had happened, but I couldn't help it. Once I started, I couldn't stop. I'd faced down a possible date rapist and an alien horde hellbent on sucking up Daemon's essence. Crazy sauce.

His laughter joined mine until tiny tears tracked down my cheeks. The sound of his laughter faded as he reached over, chasing the drops with his finger. I stilled, staring at him. His fingers left my cheek, but his gaze remained locked on me.

"What you did back there? It was sort of amazing," he murmured.

A sweet thrill jolted me. "Right back atcha. Are you sure you're not injured?"

Damon's crooked grin returned. "No. I'm fine, thanks to you." He shifted, turning off the lamp beside the bed before settling again.

I searched for something to say in the darkness. "Am I glowing?"

"Like a Christmas tree."

"Not just the star?"

The bed moved a little, and I felt his hand brush my arm. "No. You're super bright. It's kind of like looking at the sun."

Now that was odd. I held up my hand, faintly able to see the outline of it in the darkness. "It's going to be hard for you to sleep then."

"Actually, it's kind of comforting. It reminds me of my own people."

I turned my head, and he was lying on his side, watching me. A flutter formed in my chest. "The whole obsidian thing? You never told me about that."

"I didn't think it would be necessary. Or at least I'd hoped it wouldn't be."

"Can it hurt you?"

"No. And before you ask what can, we don't make a habit of telling humans what can kill us," he replied evenly. "Not even the DOD knows what's deadly to us. But the obsidian negates the Arum's strengths. Just like the beta quartz in the Rocks throws off a lot of the energy we put off, but with obsidian, all it takes is a piercing and...well, you know. It's the whole light thing, the way obsidian fractures it."

"Are all crystals harmful to the Arum?"

"No, just this type. I guess it has something to do with the heating and cooling. Matthew explained it to me once. Honestly, I wasn't paying attention. I know it can kill them. We carry it on ourselves whenever we go out, usually hidden. Dee carries one in her purse."

I shuddered. "I can't believe I killed someone."

"You didn't kill *someone*. You killed an alien—an evil that would've killed you without thinking twice. That was going to kill me," he added as an afterthought, absently rubbing his chest. "You saved my life, Kitten."

Still, knowing that the guy had been evil didn't change how it settled in my stomach.

"You were like Snowbird," Daemon said finally.

His eyes were closed, face relaxed. It was possibly the first time I'd seen him so...open. "How do you figure?"

A small smile played across his lips. "You could've left me there and ran, like I said. But instead you came back and you helped me. You didn't have to."

"I...I couldn't leave you there." I averted my gaze. "It wouldn't have been right. And I would've never been able to forgive myself."

"I know. Get some sleep, Kitten."

I was tired, exhausted, but it felt like the bogeyman was waiting outside the door. "But what if the last one comes back?" I paused, realizing a new fear. "Dee's with Mr. Garrison. He knows I was with you when they attacked. What if he turns me in? What if the DOD—"

"Shh," Daemon murmured, his hand finding mine. His fingers brushed over the top of mine. Such a simple touch, but I felt it all the way to my toes. "He won't come back, not yet. And I won't let Matthew turn you over."

"But—"

"Kat, I won't let him. Okay? I promise you. I won't let anything happen to you."

The fluttering was there again, but now it felt like a dozen butterflies had taken flight at once. I tried to stamp down the feeling. Alien business aside, Daemon and I...well, we were like magnets that repelled one another. Feeling anything other than annoyance toward him wasn't possible, but that damn fluttering was there.

I won't let anything happen to you.

My chest swelled. His touch seared me. Those words filled me with a longing that was overwhelming, unexpected. And it felt good being next to him. My body relaxed. Seconds, maybe minutes later, I drifted off to sleep beside the one boy I couldn't stand.

Just before sleep claimed me, my last thought was whether I would wake up in the morning beside this Daemon or the jerk Daemon.

Chapter 25

When I awoke the following morning, the sun had crested the mountains surrounding the valley. I really wasn't on my side of the bed anymore. Hell, I wasn't on the bed. Half of my body was sprawled across Daemon's chest. Our legs were tangled together under the comforter. One of his arms was around my waist like a band of steel. My hand was on his stomach. I could feel his heart beating under my cheek, steady and strong.

I lay there, my breath in my throat.

There was something intimate about being wrapped around one another in a bed. Like lovers.

A sweet, hot fire washed over my skin, and I squeezed my eyes shut. Every inch of me was hyper-aware of him. Of how my body fit against his, the way his thighs were pressed against mine, the hardness of his stomach under my hand.

My hormones kicked in with the power of a dropkick to

the stomach. Heated lightning zipped through my veins. For a moment, I pretended. Not that we weren't two different species, because I didn't see him that way, but that we actually liked one another.

And then he shifted and rolled. I was on my back, and he was still on the move. His face burrowed into the space between my neck and shoulder, nuzzling. Sweet baby Jesus… Warm breath danced over my skin, sending shivers down my body. His arm was heavy against my stomach, his leg between mine, pushing up and up. Scorched air fled my lungs.

Daemon murmured in a language I couldn't understand. Whatever it was, it sounded beautiful and soft. Magical. Unearthly.

I could've woken him up but for some reason I didn't. The thrill of him touching me was far stronger than anything else.

His hand was on the edge of the borrowed shirt, his long fingers on the strip of exposed flesh between the hem of the shirt and the band of the worn pajama bottoms. And his hand inched up under the shirt, across my stomach, where it dipped slightly. My pulse went into cardiac territory. The tips of his fingers brushed my ribs. His body moved, his knee pressed against me.

I gasped.

Daemon stilled. No one moved. The clock on the wall ticked.

And I cringed.

He lifted his head. Eyes like pools of liquid grass stared at me in confusion. They quickly cleared, though, turning sharp and hard within seconds.

"Good morning?" I squeaked.

Using his powerful arms, he lifted himself up. His eyes never left mine. Daemon seemed to drag in a deep breath. I wasn't sure if he let it out. Something passed between us, unspoken and heavy. His eyes narrowed. I had the funny feeling that he was sizing up the situation and somehow I was to blame for his sleepy—albeit really, really nice—fondling.

Like any of this was my fault.

Without saying a word, he disappeared above me. The door opened and slammed shut behind him without my even catching a glimpse of him.

I stayed there, staring at the ceiling, heart pounding. Cheeks flushed, my body way, way too hot. Not sure of how much time passed, but the door opened again, at normal human speed.

Dee popped her head in, her eyes wide. "Did you two…?"

Funny that out of everything that had happened in the last twenty-four hours, *that* was the first question she asked.

"No," I said, barely recognizing my own voice. I cleared my throat. "I mean, we slept together, but not *slept*, slept together."

I rolled over, burying my face into a pillow. It smelled like him—crisp and warm. Like autumn leaves. I groaned.

• • •

I was sure that if someone had told me I'd find myself sitting in a room with half a dozen aliens on a Saturday afternoon, I would've told them to get off the drugs. Yet, here I was, sitting in a recliner in the Black household, legs tucked under me but ready to run for the door if necessary.

Daemon was perched on the arm of the recliner, arms

folded over his chest. The very chest I'd woken up on. A flush crept up my throat. We hadn't spoken. Not a single word, which was okay by me.

But his current position had been duly noted by everyone. Dee looked oddly smug. A deep, unforgiving scowl had settled on Ash's and Andrew's faces, but the fact I was here overshadowed any reason why Daemon could be playing guard dog.

Mr. Garrison had come up short. "What is she doing here?"

"She's lit up like a freaking disco ball," Ash said accusingly. "I could probably see her from Virginia."

Somehow, she made the whole glowing thing sound like I was covered in boils instead of light. I glared at her openly.

"She was with me last night when the Arum attacked," Daemon responded calmly. "You know that. Things got a little...explosive. There was no way I could cover what happened."

Mr. Garrison ran a hand through his brown hair. "Daemon, of all people, I expected you to know better, to be more careful."

"What the hell was I supposed to do exactly? Knock her out before the Arum attacked?"

Ash arched a brow. The look on her face said it wasn't such a bad idea.

"Katy has known about us since the beginning of school," Daemon said. "And trust me when I say I did everything possible to keep her from knowing."

One of the Thompson boys sucked in a sharp breath. "She's known this entire time? How could you allow this,

Daemon? All of our lives have been in the hands of some human?"

Dee rolled her eyes. "Obviously she hasn't said a word, Andrew. Chill out."

"Chill out?" Andrew's scowl matched Ash's perfectly. And now I knew which one was Andrew, I could tell them apart. Andrew had an earring in the left ear. Adam, who was quiet, did not. "She's a stupid—"

"Be careful with what you say next." Daemon's voice was low but carried. "Because what you don't know and what you can't possibly understand will get a bolt of light in your face."

My eyes widened, as did pretty much everyone's in the room. Ash swallowed thickly and turned her cheek, letting her blonde hair cover her face.

"Daemon," Mr. Garrison said, stepping forward. "Threatening one of your own for her? I didn't expect this from you."

His shoulders stiffened. "It's not like that."

I took a deep breath. "I'm not going to tell anyone about you guys. I know the risks to you and to me if I did. You all don't have anything to worry about."

"And who are you for us to trust?" Mr. Garrison asked, his eyes narrowed on me. "Don't get me wrong. I'm sure you're a great girl. You're smart and you seem to have your head on straight, but this is life or death for us. Our freedom. Trusting a human is not something we can afford."

"She saved my life last night," Daemon said.

Andrew laughed. "Oh, come on, Daemon. The Arum must've knocked you around. There is no way a human could've saved any of our lives."

"What is it with you?" I snapped, unable to stop myself. "You act like we're incapable of doing anything. Sure, you guys are whatever, but that doesn't mean we're single-celled organisms."

A choked laugh came from Adam.

"She did save my life." Daemon stood, drawing everyone's attention. "There were three Arum that attacked, the brethren of one I killed. I was able to destroy one, but the two overpowered me. They had me down and had already begun reaching for my powers. I was a goner."

"Daemon," Dee said, paling. "You didn't tell us any of this."

Mr. Garrison still looked doubtful. "I don't see how she could've helped. She's a human. The Arum are powerful, amoral, and vicious. How can one girl stand against them?"

"I'd given her the obsidian blade I carry and told her to run."

"You gave her the blade when you could've used it?" Ash sounded stunned. "Why?" Her eyes darted to me. "You don't even like her."

"That may be the case, but I wasn't going to let her die because I don't like her."

I flinched. Dayum. An ache started in my chest, like a burning coal, even though I didn't care.

"But you could've been hurt," Ash protested. Fear thickened her voice. "You could've been killed because you gave your best defense to her."

Daemon sighed, sitting back down on the arm of the recliner. "I have other ways to defend myself. She did not. She didn't run like I told her. Instead she came back and she killed the Arum who was about to end me."

Reluctant pride shone in my bio teacher's eyes. "That is… admirable."

I rolled my eyes, starting to get a headache.

"It was a hell of a lot more than admirable," Dee interjected, staring at me. "She didn't have to do that. That has to account for more than being admirable."

"It's courageous," Adam said quietly, staring at the throw rug. "It is what any of us would've done."

"But that doesn't change the fact that she knows about us," Andrew shot back, casting his twin a scornful look. "And we are forbidden from telling any human."

"We didn't tell her," Dee said, stirring restlessly. "It kind of happened."

"Oh, like it happened last time." Andrew rolled his eyes as he turned to Mr. Garrison. "This is unbelievable."

Mr. Garrison shook his head. "After Labor Day weekend, you told me that something occurred but you took care of it."

"What happened?" Ash asked, obvious this was the first she'd heard of anything. "You're talking about the first time she was glowing?"

I was like a glowworm, apparently.

"What happened?" asked Adam, sounding curious.

"I walked out in front of a truck." I waited for the inevitable "duh" look, which I got.

Ash stared at Daemon, her blue eyes growing to the size of saucers. "You stopped the truck?"

He nodded.

A crestfallen look appeared on her face as she looked away. "Obviously that couldn't be explained away. She's known since then?"

I figured this wasn't the time to mention that I had my suspicions before then.

"She didn't freak out," Dee said. She listened to us, understood why it's important, and that's it. Until last night, what we are hasn't even been an issue."

"But you lied to me—both of you." Mr. Garrison leaned against the wall, in a space between their TV and an overstocked bookcase. "How am I to trust you now?"

A dull, stabbing pain flared behind my eyes.

"Look, I understand the risk. More than any of you in the room," Daemon said, rubbing his chest where the Arum had shoved his shadowy hand. "But what is done is done. We need to move forward."

"As in contacting the DOD?" Andrew asked. "I'm sure they'd know what to do with her."

"I'd like to see you try that, Andrew. Really I would, because even after last night, and I'm not yet fully charged, I could still kick your ass."

Mr. Garrison cleared his throat. "Daemon, threats aren't necessary."

"Aren't they?" Daemon asked.

A heavy silence fell in the room. I think Adam was on our side, but it was clear that Andrew and Ash weren't. When Mr. Garrison finally spoke, I had a hard time meeting his gaze.

"I don't think this is wise," he said. "Not with what…with what happened before, but I'm not going to turn you over. Not unless you give me reason to. And maybe you won't. I don't know. Humans are such…fickle creatures. What we are, what we can do, has to be protected at all costs. I think you understand that." He paused, clearing his throat. "You're safe, but we aren't."

Andrew and Ash looked less than thrilled by Mr. Garrison's decision, but they didn't push it. Other than exchanging looks with one another, they moved on to how to deal with the last Arum.

"He won't wait. They're not known for being patient," Mr. Garrison said, sitting down on the couch. "I could contact the other Luxen, but I'm not sure if that would be smart. Where we may be more confident in her, they won't be."

"And there's the problem that she's a megawatt light bulb right now," Ash added. "It doesn't even matter if we don't say anything. The moment she goes anywhere in town, they are going to know that something big happened again."

I scowled at her. "Well, I don't know what I'm supposed to do about that."

"Any suggestions?" Daemon said. "Because the sooner she's not carrying a trace, the better all of this is going to be."

Yeah, because I bet he was looking forward to babysitting me again.

"Who cares?" Andrew said, rolling his eyes. "We have the Arum issue to worry about. He's gonna see her no matter where we put her. All of us, right now, are in danger. Any of us near her are in danger. We can't wait around. We have to find the last Arum."

Dee shook her head. "If we can get the trace off her, then that will buy us time to find him. Getting rid of the trace should be the first priority."

"I say we drive her out to the middle of nowhere and leave her ass there," Andrew muttered.

"Thanks," I said, rubbing my temples. "You're so very helpful with all of this."

He smiled at me. "Hey, just offering my suggestions."

"Shut up, Andrew," Daemon said.

Andrew rolled his eyes.

"Once we get the trace off her, she'd be safe," Dee insisted and tucked her hair back, face pinched. "The Arum don't mess with humans, really. Sarah...she'd been in the wrong place at the wrong time."

They launched into another discussion about what was more important: locking me up somewhere, which didn't make sense because my light could be seen through anything, or trying to figure out a way to make the trace fade other than killing me. And I seriously think Andrew believed that was a valid consideration. Asshole.

"I have an idea," Adam said. Everyone looked at him. "The light around her is a byproduct of us using our power, right? And our power is concentrated energy. And we get weaker when we use our powers and use more energy."

Mr. Garrison blinked, his eyes sparking with interest. "I think I'm following you."

"I'm not," I muttered.

"Our powers fade the more we use them, the more energy we exert." Adam turned to Daemon. "It should work the same with our traces, because the trace is just residual energy we are leaving on someone. We get her to exert her own energy; it should fade what's around her. Maybe not completely, but get it down to levels that aren't going to draw every Arum on Earth to us."

That hardly made any sense to me, but Mr. Garrison was

nodding. "It should work."

Daemon scratched his chest, his expression doubtful. "And how are we going to get her to exert energy."

Andrew grinned from across the room. "We could take her out to a field and chase her around in our cars. That sounds fun."

"Oh, fuc—"

Daemon's laugh cut me off. "I don't think that's a good idea. Funny, but not a good idea. Humans are fragile."

"How about I shove my fragile foot up your ass," I said, irritated. My head was pounding, and I didn't find a single one of them funny. I pushed Daemon off the arm of the chair and stood. "I'm getting a drink. Let me know when guys come up with anything that won't potentially kill me in the process."

Their conversation continued as I hurried from the room. I wasn't thirsty. I just had to get out of there, away from them. My nerves felt shot. Entering the kitchen, I ran my hands through my hair. Blissful silence eased some of the pounding in my head. I squeezed my eyes shut until small spots danced behind my closed lids.

"I figured you'd be hiding in the kitchen."

I yelped at the sound of Ash's quiet voice.

"Sorry," she said, leaning against the counter. "I didn't mean to scare you."

Not sure if I believed that. "Okay."

Up close, Ash was the kind of beautiful that made me wish I could drop twenty pounds and run to the nearest makeup department. She knew it, too. There was a confidence in the tilt of her chin. "This must be a lot for you to handle, learning everything and then facing what you did last night."

I eyed her warily. Even though she wasn't trying to snap my head off, I wasn't going to relax. "It's been different."

A faint smile crossed her pouty lips. "What did that TV show say? 'The truth is out there.'"

"*X-Files*," I told her. "I've wanted to watch *Close Encounters of the Third Kind* ever since I found out. Seems like the most realistic of all the alien movies."

Another small smile and then she looked up, meeting my eyes. "I'm not going to pretend we're ever going to be best friends or that I trust you. I don't. You did dump spaghetti on my head." I winced at that, but she went on. "And yeah, maybe I was being a bitch, but you don't understand. They are all I have. I'll do anything to keep them safe."

"I would never do anything to put them in danger."

She moved closer, and I fought every instinct to back up. I held my ground. "But you already have. How many times has Daemon intervened on your behalf, run the risk of exposing what we are and what we can do? You being here is putting each of us at risk."

Anger tore through me like a fire. "I'm not doing anything. And last night—"

"Last night you saved Daemon's life. Great. Good for you." She tucked her uber-straight hair behind her ear. "Of course, Daemon's life wouldn't have needed saving if you hadn't led the Arum straight to him. And what you think you have with Daemon, you don't."

Oh, for the love of babies everywhere. "I don't think I have anything with Daemon."

"You like Daemon, don't you?"

Smirking, I grabbed a water bottle off the counter. "Not really."

Ash cocked her head to the side. "He likes you."

My heart didn't do a stupid little leap in my chest. "He doesn't like me. You even said so yourself."

"I was wrong." She folded her slender arms as she studied me intently. "He's curious about you. You're different. New. Shiny. Boys—even our kind—like shiny new toys."

I took a long drink of the water. "Well, this is one toy he has no intention of playing with." When he was awake that is. "And really, the Arum…"

"The Arum will end up killing him." Her tone didn't change one bit. It remained flat, emotionless. "Because of you, little human. He will get himself killed protecting you."

Chapter 26

"Honey, are you sure you're feeling okay?" Mom hovered over the couch, frowning. She'd been at it all day since I'd woken up. "Do you need anything? Some chicken soup. Hugs? Kisses?"

I laughed. "Mom, I'm fine."

"You sure?" she asked, pulling the afghan over my shoulders. "Did something happen at the dance?"

"No. Nothing happened." Nothing if I didn't count the billion text messages Simon had sent me, apologizing for how he'd acted, and the attack of the killer aliens afterward. Nope. Nothing at all. "I'm okay."

I was tired after spending most of Saturday in a house full of arguing aliens. Two of them didn't trust me. One of them thought I was going to be the death of Daemon. Adam didn't seem to hate me, but he wasn't overly friendly. I'd snuck out before the pizza they ordered arrived. Ash had been right.

They were a family. All of them, and I didn't fit.

When Mom left for work, I snuggled down and tried watching a movie on Syfy, but it turned out to be about an alien invasion. Their aliens weren't beings of light, but giant insects that ate humans.

I turned the channel.

It was pouring outside—so hard I could barely hear anything over it. I knew Daemon would be nearby, especially until they figured out how to get me to exert enough energy to fade the trace. All of their suggestions involved the outdoors and extreme physical exertion, which wasn't happening today.

The sound of rain was lulling. After awhile, my eyes were too heavy to keep open. As I was about to doze off, a knock on the door jarred me.

I threw the afghan off and padded over to the door. Doubting the Arum would knock, I opened the door. Daemon stood there, barely wet even though rain fell in sheets behind him. There were a few darker dots of gray across the shoulders of his long-sleeved shirt. I bet he used super-alien speed. Who needed an umbrella? And why in the hell was he in jogging pants?

"What's up?"

"Are you going to invite me in?" he asked.

Pressing my lips together, I stepped aside and let him in. He moved past me, scanning the rooms. "What are you looking for?"

"Your mom's not home, right?"

I shut the door. "Her car's not outside."

His eyes narrowed. "We need to work on fading your

trace."

"It's pouring outside." I moved past him, grabbing the remote to turn the TV off. Daemon beat me to it. The thing switched off before I pressed the button. "Show-off," I muttered.

"Been called worse." He frowned and then laughed. "What are you wearing?"

I glanced down, cheeks flaming. One thing I wasn't wearing was a bra. Christ, how could I forget? "Shut up."

He laughed again. "What are they? Keebler elves?"

"No! They're Santa's elves. I love these pajama bottoms. My dad got them for me."

His smug grin faded a little. "You wear them because they remind you of him?"

I nodded.

He didn't say anything. Instead, he shoved his hands into the front pockets of his jeans. "My people believe that when we pass on, our essence is what lights the stars in the universe. Seems stupid to believe in something like that, but when I look at the sky at night I like to think that at least two of the stars out there are my parents. And one is Dawson."

"That's not stupid at all." I paused, surprised by how touching that belief actually was. Wasn't it the same as ours, believing our loved ones were in heaven watching over us? "Maybe one of them is my dad."

His eyes met mine then flitted away. "Well, anyway, the elves are sexy."

And a serious, deep moment effectively smashed into nothing. "Did you guys come up with another way to fade the trace?"

"Not really."

"You're planning on making me work out, aren't you?"

"Yeah, that's one of the ways of doing it."

I sat on the couch, quickly growing irritated. "Well, there isn't much we can do today."

"You have a problem going out in the rain?"

"When it's almost the end of October and cold, yes I do." I plucked up the afghan and placed it in my lap. "I'm not going out there and running today."

Daemon sighed. "We can't wait around, Kat. Baruck is still out there and the longer we wait, the more dangerous it is."

I knew he had a point, but still, running around in the cold ass rain? "What about Simon? Did you ever tell the others about him?"

"Andrew is keeping an eye on him. Since he had a game yesterday, it faded most of his trace. It's very faint now. Which proves that this idea is going to work."

I snuck a peek at him. Instead of seeing the stoic expression, I saw the one from yesterday morning. The look in his eyes before he realized he was in bed with me. My body warmed. Stupid, stupid hormones.

He reached behind him and pulled out the obsidian blade. "This is another reason why I stopped over."

The obsidian was shiny, glossy black as he laid it on the coffee table. It wasn't glowing a mottled red like it had been when near the Arum.

"I want you to keep this with you, just in case. Put it in your backpack, purse, or whatever you carry."

I stared at it a moment. "Seriously?"

Daemon avoided my eyes. "Yeah, even if we manage to get the trace to fade, keep this on you until we finish off Baruck."

"But don't you need it more than I do? Dee?"

"Don't worry about us."

Harder said than done. I stared at the obsidian, wondering how in the world I was supposed to stash this thing in my bag. "Do you think Baruck is still here?"

"He's still around, yes," he stated. "The beta quartz throws our presence off, but he knows we're here. He knows I'm here."

"Do you think he's going to come after you?" For some reason, my stomach got tipsy at that thought.

"I killed two of his brothers and gave you the means of killing the third." He was totally at ease discussing the fact that there was a deranged alien out to kill him. He had balls. I liked that about him. "Arum are vengeful creatures, Kitten. He won't stop until he has me. And he will use you to find me, especially since you came back. They've been on Earth long enough to recognize what that can mean. That you would be a weakness to me."

"I'm not a weakness. I can handle myself."

He didn't respond, but the intensity in his gaze seared me to the core. My confidence crumbled piece by piece. To him I was a weakness, and maybe even Dee believed that. The rest of the Luxen sure did.

But I killed an Arum...while his back was to me. Not like I'd been ninja stealth.

"Enough talking. We have stuff to do now," he said, glancing around. "I don't know what we can do in here that will make a damn bit of difference. Maybe jumping jacks?"

Jumping jacks without a bra was so not going to happen. Ignoring him, I opened up my laptop on the coffee table and checked out my last post. I filmed an "In My Mailbox" after I'd gotten back yesterday, needing the comfort of books and my blog to remind me what "normal" felt like again. It was short since I only had two books. And I looked like crap. What had possessed me to wear pigtails?

"What are you looking at?" he asked.

"Nothing." I went to close the lid, but it wouldn't budge. "Stop using your freaking object thing on my laptop. You're going to break it."

He cocked an amused brow and sat beside me. I still couldn't close it. And the mouse wouldn't move. I couldn't even shut down the damn website. Leaning forward, Daemon tilted his head to the side. "Is that you?"

"What does it look like?" I hissed.

A slow smile crept over his face. "You film yourself?"

I took a deep and slow breath. "You make it sound like I'm doing a live perv show or something."

Daemon made a sound in the back of his throat. "Is that what you're doing?"

"That was a stupid question. Can I please close it now?"

"I want to watch it."

"No!" The idea of him watching me geek out over the books I'd bought in the last week horrified me. There was no way he'd understand.

Daemon cast me a sidelong glance. My eyes narrowed as I turned back to the screen. The little arrow moved over the page and clicked on the play button.

"I hate you and your freaky alien powers," I muttered.

A few seconds later, the video started and there I was, in all my book nerd glory, shoving cover after cover in front of my crappy webcam. A few bookmarks showed. And I even worked in a totally cool Diet Pepsi product placement. Thank God I wasn't singing in this video.

I sat there, arms folded, and waited for the inevitable slew of smartass comments. Never in my life did I hate Daemon more than at that moment. No one I knew in real life paid attention to my blog. Books were a passion I shared with virtual friends. Not Daemon. It wigged me out knowing he was watching this.

The video ended. Voice low, he said, "You're even glowing in the video."

Mouth clamped shut, I nodded. And I waited.

"You really have a thing for books." When I didn't respond, he closed the laptop without touching it. "It's cute."

My head whipped around to him. "Cute?"

"Yeah, it's cute. Your excitement," he said, shrugging. "It was cute."

I think my jaw hit the carpet.

"But as cute as you are in pigtails, that's not going to do anything to fade the trace on you." He stood and stretched. Of course his shirt had to ride up, drawing my eyes. "We need to get this trace off you."

I was still stunned over the fact he hadn't made fun of me, rendered speechless by it, shocked to the core. He just earned a few bonus points.

"The sooner we get the trace off you, the less time we have to spend together."

And there went the points. "You know, if you hate the idea of being around me, why doesn't one of the others come over here and do this? I actually prefer any of them to you, even Ash."

"You're not their problem." His eyes locked with mine. "You're my problem."

My laugh was harsh. "I'm not your problem."

"But you are," he reasoned gamely. "If I had managed to convince Dee not to get so close to you, none of this would've happened."

I rolled my eyes. "Well, I don't know what to tell you. There isn't much we can do in here that's going to make a difference, so we might as well count today as a loss and spare each other the pain of breathing the same air."

He shot me a bland look.

"Oh, yeah, that's right. You don't need to breathe oxygen. My bad." I shot to my feet, itching for him to be out of my house. "Can't you just come back when it stops raining?"

"No." Daemon leaned against the wall, folding his arms. "I want to get this over with. Worrying over you and the Arum isn't fun, Kitten. We need to do something about this now. There are things we can do."

My hands curled into fists. "Like what?"

"Well, the jumping jacks for…an hour or so should do it." His gaze dropped. Something flickered in his eyes. "You may want to change first."

The urge to cover myself was strong, but I resisted. I wasn't going to cower from him. "I'm not doing jumping jacks for an hour."

"Then you could run around the house, up and down the

stairs." He paused, his smug grin turning wicked as his eyes met mine. "We could always have sex. I hear that uses up a lot of energy."

My mouth dropped open. Part of me wanted to laugh in his face. There was a part of me offended that he would suggest something so ridiculous, but there was another part that liked the idea. Which was so, so wrong it wasn't even funny.

Daemon waited.

"That will never happen in a million years, buddy." I took a step forward, raising my pointer finger at him. "Not even if you were the last—wait, I can't even say last human on the face of this Earth."

"Kitten," he murmured lazily. A clear warning in his eyes.

I ignored it. "Not even if you were the last thing that looked like a human on the face of this Earth. Got that? Capiche?"

He tilted his head to the side, and several locks of hair slid over his forehead. Daemon smiled, a wealth of danger in the tilt to his mouth, but I was on a roll now.

"I'm not even attracted to you." *Lie. Ding! Ding! Lie.* "Not even a little bit. You're—"

Daemon was in front of me in a flash, not an inch from my face. "I'm what?"

"Ignorant," I said, taking a step back.

"And?" He matched my step.

"Arrogant. Controlling." I took another step back, but he was still in my personal space and then some. "And you're... you're a jerk."

"Oh, I'm sure you can do better than that, Kitten." His

voice was low as he inched me backward. I barely heard him over the pounding rain and the thundering of my heart. "Because I seriously doubt you're not attracted to me."

I forced a laugh. "I'm totally not attracted to you."

Another step forward on Daemon's side, and my back was against the wall. "You're lying."

"And you're overconfident." I inhaled, but all I smelled was *him*, and that did funny things to my stomach. "You know, the whole arrogant thing I mentioned. Not attractive."

Daemon placed his hands on each side of my head and leaned in. A lamp was on one side of me, and the T.V. on the other. I was trapped. And when he spoke, his breath danced over my lips. "Every time you lie, your cheeks turn red."

"Nuh-uh." Not the most eloquent thing I'd ever said, but it was the best I could come up with.

His hands slid down the wall, stopping beside my hips. "I bet you think about me all the time. Nonstop."

"You're insane." I pressed back against the wall, breathless.

"You probably even dream about me." His gaze lowered to my mouth. I felt my lips part. "I bet you even write my name in your notebooks, over and over again, with a little heart drawn around it."

I laughed. "In your dreams, Daemon. You're the last person I think—"

Daemon kissed me.

There wasn't a moment of hesitation. His mouth was on mine, and I stopped breathing. He shuddered and there was a sound from the back of his throat, half growl, half moan. Little shivers of pleasure and panic shot through me as he deepened the kiss, parting my lips. I stopped thinking. I pushed off the wall, sealing the tiny space between us, pressing against him, digging my fingers into his hair. It was soft, silky. Nothing else about him felt that way. I sparked alive, my heart swelled to the point of near bursting. The rush of sensations crawling across my body was maddening. Scary. Thrilling.

His hands were on my hips, and he lifted me up as if I were made of air. My legs wrapped around his waist, and we moved to the right, knocking into a floor lamp. It toppled over, but I didn't spare it another thought. A light popped somewhere in the house. The TV turned on, then off, back on. Our lips remained sealed. It was like we couldn't get enough of each other. We were devouring one another, drowning in each other.

We'd been building up to this for months, and oh my God was it worth the wait. And I wanted more.

Lowering my hands, I tugged at his shirt, but it was stuck under my legs. I wiggled down until my feet were on the floor. Then I got a hold of his shirt and yanked it up. He broke apart long enough to pull it over his head and toss it aside.

His hands slid around my head, pulling me back to his mouth. There was a cracking sound in the house. A fissure of electricity shot through the room. Something smoked. But I didn't care. We were moving backward. His hands were moving down, under my shirt, his fingers skimming over my skin, sending a rush of blood to every part of my body. And my hands went down. His stomach was hard, dipped and rippled in all the right places.

And then my shirt joined his on the floor. Skin against skin. His hummed, brimming full of power. I ran my fingers down his chest, to the button on his jeans. The back of my legs hit the couch and we went down, a tangle of legs and hands moving, exploring. Our hips were molded together and we moved against one another. I think I whispered his name, and then his arms tightened around me, crushing me against his chest and his hands slipped between my legs. And I was swimming in raw sensations.

"So beautiful," he murmured against my swollen lips. And then he was kissing me again. The deep kind of kisses that left little room for thought. There was only feeling and wanting. That was all. I wrapped my legs around his hips, pulling him closer, telling him what I wanted with my soft moans.

Our kisses slowed, becoming tender and infinitely more. It was like we were getting to know each other on an intimate level. I was breathless and dazed, unprepared for all of this, but my body ached for more than just kisses and touching—for more of him. And I knew he did, too. His powerful body shook like mine. It was easy to get lost in him, lost in this connection between us. The world—the universe—ceased to exist.

And then Daemon stilled, his breath coming out in rough gasps as he pulled back, lifting his head. My eyes opened slowly, dazed. His pupils were white, glowing from within.

Daemon took a deep breath. An eternity seemed to pass as he stared down at me, his eyes wide, and then he pieced himself back together. The light went out. His jaw hardened. A mask slipped over his face. The arrogant half smile I disliked so much tipped up one corner of his swollen lips. "You're barely glowing now."

Chapter 27

I hated Daemon Black—if that was even his real name—with a vengeance that equaled the solar power of a thousand suns. *You're barely glowing now.* He left after that, grabbing his shirt off the floor and sauntering out of my house.

The son of a bitch blew up my laptop.

That was what had been smoking. His alien mojo apparently has a major affect on lights and most electronics. Now I had to rely on school computers to update my blog. Ugh. And I'd spent a good hour after I peeled myself off the couch replacing light bulbs in the house. Luckily, the T.V. hadn't been fried.

But my brain had. What had I been thinking? *Doing?* It had to have been all the arguing between us. That was the only explanation for why there was such a massive explosion from such a heavy make-out session. And he wasn't as unaffected as he pretended. No one could fake *that*.

My glow had faded to a small trace, much to everyone's amazement. Imagine trying to explain how that happened. And I'm sure he couldn't wait to share the info.

I hated him.

Not just for the fact he'd proven me a liar, or that I now had to wait until my birthday for a new laptop, or the fact Dee was highly suspicious of how my glow faded, but because of what he made me *feel*, for making me *admit* it out loud, too.

And if he poked me in the back with a pen one more freaking time, I was going to throw him in front of an Arum.

My cell phone buzzed in my backpack as I walked to my car, hunkered down against the unforgiving wind sweeping down from the Rocks. Without looking, I knew it was another text from Simon. For the last week he'd been texting his apologies over and over again. He didn't dare talk to me in class or public, not with Daemon's threat looming over his head. I wasn't forgiving him anytime soon. Drunk or not, it wasn't an excuse for being an overbearing ass who didn't understand the word "no".

"Katy!"

I jumped at the sound of Dee's voice. Shouldering my bag, I turned and waited.

As always, Dee looked amazingly beautiful. Today she'd worn skinny dark denim jeans and a lightweight turtleneck. With her glossy black hair and bright eyes, she was stunning. Her smile was wide and friendly, but it quickly faded as she neared me.

"Hey, I didn't think you were going to stop," she said.

"Sorry. I was lost in my thoughts." I started walking again, spying my car. "What's up?"

Dee cleared her throat. "Are you avoiding me, Katy?"

I'd been avoiding all of them, which was hard. They lived next door. They were in my classes. They sat with me at lunch. And I missed Dee. "No."

"Really, because you haven't been very talkative since Saturday," she pointed out. "Monday you didn't even sit with us at lunch, claiming you had to study for a test. Yesterday, I don't think you said two words to me."

Guilt twisted my insides. "I've been...out of it."

"It's too much, isn't it? What we are?" Her voice was small, childlike. "I was afraid this would happen. We're huge freaks—"

"You're not freaks," I said, meaning it. "You guys are... more human than you give yourselves credit for."

Dee seemed relieved to hear that. She darted in front of me. "The boys, they're still looking for Baruck."

I sidestepped her and opened my car door. The obsidian blade bounced around in the compartment on the side of the door. Carrying it in my backpack had made me feel like I was going to shank a student or something. So in my car it went. "That's good."

She nodded. "The boys are going to continue searching and keep an eye on things, and both you and Simon barely have any traces on you now." Dee paused. "I'd still like to know how that happened so quickly."

My stomach twisted. "Uh, yeah, there was a lot of... physical activity."

Her brows inched up her forehead. "Katy..."

"Anyway," I said quickly. "That's all good—the trace

fading from Simon, especially since he has no clue about any of this, so I'm glad, creeper-ness aside."

"You're rambling," she said, grinning.

"Yeah, kind of."

"So what are you doing tomorrow?" she asked, hopeful. "It's Saturday *and* Halloween. I thought maybe we could rent a bunch of scary movies."

I shook my head. "I promised Lesa I'd give out candy with her. She lives in a subdivision, so…" Hurt flickered across Dee's face. What was I doing? Dissing a friend because of her jackass brother? That wasn't me. "I can come over afterward, and we can watch movies if you want?"

"If you want?" she whispered.

Leaning over, I hugged her slim shoulders. "Of course I want. Just make sure you get tons of popcorn and candy. Those are a requirement."

Dee returned the hug. "That I can do."

I pulled back, smiling. "Okay. I'll see you tomorrow night then?"

"Wait." She grabbed my arm, her fingers cold. "What happened between you and Daemon?"

I willed my face blank. "Nothing happened, Dee."

Her eyes narrowed. "I know better, Katy. You would've had to do major running around to burn off most of the trace in one afternoon."

"Dee—"

"And Daemon has been acting grumpier than normal. Something happened between you two." She brushed her hair out of her face, but the curls sprung right back. "I know you said you guys didn't do anything that one time, but…"

"Seriously, nothing happened. I promise." I climbed into my car, forcing a smile. "I'll see you tomorrow night."

She didn't believe me. I didn't believe myself, but what could I say? Admitting what went down between Daemon and me wasn't something I wanted to share with his sister.

• • •

Every Halloween I missed being a kid, getting to dress up and eat tons of candy. The only thing I got to do now was... eat tons of candy. Not half bad.

Lesa laughed as I dug out another box of Nerds. "What?" I elbowed her. "I love these things."

"And mini Hershey bars, Kit Kats, bubble gum, Star-bursts—"

"Look who's talking!" I gestured to the pile of wrappers on the steps beside *her* feet. "You're a freaking candy monster."

We stopped while a small child shuffled up the steps, dressed like a member of Kiss. Odd costume choice.

"Trick or Treat!" the little boy cried.

Lesa fawned all over him and gave him several pieces of candy. "You are so not here for the kids," she said, watching the little boy run back to his parents.

I popped a piece of caramel in my mouth. "What gave you that idea?"

"Did you think that little boy was cute?" She moved the bowl away from me.

I shrugged. "Guess so. I mean, he kind of smelled like...I don't know. Kid."

Lesa busted out laughing. "Do you like kids?"

"Kids scare me." A mummy and vampire approached us. Lesa cooed over them until they scampered away. "Especially the little ones," I continued, scowling when I saw there weren't any Nerds left. "They jabber and stuff, and I have no idea what they are saying, but your little brother is super cute."

"My little brother craps himself."

I laughed. "Well, maybe it's because he's, like, only one?"

"Whatever, it's still gross." She handed some candy over to a cowboy with an arrow through his head. Sweet. "So what's your deal been?"

"My deal?" Like a ninja, my hand shot out and snatched a roll of Smarties. "I don't have a deal."

"You're so full of it." It was so dark out, I couldn't make out her eyes. Her subdivision didn't believe in street lamps. "You've been an angst-ridden teenage girl, like the kind in the books I read, all week."

I rolled my eyes. "Have not."

She nudged me with her knee. "You haven't been talking to anyone, especially not Dee. And that's weird, because you guys are close."

"We still are." I sighed, squinting into the encroaching darkness. Shapes of parents and their kids walked along the side of the streets. "I'm not mad at her or anything. I'm going over to her house after I leave here."

Lesa cradled the bowl. "But?"

"But something happened with her brother," I said, caving in to the need to talk to someone about what happened.

"I knew it!" she screamed. "Oh my God, you have to tell me *everything*! Did you guys kiss? Wait. Did you have sex?"

A parent of a fairy shot her a dirty look as she ushered her child off Lesa's porch.

"Lesa, seriously, chill."

"Whatever. You have to tell me. I will hate you forever if you did but don't tell me. What does he smell like?"

"Smell like?" I scrunched up my face.

"You know, he looks like he'd smell good."

"Oh." I closed my eyes. "Yeah, he does smell good."

Lesa sighed dreamily. "Details. Now."

"It's nothing big." I picked up a fallen leaf, twirling it. My lips tingled, thinking about his kiss. "He came over last Sunday and we kissed."

"That's all?" She sounded so disappointed.

"I didn't sleep with him. Jeez. But...it was pretty heavy." I dropped the leaf and ran a hand through my hair, tugging it back. "We were arguing and the next thing I know—BAM. We're going at it."

"Geez, that's...that's hot."

I sighed. "Yeah, it kind of was. But then he left abruptly."

"Of course, because you guys have this fiery passion that explodes, and he couldn't take the heat."

I gave her a bland look. "We don't have anything."

Lesa ignored me. "I was wondering how long it would last with you two antagonizing each other."

"I don't antagonize him," I muttered.

"What did you guys argue about?"

How could I explain? That we'd only goaded each other into doing something because I'd said I wasn't attracted to him and he needed to kill my glow? Yeah, not happening.

"Katy?"

"I don't think he meant to kiss me," I said finally.

"What? Did he slip and fall on your mouth? Those things are known to happen."

I giggled. "No. It's just that he seemed pissed off about it afterward. No, he *was* pissed."

"Did you like bite his tongue or something?" Lesa tucked her hair back, frowning. "There has to be a reason why he was mad afterward."

Since it was getting late and the kiddos few and far between, I grabbed the bowl from her and starting fingering through the leftovers. "I don't know. I mean we haven't talked about it. He literally left afterward, and all he's done since then is poke me with his pen."

"Probably because he wants to poke you with something else," she said dryly.

My eyes bugged. "I can't believe you said that."

"Whatever." She waved her hand in the air. "He's not back with Ash, right? I mean, those two are—"

"On and off—I know. I don't think so. It doesn't matter." I popped a piece of candy in my mouth. At this rate, I was going to be rolling off Lesa's porch. "It's just that..."

"You like him," she finished for me.

I shrugged, moving on to a Snickers bar. Did I like him? Maybe. Was I attracted to him? Obviously. I'd been seconds away from getting buck-naked with him. "It's the most messed up thing, ever. No one on this planet pisses me off more than him, but...Ah, I don't want to talk about this." I snatched the bag of Skittles back. "Anyway, how are things with Chad?"

"You're changing the subject. I am not fooled."

Not looking up, I rooted around in the bowl. "You guys went out last night, right? Did he kiss you? Does *he* smell good?"

"Chad does smell good, actually. I think he wears a newer version of Old Spice. Not the kind my dad wears, because that would be gross."

I laughed. We chatted for a little while then I left and headed home. Dee had the entire house decked out in carved pumpkins that hadn't been there when I left earlier. She pulled me inside, a strange smell in the air.

"What is that?" I wrinkled my nose.

"I'm baking pumpkin seeds," she exclaimed. "Have you tried them?"

I shook my head. "No. What do they taste like?"

"Like pumpkin."

Of course she was actually baking them. The pale seeds were on a baking sheet, but it was her hands doing the baking and not the stove. Pumpkin guts were scattered all over the newspaper-covered table.

"I'm going to borrow your hands during the winter, when ice is caked on my windshield."

Dee laughed. "I have no problem with that."

Grinning, I shuffled over to the stack of movies on the counter. I scanned the spines, laughing. "Oh my God, Dee, these movies are awesome."

"I thought you would like the combination of the *Scream* and *Scary Movie* series." She moved her hands over the baking sheet. The seeds popped and jumped. Cinnamon filled the air. "We'll leave the *Halloween* movies until later."

I glanced at the door. "Um, is Daemon here?"

"No." She grabbed the sheet, dumping the seeds into a ball decorated in bats and skulls. "He's out with the guys, seeing if they can get Baruck to show himself."

Taking our snacks and movies into the living room, I thought about what she said. "Are they purposely trying to get him to show himself? Like they want to fight him?"

A DVD flew from the stack to her hand. She nodded. "Don't worry. Daemon and Adam are checking around town. Matthew and Andrew are out in the country. They'll be okay."

Unease turned my stomach. "Are you sure?"

Dee smiled. "This isn't the first time they've done something like this. They know what they're doing. It'll be okay."

Sitting back against the couch, I tried not to worry. It was hard, especially since I'd seen the look in Baruck's eyes. Dee settled in next to me, and I tried a few pumpkin seeds. Not bad. We'd made it through the first *Scream* movie when her cell rang.

Raising her hand, Dee flicked it and the cell flew off the table and landed in her hand. She answered with a roll of her eyes. "This better be good, Daemon, because—" Her eyes widened. She shot to her feet, her free hand clenching. "What do you mean?"

My stomach turned to liquid as I watched her edge around the coffee table.

"Katy is with me, but her trace is barely noticeable!" Another pause and then her face paled. "Okay. Be careful. I love you."

As soon as she tossed the phone to the recliner, I stood. "What's happening?"

Dee faced me. "They spotted Baruck. He's heading this way."

Chapter 28

Of course that didn't mean he was coming right here, but there was a chance—a big chance—that he was. Enough so that Dee prowled the length of the living room like a caged tiger. She wasn't afraid, but ready to do battle.

"If Baruck comes here, can you fight him?" I asked.

Dee passed me a steely look. She was a totally different person, morphing into a badass warrior princess. How come I'd never seen this side of her? "I'm not as quick or as powerful as Daemon, but I'll be able to hold my own until Daemon gets here."

My stomach dropped. Hold your own wasn't enough. What if Daemon didn't get here in time? Dee stopped in front of the window, her slim shoulders squared. It hit me all at once. Everything Daemon had been worried about was coming true. I was a weakness—a liability to Dee. I couldn't—I *wouldn't* let that happen.

"Is my trace strong enough that he'd see me inside your house?"

She paused. "Not really."

"What about from the main road? The woods?"

There was a pause. "I don't know, Katy, but I'll stop him before he gets to you."

"No. I have an idea." I stepped forward, almost knocking over the stack of DVDs. "It's kind of crazy, but it could work."

Her eyes narrowed. "What?"

"If you make my trace stronger, I can definitely lead him away from here. Then he won't come here and Daemon—"

"Absolutely not," she said, whirling around. "Are you insane?"

"Maybe," I said, biting my lip. "Look, it's better than sitting here with me when I could very well lead him right back to your house! And then he'll know where you guys live! What then? You won't ever be safe. I need to lure them away from your home."

"No." Dee shook her head. "I can't do that. I can fight—"

"There's nothing else I can do! I can't fight him and what if he escapes? What if he tells others where you live?" Daemon's words came back to me. *You would be a weakness to me.* Except I wouldn't be his weakness, I'd be Dee's. I couldn't live with that. "And I'll be a liability. Baruck will know that. You have to stay here. If Baruck finds us together, he'll use me to destroy you. The best plan is for me to lure the Arum away and let the guys meet me in the field and take him down together."

"Katy—"

"I'm not taking no for an answer! We don't have much time." I moved to the door, grabbing my keys and cell phone. "Light up. Do the crazy balls of light thing. That seems like it worked last time. I'll head…I'll head to where the field party was! Tell Daemon that's where I'm going." When she stood there, staring at me, I yelled, "Do it!"

"This is insane." Dee shook her head, but she stepped back and started to blur out. A second later she was in her true form, a beautiful silhouette of light. *This is insane*, her voice whispered in my thoughts.

I'd stopped thinking. "Hurry."

Two balls of crackling light formed in her outstretched arms. They shot around the room, blowing the lights and the TV, but ended up bouncing off the walls harmlessly. The fine hairs on my body stood as static filled the air.

"Am I glowing?" I asked.

Like the sun.

Well, that worked. Taking a deep breath, I nodded. "Call Daemon and tell him where I'm going."

Be careful. Please. Her light began to fade.

"You, too." I turned and raced out of the house toward my car before I could think twice about what I was doing.

Because this was absolutely insane—the craziest thing I'd ever done. Worse than giving a one-star review, scarier than asking for an interview with an author I'd give my firstborn to eat lunch with, more stupid than kissing Daemon.

But this was all I could do.

My hands were shaking when I shoved the key into the ignition and backed out of the driveway, narrowly missing Dee's Volkswagen. I hit the gas, squealing out onto the main road. I was clenching the steering wheel like a granny, but driving like I was trying out for NASCAR.

I kept glancing in my rearview mirror as I flew down the highway, expecting to find Arum chasing after me. But every time I checked, the road was empty.

Maybe this hadn't worked? Oh God, what if Baruck continued to the house and found Dee? My heart leapt into my throat. This was a stupid, stupid idea. My foot faltered on the gas pedal. At least he wouldn't be able to use me to get to Dee.

My cell rang from the passenger's seat. Unknown Caller? Now? I almost ignored it, but I grabbed it and answered anyway. "Hello?"

"Are you out of your freaking mind?" Daemon yelled into the phone. I winced. "This has to be the stupidest thing—"

"Shut up, Daemon!" I screeched. The tires swerved a little into the other lane. "It's done. Okay? Is Dee okay?"

"Yes, Dee's okay. But you're not! We've lost him, and since Dee said you're glowing like a goddamn full moon right now, I'm betting he's after you."

Fear spiked my heart rate. "Well, that was the plan."

"I swear on every star in the sky, I'm going to strangle you when I get my hands on you." Daemon paused, his breath heavy on the phone. "Where are you?"

I glanced out the window. "I'm almost to the field. I don't see him."

"Of course you don't see him." He sounded disgusted. "He's made of shadows—of *night*, Kat. You won't see him until he wants you to."

Oh. Well. Shit.

"I can't believe you did this," he said.

My temper snapped under the fear. "Don't you start with me! You said I was a weakness. And I was a liability back there with Dee. What if he came there? You said so yourself he'd use me against her. This was the best I could do! So stop being such a damn jerk!"

There was such a gap of silence I thought he'd hung up on me, but when he spoke, his voice was strained. "I didn't mean for you to do *this*, Kat. Never something like *this*."

His voice sent shivers through me. My eyes darted over the blurred shapes of trees. I drew in a deep breath, but it got stuck. "You didn't make me do this."

"Yeah, I did."

"Daemon—"

"I'm sorry. I don't want you hurt, Kat. I can't—*I can't* live with that." Another stretch of silence passed while his words sunk in and then, "Stay on the phone. I'm going to find a place to ditch the car and I'll meet you there. It won't take more than a few minutes to get there. Don't get out of the car or anything."

I nodded as I pulled the car to a stop inside the field. The moon rolled behind a cloud, turning everything pitch black. I couldn't see anything. A horrifying, sick feeling settled in my stomach. Reaching down, I grabbed the obsidian blade and held it tight. "Okay. Maybe this wasn't the strongest idea."

Daemon barked a short, harsh laugh. "No shit."

My lips twitched as I glanced in the rearview mirror. "So, um, the not living with your—"

There was a shadow there that looked...more solid than the rest. It moved through the air, thick like oil, slipping over the trees, spreading along the ground. Tendrils reached the back of the car, sliding over the trunk. My throat dried, lips parted.

The blade warmed in my hand. "Daemon?"

"What?"

My heart thudded. "I think —"

The automatic locks unlocked and my driver's door flew open. A scream came out. One second I was holding the phone and the next I was flying to the ground, my fingers almost losing their grip on the blade. Pain shot through my arm and side as I hid the blade behind me.

I lifted my eyes. My gaze traveled over black pants and the edges of a leather jacket. Pale face. Strong jaw and a pair of sunglasses covered the eyes even though it was night.

Baruck smiled. "We meet again."

"Shit," I whispered.

"Tell me," he said, bending down and lifting a strand of my hair. His head swiveled to the side as he talked, moving back and forth like a bird. "Where is he?"

I swallowed thickly as I scrambled back across the ground. "Who?"

"You're going to play dumb with me?" He stepped forward and removed his sunglasses, slipping them inside his jacket. His eyes were black orbs. "Or are all humans just so stupid?"

My chest rose and fell sharply. The blade was only good in his true form. And it was burning through the leather, stinging my hand.

"I want the one who killed my brothers."

Daemon. My entire body was shaking. I opened my mouth

but nothing came out.

"And you...you killed one of them, protecting *him*." He flickered out. There was my chance, but before I could move, he solidified in front of me. "Take me to him or I will make you beg for death."

I shook my head, tightening my hand. "Screw you."

He faded out, becoming a mass of dark and twisted shadows. Lunging to my feet, I let out a battle-worthy scream and swung my arm around, aiming for the center of the black goo. The blade burned bright, the color of hot coals.

My jab never landed.

A smoky hand caught my arm. The touch was bone-chillingly cold. His voice was an insidious whisper among my thoughts, like a snake slithering inside my head. *Do you think I'd fall for that? Pleassse...*

He twisted. I heard the CRACK before I felt the pain. My fingers twitched and the blade fell to the ground, shattering into a dozen shards like nothing more than fragile glass. I screamed as a wave of pain crippled me.

That wassss for my brother.

A shadowy hand circled my neck and lifted me off my feet. *And thisss isss becaussse you annoy me.*

Baruck threw me backward. I hit the ground hard and then slid several feet through trampled corn. Stunned, I stared up at the pitch-black night sky.

Tell me where he isss.

Gasping for air, I rolled onto my feet and took off for the trees. I *ran*. Holding my arm protectively against my chest, I ran as fast as I could, my sneakers slapping against the hard-packed ground and crushing grass and fallen leaves. I didn't look back. Looking back would be *bad*. I tore through the woods, smacking at the low-hanging branches. Déjà vu floated through me as I stumbled over exposed roots and the uneven ground.

Baruck came out of nowhere, moving past in a blur of shadows. He solidified right in front of me, throwing me off. I skidded to a stop, spinning around. He was there, too, and he knocked me to the ground.

"Did you get it out of your system, yet?" A cruel smile formed on his pale lips. "Or do you want to run more?"

I scrabbled across the dirt as I gulped in every ragged breath I could. The horror made it hard to gain any sense of control. I was out of time.

Baruck lashed out. His arm didn't hit me, but I flung back and landed with a dull thud on the ground. The air knocked out of my lungs. Small rocks dug painfully through my jeans.

He reached down, sinking his hand in my hair and coiling it around his fist. I bit down on my lips to stop from crying out as he dragged me behind him. Material around my knees tore open. Pain radiated through me, threatening to consume me. I was sure he would pull every strand of my hair while ripping the skin off my knees.

He gave another painful yank, and I yelped. "Oops." He stopped. "I always forget how painfully frail your kind is. I don't want to accidentally pull your head off." He then laughed at his own remark. "Not yet, at least."

I grabbed his arms with my good hand, trying to lessen the pull, but it wasn't much help. He brought me into the path of branches, roots, and boulders. My muscles were screaming in protest and I hunched over, beginning to feel dizzy and moments away from succumbing to the pain.

"How are you doing down there?" he asked conversationally. Baruck abruptly pulled my head up. Sharp pain shot down my neck and back. "Doing well, I see." He stopped, and I fell the small distance to the ground. We were near the edge of the woods again. He loomed over me. "Tell me where he is."

I put my skinned up hand on the ground, panting. "No."

His booted foot jerked up, slamming into my side. I knew something broke. Something pretty damn bad, because there was wet warmth running under my shirt.

Tell me.

Wincing, I curled up. The coldness of his true form chilled my very soul.

He came closer. *There are worssse things than what isss physisscal. Perhapsss that will motivate you.*

Baruck grabbed me by the throat again, lifting me onto the tips of my toes. He leaned in and roughly pulled me against him. His face was inches from mine, consuming my world.

I can take your esssence; drain you until your heart ssstopsss. It does nothing for me, but jussst imagine the ssslow unending pain. Tell me where he isss.

I wasn't brave, but I wasn't going to turn Daemon over to him. If Baruck defeated him, he'd go after Dee next. I'd never be able to live with myself. I wasn't that weak of a person. I wasn't a liability out here.

I said nothing.

He pulled back and shoved his hand into my midsection. I could feel *it*—his shadowy hand inside me, turning every cell cold. The small space of air between us constricted and pulled. The air in my lungs came out in a painful rush.

Just like that, I could no longer breathe.

My lungs seized as he continued to breathe in my air. The burning in my throat and lungs turned quickly to a scorching fire as sharp pain radiated out over every limb. Every cell in my body screamed, begged for relief, and in protest as my heart stuttered abnormally. It wasn't precious oxygen that he stole from me, but the very energy that kept me alive. I was losing strength fast, and the panic that was consuming me hadn't helped. My hands were numb and my one good arm hung limply at my side. Everything slowed and the pain dulled a little. I vaguely felt his hand leave my throat, but I could not move. His powers had me hooked to him as he fed.

He said something, but I could no longer distinguish the words. I was so tired, so heavy, and only the fiery pain in the pit of my stomach kept me from slipping away. My eyes drifted shut of their own accord, and I felt him take another heavy inhale and the pain flared again.

Something snapped within me, like a cord stretched too thin. It broke and recoiled with relentless speed. A flash of bright pale blue light exploded behind my closed lids, and I was momentarily blinded. A roaring sound invaded my ears. Death had come for me.

Death sounded painful, angry, and desperate. Not peaceful. I thought that was unfair. After all that had happened, couldn't death have welcomed me with warm arms and visions of my dad waiting for me?

Without warning, a figure crashed into us and sent me spiraling to the ground in a messy heap. With intense effort, I peeled my eyes open and saw him crouched like an animal in front of me.

Daemon growled in fury as he rose, standing over me like an avenging angel, swathed in light.

Chapter 29

Baruck's mad laughter echoed and bounced around my skull. "You've come to die with her? Perfect. That makes this so much easier, because I think I might have broken her."

Daemon shadowed Baruck's wild movements, fading out and taking on his true form—the form he could be killed in.

"She tasted good, too. Different somehow," he taunted. "Not like a Luxen, but still worth it in the end."

Launching himself at Baruck, Daemon threw him several feet away with one powerful blast of light from an outstretched arm. "I'm going to kill you."

Baruck rolled on to his back, nearly choking with laughter. "You think you can take me, Luxen? I have devoured those stronger than you."

Daemon's howl of anger drowned out whatever else Baruck might have said, and he sent another blast of light at him. I felt the ground beneath me tremble as I managed to raise myself up onto my elbows. Each movement, no matter how small, sent sharp stings all through me. I could feel my heartbeat, the struggle behind it. Streaks of lights danced within the darkness of the Arum. They exchanged blows without even touching one another.

Bright, orangey balls of fire formed on the tips of Daemon's hands. They shot out past Baruck, fizzling out before they slammed into trees. The world turned amber and gold. Heat blew back at me. Embers crackled in the air, fading before hitting the ground.

Each strike sent the ground into motion, knocking me back down, face-first into the damp, itchy grass with a grunt. Pushing myself up, I saw a streak of light moving over the field, much like a falling star but shooting across the ground at a dizzying speed.

The light shot between Daemon and Baruck, fizzing out as it reached me. Warm hands gripped my shoulders and lifted me. "Katy, talk to me," Dee begged. "Please talk to me!"

Nothing happened when I tried to talk. No words came out.

"Oh my God." Dee was crying, her tears falling from her beautiful face and landing on my nearly silent chest. She pulled me into her thin arms as she screamed for her twin.

Daemon turned from the battle at the same time Baruck did. With one look, a bolt of darkness shot straight for us, knocking Dee back. She screamed out in pain and rolled to her knees. She looked up, her eyes glowing an intense white.

She rose to a crouch, her human form fading into crackling light.

Daemon struck back harder, and the ground rumbled. Baruck dodged Daemon's attack and went after Dee. Screaming in fury, she rushed Baruck.

He caught her again. For a second, darkness swallowed her, and then she crumbled to the ground in a twitching heap. Daemon charged Baruck, tackling him to the ground in a rage that was so potent it fueled everything around him. From the branches that shook, to the dead leaves falling like macabre rain, to the ground beneath me. The air crackled with power.

I felt it in my bones. Groaning, I staggered to my feet and sucked in a breath. I wasn't going out this way. My friends weren't going out like this.

Dee was on her feet, flickering in and out. Blood trickled from her nose. She shook her head and stumbled forward.

I saw what was going to happen next through a very narrow lens. Things seemed to slow down. I rushed forward as Daemon glanced over his shoulder at his sister. Baruck pulled his arm back, preparing another stream of matter. The image of the tree snapping in half along the road flashed before me.

Rushing forward, I crashed into the light that was Dee the moment Baruck released the blast of energy. Darkness surrounded me, and I heard a scream—a piercing scream that wasn't mine. And then I was flying—really flying. The sky was rolling, stars and darkness, over and over. The entire world shimmered.

I hit the ground hard, already knowing it was too late.

A body crashed next to mine. A limp, slender arm fell against mine. Dee. I hadn't been quick enough. The arm warmed against mine, becoming less…solid. Her light cast upon me. Sorrow cut through me like a thousand double-edged razor blades. She wasn't moving, but I could see her chest moving, slow and shallow.

Distracted, Daemon turned and made a fatal mistake. *You'll get him killed*, Ash had said. Baruck reared his arm back and his blast caught Daemon in his back. He went up, spiraling through the air, flickering in and out of human form. He landed only a foot from us.

Baruck laughed and shifted into his shadowy form. *Three for one ssspecial.*

Tears burned my eyes as my cheek nestled against the damp grass. Daemon tried to sit up, but he collapsed onto his back, his face contorting in pain.

It'sss over. All of you will die. Baruck advanced.

Daemon turned his head toward me. Our eyes locked. There was so much regret in that one look. His face faded out, blurred and unrecognizable. He couldn't hold his human form. Seconds later, and he was in his true form. The shape of a man encased in the most beautifully intense light.

One arm extended out toward me, forming fingers. Heart breaking, I reached out and my fingers disappeared in his light. Warmth encircled my fingers, the slightest pressure of Daemon's hand wrapping around mine. He squeezed, as if to reassure me, and a sob caught in my throat.

Daemon's light flickered but continued climbing up my arm, wrapping me in his intense heat. Like the day of the first Arum attack, in the wake of his warmth, my body began knitting itself back together.

Daemon was using the last of his strength to save me.

"No!" I shouted, but it came out no more than a hoarse whisper. I tried to pull my hand away, but Daemon refused to let go. And he didn't know what I did...I was too hurt to be saved. He should have taken the last of his strength to save himself. Or save Dee...

I pleaded with him with my eyes, but he squeezed my hand tighter.

This wasn't fair. It wasn't right. They didn't deserve this. *I* didn't deserve this. Pain and hatred welled in me. I would die, my friends would die, my mother would be lost, and Daemon.... I couldn't even understand the purpose behind all of this. The Arum's greed for power? Was it worth all these lives? The injustice of it all tore at me and a surge of energy that came from deep within me, jolted through my body.

I wasn't going to die like this. Neither were Daemon and Dee, not in some Podunk field in bumfuck West Virginia.

Using the strength Daemon had given me, I pushed myself to sit up and grabbed Dee's heated arm, keeping ahold of Daemon, willing them to get up, willing them to fight.

Baruck moved toward Daemon's light. Of course he'd take him out first—the most powerful. He'd be tweaking for hours. I wasn't even a blip on his radar at this point.

Daemon's hand spasmed and his light flared as the edge of Baruck's shadow rippled over him.

And something, something unexpected happened.

A pulse of light went through him, shining so bright that I winced. It arced high in the air, crackling and spitting. It found its other half, recognizing the form beside me. The same was happening with Dee's light even though she was unconscious. Her light blazed, connected with Daemon's.

Baruck's shadow halted.

The arc of light pulsed above and shot *down*, right into the center of my chest. The impact felt like it sent me deep into the ground, but...I was lifted off the ground, hair flying out around me. Power built between the three of us. It sparked, and out of the corner of my eye I saw both of them return to human form. Dee slumped on the ground, moaning softly, Daemon pushing to his knees, turning toward me.

But I...I was hovering. At least, that was how it felt. I didn't concentrate on that or even what Daemon was doing. It was only Baruck and me.

I wanted him to go away, to disappear. I wanted his very presence wiped clean from this earth. I wished for it more than anything I have ever desired. Every fiber of my being was centered on him. I pulled everything within me: every fear, every tear I'd shed for Dad, and every moment in my life where I was a *bystander*.

Power coiled inside me, wrapped through my very core. With a wild battle cry, I let it go. The cord snapped, and the recoil occurred outside of me.

The sky above us erupted in white lightning. I felt *it* leave, and I heard the old trees around us creak and groan as it rushed over them. The strong oaks, with no place to hide, bent to its power. The flash of light followed true to its target, washed through Daemon and Dee, and slammed Baruck in the chest.

His shadow form jerked. There was a loud snapping sound, and the light exploded once more, enveloping him completely.

Daemon stumbled backward and shielded himself from the explosion. The light flared, then quickly receded, and without a single word, Baruck was no more. Daemon slowly lowered his arm and stared blankly at the empty spot. He turned toward me. His voice was barely a whisper. "Kat?"

I was on my back before I realized it. The dark sky above began to blur. I didn't know what happened or what I did, but I could feel the power as it slipped out of me, and along with it, something more important.

I felt *nothing*, and let out a tired breath. It made this rattling sound that I knew should concern me, but I didn't think to care. There was this darkness again, a different kind than the Arum's. This was softer, numbing.

Daemon fell to his knees beside me, pulling me into his strong, solid arms. "Kat, say something insulting. Come on."

Off in the distance I could hear Dee stirring and rising to her feet, panic filling her voice. Without a glance back, Daemon gently moved his fingers over my face and spoke. "Dee, go back to the house now. Get Adam—he's out there somewhere."

Dee's arms were wrapped around her waist, and she was bent at an angle that alluded to a cracked rib or two. "I don't want to leave. She's bleeding! We have to get her to a hospital."

I was bleeding? Huh. I hadn't known. I felt wetness on my face: under my lips, my nose, and there was a strange dampness around my eyes, but it didn't hurt. Was I crying? Was it blood? I could feel Daemon around me, but it all seemed far away.

"Go back to the house now!" Daemon yelled and his grip

around me tightened, but his voice softened. "*Please*. Leave us. Go. She's okay. She…she just needs a minute."

Such a damn liar. I wasn't okay.

Daemon turned his back to her, pushing the tangled waves of hair out of my face. Only after she'd left, did he speak softly to me. "Kat, you're not going to die. Don't move or do anything. Just relax and trust me. Don't fight what's about to happen."

I watched as Daemon lowered his head. He rested his forehead against mine. His form faded out and he slipped into his true body. My eyes fluttered shut against the intensity of his light. The heat was almost too much. I was too close to it.

Hold on. Don't let go. His voice came through. *Just hold on.*

I felt myself sink deeper, and his hand cradled my head. Daemon exhaled long and steady against my lips. Warmth spread from him to me, slowly moving down my throat and into my lungs, filling me with such glorious heat that I knew there was no better way to let go than this.

Like a balloon that was slowly being inflated, I began to rise. My lungs filled as his heat spread through every vein and my fingers began to tingle. The pressure in my head subsided. I swam in the intoxicating feeling that inundated me. My senses started to process the things around me again, and I was no longer in this numb and dim world.

He continued until I was able to move in his arms. I pulled myself up, gripping his arms, following him out of the dark abyss. I reached for him blindly. My lips brushed his and my world exploded in feeling. They shifted until I was able to comprehend and make sense of some of it. And they weren't mine, not entirely.

What am I doing? If they find out what I've done...but I can't lose her. I can't.

I gasped for air, floored by the knowledge that I was hearing Daemon's thoughts. He was talking to me—not like before when he was in his true form. This was different, like his thoughts and feelings were dancing around mine. Fear beat at me, as did something softer, even more powerful than fear.

Please. Please. I can't lose you. Please open your eyes. Please don't leave me.

I'm here. I opened my eyes. *I'm here.*

Daemon jerked back, the light fading slowly, slipping out of me, over my skin and back into him.

"Kat," he whispered, sending shivers through me. He sat back with me still nestled against his chest. I felt his heart thunder violently, beating at the same rate as mine, in perfect sync.

Everything around us seemed...clearer. "Daemon, what did you do?"

"You need to rest." He paused, his voice throaty, weary. "You're not a hundred percent. It will take a couple of minutes. I think. I haven't healed anything on this level before."

"You did at the library," I murmured. "And at the car..."

His head lowered against mine. "That was just to help with a sprain and bruises. That was nothing like this."

The arm that had been broken didn't even ache as I lifted it. I turned my head toward him, my cheek brushing his. I stared in amazement at the bent trees that folded around us in a perfect circle. My gaze fell to the ground and settled on the space Baruck once stood. The only trace of him was the scorched earth he left behind.

"How did I do that?" I whispered. "I don't understand."

He buried his head in the crook of my neck, breathing in deeply. "I must've done something to you when I healed you. I don't know what. It doesn't make sense, but something happened when our energies joined. It shouldn't have affected you—you're human."

I was beginning to wonder about that.

"How are you feeling?" he asked.

"Okay. Sleepy. You?"

"The same."

I watched in silence as his curious eyes followed his thumb over my chin, and he traced along my lower lip.

"I think, for now, it would be best if we kept this between ourselves—the whole healing thing and what you did back there. Okay?"

I nodded, but stilled as his hands drifted around my face, removing the smudges our battle had left behind.

A tumble of black waves shifted over his forehead and a smile spread across his face, reaching his eyes, deepening them to a brilliant green. His fingers splayed across my cheeks and his head slanted, and I couldn't help but think of what I'd overheard as his mouth brushed against mine. There was an infinitely tender quality to his soft kiss. It reached deep inside me, sending my heart into overdrive. It was innocent, intimate. Soul-burning as he tipped my head back and explored my lips as if it was the first time we'd kissed.

And maybe it was—a real kiss.

When he finally pulled back, he laughed unsteadily. "I was worried that we'd broken you."

"Not quite." My gaze moved over every inch of his weary face. "Did you break yourself?"

He snorted. "Almost."

I took a breath, a little dizzy. "What now?"

A slow, tired smile pulled at his lips. "We go home."

Chapter 30

It literally hurt deep inside not being able to post my "Waiting on Wednesday", but I still had several weeks before my birthday. And even though Dee would let me borrow her computer, I didn't want to use it for that. Pouting, I grabbed the can of soda out of Dee's fridge and went back into the living room.

Aliens could sure eat a lot of food.

"Do you want more pizza?" Dee offered, staring at the last slice with such longing that I was beginning to think that she and Adam needed to re-evaluate their relationship.

I shook my head. Dee had eaten enough to feed a small starving village and frankly, I wasn't hungry. Eating while Dee and Adam stared at me was getting tedious and uncomfortable. Dee didn't think I noticed, and Adam was currently on pause from asking another question about what happened that night with Baruck.

As far as everyone knew, Daemon had killed Baruck and I hadn't been injured as badly as Dee had thought. Somehow Daemon had convinced her that I was just stunned. I peeked at them.

But it had been me—I'd killed someone. Again.

Surprisingly, the thought didn't fill me with the same amount of dread and sickness as it initially did. Over the last couple of days, I'd come to a certain understanding with my actions. It was a level of shaky acceptance that made it easier to swallow even if I would never forget.

It was either him or me and my friends.

The alien asshat had to go.

Everyone was still staring. Lovely.

Dee sat down next to me and took a sip of her soda. Convinced or not, Dee knew something was up when I returned with Daemon that morning...and something was.

She nudged my leg with hers, gaining my attention. "Are you feeling okay?"

If I had a dollar for every time she asked that question, I'd have a new laptop already. It wasn't like I didn't know I was lucky to be alive, and I should be suffering from post-traumatic stress, but I did feel fine. I never felt physically better, to be honest. I felt like I could go out and run a marathon or climb a mountain. I didn't want to look into the reason for that too closely. Enough things had already successfully freaked me out.

Someone cleared his throat, jarring me out of my thoughts. I looked up to see Dee and Adam staring at me expectantly. I couldn't remember what they wanted. "What?"

Dee smiled a little too brightly. "We were wondering how

you were handling things? If you are worried about there being more Arum."

"Oh, do you think there will be?" I immediately responded.

"No," Adam reassured me. Ever since the battle with Baruck, he actually started talking to me. It was a nice change in things. Ash and Andrew were a different story. "We don't think so."

I shifted uncomfortably and my skin itched. I wasn't sure how long I could sit here with them staring at me at me like I was an experiment gone wrong.

"I thought you said Daemon would be back soon?" Adam settled in the recliner.

Dee's eyes shifted from Adam to me. "Daemon should be here any minute."

I hadn't seen Daemon since that morning. I'd asked Dee several times where he had gone, but she never answered me. Eventually, I gave up pestering her.

The two of them started talking, making plans for Thanksgiving break coming in a few weeks. I zoned out, like I'd been doing for the last three days. It was strange. I couldn't concentrate. I felt off, like I was missing a part of me.

Warmth slipped over my skin, like a warm breeze. It came out of nowhere. I looked up, seeing if anyone else noticed what I'd felt. They were still talking. I shifted on the couch as the feeling increased.

Dee's front door opened, and my breath caught in my throat.

Within seconds, Daemon entered the room. His hair was a tousled mess and there were shadows under his eyes. Without saying a word, he dropped onto the couch, his heavy lashes hiding his eyes, but I could feel his stare.

"Where have you been?" I asked in a voice that sounded shrill to my own ears.

Silence fell while two more sets of beautifully odd eyes settled on me. I felt my cheeks turn hot and I leaned back, feeling like an idiot. I folded my hands and kept my eyes pinned to them. What a way to draw attention to myself.

"Well hello, honey, I've been out boozing and whoring. I know, my priorities are pretty off."

My lips thinned at his sarcastic response. "Dick," I muttered.

Dee groaned. "Daemon, don't be a jerk."

"Yes, Mommy. I've been with another group, searching the whole damn state to make sure there aren't any Arum that we're not aware of," Daemon said, his deep voice soothing a weird ache within me at the same time I wanted to thump him upside the head.

Adam leaned forward. "There aren't any, right? Because we told Katy she didn't have anything to worry about."

His eyes left me briefly. "We haven't seen a single one."

Dee hooted happily and clapped her hands. She turned to me, her smile genuine this time. "See, nothing to worry about. Everything is over."

I smiled back at her. "That is a relief."

I heard Adam talking to Daemon about his trip, but it was hard to pay attention. I closed my eyes. Every cell in my body was aware of him, like that day in my living room but on a different level.

"Katy? Are you even here, right now?"

"I think so." I forced a smile for Dee's sake.

"Have you guys been driving her crazy?" Daemon asked, sighing. "Bombarding her with a million questions?"

"Never!" cried Dee. Then she laughed. "Okay. Maybe."

"Figured," Daemon muttered, stretching out his long legs.

Unable to stop myself, I turned toward him. Our eyes locked. The air between us seemed to stretch with heat and electricity. The last time I'd seen him, we'd been kissing. And I had no idea where that left us.

Dee shifted next to me, clearing her throat. "I'm still hungry, Adam."

He laughed. "You're worse than I am."

"True." Dee hopped to her feet. "Let's go to Smoke Hole. I think they are having homemade meatloaf." She edged around me, leaned down, and gave Daemon a peck on the cheek. "Glad you're back. I've missed you."

Daemon smiled up at his sister. "Missed you, too."

When the door shut behind Dee and Adam, I let out the breath I'd been holding. "Is everything really okay?" I asked.

"For the most part." He reached out with one hand, running his fingers over my cheek. Daemon sucked in a sharp breath. "Hell."

"What?"

He sat up and scooted closer, his leg pressing against mine. "I have something for you."

Not what I was expecting. "Is it going to blow up in my face?"

Leaning back, he chuckled and reached into the front pocket of his jeans. He pulled out a small leather pouch and handed it to me.

Curious, I pulled on the little string and carefully emptied the pouch into my palm. I glanced up, and when he smiled, I felt my heart turn over. It was a piece of obsidian about three inches long, polished and shaped into a pendant. The glass was shiny black. It seemed to hum against my skin, cool to the touch. The silver chain it hung from was delicate, spiraling over the top of the pendent. The other edge was sharpened into a fine point.

"Believe it or not," Daemon said, "even something as small as that can actually pierce Arum skin and kill them. When it gets really hot you'll know an Arum is nearby even if you don't see one." He carefully picked up the chain, holding the clasps. "It took me forever to find a piece like this since the blade turned to crap. I don't want you to take this off, okay? At least when...well, for the most part."

Shocked, I pulled my hair out of the way and twisted around, letting him hook the necklace around my neck. Once it was clasped, I faced him. "Thank you. I mean it, for everything."

"It's not a big deal. Has anyone asked you about your trace?"

I shook my head. "I think they're expecting to see one because of all the fighting."

Daemon nodded. "Hell, you're bright as a comet right now. The sucker has got to fade or we'll be back to square one."

A slow heat built inside me. Not the good kind. "And what is square one, exactly?"

"You know, us being...stuck together until the damn trace fades." His gaze flickered away.

Stuck together? My fingers dug into my denim-clad

knees. "After everything I've done, us being around each other is being *stuck* together?"

Daemon shrugged.

"You know what? Screw you, buddy. Because of me, Baruck didn't find your sister. Because of what I did, I almost died. You healed me. That's why I have a trace. None of this is my fault."

"And it's mine? Should I have left you to die?" His eyes burned now, like emerald pools. "Is that what you wanted?"

"That's a stupid question! I don't regret that you healed me, but I'm not dealing with this hot and cold shit from you anymore."

"I do believe you protest too much with the whole liking me part." A wry grin twisted his lips. "Someone sounds like they are trying to convince themselves."

I took a deep breath and let it out slowly. As much as it bothered me to say this, because there was a part of me that wanted him, I did. "I think it would be best if you'd stay away from me."

"No can do."

"Any of the other Luxen can watch over me or whatever," I protested. "It doesn't have to be you."

His eyes met mine. "You're my responsibility."

"I am nothing to you."

"You're definitely something."

My palms itched to have a close encounter of the bitch-slap kind with his face. "I dislike you so very much."

"No. You don't."

"Okay. We need to get this trace off me. Now."

A wicked smile played over his lips. "Maybe we can try

making out again. See what that will do to this trace. It seemed to work last time."

My body liked the idea. I, however, did not. "Yeah, that's not going to happen again."

"It was just a suggestion."

"One that will never. Happen," I bit out each word deliberately. "Again."

"Don't act like you didn't have as much fun—"

I smacked him in the chest hard. He only laughed, and I started to push off, but...*wait.* I pressed my hand against his chest as I stared at him.

Daemon arched a brow. "Are you feeling me up, Kat? I'm liking where this is heading."

I was—nice chest and all— but that wasn't the point. His heart beat against my palm, a strong tempo that was slightly accelerated. *Thump. Thump, thump. Thump.* I placed my other hand against my own chest. *Thump. Thump, thump. Thump.*

I started to feel dizzy. "Our heartbeats...they're the same." Both of our hearts were racing now, completely synchronized. "Oh my God, how is this possible?"

Daemon started to look pale. "Oh crap."

My lashes lifted. Our eyes locked. The air seemed to spark around us, filled with tension. Oh crap, indeed.

He placed his hand over mine and squeezed. "But it's not too bad. I mean, I'm pretty sure I morphed you into something and this whole heart thing proves we must be connected." He grinned. "Could be worse."

"What could be worse exactly?" I asked, stunned.

"Us being together." He shrugged. "It could be worse."

Part of me wasn't sure I'd heard him right. "Wait a sec. You think we should be together because of some kind of freaky alien mojo that has connected us? But two minutes ago you were bitching about being *stuck* with me?"

"Yeah, well, I wasn't bitching. I was pointing out that we are stuck together. This is different…and you're attracted to me."

My eyes narrowed. "I'll get back to that last statement in a second, but you want to be with me because you now feel… forced?"

"I wouldn't say forced exactly, but…but I like you."

I stared at him. It was all too easy to recall what I'd overheard when he'd healed me. Part of me had thought that maybe what he'd felt was real, but maybe it was the product of whatever the hell he'd done. That made sense considering what he was saying.

Daemon frowned. "Oh no, I know that look. What are you thinking?"

"That this is the most ridiculous declaration of attraction I've ever heard," I said, standing. "That is so lame, Daemon. You want to be with me because of whatever crazy stuff that had happened?"

He rolled his eyes as he stood. "We like each other. We do. It's stupid that we keep denying it."

"Oh, this is coming from the dude who left me on the couch *topless*?" I shook my head. "We don't like each other."

"Okay. I should probably apologize for that. I'm sorry." Daemon took a step forward. "We were attracted to each other before I healed you. You can't say that's not true, because I've always…been attracted to you."

I took a step back. "Being attracted to me is as lame a reason to be with me as the fact we're stuck together now."

"Oh, you know it's more than that." He paused. "I knew you would be trouble from the start, from the moment you knocked on my door."

I laughed dryly. "That thought is definitely mutual, but that doesn't excuse the split personality thing you've got going on."

"Well, I was kind of hoping it did, but obviously not." He flashed a quick grin. "Kat, I know you're attracted to me. I know you like—"

"Being attracted to you isn't enough," I said.

"We get along."

I gave him a bland look.

Another flash of his teeth as his lips spread. "Sometimes we do."

"We have nothing in common," I protested.

"We have more in common then you realize."

"Whatever."

Daemon caught a piece of my hair and wrapped it around his finger. "You know you want to."

The memory of the sweet kiss we'd shared in the field returned. Frustrated, I snatched my hair back and focused. "You don't know what I want. You have no clue. I want a guy who wants to be with me because he actually *wants* to be. Not that he's forced to be out of some kind of twisted sense of responsibility."

"Kat—"

"No!" I cut him off, balling my hands into fists. *Come on, Kittycat, don't be a bystander.* I wasn't going to be a bystander anymore, which meant not caving to Daemon. Not when his reasons for wanting me were so lame they made a top ten list. "No. Sorry. You have spent months being the biggest jerk to me. You don't get to decide to like me one day and think I will forget all of that. I want someone to care for me like my dad cared for my mom. And you aren't him."

"How can you know?" His eyes flashed, turning them into brilliant jewels.

Shaking my head, I turned toward the back door. Daemon appeared in front of it, blocking my exit. "God, I hate when you do that!"

He didn't laugh or smile like he normally would. His eyes were wide and bright, consuming. "You can't keep pretending that you don't want to be with me."

I could—I would try, even though deep down, I did want to be with him. But I wanted him to *want me*, not because we were stuck together or because somehow we were connected. I'd always liked the glimpses of the real him. That Daemon I could be with—I could *love*. But that Daemon never stayed around long, pushed out by his never-ending duty to his family and race. Saddened by that, I pressed my lips together.

"I'm not pretending," I said.

His eyes searched mine. "You're lying."

"Daemon."

He placed his hands on my hips and tugged me forward carefully. His breath stirred the hair around my temple. "If I wanted to be with…" he started, his hands tightening. "If I wanted to be with *you*, you'd make it hard wouldn't you?"

I lifted my head. "You don't want to be with me."

His lips twitched into a smile. "I'm thinking I kind of do."

Parts of my body liked that. My chest swelled. Insides knotted. "*Thinking* and *kind of* aren't the same thing as knowing."

"No, it's not, but it's something." His lashes lowered, shielding his eyes. "Isn't it?"

I thought of the love my mom and dad had again. I pulled away, shaking my head. "It's not enough."

Daemon's eyes met mine and he sighed. "You *are* going to make this hard."

I didn't say anything. My heart was thumping as I sidestepped him and headed for the front door.

"Kat?"

Drawing in a deep breath, I faced him. "What?"

A smile parted his lips. "You do realize I love a challenge?"

I laughed under my breath and turned back to the front door, giving him a one-fingered salute. "So do I, Daemon. So do I."

. . .

Keep reading for bonus scenes from
Daemon's point of view...

Acknowledgments

Obsidian wouldn't even be a glimmer in my eyes without Liz Pelletier. Simply put, you're the best. Seriously. Funny how one email can turn into this crazy idea within minutes, hours...and then days—wait, hours? And you're like an editing ninja. Thank you.

Thank you to the wonderful, awesomely awesome team at Entangled Publishing. Heather Howland—I love the buns atop your head in your Twitter avatar. Have I told you that before? Thank you to Suzanne Johnson for turning my manuscript into a lovely Christmas tree during copyedits, Heidi Stryker—a huge thanks to you for being the first intern to read *Obsidian* and think, "Wow, this doesn't suck."

A shout out to my publicist Misa—thank you for handling everything that you do. A big thank you to Deborah Cooke. You are amazing and I am humbled!

To my agent Kevan Lyon—you are a dream come true.

Special thanks to agents Rebecca Mancini and Stephanie Johnson. Whenever I hear your names, I get all warm and fuzzy inside.

To my family and friends, thank you for not disowning me when I don't answer your calls or pay attention when you're talking. I know I get lost in my head from time to time, so thank you for being patient.

Lesa Rodrigues and Cindy Thomas—you guys kept me sane while writing *Obsidian*. To Carissa Thomas for liking to mess around with pictures of hot guys and make my blog all steamy, thank you.

Julie Fedderson—you're the best crit partner and cheerleader in the world.

And a huge, GIGANTIC thanks to all the book bloggers out there who helped reveal the cover of *Obsidian* and spread the word. I heart each and every one of you.

Bonus Material

Scenes from Daemon's point of view!

"Uh-oh spaghetti-o's"

Daemon

The moment I walked into trig class, I saw Kat. Kind of hard to miss with that whitish glow surrounding her. I spotted a couple of seats empty on the other side of class and knew that's where I should go.

Instead, I switched my notebook to my other hand and headed straight down the aisle where she was seated. She kept her eyes glued to her notebook, but I knew she was aware of me... The faint blush along the tips of her cheekbones gave her away.

I grinned.

But then my gaze slid to the awkward splint covering her slender arm, and my grin faded. Potent rage swept through me at the reminder of how close she'd come to becoming an

Arum's playtoy. My teeth gnashed together as I stalked past and fell into the seat behind her.

Images assaulted me of how she'd looked after the Arum attack — shaken, terrified, and so tiny in my shirt as we waited for the useless police to show up. If anything, this should've served as a reminder to get my ass up and move to a different seat.

I pulled a pen out of the spiral ring on my notebook and poked her in the back.

Kat glanced over her shoulder, biting her lip.

"How's the arm?" I asked.

Her features pinched, and then her lashes swept up, her clear eyes meeting my stare. "Good," she said, fiddling with her hair. "I get the splint off tomorrow, I think."

I tapped my pen off the edge of the desk. "That should help."

"Help with what?" Wariness colored her tone.

Using the pen, I gestured to the trace surrounding her. "With what you've got going on there."

Her eyes narrowed, and I remembered she couldn't see how she was lit up like a Christmas tree. I should have cleared things up, but it was so much fun getting a rise out of her. When it looked like she was two seconds from smacking me upside the head with her splint, I couldn't help myself.

I leaned forward, watching her eyes flare. "Less people will stare without the splint is all I'm saying."

Her lips thinned in disbelief, but she didn't look away. Kat met my stare and held it. Not backing down — never backing down. Reluctant respect continued to grow inside me, but underneath that, something else was developing. I was two seconds from kissing that pissed off look right off her face. I wandered what she'd do. Hit me? Kiss me back?

I was betting on the hitting part.

Billy Crump let out a low whistle from somewhere off to the side of us. "Ash is going to kick your ass, Daemon."

Kat's eyes narrowed with what looked a lot like jealousy. I smiled. I might just need to change my bet. "Nah, she likes my ass too much for that."

Billy chuckled.

I tipped my desk down, bringing our mouths within the same breathing space. A flash of heat went through her eyes, and I so had her. "Guess what?"

"What?" she murmured, her gaze dropped to my mouth.

"I checked out your blog."

Her eyes shot back to mine. For a second they were wide with shock, but she was quick to smooth her expression. "Stalking me again, I see. Do I need to get a restraining order?"

"In your dreams, Kitten." I smirked. "Oh wait, I'm already starring in those, aren't I?"

She rolled her eyes. "Nightmares, Daemon. Nightmares."

I smiled, and her lips twitched. Dammit, if I didn't know better, I'd think she liked our little fights, too. The teacher started calling out roll, and Kat turned around. I sat back, laughing softly.

Several of the kids were still watching us, which kind of knocked the sense back into me. Not that I was doing anything wrong. Teasing her wouldn't bring the Arum to us or put her in danger—or my sister. When the bell rang, Kat bolted from the class. Shaking my head, I grabbed my notebook and headed out into the throng of students.

During a class exchange an hour later, I ran into Adam who fell in step beside me. "There is talk."

I arched a brow. "Talk about what? How everyone drives trucks around here? Or how cow tipping really is a pastime? Or how my sister is never, ever going to seriously get with you?"

Adam sighed. "Talk about Katy, smartass."

Schooling my features, I stared straight ahead as we navigated the crowded halls. Both of us were a good head or so taller than most. We were like giants in the land of humans.

"Billy Crump's in your—"

"Trig class? Yeah, I know that already."

"He was talking in History about you flirting with the new girl," Adam said, sliding past a group of girls who were openly staring at us. "Ash overheard him."

With each passing second, my annoyance was hitting an all new high.

"I know you and Ash aren't seeing each other anymore."

"Yep." I grit my teeth.

"But you know how she gets," Adam continued quickly. "You better be careful with your little human—"

I stopped in the middle of the hall, two seconds from throwing Adam through a wall. Kids shuffled around us as I spoke barely above a whisper. "She's not my little human."

Adam's gaze was unflinching. "Fine. Whatever. Out of everyone, I don't care if you took her into the locker room and did her, but she's glowing...and so are your eyes. And all of this is familiar."

Shit. On. A. Brick. Striving for patience I wasn't known

for, I started walking, leaving Adam behind. I needed to stay the hell away from Kat. And that would keep her away from the rest of the Luxen, namely Ash.

When was the moment Katy became different from the herd—from the rest of the humans? Someone I wanted to know? And Adam was right. All of this was familiar, except we'd had this conversation with Dawson over Bethany.

Dammit. This was not happening.

I glided through the rest of my classes bored out of my freaking mind. Many times last year, I tried to convince Matthew to get me a forged high school diploma. No such luck there. The DOD probably thought school was a privilege for us, but what they taught couldn't keep my interest. We learned at an accelerated rate, leaving most humans in the dust. And the DOD would have to approve my request to go to college if that's what I decided. Hell, I wasn't even sure I wanted to go to college. I'd rather find a job where I got to work outside—something that didn't include four small walls.

When lunch rolled around, I was half tempted to call it a day. School wasn't the same without Dawson. His exuberance for everything, even the mundane, had been contagious.

Not hungry, I grabbed a bottle of water and headed to the table. I sat beside Ash and leaned back, picking at the label on the bottle.

"You know," Ash said, leaning against my arm. "They say what you're doing is a sign of sexual frustration."

I winked at her.

She grinned and then turned back to her brother. That was the thing about Ash. Even though we'd dated on and off for years, she could be cool...when she wanted to be. Neither of us was really into each other, not the way Dawson had been with Bethany or as we should be.

Lifting my eyes, I immediately found Kat in the lunch line. She was talking to Carissa—the quieter of the two girls in trig. My gaze dropped down to her flip flops and slowly worked my way back up.

I think I loved those jeans. Tight in all the right places.

It was amazing really—how long Kat's legs looked for someone so short. I couldn't figure out why it seemed the way.

Ash's hand dropped on my thigh, drawing my attention. Warning bells went off. She was so up to something. "What?" I asked.

Her bright eyes fixed on mine. "What are you looking at?"

"Nothing." I focused on her, anything to keep her interest off Kat. As feisty as the little kitten was, she was absolutely no match for Ash. I sat the bottle aside, swinging my legs toward her. "You look nice today."

"Don't I?" Ash beamed. "So do you. But you always look yumtastic." Glancing over her shoulder, she then turned back and slid into my lap faster than she should have in public.

A couple of the boys at a neighboring table looked like they would've traded in their moms to be in my position. "What are you up to?" I kept my hands to myself.

"Why do you think I'm up to anything?" She pressed her chest against mine, speaking in my ear. "I miss you."

I grinned. "No, you don't."

Pouting, she slapped my shoulder playfully. "Okay. There are some things I miss."

About to tell her that I had a good idea of what that thing

was, Dee's jubilant shriek cut me off.

"Katy!" she yelled.

Cursing under my breath, I felt Ash stiffen against me.

"Sit," Dee said, smacking the top of the table. "We were talking about—"

"Wait." Ash twisted around. I could picture the look on her face. Lips turned down, eyes narrowed. All that equaled bad, bad times. "You did not invite her to sit with us? Really?"

I focused on the painting of the PHS mascot—a red and black Viking, complete with horns. Please don't sit down.

"Shut up, Ash," Adam said. "You're going to make a scene."

"I'm not 'going to make' anything happen." Ash's arm tightened around my neck like a boa constrictor. "She doesn't need to sit with us."

Dee sighed. "Ash, stop being a bitch. She's not trying to steal Daemon from you."

My eyebrows shot up, but I kept up the prayer. Please don't sit down. My jaw locked. Please don't sit here. If she did, Ash would eat her alive out of pure spite. I'd never understand girls. Ash didn't want me anymore, not really, but holy hell if someone else did.

Ash's body started to vibrate softly. "That's not what I'm worried about. For real."

"Just sit," Dee said to Katy, her voice tight with exasperation. "She'll get over it."

"Be nice," I whispered in Ash's ear, low enough for only her to hear. Ash smacked my arm hard. That'll leave a bruise. I pressed my cheek into her neck. "I mean it."

"I'll do what I want," she hissed back. And she would, too. Worse than what she was doing now.

"I don't know if I should," Kat said, sounding incredibly small and unsure.

Every stupid, idiotic thought in my head demanded that I dump Ash out of my lap and get Kat out of here, away from what surely was going to end up being horrible.

"You shouldn't," Ash snapped.

"Shut up," Dee said. "I'm sorry I know such hideous bitches."

"Are you sure?" Kat asked.

Ash's body trembled and heated up. Her skin would be too warm for a human to touch without realizing something was different, wrong even. I could feel her control slipping away. Exposing herself wasn't likely, but she appeared mad enough to do some damage.

I turned my head to look at Kat for the first time since I'd seen her in the line. And I already knew I was going to hate myself for what I was about to say, because she didn't deserve this. "I think it's obvious if you're wanted here or not."

"Daemon!" My sister's eyes filled with tears, and now it was official. I was irrevocably a dick. "He's not being serious."

"Are you being serious, Daemon?" Ash twisted toward me.

My gaze held Kat's, and I clamped down on everything. She needed to leave before something shitty happened. "Actually, I was being serious. You're not wanted here."

Kat opened her mouth, but she didn't say anything. Her cheeks had been pink—the way I liked them—but the color faded quickly. Anger and embarrassment filled her gray eyes. They glistened under the harsh lights of the cafeteria. A sharp pierce sliced through my chest, and I had to look away—because I had put that look in her eyes. Clenching my jaw, I focused over Ash's shoulder on that stupid mascot again.

In that moment, I wanted to punch myself in the face.

"Run along," Ash said.

A few snickers sounded and anger whipped through me, heating my skin. It was ridiculous that I was pissed that other people were laughing when I'd embarrassed her, hurt her more than anyone.

Silence fell over the table, and relief was imminent. She had to be leaving now. There was no way—

Cold, wet, and sloppy stuff plopped on the top of my head. I froze, aware enough not to open my mouth unless I wanted to eat…spaghetti? Did she…? Sauce covered noodles slid down my face, landing on my shoulder. One hung off my ear, smacking me against the neck.

Holy shit. I was dumbfounded as I slowly turned to look at her. Part of me was actually…amazed.

Ash leaped from my lap, shrieking as she shoved her hands out. "You…You…"

I plucked one of the noodles off my ear and dropped it on the table as I peered up at Kat from underneath my lashes. The laugh came up before I could stop it. Good for her.

Ash lowered her hands. "I will end you."

My humor vanished. Jumping up, I threw an arm around Ash's waist. "Calm down. I mean it. Calm down."

She pulled against me. "I swear to all the stars and suns, I will destroy you."

"What does that mean?" Kat balled her hands, glaring at the taller girl like she wasn't afraid of her one bit, and she should've been. Ash's skin was scorching hot, vibrating just beneath the surface. At that moment, I really started to doubt she'd not do something stupid and reveal us in public. "Are you watching too many cartoons again?"

Matthew stalked over to our table, his eyes connecting with mine for a moment. I'd hear about this later. "I believe that's enough," he said.

Knowing not to argue with Matthew, Ash sat down in her own seat and grabbed a fistful of napkins. She tried to clean up the mess, but it was pointless. I almost laughed again when she started stabbing at her shirt. Sitting down, I knocked a clump of noodles off my shoulder.

"I think you should find another place to eat," Matthew said to Katy, voice low enough that only the people at our table could hear. "Do so now."

Looking up, I watched Kat grab her book bag. She hesitated, and then she nodded as if in a daze. Turning stiffly, she stalked from the cafeteria. My eyes followed her the whole way out, and she kept her head held high.

Matthew turned from the table, probably off to do some damage control. I wiped the back of my hand down my sticky cheek, unable to stop myself from laughing softly.

Ash smacked me again. "It's not funny!" She stood, hands shaking. "I can't believe you think that was funny."

"It was." I shrugged, grabbing my water bottle. Not like we didn't deserve it. Looking down the table, I found my sister staring at me. "Dee..."

Tears built in her eyes as she stood. "I can't believe you did that."

"What did you expect?" Andrew demanded

She shot him a death glare and then turned those eyes on me. "You suck. You really freaking suck, Daemon."

I opened my mouth, but what could I say? I did suck. I'd acted like an ass, and it wasn't like I could defend that. Dee had to understand that it was for the best, but when I closed my eyes, I saw the hurt in Kat's eyes and I wasn't so sure I'd done the right thing...at least the right thing by her.

"The Morning After"

Daemon

I wasn't sure if I was dreaming, but if I was, I didn't want to wake up. The scent of peach and vanilla teased me, invaded me.

Kat.

Only she smelled that wonderful, of summer and all the things I could want and never have. The length of her body was pressed against mine, with her hand resting on my stomach. The steady rise and fall of her chest became my entire world, and in this dream—because it had to be a dream—I felt my own chest matching her breaths.

Every cell in my body sparked and burned. If I was awake, I'd surely take on my true form. My body was on fire.

Just a dream, but it felt real.

I couldn't resist sliding my leg over hers, burrowing my head between her neck and shoulder, and inhaling deeply. Divine. Perfect. Human. Breathing became more difficult than I'd ever imagined. Lust swirled through me, heady and consuming. I tasted her skin—a slight brush of my lips, a flick of my tongue. She felt perfect underneath me; soft in all the places I was hard.

Moving over her, against her, I loved the sound she made—a soft, wholly feminine murmur that scorched every piece of me. "You're perfect for me," I whispered in my own language.

She stirred, and I dreamt her responding, wanting me instead of hating me.

I pressed down, sliding my hand under her shirt. Her skin felt like satin underneath my fingertips. Precious. Prized. If she was mine, I'd cherish every inch of her. And I wanted to. Now. My hand crept up, up, up.

Kat gasped.

The dreamy cloud dissipated with the sound I felt all the way through me. Every muscle locked up. Very slowly, I pried my eyes opened. Her slender, graceful neck sloped before me. A section of skin was pink from the stubble on my jaw...

The clock on the wall ticked.

Shit.

I'd felt her up, in my sleep.

I lifted my head and stared down at her. Kat watched me, her eyes a smoky, wonderful gray and questioning. Double shit.

"Good morning," she said, her voice still rough with sleep. Using my arm, I pushed up and even then, knowing that none of it had been a dream, I couldn't look away from her, didn't want to. An infinite need was there, in her, in me. Demanding that I kneel to it, and I wanted to—dammit, did I ever want to.

The only thing that got to me, that cleared the layers of lust and idealistic stupidity out of my head, was the trace shimmering around her. She looked like the brightest star.

She was in danger. She was a danger to us.

With one last look, I shot across the room with inhuman speed, slamming the door behind me. Every step away from that room, from that bed, was painful and stiff. Rounding the corner, I almost ran into my sister.

Dee studied me, eyes narrowed.

"Shut up," I muttered, heading past her.

"I didn't say anything, jerk-face." Amusement betrayed her words.

Once inside my bedroom, I quickly changed into a pair of sweats and slipped on my sneakers. Running into my sister cooled most of me down, but there was a raw edge to my nerves and I needed to be out of this house, away from her.

Not even bothering to change my shirt, I picked up speed, shooting through the house and out the front door. The moment my sneaks touched the porch, I took off and darted into the woods in a burst of speed. Overhead skies were gray and bleak. Drizzle pelted my face like a thousand tiny needles. I welcomed it, pushing and pushing until I was deep in the woods. Then I shed my human skin, taking my true form as I shot between the trees, moving until I was nothing more than a streak of light.

This was wrong. Think of Dawson. Look at what

happened to him. Did I want to take the same risk? Leave Dee all alone? But even now I could feel her skin, taste it— sweet and sugary like candy. Hear that wonderful sound she made over and over again, haunting every mile I put between us.

An idea began to form—one that Dee would hate, but I didn't see any other option. I could go to the DOD and request a move to one of the other communities. We'd be giving up our home, leaving our friends behind and Matthew, but it would be for the best. It was the right thing to do. Dee would be safe.

It would keep Kat safe.

Because Dee couldn't stay away from her and neither could I. But no matter where I went, what I was running from would still be with me—Kat. She wasn't just back in the house, in that bed. She was with me now, inside me. And there was no outrunning that.